<small>PRAISE FOR</small> Jayne Anne Phillips's

Night Watch

"There are dozens of passages in *Night Watch* that deliver moments so vivid, so full of sensory awareness, that they demand both immediate rereading and the folding down of the appropriate page's corner so they can be revisited. Read this book for those passages. Read it to learn a history you didn't know you didn't know. . . . Read *Night Watch* to be enlightened." —*Washington Independent Review of Books*

"Phillips is at the top of her game in *Night Watch*, devising a mesmerizing plot. . . . A portrait of a family in peril . . . which rivals [Phillips's previous novel] National Book Award finalist *Lark and Termite*." —*Pittsburgh Post-Gazette*

"Phillips's depiction of a ravaged world . . . feels true to the profoundly destabilising nature of her subject. . . . With this excellent novel, Phillips has brought a little more of this foundational American episode into the light." —*The Guardian*

"*Night Watch* is escapist in the best sense of the word, allowing readers to immerse themselves in the experience of a distant era and identify deeply with the struggles of the people who lived through it." —*BookPage*

"A superb meditation on broken families in post–Civil War West Virginia. . . . The bruised and turbulent postbellum era comes alive in Phillips's page-turning affair."
—*Publishers Weekly* (starred review)

Jayne Anne Phillips

Night Watch

Jayne Anne Phillips is the author of six novels, including *Night Watch*, *Quiet Dell*, *Lark and Termite*, *Mother-Kind*, *Shelter*, and *Machine Dreams*, and two widely anthologized story collections, *Fast Lanes* and *Black Tickets*. *Quiet Dell* was a *Wall Street Journal* and a *Kirkus Reviews* Best Fiction selection. *Lark and Termite*, winner of the Chicago Tribune Heartland Prize, was a finalist for the National Book Award, the National Book Critics Circle Award, and the Prix Médicis étranger (France). *Machine Dreams*, chosen as one of twelve *New York Times* Best Books of the Year, was a finalist for the National Book Critics Circle Award. *Black Tickets*, awarded the Sue Kaufman Prize for First Fiction from the American Academy of Arts and Letters, is often cited as a book of stories that influenced a generation of writers. The recipient of Guggenheim, National Endowment for the Arts, Howard, Bunting, and Rockefeller Foundation Fellowships, Jayne Anne Phillips is a member of the American Academy of Arts and Letters. Information, essays, and text source photographs on her fiction can be viewed at her website, www.jayneannephillips.com.

Night Watch

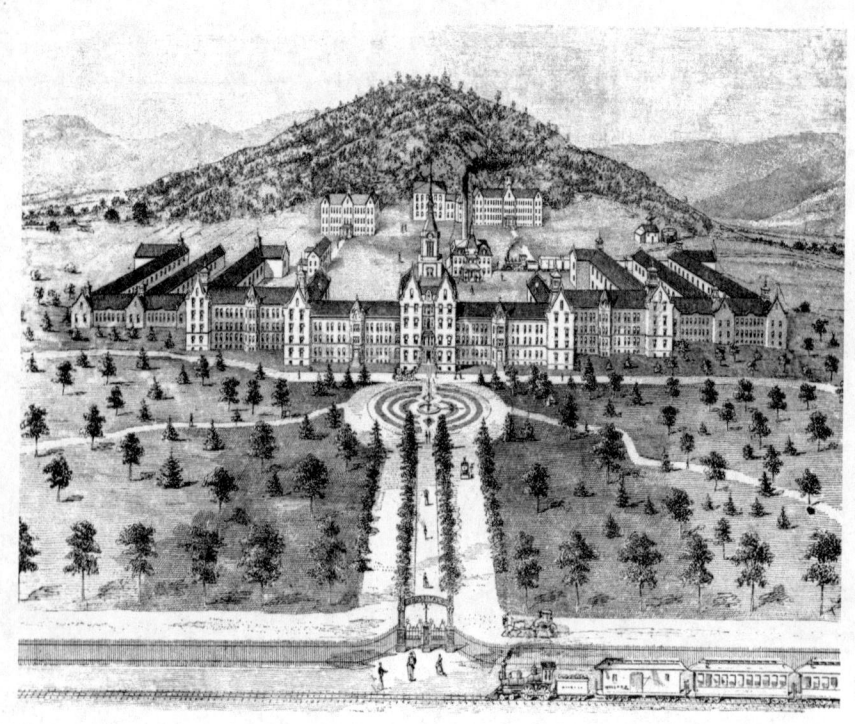

Trans-Allegheny Lunatic Asylum, Weston, West Virginia

Night Watch

Jayne Anne Phillips

VINTAGE BOOKS

A DIVISION OF PENGUIN RANDOM HOUSE LLC

NEW YORK

FIRST VINTAGE BOOKS OPEN-MARKET EDITION 2024

Copyright © 2023 by Jayne Anne Phillips

All rights reserved. Published in the United States by Vintage Books, a division of Penguin Random House LLC, New York, and distributed in Canada by Penguin Random House Canada Limited, Toronto. Originally published in hardcover in the United States by Alfred A. Knopf, a division of Penguin Random House LLC, New York, in 2023.

Vintage and colophon are registered trademarks of Penguin Random House LLC.

Portions of this work first appeared in different form in *Oxford American*, *Conjunctions*, and *Narrative* magazine.

The Library of Congress has cataloged the Knopf edition as follows:
Names: Phillips, Jayne Anne, [date] author.
Title: Night Watch : a novel / Jayne Anne Phillips.
Description: First edition. | New York : Alfred A. Knopf, 2023.
Identifiers: LCCN 2022039327 (print)
Subjects: LCGFT: Novels.
Classification: LCC PS3566.H479 N54 2023 (print) | DDC 813/.54—dc23
LC record available at https://lccn.loc.gov/2022039327

Vintage Books Open-Market ISBN: 979-82-17-00702-8
eBook ISBN: 978-0-451-49334-7

Book design by Maggie Hinders

vintagebooks.com

Printed in the United States of America
10 9 8 7 6 5 4 3 2 1

For my grandfathers,

Warwick Phillips (Sept. 15, 1886–Aug. 1, 1919)
of Roaring Creek, West Virginia,

James William Thornhill (July 31, 1867–Aug. 21, 1943)
of Buckhannon, West Virginia,

and for my grandmother Grace Boyd Thornhill's "Great Aunt Jenny,"
who welcomed her husband home from incarceration in Richmond's infamous
Libby Prison in 1865

Contents

I am interested in what prompts and makes possible this process of entering what one is estranged from.

—TONI MORRISON, *Playing in the Dark: Whiteness and the Literary Imagination*

West Virginia should long since have had a separate State existence. The East has always looked upon that portion of the State west of the mountains, as a territory in a state of pupilage . . . Our State is the child of the rebellion; yet our peace, prosperity and happiness, and . . . that of the whole country, [depends] on the speedy suppression of this attempt to overthrow the Government of our fathers; and it is my duty, as soon as these ceremonies are closed, to proceed at once to aid the Federal authorities in their efforts to stay its destructive hand.

—GOVERNOR ARTHUR I. BOREMAN, *First Inaugural Address, State of West Virginia, Wheeling, West Virginia, June 20, 1863*

I cannot give you an idea of half the horrors I have witnessed and yet so common have they become that they do not excite a feeling of horror.

—LIEUTENANT CHARLES HARVEY BREWSTER, *Tenth Massachusetts Infantry, May 1864, The Civil War: The Final Year, Told by Those Who Lived It, ed. Aaron Sheehan-Dean*

I'm saying it's all inside us, the whole war.

—DENIS JOHNSON, *Tree of Smoke*

PART I

1874

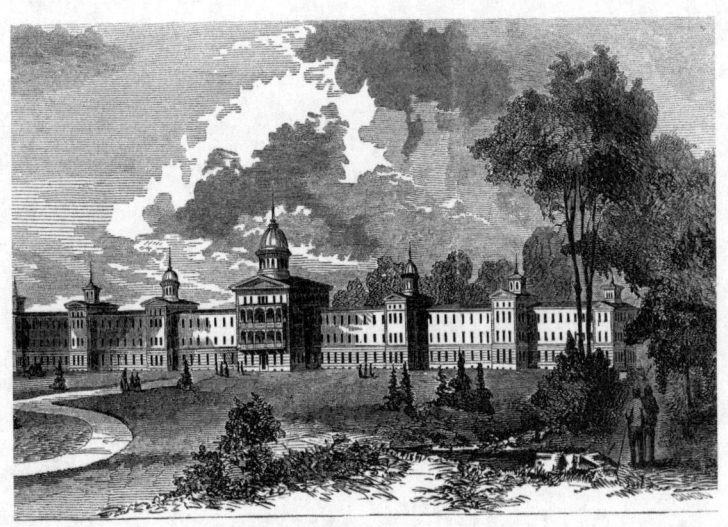

STATE HOSPITAL FOR THE INSANE FOR 250 PATIENTS.

IT IS AMONG THE MOST PAINFUL features of insanity, that in its treatment, so many are compelled to leave their families; that every comfort and luxury that wealth or the tenderest affection can give, are so frequently of little avail . . . The simple claims of a common humanity should induce each State to make a liberal provision for all its insane . . . especially as regards the poor.

— DR. THOMAS STORY KIRKBRIDE, 1854
On the Construction, Organization, and
General Arrangements of Hospitals for the Insane

ConaLee

A JOURNEY
APRIL 1874

I got up in the wagon and Papa set me beside Mama, all of us on the buckboard seat.

Hold her hand there, he said to me, like she likes. Sit tight in. Keep her still.

I saw him lean down and rope her ankle to his. I was warm because he made me wear my bonnet, to keep my skin fine and my eyes from crinkling at the corners. In case someday I turned out after all.

Talk to her, he said. Tell her she'll like it where she's going. A fine great place, like a castle with a tower clock. Tell her.

You'll like it, Mama, I said. A fine place like a castle, built from stone.

Tell her about them palms.

Palm trees in pots, Mama, and velvet sofas, like in a city hotel.

And don't call her Mama, he said. Don't you see how she's dressed?

He'd got the dress from a widow man who was giving away his dead wife's carpetbag and clothes, the petticoats, silk underthings, the skirts, the satin bodice and jacket with bell sleeves, a net for her hair with a pearl comb fastener. Our neighbor had pulled Mama's dark locks up in bundle braids, like the page from *Godey's Lady's Magazine* we kept nailed on the wall.

You know what to call her, he said. Don't fail in't.

You said call her Miss Janet. Though it is not her name.

It is her name now. Her old name won't do her good. She's a quality woman alone in the world. Call her by her name.

I will, just in a minute. Catchin my breath.

But I put my hand on hers. She was clasping her knee so hard I could feel her shake. I was out of breath from carrying the babbies to the neighbor women. One of them would take the boy because he was walking and talking, and the boy twin if she got both boys. The other woman would take the girl twin, so that was a separate trip, pulling the drag with the bags of flour and salt. I guessed we were going to be gone some days, driving over to Weston. Papa had packed a grip and had him a bedroll. I had my leather bag of fancy dress buttons, folded up under my woolsey jacket. I was wearing my trousers, as like I was going to feed the chickens.

Papa, who's going to feed the chickens while we're gone, and find the eggs?

That neighbor woman, he said. That took the girl twin.

Mama never named the babbies. We only called them so— the babbies, and she nursed all three. The twins weren't but twelve weeks. I had marked the weeks, a line through every Sunday since February 1. It was that eve we brought them, Papa and me, and he cut the cords with a hot knife. No one else came to help. Not even Dearbhla, our neighbor granny a ridge above—Papa forbade her near us. Mama made noise, sounds and words. I was hopeful she would talk normal after, like she did before Papa came, way before, it seemed. But she only made those sounds and lay abed since. I would bring the new ones to her from the drawers I lined with blankets. She'd so much milk, hard as stones and pushing her clothes away, until I just left the babbies in the bed to suckle. The older one was walking by then but he crowded in and took his turn.

The road was shade and sun, and shade and sun. Early spring, a chill edging the tallest pines.

Talk to her, Papa said, like I told you.

There's a clock tower that keeps the time for the town, I told her. And a great lawn with a fishpond. Paths and flower beds.

We had the cow then and I gave her milk with egg beaten in. Now and again she said a word, clear as anything. Bell, she said, or goose. A game like rock, scissors, paper. Or did she want a bell. I gave her a jingle bell from a harness in the shed, but she only laid it aside. There was no goose. I had all I could do to change the nappies, soak and wash and hang them, flags from a line on the porch.

Her name, he said.

Miss Janet, you will like to walk on the paths. Quality ladies are there. Everyone their own room, Papa says. Like a hotel. Resting. No more chores. Fresh breads and butter. Got their own bakery and dairy, and buy food fresh from the farmers. Corn, tomatoes, meats.

Mama had not done chores, not for the longest time. She turned her head as we rode along, tilting her face slow to one side, then to the other. The earbobs I found in her jacket pocket had little tassels that matched the bodice of the dress and she could feel the gold threads touch the line of her jaw. The way she held her shoulders squared, and stayed so still but to stand and move where you led her, made her look proud. As though naught concerned her. It was that gave him the idea, surely, and the widow man throwing out the clothes. And the cow going down. The cow was on her knees and I'd no time to

walk up the ridge to Dearbhla, to fetch one of her root or marrow tonics. Papa was ever away and came back from town of
an evening, with lamp oil and bread and cheese. Or he stayed
in the woods, hunting. Rabbits, pheasant, turkey. He'd got the
clothes in town. Just in time, he said, and all was in motion so
fast, with farming out the babbies so she could have her rest.

We will come to visit you, Miss Janet, I said. Even the babbies. We will bring them to see you, dressed nice. And you
resting while they grow.

No need to worry about any babbies now, Papa said. And
began to whistle a tune.

I leant against Mama, my head to her shoulder, and she
leant against me, her face to the top of my head. It was how
we slept at night sometimes. She liked her pillows behind her,
and me near beside her, to lift up the babbies. The wagon was
lurching gentle and I fell asleep, my dreams twisting off, wisps
of all she wanted to tell me and had no strength to say. We
slept that way, sealed as shells, while the sun dropped lower
and the summer gloaming came up from the fields. Today was
April and I knew it, even as the wagon groaned and shifted
and he was pulling off the road. You stayed off the roads if
you stopped then, out of sight, if you left our mountain cover.
I could feel the shade of the beech he pulled us under before
I opened my eyes, a beech so big it spread a shelter wide as a
circus tent, the long dappled branches grown right down to
the ground. The new grass underneath was soft and green as
fairy grass.

We could live here, I said.

He'd braked the wagon and staked the horse to graze. Then
he was up beside me and lifting her to the back. He gave me a
bag of dried apple slices. There's your supper, he said. You sit
here and face front. Stay hushed.

I could feel him lay her down, his weight shifting about her,
and hear him loosen her clothes. I'd packed her bodice with
clean rags, last of the babbies' nappies. No milk on those qual-

ity clothes. That's what he was about. Those babbies would be crying for her. I heard her breathe a half sigh of relief, the sound she made in the hard latch of their suckle. Their pale fists would drift over her until their fingers opened, but his hands were on her now, and his mouth, taking their sustenance. My face was afire. I couldn't see naught in front of me and thought I heard the babbies howling across the fields. The branches of the beech stirred in one part, then another, shielding all from sight. Just in a while the wagon began to rock and I wanted to climb down. I tried to move but heard his strangled whisper: *Stay still.* I never knew if he said it to her or to me. I would see things shift sometimes, and go tight and clear and strange. Just now, threads of seed on floating strands glimmered, lifting the tree's canopy in a ruffling wave I knew could not happen but in my sight. The fields turned gold then, and the grass was lit and sharp. Shining blades pulled at the twilight, pulling it down, firing red and blue and red before the bright white inside the colors pierced me through.

. . .

I was laid out flat beside her when I woke, and the sky was full dark. Her head on my chest felt warm and hard as a rock in the sun. I wondered was she fevered but I was only cool from not moving, and calm in my mind. I would have such sleeps and wake up where I'd been, only time had slipped, a little time or more. Time I'd lost and could not know. It was empty there but full and floating, and wiped out every pain. Dearbhla said I gave myself what I needed, that I never had such "rests" before Papa came. Even when I woke, I was so peaceful that I had to think of moving. All was stars above us, nothing but stars in the inky black, for we were on the open road. Just then I was falling up, into the night sky that seemed to draw away, turning like a cup. A shooting star crossed the handle of the Dipper. I could see Orion's Belt and moved her from me, to sit up and look for Betelgeuse and Bellatrix. I knew my constellations if I traced one to another, to see them whole like pictures on a plate.

He called me up to him then. Here, he said, Connolly.

I climbed up beside him. Cold, I shivered into myself and pulled on my woolsey jacket. I told him I wished I'd dressed nicer.

Yer fine as you are, Papa said.

We were moving along a bare hill, and the fields as far as I could see were flat and chopped. Someone had burned them, cleared the crop and left the chaff. Burned and not harvested. Some mite or fungus could eat a crop and leave a poison for the next. Farmers burned it all with torches. Some days ago it seemed, but there'd been no rain to take the smell. Charred popcorn it smelled like, dirt-damp, a soil smell coming up in mist and dew on the singed air. The road emptied along through it, dusty, yellow with moon glow.

Puts me in mind of the War, Papa said. Mighty lonely when it's burnt and dead, far as you can see. It's how we did it, burned them out.

And they burned us out, I said.

That they did, he said, but they never found you, back along that ridge.

I didn't say they had found us, and more times than I knew. Mama would hide me in the root cellar, once with a handful of carrots she ripped from the ground as we ran. Don't come out no matter what, until I fetch you! And she dropped me in. She told me, when she was still talking, never to tell about the War. No matter who won, it didn't do to say what had happened. The Secessionists lost, I knew, and the Abolitionists won, but they were all ragged, drifting men.

That little cabin, Papa said, deep in the cover. Not much to see, but full forested and a steep climb. Nothing level for any farm a'tall. Don't know how you managed.

Mama had a bigger garden, I said, in patches, all along. Two cows and more chickens then, and the neighbor women traded one thing for another. Dearbhla took the buckboard to town and sold her roots and tonics.

Told you not to speak of that old woman, Papa said.

Just to say, Mama wasn't like she is now.

That a fact, he said. Well. Sometimes the strain eases and what's held together falls apart. Good thing I come by when I did.

The sound of the wagon groaning along was a lull. Whenever I tried to think on it, I could not remember when he came home. I knew of a homecoming picnic at the church, with banners in the trees and fife and drum, maybe around that time. But that was not it. We never went near church after he came.

A few things to tell you, he said. A girl that hasn't got her monthlies yet cannot get with child. And a woman suckling infants cannot get with child. Miss Janet will not get with child.

But she did, I said. When the chap was small and suckling.

The chap was sitting up. Six month he was. That was too late. Now is not too late. Those little ones are a ways from sitting up.

I didn't say anything, only looked before us to where the road turned.

That chap, he said, and laughed. Like a mountain goat. Walking and yammering so young. He's mine, all right.

We're all yours, I said.

A bank of trees came up in the distance, long like a huddle of shapes. They straightened taller along both sides of the road as we came on.

He gave me the harmonica from his pocket. Play me a tune real quiet, he said.

I played "Camptown Races," slow as a hymn, so that only we could hear.

Keep that mouth organ, he said. You play it better than most.

We were off the mountain some time now, into the valley.

The trees were willows standing up one after another, droop-
ing their tendril branches. We were in a glade and the burnt
fields strung out behind us.

.   .   .

Clouds came off the ground as we got toward dawn. The stars
faded all but one or two. Mama would be as alone. I wouldn't
be there to hear her say my name, and other words she spoke
now and again. As only I hadn't been so rushed, I could have
brought her books, to remind her of home. Brought to *this
place* in saddlebags she'd said. But Mama's books were mine,
too—I'd writ *ConaLee* in every one, and listed them in my
mind:

My set of McGuffey's primers, that were hers.
Mr. Noah Webster's dictionary. Open to a page, pick a
word, eyes closed.
Our Bible.
Myths of Ancient Times, the Minotaur and Cyclops, one
stumbling in dark caves, the other with his blinded eye.
Water-Babies: Fairy Tale for a Land-Baby, dragonflies and
darting trout and little Tom.
My *Wordsworth*.
My *Tennyson*.
My *History of the American States.*
Oliver Twist, by Mr. Charles Dickens.
A Christmas Carol. In Prose. Being a Ghost Story of Christmas,
by the same Mr. Dickens. We acted out the parts every
Christmas, with Dearbhla for audience.
Aesop's Fables.
Sonnets of Shakespeare. Mama knew some by heart and
taught me to read the words.
Geographies of the World.
Constellations and Their Stories.

Now the stars were gone. Dearbhla always said that she could see me through them. I played my harmonica, sounds that only breathed, and shut my eyes. In a while I could hear little trills between the sounds, and then the sounds were water. Rills of water came up under us, on a bridge. Air circled like swallows from a cave. He stopped just the other side to fill the canteens and water the horse from the feedbag. Water poured through it and the mare lowered her head to beat the dripping to the ground. He poured water over her till her mane was wet and flat and smoothed her flanks, moving the harness and the reins. He knew animals and handled them all the same, strong and sure, whether he wrung a chicken's neck or coaxed a horse from a ditch. For all his whistling or rare look of favor, his hands moved you here or there. I walked down under the bridge to the stream, to wash and drink and relieve myself where he couldn't see. I thought I would bring Mama and pull up her skirts for her to crouch as silent. The brook was loud and fresh by the rattling water, a bell of sound beneath the bridge, her bell it could be, like the word she said, and no one else near. I wished we could abide here, small and hidden as the water sprites that live in rocks and pools.

But when I went back up, he had got her out of the wagon. Her drawers were off. He had a way of leaning back against a wall or porch rail and now the wagon, holding her fast with her clothes bunched up over her head. She was a blind thing in a sack with her arms flung up and trapped. He'd arched her out before him to aim her like a vessel; he did it when she made water and he was there to know, or decide she must. She was so white and pale on her thighs, still with a pouch of belly from the twins. He watched her while she couldn't move and spat in his hand to clean her.

I could have taken her to the stream, I said.

And muddy her clothes? Them delicates are silk.

She knew what to do when I took her to the privy, or sat her on the chamber pot by her bed. The house was one big room.

Days or nights, he would tell me what was private, when not to look, but he never said this was private and did it when I was near, calling me back if I turned away.

He called me now. Come and help with her drawers.

He watched me pull them up, then he stood her on her feet. He let down every layer of skirts and her arms came down to hold her breasts. She would be aching again or nearly, and she looked around her.

We got to get on, Papa said. Help her into the wagon and keep the dust from her skirts. You sit up with me.

.　.　.

Dusk of the second day, I could see the glow of a town but knew he wouldn't go through it. He found dirt roads and meadow trails, and kept a pair of clippers for snapping barbed wire. He could twist it back together and leave no sign of passage. He liked to say about all he knew. Staying hid so you could see and not be seen. Which roots and leaves to eat if you stayed hid. How to fish with a bent safety pin and a length of rush, with the white grubs that lived under rocks for bait. How to see the holes where animals lived. How to set a trap from lengths of green sapling so thin even a child could bend them, and so sharp they pierced the flesh. How to find the North Star. Never to live in a town, but always on country land, deep in shelter, where few passed. Like where we lived, high on the ridge. I supposed he'd put us there, and so knew where to find us.

What could that town be? I asked him. There, between the hills.

Not Weston, he said. Not yet. We'll go around.

You always know how to go.

I know my way, he said. Been through here. Even to Weston, back in '64 with Witcher's Raiders. The Asylum was half built, already like a castle. Camp Asylum, it was then, with the Union boys just pulled out. We took all the blankets and every scrap from the larder. The South was eating bark by then, and what-ever we could steal. Here, take the reins. Give me that mouth organ.

The horse went on. Papa leaned back, pushed his hat low, and played an air.

Then he was quiet. Napping. Catnapping he called it, how you kept going when you were on the move. Awake and asleep, he said. But I felt alone, driving the wagon. We were under a stand of pines, so close I could smell the needles on the boughs. A great owl looked down at me, blinking its round orange eyes. Huge they were. The lids seemed to stutter to open wide again. The owl drew up, fluffed its white chest to twice the size, and opened its sharp beak. A tongue darted out but the echoing sound seemed to come from everywhere. Then the great wings spread and gathered, rowing the air like water. The owl flew over me and was gone. I saw that its white feathers were dappled with black.

Papa startled. What was that?

An owl, I said. Flew out from the trees, straight across.

Screecher, was it?

Might have been.

He took the reins. Or maybe a barn owl. Good omen, they say. You wouldn't have seen one before cause you never had a barn.

Did you?

Did I what?

Ever have a barn?

Course I had a barn, he said, now and again. You and your mama, sure never had a barn. He clicked his mouth at the horse and snapped the reins, picking up the pace.

I was thinking we were far from any barns out here, and a name was not a given. He'd named Mama to suit himself—called her Mrs. until she was Miss Janet. And said my name wrong, Connolly instead of ConaLee. But a name meant noth-ing to the owl. It lived wild, and hunted in the woods for mice and birds' eggs, and might live in these very pines. Papa didn't know. He'd not seen the owl nor felt its gaze.

Are we nearly there? I asked him.

Soon, he said. After a while he told me to go back to her and press out her milk, careful, to keep her clothes clean. I crawled over the buckboard seat into the back and lay beside her. She always knew me when we were alone, and put her hands on my shoulders now for me to pull her bodice loose. She was hard and sore. I held the rags to one breast and pushed gentle on the other. Milk fanned in blue threads across my face. I made a palmed bowl of a flour sack and kept it tight against her. It didn't take long because I knew exactly how. After, I could feel the sticky sweetness on my cheek and kept my hand on my face when she pulled me to her. I fell asleep hungry and heard the babbies, crying far off, like the sound of them would follow us forever.

· · · ·

Just after dawn, we stopped and I sat up. Papa had braked the buckboard on a wide dirt road. A railroad track lay to one side, then a thin run of stream, and the back of the town. To the other side was a great lawn. The broad gravel path of the entrance led far back to the castle, and the stone walls, four or five stories high, went off to both sides as far as I could see. Straight paths crisscrossed the grounds but the widest one led to the huge front doors. There was a circle halfway on, with a fountain and round pool in the middle, and benches arranged around it. Then the path led to the stone steps and arched doors of the building. It looked as though there would be many doors, for the long wings and many windows, with cupolas topping the roof, but there was just one door, bigger than any I'd seen, with oval leaded glass windows on each side, and a leaded glass pyramid for a transom window. A wide palace door for a prince or princess. All was silent. The sky was rosy. It was first light, and the stone walls looked more blue than gray. There was the clock tower, and above it a spire like a church. No cross, only a point.

Didn't I tell ye? Papa said. Two hundred feet tall.

It's a wonder, I said.

He gave me a round mirror small as my hand. Neaten up, he said. Get the sleep from your eyes. Wake her and make sure she looks well. Her hair needs held fast, and her skirts must fall right. And give me back that mirror. Had it since I came to these parts—my lucky charm, if I do say.

She stood when she saw us looking at her. He stood and reached across to tighten her bodice. Then he shook out her skirts and buttoned the clasps at her waist to show her form. She looked an hourglass, with her full front and wasp's middle, and her skirts flared in their circle.

I turned to see where she would go. There was no gate, as though the way was always open. The sign was written in brass script: *Trans-Allegheny Lunatic Asylum*. No one stirred, within or without.

It is for all the best people, Papa said. Quality people. Long as she's silent, she's as good a quality as any.

She's not a lunatic, I said. She says words to me some days.

Words? They will know she needs rest, and a cure. They think of cures in these places. He glared at me. Get to it, he said. Help her. A woman of quality is assisted.

I climbed down, still clutching the little mirror. He gave me her carpetbag and I reached up for her hand. He held her elbow until she was down. She stood beside me, still as a deer, listening. Not to him but to the stones of that building that flared up and out and went on to either side. A patchy mist came up around the stone, the cupolas and blank windows, the tall pines and oaks, and the empty benches on the grounds.

Should I walk with her inside? I asked.

She's not going in without you, he said. Then he sat back

down, put the reins aside, and fixed me in his gaze. Connolly, he said. How old are you?

He should have known but I told him. I'll be thirteen at the end of December. Born after you went away.

Born in '61, the year both sides mustered troops. Tall for your age but right puny. Too skinny for a man to take on. I considered it. But you'll stay with her.

Here?

This is home. There's nothing back there. It's all give away.

It's give away?

Are you listening to me?

Yes sir, I said, for he liked to be addressed such.

He leaned down and pointed his finger at me until he touched my throat, just at the little notch of bone. Then listen, he said. I am not yer Papa, nor have I ever been. I never laid eyes on you or your mama till I came upon you, and you don't know my name.

It was true. She had never called him a name. Only at first he bade us call him Papa and she never said different.

No woman teched in the head is going to raise three young ones, he said, with no cow and no man and no one but you to help. I can't help her nor stay away from her.

I swallowed once and felt his finger press harder. I thought to choke but held my breath.

So don't be looking for me, he said, or tell anyone where you come from. I only rode you here as a kindness. You was walking along the road, and because she is a quality woman in need of refuge, I rode you here. It was on my way. Tell me so.

You rode us here, I said. It was on your way.

Her milk will dry up in a week. Until then you keep it secret. You know what to do. Miss Janet is a quality woman with no dependents nor family. You are not her family, but a servant. Nowhere to go but with her. If they say you can't stay, tell them you have fits.

I don't.

You do, and they will know it soon enough. Those lights you see. Not everyone sees lights. Say you need a room near hers, to keep her calm. Across the hall or just beside. Don't ever argue or make a fuss, or they will separate you.

Sir? I said.

Times is hard, he said, and flicked the reins. You'll tell the story.

The wagon was moving off and his words drifted back with the dust.

THE NUMBER OF INSANE confined in one hospital, should not exceed two hundred and fifty . . . as a crowded institution cannot fail to exercise an unfavorable influence on the welfare of its patients.
— DR. THOMAS STORY KIRKBRIDE, 1854

ConaLee

NIGHT WATCH

I wished so hard we had arrived at night when no one could see us, for me to think on our situation, but the sky had lightened and there was no time. I put the little mirror in my pocket, hoisted Mama's carpetbag, and took her arm. We walked slowly along the gravel path.

Miss Janet, I said. We will stop at this place, to break our journey. Many stop here to rest a few weeks. I hope to stay near you.

She lifted her skirts a bit in the front, like any lady would on a walk that wasn't paved. We came to the circular pool, and Mama turned to walk round it, rather than going on. The sides of the pool were layered brick, and a black iron pedestal held the fountain aloft. Water bubbled in a spray, spilling gentle from fountain to pedestal to pool. It was soundless, and curious. I wanted to climb on the bricks and sit by the side of the pool to hear the water. Papa had said there were fish. Surely it wasn't so. I turned to move on but Mama had sat down on a wrought iron bench. I sat beside her, wondering if anyone was watching. If someone asked I would say she found the grounds so green and calming, even this early. The curved iron benches were placed every few feet.

There was no use asking her about Papa, if it was true, or lies that had to do with too many infants and winter coming on. We didn't live in sight of any neighbors, and the small farms deep into the ridges were deserted regular in the War years, occupied, deserted again. We'd no relatives I knew of, and only Dearbhla for family. We lived in Virginia but now we were not Virginia. I knew from Papa that the name of our state had changed more than once, that West Virginia had betrayed the South and stood for the Union. If Papa was for the South, I was for the Union, and Mama was surely with me, even if she valued the flow blue plate that showed Charleston's South Carolina harbor, with the broad rivers and clouded sky. It hung above the iron sink in a wire frame, the little waves of the water and the compass points held fast in metal teeth. Give away now, like everything else.

If he was not my papa, nothing was his to give away, except the babbies, and they were Mama's as well, and mine. I wondered could I go for the sheriff, in this strange place. No. The winter would be cold. I could not warm it. I heard it coming nearly, the way it blew into the mountains and rattled the trees in the hollows, clattering, billowing, swole with snow, and I looked out across the lawn. A rabbit moved in the grass, sat up to scent the air, and raced toward the building in a blur. As it was we must knock at the vast black door and have it opened to us.

．．．

I could not bring myself to pull the bell cord and wake anyone, but I stood Mama just beside me and knocked. I could scarcely hear the sound myself. My hand seemed a crumpled moth on the huge black door, tapping, tapping again, but I would not pound or insist. I was only whispering to one who must have seen us, the person or persons on night duty. Someone, through one of the rows and rows of windows, must have seen us arrive. Surely that person must let us in or turn us away.

I waited a moment as though in courtesy, and began to knock again. So it went on until I wished I was that rabbit, fleet and small, with my secret warren close by. I felt Mama reach for me and I put my arm about her waist. I was near her height but her weight seemed twice mine and she was wore out, up from bed so seldom, and confined in the rattling, bumping wagon almost two days, to sit or lie in the sun or the dark, always tied at the ankle lest she might flee or resist. Perhaps she'd sat down before the fountain, unable to walk farther. The thought so frightened me that I knocked again, and did not stop knocking. I'd not slept much and imagined the owl from the night pines, flying suddenly near me at the towering door, as though to strike with sharp talons. The owl's call seemed to echo all around.

But I heard the sound of locks opening, and bolts sliding, and the door half opened. A tall man, broad in the shoulders, stood looking down at us. He was dressed almost like a train conductor, all in black, and his cap was round, with a round bill. He wore a patch that covered his right eye from brow to cheekbone, with a livid scar beneath. It was not so fearful or unusual then, especially in the towns, to see the bandaged or maimed. They weren't able-bodied and couldn't go back to the farms. So many amputees and injured soldiers from the War, most of them young, survived wounds that killed older men. I could not tell if this man was young. Everyone seemed old to me, and I counted myself among them. I'd not grown up with children. My mother was past her thirtieth year, and I was more like her sister, these years past, than her daughter. Papa would call me the old biddy, and her the fairy queen.

I made my voice steady. Good day, I said. I have brought Miss Janet—for her rest and cure.

The staff does not receive at this hour, he said. You must come back after nine.

Sir, I'm sorry for the early hour. But we have traveled such a way—

I felt myself thrown forward then, for my mother had fallen against me with all her weight. I was half in the entrance, my ribs hard against the marble doorstep, and felt him lift her from me as the door swung wide. He pulled me to my feet with one hand as he shut the door behind us and threw the bolt into place. Then he was carrying her across the round, empty room, so vast it seemed, as though she was a child.

I ran after them with her carpetbag, trying to keep pace. She's faint, I was saying. We've not had much to eat or drink—

He'd stopped though, and put her on a chaise, and taken a vial from his pocket. Hartshorn spirits, he said, ammoniac, to revive her. He took the small cork from the vial and held it to her nose.

She started and drew in her breath, gasping, and opened her eyes on his face that was close to hers. Her gaze widened as though she knew him. Of course she didn't, but I was grateful she didn't call out or seem afraid. I saw now that his eye patch wasn't made of cloth but of something harder, rounded tin or metal covered with felt, held in place with a strap. A scar like an angry bloom was on his temple and disappeared under his cap and shaggy black hair, but she seemed to sense a sudden protection or counsel. Then he stepped back and she looked wildly around as though she'd no memory of how we arrived at such a place. She saw the whole length of the room behind me.

I reached down to grasp her shoulder. Miss Janet, I remembered to say, you were faint. We have come to the Asylum, for your rest—

I'll call the Matron, said our benefactor. The cooks are not in yet, but I've some victuals set out. I'm O'Shea, the Night Watch. Can you walk, Miss? He looked at me when she didn't answer. Girl, he said, if you'll bring her. And he turned on his heel.

We crossed the wide floor of the round room, round as the clock tower some three floors above. Furniture, sofas and wing chairs, were placed along the wall as though folks might conversate in this big wide place. Our shoes, Mama's and mine, clicked on the marble floor. His footsteps were silent, and such a big man. Then I saw that he'd thick woolen covers tied over his boots.

He motioned that we should wait on a wooden bench beside an alcove that seemed to lead to a private room. He brought us two bowls of coffee with milk. An odd-looking child stayed close beside him. An undersized boy he seemed, with one blue and one milky eye, veiled nearly white across the pupil. He wore a woman's long duster over his clothes and his cloudy swirl of light hair fell to his shoulders. The man seemed not to notice him, then said, Boy, reproving him for staring at us. They repaired to the alcove. The Night Watch came back with a plate of cold johnnycakes spread with sorghum molasses. We ate from the plate on my lap, despite the empty chairs and settees, with little tables before them, all about the large room. The coffee was nearly hot and we drank it down. The dense cornmeal of the fried cakes tasted fresh and I cut them up for sharing. I put a fork in Mama's hand. After a moment, she glanced up at the tall man and began to eat. I fed myself and he stood just near, as though we were meant to eat quickly, and he reached for the plate when we heard a heavy tread on the stairwell over our heads. I put a last forkful in her mouth as he removed the plate and cutlery in haste. Wiping my mouth with my hand, and Mama's as well, I thought of Papa's hand and pushed the thought away like a black whelm that might overtake us. He was not here. This could not be home, but it might be refuge if I could stay near her. I stood, my hand on Mama's elbow to be sure she did the same, and looked for the man who'd admitted us. He must have summoned someone and waited now, respectful. The child was nowhere to be seen.

———

> The objection to a night watch . . . simply shows that incom-
> petent persons have undertaken to perform this duty . . .
> [They] should accustom themselves to open doors . . . in
> the most quiet manner . . . and they should always wear
> woolen shoes when passing through the wards.
> —DR. THOMAS STORY KIRKBRIDE, 1854

Weed

SAYS AND KNOWS

Slides, turns, runs and slides in the ward halls at night, socks on his boots like a Night Watch, silent one hallway to another. Follows the Night Watch, out of sight or close-up, till he points, Stop. Lets Weed cling to one strong fist, swing to and fro, up and down. Featherweight Weed. Then back to rounds. Night Watch in the men's wards, rounding, he says, peering through slots in doors, each sleeper, talker, rumbler. Weed following, secret, only allowed in Gentlemen's Ward D, waiting at corners while the Night Watch checks farthest wards and locked steel gates. Weed moves from settee to wing chair, slides here, there, then down against a wall to wait. The Night Watch talks to the Nurse Attendants, big men with soft voices. Weed plays with the yarn in his pocket, a bit of twig and his round lead spoon, digger spoon with no handle. Furls yarn around the digger till the twig steals it back, furling one to another till his gaze settles. Sleeps with his eyes half open, feels the soft heavy tread of the Night Watch through the floor, stopping at each door again in Gentlemen's Ward D. D for debonair, joke the gentlemen, E for exemplary, nodding to their fellows at games, regimens, summerhouses on the Great Lawn. F for frightful, those not allowed privileges. Weed, allowed here, there, slides through the big ward doors that Night Watch locks behind them, slides round, wide across the rotunda room to the curtained alcove tucked under the women's wards stairwell. Night Watch seeing to the breakfast the cooks leave for him in tin boxes, and cold water, milk, in the half-size icebox. Furry dark in the alcove while the big wide room beyond begins to stripe with light. Weed hears the knocking first. Slides across behind Night Watch to the massive entrance and stands aside, stick still, peering through one of the narrow leaded glass windows to the side of the door. Pink edge in the dawn sky. A lady in fine dress, a girl, pounding. Night Watch orders him to the alcove. You stay there, boy, no sound. Hear me? Weed slides across the polished floor, stays behind the curtain. He can't see, only listen, until the Night Watch seats them near. Gives them the coffee milk and breakfast he would have shared with Weed. Weed stays still behind the curtain. Watching like he does. The lady in fine dress is like a girl and the girl has charge of her, cutting up the griddlecakes. The lady glances at Weed. He knows she sees through the curtain altogether. Quick, sharp, she flicks her gaze at the Night Watch. She knows and watches, then looks away, shut tight. She's the one will stay. The girl will leave. They leave them, so they do, so Hexum the head cook says, they bring them and leave them flat. Left, they stay. Weed pulls at the frowsy collar of his duster, rolls the pilled bits in his neck, to his face. Warm, worn soft, dust smell, barn smell. Hold to a thing, a smell. 'Twas yer blanket once,

Pet, pulled it from 'er and wrapped you in it. Weed knows the pen in Hexum's room is where she kept him, a scrubbed-clean slatted pen from the dairy for new calves while their mothers were milked. Like a small room it was, taller than him, and she has it still for he likes to climb in while she drapes a sheet over top, hunkers her bulk on hands and knees to look in at him. In yer cave are ye Pet? For ole Hexum raised ye, didn't I now, till you was big enough to raise yerself. Scuttle about, no sounds but yer whispers and hums. Too strange for a foundling, an wi' yer one blue eye. But Hexum knows ye see brighter than any jay or crow. Spot a shining across a field, you do, coax a mouse from a hole by looking. Ah, Weed, you do well. Show yerself, ye fast boy. And so he does. Steps out and shows himself to the girl. The Night Watch doesn't see. But Weed knows. Some stay. Some are left. The girl will go. Out the thick wall of door, down the stone steps, away on the graveled paths, the fountain silver splashing, out to the road and the town. Some stay, in the hallways and rooms, the gardens, walk the woods and orchard till they sleep deep in the graveyard. Those old ones, some young ones, his mam no-named among them, stay longest. Numbers only. Long and long, flat rows. He hears then, Matron's heavy tread a stairwell above. Steps back. Still, stillest. The velvet curtain hides him while he peers through, sees Night Watch hide in plain sight, looking past Matron, past the air she pulls with her, the day that goes tighter. Matron turns and goes and pulls the girl behind her. Matron has the girl, not touching, pulling her along, the lady following.

———

MATRONS . . . Some able hospital physicians amongst us have proposed having no Steward or Matron, but this suggestion, I presume, has arisen from difficulties . . . which have no doubt originated from improper persons having been selected for these stations. . . .

—DR. THOMAS STORY KIRKBRIDE, *1854*

ConaLee

MRS. BOWMAN

She was well fleshed and broad, like a square that could not be moved. Just as we stood, she appeared through the double doors that concealed the stairs, nodded, and turned to show the way. She'd no doubt we'd follow. Her long apron and dress were black, with a bit of white sheer at the throat. A puff of the same sheer white stood atop her head and thick gray braids. She led us to an office with *Reception* on the door, and sat herself behind a big desk. Three chairs were drawn up. I sat Mama in the chair to the left and took the chair just across, my back straight and tense. The woman looked down to fetch a small ledger from her apron and I glanced at Mama to see that she was sitting forward too. Her gaze wandered as though she saw another room entire, or no room at all, but she held very still.

The woman in black looked up from her ledger and peered at me over her glasses. Good day, she said. I'm sure you are fatigued.

Oh yes, ma'am. Thank you for the coffee. The johnnycakes and molasses warmed us after our journey.

She looked at me so strange. It seemed I'd spoken out of turn about the food and I thought not to mention the little boy.

I am Mrs. Bowman, she said after a moment, Hospital Matron in charge of Ward attendants, domestics, and house-keeping. As the hour is early, I will interview you. It is five, and the attendants come on duty at six to ready our patients for breakfast. I will come for you by noon, and deliver you to our Physician Superintendent, Dr. Thomas Story. He will consult as to diagnosis and treatment.

Dr. Story?

Yes, dear. Do you know of him?

No. It's—not a usual name.

He is a Quaker, from Philadelphia.

I nodded, for she seemed pleased to say it. I knew little of Philadelphia. I knew Quakers had no confessor, nor even a pastor.

The name is quite usual there. He trained under his uncle, Dr. Thomas Story Kirkbride of the Pennsylvania Hospital, as did I. You were admitted by our Night Watch, Mr. John O'Shea. Mrs. Hexum sees to the kitchen and dining rooms. Dr. Story alone decides upon a daily regimen for each female patient, and consults concerning the men's wards.

Yes, ma'am. I hope I might stay with Miss Janet . . . to help her . . .

Are you State residents, then? Can you prove such?

We are, ma'am. We rode two days to arrive here.

The Night Watch, Mr. O'Shea, saw a wagon deliver you to the Hospital. Near dawn, he said. Your family should have come in to register you.

He is not family. He saw us walking along the road and brought us here. It was on his way, he said, and he saw that Miss Janet is a woman of quality, in need of refuge. She barely speaks, you see.

She's mute, then? From birth?

No. Not from what I was told.

Is she healthy, otherwise? Most arrive with a doctor's report. We do not examine or treat physical disorders here.

Yes, she's healthy. She just . . . got quiet, alone, with the War and all. I worked for a neighbor family that's moved North now, to live with kin. They bade me look in on Miss Janet, and take meals to her. She stayed to home, after the War. Then her house burned, and well, there was nothing left. She commenced to walking, and I caught up to her. She would not turn back and so we kept on. The man in the wagon, he said to bring her here. He said it was a fine place where she could rest, with quality people.

His name? She looked down at her ledger, quill in hand.

He never said. We were only riding, in the back of the wagon. All he said, was, a refuge, for quality—

We treat all here, she said, according to what each requires.

Mrs. Bowman, I said. I have brought Miss Janet and I hope to help care for her. She's used to me.

You are not afflicted yourself.

Oh, no ma'am.

Your name?

Connolly.

How old are you, Miss Connolly?

Sixteen, but I've worked since I was little.

And your given—your Christian name?

Eliza, I said, for the name came to me.

Mama blinked as though Eliza was not the name to choose. I held my breath . . .

Mrs. Bowman leaned forward.

Yes, I said then, I'm Eliza.

What experience have you?

Cooking, ironing, cleaning, I said, reading to the sick and such. I'm young, but I'm a hard worker. And I've a calling for work with the anxious or confused.

Mrs. Bowman nodded. And your references?

I don't— The family I worked for, left sudden to move North. And the same day, the fire— Miss Janet's home was the finest in the neighborhood. It was all confusion, and I went after her, fearing for her safety. She is my reference, I would say. I have kept her calm over two days, with little rest or comfort, and brought her here.

I wondered I could lie so well. A liar was evil. But all stories were lies and I knew so many. I knew what not to say to anyone come by our ridge. We were far away now. How would we ever get back? I pressed my fingernail hard into my palm to stop thinking of it.

Mrs. Bowman made no comment but to address Mama. Miss Janet, she said. Is "Janet" your Christian name, or your surname?

Tell her, I thought. Tell her your name. I was near grown and didn't know her given name, or our surname, for Dearbhla would never say it, and she called Mama "My One," never a Christian name. But Mama only looked at me. A trembling smile came to her mouth.

Miss Janet, said Mrs. Bowman. Do you know Eliza?

Mama inclined her head toward me, and held out her hand to seek mine. Tears wet her eyes.

I don't mind to share a room with her, I said. A pallet on the floor is all I need. She's fragile, and quiet. I wouldn't want anyone to . . . bother her and her not able to say.

Miss Connolly, the men's and women's wards are completely separate, of course. Meals are served first to the women, then to the men. Even the walking trails, for taking the air behind the Asylum, are segregated. And we pride ourselves that every patient has a private room with window and transom. Ventilation and mountain air, exercise and routine. For this morning, you may accompany Miss Janet to her room, but by this evening, we must sort out your situation.

I see. And I thank you, very much, Mrs. Bowman.

I will take you up, she said, to Women's Ward B. Those in Ward C must earn privileges. The calmer women patients reside in wards A or B, provided they take part in activities and treatment.

It was as though a bit of ice lodged tight in my throat. Miss Janet must take part. But we were up and moving out of the office, across the marble floor of the great round room, through the silent doors that concealed the stairwell. Mrs. Bowman went on before us, mounting the stairs, and Mama held to my arm, her eyes cast down. I grasped the rolled mahogany banister and looked up to see it loop floor after floor to the top. Tones of pale color shone between the carved balusters— rose and yellow and blue. Each floor seemed different from the next in shades that might lighten shadows or calm the infirm. The very top seemed dark even in daylight, and I felt dizzy to think of standing near it to look down rather than up. We came to the first broad landing, with the rose-colored plaster walls and the brass wall plaque inscribed *Ward A*. I saw that the doors to the wing opposite were barred with a thick plank and set with locks. We continued on, up the stairs, and I hoped Mrs. Bowman's questions had ended for today. Any details of our story had left my mind. The staircase seemed a last means of retreat and I only helped Mama keep the pace, following Mrs. Bowman's solid black form. I thought of her tilting backward and crushing us both, but we came to the second landing. I didn't look at the barred wing opposite. But the walls were a pretty pale yellow and the brass wall plaque by the thickset door read *Ward B*. Mrs. Bowman took a ring of skeleton keys from her apron and fit one to the door of the yellow ward. She swung the door open.

We enter here, she said. I must lock up behind us.

We walked past her into Ward B, a wide hallway that went on such a way, with sections marked by beamed wooden archways. The hardwood floors were covered by one rug after another, round rugs for each parlor space, square rugs between, with sofas and rocking chairs along the walls. The hallway was so wide that it seemed a very long, pale yellow room, and the arches and trim of the high ceilings were sky blue. It was true what Papa said about the palms, all set about in big pots, and many other leafy plants as large as small trees. Light streamed through from double doors at the very end. The globes of the ceiling fixtures glowed with gaslight.

This way, said Mrs. Bowman, her voice low. Nurses will be coming soon to wake everyone. Wards A and B breakfast at six, with some from Ward C.

What pretty colors, I said, taking care to whisper.

It is all Dr. Story's design, she answered, and paused at a door midway down. Your arrival was unexpected, and we've not made preparations but to fill the water pitcher. We may locate you elsewhere, Miss Janet, if you stay on, but for now this room is made up and will afford you a rest.

Again the ring of keys, the door unlocked.

The room was light blue, small and spare, with a narrow

bed along one wall made up in white sheets and counterpane, a folded patchwork quilt at the foot. Two tall windows with broad sills were hung with tied-back curtains of some thin yellow fabric. A small round pillow of the same yellow sat as though prized at the head of the bed. The bars on the windows were so thin and close together that they seemed the mullions of the glass panes. A small trunk sat by the bed, and a girl's round mirror, edged in plaster roses, stood in the far window. The deep windowsill behind the bed held what seemed a makeshift altar—a hinged wooden frame, carved with an arch, opened on a small figurine of an angel. Later I would see that the angel was plaster washed free of color, hung on a rude nail.

Mrs. Bowman was speaking. I could barely attend her words.

This room, she said, was occupied by an elderly, infirm gentlelady who passed away. She had no home but here, so her few possessions as yet remain.

We nodded to Mrs. Bowman, and she to us, and she closed the door shut behind her. I heard the lock click. We could not get out and no one could get in. I turned to Mama and she turned to me, still holding my hand. I undid her jacket clasps, and helped her out of her skirts. These I folded with care and lay across the one straight chair. We stepped together then, as though in a dance of certain measure, to the narrow bed and lay down upon it. We held the small round pillow between us and slept, safer, it seemed, than we had ever been.

CLASSIFICATION—The least excited—what is commonly
called the best class of patients—should occupy the upper
stories and be nearest the center building . . . Patients are
often much interested in the delusions of their neighbors,
and by their efforts to relieve the afflictions of others, frequently do much towards getting rid of their own.
—DR. THOMAS STORY KIRKBRIDE, *1854*

ConaLee

THEE AND THINE

I dreamed I was walking on a street, holding the three babbies.
They clung to me, but my arms seemed to hold no weight.
The babbies seemed even to lighten my step, so that I barely
trod the cobblestones of a sunny street I'd never seen. We came
to the corner. Then I saw them across the way, nearly grown,
and my empty arms ached. I heard the sounds of a milk cart,
the clomp of a horse, the rundle past of our buckboard that
took me from them, but all those were only shadows, whilst
the children were real. They looked at me but did not know
me. I woke despairing, clasped in my mother's embrace and
the scent of her milk. Her body remembered them even if she
didn't. I clasped the bedsheet to her breasts and felt it dampen.
I'd no timepiece but the light in the room had changed. We
must wash and dress, but I only wanted to lie still and call
back the babbies I might never see again. I thought on the feel
of them against me. All he give away. Lest I lose my breath,
I recalled for myself a cipher of things lost, not persons. I'd
nothing but the clothes I wore, and so visioned, in the order I
recalled them, my muslin dress, my worsted wool, my woolen
socks, three pair. My better shoes, that were Mama's. My win-

ter cloak made by Dearbhla. I visioned my chickens and the names I gave them. Four God's Eyes from Dearbhla. My slate and chalks. My ruler and abacus. My inkwell and quill pen, that was Mama's.

I never went to any school but hers. We read at night, Mama to me and I to her, standing and reciting. She said it was our only theater, and winter evenings were given to lessons. We were hiding from the War and men leaving the War, Mama said, hiding our chickens and cows and provisions, staying out of the town. She shared our buckboard with Dearbhla, our granny neighbor who lived on the ridge above us, to sell her ramps and ginseng and medicine powders of a Saturday when the road was passable. Dearbhla brought us salt and flour and cornmeal from town, and I collected her a dozen eggs a week from our chickens. She made me a God's Eye every birthday: skinned sticks and sinew and corn silk, with threads or twine for color. Mama hung them over my pallet, one for each year, and told me back then that if I found myself alone, I must go to Dearbhla, that some feared her land and woods, and the fear might keep me safe. I wasn't allowed to learn her cures. Dearbhla could take away a headache or the flux, but she said her powders and tinctures were nothing but what grew hereabouts. She helped bring the first babe, the little chap. Then Papa told her to stay away and keep her potions and spells. He tore down the God's Eyes and buried them in the garden. I found some broken pieces and sewed them between my blankets to be near me every night. I wished now I could see what Dearbhla saw, to see how to be home again, and keep us from this trouble! Irish hag, Papa called her, bogtrotter, medicine bone, woods witch. Dearbhla soaked rabbit bones, and fox or coyote bones, even bird bones, in fox urine to turn deer from the gardens, or wrapped chicken bones in braided jimsonweed to keep bad luck distant. She hung clean, polished bones from her house and porch rafters to catch good fortune. They talked in the wind, wheeled about in storms.

Dearbhla would say that she and my mama were the same. But Dearbhla was old, strong and lean as a man. Her face was lined and freckled and she smelled of woodsmoke even in summer. Her long gray hair hung in plaits thick as sheep's wool that I loved to lean my face against when she unbound them. She covered them in the crown of her man's brimmed hat, wore sack skirts or trousers she sewed herself, and tromping boots. She was ever foraging roots and herbs, and gathering bones to dry in her shed.

First day of July last, a night rain had set the creeks to running. The chap was a year old that day. I tied him to my front in Mama's shawl and walked up the ridge to Dearbhla. Papa forbade her coming near, and me from going to her, but he was gone to town. Mama was with child again, her belly already swole. She wouldn't walk or talk, and only ate if I fed her with the spoon.

Dearbhla's cabin and porch were like ours, like someone had set down two of the same amongst the trees, but her porch was hung with big God's Eyes made of sapling limbs and long feathers, some with bells or broken porcelain bits that rattled in a breeze. Her dogs set to barking and stopped when they knew it was me. Papa would say she raised bobcats from kittens and kept them in a den she made in the rocks. We heard them some nights, screaming like banshees. Papa would go out then and fire his gun in the dark, saying he'd get him a biddy witch, a filthy mick. Then he'd drink whiskey and fall asleep outside like Dearbhla had cast him down from way up on her ridge.

I came up along the blackberry bramble that edged her woods, and she came down the path to meet me.

ConaLee, she said. Give me that chap. And she took him from me and lifted the shawl away.

Mama is bad, I said.

I know she is. My One.

I have to feed her, Dearbhla, the same as I feed him, boiled oatmeal and broth, and jerky I chew till it's soft.

I see you, ConaLee. She took my hand and led me onto the porch.

Are you conjuring me, Dearbhla? I can't hardly lift my feet.

I do not conjure, ConaLee. That is only what they say. You are wrung out from being all she has. Rest here in the hammock.

She tipped the porch hammock down to take me up. I lay back along the feather tick and sheepskins, and she put the chap in with me. I held on to him and closed my eyes and heard her go inside. Dearbhla said my name the way my mama used to, not the way Papa did, and I could smell lavender and mint and the bundled herbs she had drying, tied up all along the eaves.

She was tall and thin, Dearbhla, like a wraith, and I could sense her moving here and there, gathering food in a wooden bowl, grinding and fixing. Then I was asleep and saw her gliding amongst the trees. I looked into the hills and valleys and rippling streams with her eyes, like she clasped me to her, rising and falling. Then I felt her strong hand at the back of my neck, holding my head up.

ConaLee, drink this. Sweet with berries and honey.

I could taste the bitter underneath, but I drank nearly all, and gave some to the chap. For your birthday, my babbie, I told him.

This boy have a name yet?

Mama never named him, Dearbhla, because she hardly talks. Papa calls him Chap and put a gate across the steps to keep him on the porch. I step over to fetch water. And now there's a new one coming, soon, it must be. She is swole up and won't hardly move from the bed.

In three month, Dearbhla said. More than one. Two babbies.

No, I said. How can I bring two—

Just like before, she said, when you helped me. The girl is like you, born with a caul. You must tear it away in one piece and burn it in the fire, just as the child takes breath.

It was like I heard old sounds, and saw a veil before me with the light behind it. You were there, I said, when I was born.

Dearbhla put her hand to my forehead. Course I was, she said. Didn't I raise your mama, and come with her to this place? Hush now.

I wished Dearbhla would conjure me, even if she said she couldn't, and keep us with her. And make Mama into a bird that could find its way to us. Dearbhla's dark eyes, deep as pools, came near. I was asleep and awake and had no thought to move.

Hear me, ConaLee. No matter what that man do, you fly to me in your mind. I hold you until he go away. For the rest, you chew these roots each morning. Never let him see.

I felt her take the so-small pouch of fancy buttons I kept hid in my clothes, and pull open its drawstring mouth. She held it up for me to see, and poured in the roots. They were white and small as grains of rice.

What are they for, Dearbhla?

To stave off your monthlies, keep your scent and sweat pure as a child's.

Dearbhla, make him leave Mama be.

I cannot keep him from her. His hook is in her. But her eye, her thought, is deep away. She will eat from your hand only.

Make him go, Dearbhla.

My One, she said, my child. She was talking to Mama, not me, but she moved her hand across my eyes, talking all the while under her breath.

I didn't try to listen. The words slipped in and out. But I knew in the long months after, to feed Mama raw eggs whipped to a froth, sweetened with warm milk and maple syrup, and marrow ground up with dried apples. I knew there would be another baby after the boy was born. I caught her and pulled the caul away, and carried her to the fire to see it burn. She wailed a wild scream as it disappeared, a sound no babe would make, a cry like a howl.

Like he was answering, Papa threw open the door to the snowy February night and ran out to shoot his pistol into the trees all round the cabin. Later he never touched the girl twin, nor the boy. He'd take up the chap, roar with him and make him laugh, but the new ones were mine to mind. I said to myself, all that winter, that Dearbhla saw them, and me, even if I could not go to her. And she could not come to me.

Here, though, the Asylum walls were thick. Our mountain, our ridge, was far away. The thick door to our room and the glass transom above were shut, and seemed to stop sound. I heard my mother stir.

Here, I told her. Sit like I'm sitting. The doctor will talk to us today.

She sat beside me on the edge of the bed, holding the sheet to her, and nodded.

You must think of talking, Miss Janet. To keep me near you. Here, I am Eliza. They will call me Eliza, or Nurse Connolly.

She only looked at me like I was mistaken, but seemed more herself already. I poured the washbowl full and cleaned her front and face with the sponge I found beside the pitcher, and splashed myself with water before rinsing her milk from the sheet. A mere portion was wet. I hung it to dry on the closet hooks, and would say she'd been sick if they asked. I saw I'd forgotten to take off her silken hairnet and combs, but they'd kept her dark plaits smooth. That was good—I'd no thought I could dress her hair in such high style. I led her to the one chair and made the bed up tight. All the while I dressed her, I talked to her. First her delicates, with clean babbie's diapers I'd brought, folded tight to catch her milk, then chemise and slip and hoop petticoat. Blouse and skirt. The short tight jacket with its ruched collar and silk buttons. She stood to help me, as though she was Miss Janet, and turned her head just so. I held up a tasseled earring and fixed it to her ear.

There, Miss Janet, I said. You must learn to do things for yourself. Give me your hand, like this.

I opened my hand, lifted hers to mine, and turned up her palm. There I placed the other earring; they were a pair, after all. She held it, looking, and I moved her to the girl's round mirror. I stood behind, lifting it up so that I looked into it over her shoulder. Slip the wire through, I said. And clip it behind.

She peered at her reflection, amazed it seemed, and turned her head to and fro, touching the long silk tassel, watching it move. She even smiled at me.

I knew I must fix the mirror to the wall so she would get used to seeing herself. I reached around her and opened the earring. There, I said, put it on.

She held it to her ear.

I had to help her close the wire.

It was still a triumph of sorts.

She stood by the window looking out as I pulled on my own dusty clothes—my chambray shirt, my woolsey jacket only to cover the shirt, my trousers. I felt of my pocket and there was the little mirror. His luck charm, Papa had said. At least I'd taken his luck, but I hid the mirror deep in Mama's carpetbag and wished for nicer clothes. I'd kept her garments clean and shaken out, but mine were dusty from chores, even before our buckboard journey. I saw my feet on the well-trod paths of home, and then rushing, nearly flying, along the narrow road to the neighbor farms, either side, with my charges. First the boys, the babbie tied to my front in the shawl, the chap riding the drag, crowded in with sacks of clothes and bedding, crowing like I'd found him a new game. Then the girl, supplies from the larder weighing down the drag. Payment I'd supposed, for taking charge until we returned. It was only widows on the ridge. The older one had lost her sons and husband in the War, and the younger, childless widow, was barren—she'd said so many a time. How would they feed the nurslings? I hadn't even thought, and babbled we wouldn't be gone long. The women said nothing, bending and hauling to rid me of my burdens, and me rushing away, for he'd put Mama in the buckboard and I was panicked he'd take her from me. He'd turned up midday and bade me dress her in the clothes, before he said we were leaving. The neighbor widow who did her hair, the younger one, smiled just as sweet. She took the lady's magazine picture torn from *Godey's* off its nail on the wall, to show that Mama's dark locks came forward just so in plaits from under her bonnet—just like the beautiful lady in gray who was arriving or leaving in the picture. She wore her gloves, and the seated woman in blue offered her a message or card. The young widow took herself off then, to make preparations for what she'd soon receive.

I put the picture of the visiting ladies, rolled tight and tied with string, in Mama's new carpetbag. Surely she'd want it— she'd told me long ago that the image was "thee and thine." I was the young visitor in gray, and she, the older lady in blue.

Their silk dresses shone and nearly rustled. Now I fetched the picture from Mama's bag and sat on the bed to unroll it. Mama sat beside me, touching the page. I liked to pretend the picture showed us in a time to come, with velvet chairs and fine rugs. The red velvet chair was as deep red, the patterned screen behind them as fine, but I saw that the lady in blue was dark eyed, in her lap a white bundle, a drawstring purse, might be, like the muslin bags that Dearbhla filled with her medicine roots and powders.

I turned to Mama. Don't ever say about Dearbhla. Not here.

She nodded, looking at me as though to mark my words, listening as she had not in many weeks.

I took my own small muslin pouch from inside my chemise, and opened it to feel for the grains of root Dearbhla had given me. I found only one left among the buttons, and put it in my mouth. Held in my teeth, worried and chewed slow, it tasted of licorice. Could be these many months, I'd swallowed a message from Dearbhla, piece by piece. Perhaps she knew of our journey. We had traveled, hard as it was, and slept, and found "asylum." Dearbhla always said that words had two meanings. Papa called me "puny," "stick straight"—I was near as tall as Mama but thin as a boy, and my monthlies had not begun. No one could keep things from happening, I was sure—but it seemed Dearbhla glimpsed what might come. Not conjure, she would say, but thought that sees between. I could not change what was. I only hoped to keep Mama safe until she was herself.

You are Miss Janet now, I told her. Whatever came before—it's not true here.

She nodded. Then she whispered, Here, we are safe.

They were four words, barely breathed, but my heart warmed. Yes, Mama! I told her. Someone will come for us, and the doctor will talk with you. His name is—Dr. Story. It's funny, nearly. We have a story, while we are here. You are Miss Janet, in need of rest and cure. You are calm now, if he asks. And you must say that Eliza—my name, here—should stay near you. Can you say it? Eliza?

She frowned, her eyes wet.

But she surely remembered Eliza, for *Uncle Tom's Cabin* was one of our winter books. She'd read me the story, cold nights by the fire, with the wind howling and snow whirling down, of enslaved Eliza crossing the river, when I was too young to read it myself. The ice *pitched* and *creaked* as Eliza *leapt* to another and *still another cake,* fleeing those who chased her. I did not know *enslaved*, I did not know *Ohio* save for the map in my *American States*, but I knew of cakes. I ate Mama's cakes for breakfast, then—they were cornmeal pancakes, but she called them cakes—and I wished for brave Eliza that the icy cakes in the river could be as soft and warm and sweet. But Eliza trod on frozen, lurching cakes that cut her feet, and *blood marked every step.*

Mama said my name, ConaLee, as like to remind me who I really was.

Yes, I said. But you must ask that Eliza stay with you. To help you. Here, I am Eliza. You know me. Eliza.

She put her hand on my cheek. My One, she whispered. Don't fear.

Mama, I told her. You see? You can speak.

Yes, to you . . .

But she would not say the name Eliza, not today. I only hoped the doctor would speak with me and let me plead our case. I took her arm as we sat together on the narrow bed, waiting for the knock on the door.

———

PART II

1864

Seventh West Virginia Volunteer Cavalry Regiment
(The Bloody Seventh), July 1861

The Sharpshooter

AFFLICTED

MAY 1864

Most days of the winter bivouac, he came alone to this narrow water, barely a stream, just a rivulet, brush and vines to one side, rushes to the other. Two broken-down rowboats rotted in a bend. The water glimmered toward Cedar Mountain. The reflection, the shimmer, put him in mind of the clear dappling ribbons tracing through the flat fields of his childhood. That the shapes of the streams were so similar confounded him, even to the gentle bends and wide-mouthed opening that tightened to a false horizon. The little boats were ruined versions of the one he'd drifted in with Eliza, tangling limbs to lie still and not be seen through the green shoots of the fields. Those moments, in all he'd traversed these three years of the War, away from her, came back to him.

If he'd gotten them farther when they'd fled, all the way north to Canada, say, but flecks of blood striped her legs. She was with child and couldn't have stood weeks more on horseback. And their isolated Allegheny ridge in frontier Virginia seemed better hid than anywhere in Massachusetts. He'd heard tell of Boston, abolitionist stronghold, from men whose horses he'd shoed and curried, Southern purveyors come to sell goods to the plantations. The coming trouble, they said, the War to defend our way of life, the Yankee devils. He wanted to be one of those devils, even before Eliza's father, on mere suspicion, had him bound, his chest branded like he was property—warning shack Irish off his daughter. The fact Dearbhla had been nursemaid to his motherless children, and raised her adopted son with them for a time, was worse insult.

A scant week later, there was no choice; they had to leave,

he and Eliza, and Dearbhla, whom he called the only mother
he'd known. Bandaged under his shirt, the wound salved
with Dearbhla's herbal paste, he'd led them in sudden flight
through a chaotic low country dusk he did not dwell upon.
They'd found the deserted cabins two months later, highest up
an Appalachian mountain ridge in the heights of the Alleghenies. Fugitives, they stayed to the ridges. Bearded, hair grown
long, speaking as men spoke in those mountains, he traded for
supplies in the valley hamlet below. Two years surcease and
safety, then the beginnings of conflagration. The valleys below
them would host the War's first skirmishes after he enlisted,
but western Virginia's heights were too steep and forested to
allow major battles, or the killing fields in Virginia and Pennsylvania he'd so far survived.

He and Eliza made no children in their refuge, those short
years before the War. She'd thought she was barren, from the
one she'd lost on the journey. It seemed a trick of fate when she
got with child just as War broke out. He was sick to go, sick to
stay, but the babe, safe only in the mountains, was more urgent
reason the War must be won. There should be a child now, if
things were well. He read Eliza's letters from the first months
again and again, but his Seventh West Virginia Volunteer
Cavalry Regiment had been pulled into the Third Brigade,
Second Infantry. Cavalry sharpshooters weren't officially des-
ignated; they ranged farther than their infantry counterparts
and moved on verbal order. Letters seldom found them, and
he mailed his own missives into a void, one camp to another.
He'd only signs such as Dearbhla might imagine to know his
family were alive. Before mustering in, he'd showed his enlistment papers to a pastor and brought him up the mountain
to make Eliza his wife under their new name, then journeyed
to open an account at the bank in Weston, the nearest larger
town. He named "family" as beneficiary and gave the small
ledger book to Dearbhla for safekeeping. He didn't want Eliza
showing herself in the towns—they hadn't use for money; they

bartered or made what they needed, but he banked part of his soldier's wages, as much as he could spare, always from a working post office in a town. The random mail he received in camp was bank receipts. He'd seen children and their stunned families streaming out of battered Fredericksburg, Chancellorsville, Gettysburg: weak, coughing children, Black and white, with rheumy eyes. But Dearbhla knew woods medicinals, plants that healed and strengthened, how to shoot and hunt, and he'd taught Eliza. No battle would find its way to them. They could be safer nowhere else.

The woods here in occupied Virginia, west of the Rapidan, were scruffy outcroppings, but he came to this ruffle of water behind the bivouac to commune with his hopes. His three-year enlistment was up but he'd reenlisted in '64; he would not go home until the War was won and the name he'd taken stayed his—legitimate, won, writ on discharge papers. He came here to imagine that paper in his hand, his chosen name in stalwart script, the War over. He fought alongside men who thought themselves his brothers and did not know him. Here at this forgotten stream, flowing hidden between brush and flowering weeds, he knew himself. Elsewhere he was never one man but two, seen, unseen, his strength doubled, his awareness keen, covert, as though one self fought for the survival of the other. He allowed his mind such thoughts, crouching to anoint his hands with pungent mustard weed crushed in the pale sap bled of broken Queen Anne's lace. He'd long ago traded his Burnside carbine for the longer range of his Enfield, and the unguent kept his hands supple, sensitive to his weapon.

The stream's reflective surface was still but for flashes of dragonfly and insect. Water bugs skated on their eyelash legs. He watched them and washed the milky paste from his hands, half closing his eyes in the afternoon sun's beckoning shadows. Message, he thought, or rebuke. He'd believed the North superior, massive, unbeatable. No one had thought it would take this long, that the South must be battered to death. He'd seen such that he wondered what world would be left, though he'd taken from it all he could, to hasten victory. He was alive because sharpshooters circled battlefields, knelt protected behind breastworks to target enemy command, lay prone in a pronged abatis of felled trees to kill enemy leading a charge. He positioned himself above battlefields to pick out, at a distance, an officer's circling saber, a feathered, broader-brimmed cap, the glinting gold buttons of a double-breasted jacket. He foraged alone at night near enemy lines, culling pickets. He'd found clear aim from near half a mile—headshots and the immediate drop. He hoped for such himself if he was to die in the coming weeks, but a quick death looked more unlikely. Grant cared nothing for special skills; he'd moved sharpshooters from one division into another and issued them regulation uniforms. He cared nothing for those who'd fought and were captured. No more prisoner exchanges; any Union man in a Southern prison would die there to deny the South her replacements. Men in camp said Grant would take Richmond this summer, just as he'd secured the Mississippi at Vicksburg and forced the Rebels deep into Georgia after Chattanooga. May it be so. The stream meandered. The sharpshooter did not pray, though holy verses, childhood hymn and phrase, played through his mind in the quiet.

. . .

All winter, the Army of the Potomac encamped west of the Rapidan, swelling their ranks while Lee's army suffered for rations in their earthworks east of the same broad river. The armies swung toward each other to no avail: Lee's October assault by way of Cedar Mountain, Meade's repulse at Manassas, Meade's day after Thanksgiving strike on rebel earthworks at Mine Run. No loss, no gain. Lee hadn't enough troops to pursue the Yankees. Rain, mud, sleet, and hail preceded snow; the deep rutted mud froze solid. Union sharpshooters, mountain natives of New England and Appalachia, went out in twos and threes, forded the shallow river in the dark, shot Rebel pickets night after night. Once they'd walked across the frozen Rapidan, leaving the horses tied to trees on the Union side. He'd shot an officer near midnight, a soldier in full uniform who'd come out to smoke with the pickets. Sharpshooters moved with the troops but they were loners, known to one another by names that described their eccentricities: Flint, for the flint he carried in his pockets to light fires in damp brush or the meager cup of a nearly vertical rock; Horse, for his ability to catch spooked Rebel horses wandering behind Yankee lines and string them together on one lead. Cherokee, they called the West Virginian, for his use of herbs as charms and salves, his skill at fastening his long legs around his mount and riding slipped to the side, holding to her mane. The blue jacket of his secondhand uniform had faded to near gray, but he wouldn't part with it—extra protection, he told the rest, on lone nights behind Confederate lines. He could talk like a Reb if surprised by enemy in the dark, and entertained in camp, telling stories in a tone-perfect South Carolina accent—Marse this and Marse that, laced with contempt. Union men had shoes and coats, at least, while some of Lee's soldiers wrapped their feet in rags and sat about in women's shawls. The Rebs had already caught every living rabbit and squirrel their side of the river. Half in number to Grant's better-supplied troops, they ate a quarter as much; rumor had it they'd surely give up by spring.

The sharpshooters laughed and cursed at their campfires. Lean men are mean men, they said. Any Reb ain't deserted by now is a killing machine, and Grant had so many men he gave not a damn if half were slaughtered. Grant was the heartless death angel come to win the War; it was whether a man of them could survive to see it. The sharpshooters carried their long Enfield rifles everywhere, volunteered to probe Confederate lines, plotted how to separate themselves from infantry once the army moved. They ate less to store up rations. They believed in Grant but didn't want to die for him, for he saw them as one nameless sacrificial tide that must turn another.

. . .

The Army of the Potomac had passed last January and February in Brandy Station. The officers' wives departed camp in March, the sutlers and their wares in April. Troops began crossing the Rapidan on the third of May at Germanna Ford, and farther down, at Ely. The fast-flung pontoon bridges were wide enough for supply wagons, but two columns of men preceded the wagons for hours, sharpshooters scattered among them. The tramping thud of more than 120,000 infantry raised a hanging cloud of dust. Waves of troops pressed forward from the river, then staggered in broken lines into an infernal close woods called the Wilderness—not a forest but miles of brushy tangle. Young trees, three to six inches round, so tight grown and numerous that a man must turn sideways to move between them, thrust upward thirty to forty feet. Scrub, brush, briar bush, sucking vines thick as a finger, tangled men at the knees. The sharpshooter, cut off from his fellows, his horse tied to a wagon far to the rear, shook his head in disbelief. His orders to target officers would be guesswork in this woods where no man could lead a charge. B'God they'd best move through in daylight and rendezvous with the wagons by nightfall. Fighting here would be a hell and brimstone of close combat, no lines possible, no way to situate above or at an angle. The fine scope on his weapon was near useless; any man on a horse would be on him before he could take aim, if a sure distance shot was even possible in this maze. But the army must stop to wait. The wagons must find passage around the gnarled Spotsylvania forest called the Wilderness, else Grant's troops risked losing their victuals, their ammunition, and the bandages and saws that served the medical tents. The sharpshooter cradled his long rifle in his arms and reflected that his horse was all he wanted; he knew how to survive without rations or biscuit and wore three days' ammunition, for he weighed every shot, up from a gully or ditch, down from a height, or from purchase in a tree. Here there were no trees big enough to lend a man height and cover, nowhere his wily mare could flatten herself on command behind rocks or ledges. He'd taught her tricks worthy of a circus horse, and she plodded now between miles of rumbling Conestoga wagons, her mane and fetlock brushed smooth. Liza, he called her, for the Eliza who was mother to his child, though no letter had caught up to him to say if the child was boy or girl.

The men were halted. They set to clearing a swath around them, felling thin trees in piles. Saplings the height of three men grew so close and narrow they'd no branches. Their ragged pointed trunks, twenty or thirty across, made flung-down triangular breastworks, the earth dug out enough that a man could crouch to reload. The sharpshooter fell to with the rest, slashing and digging, furious at the prospect of staying in these woods at night, when they ought to be finding open ground. He breathed better as they widened a space here and there down the line. All around, far as they could see: more close trees, impassable thickets. The brush and briars and winding grapevine needed close work with machetes that none of the troops possessed. Some beat passage with their short-handled shovels, effecting holes in the draped green undergrowth. The sharpshooter dug deeper inside one breastwork and another, aware that shots from direct fire would find their way through the felled trees. He considered moving alone across this Wilderness, likely miles of hard going to where the tangle gave way, and waiting for Grant's army to emerge after him. But if he left his assigned unit in the confusion of the advance, he might never locate his horse, and he was mighty partial to her; she brought him luck, and the sense of her firmly under him was some remnant of comfort. He slashed trees so quick and hard that they fell in lines. Those near him crossed the green saplings in constructions that smelled fresh in the close woods.

They set up pickets ten feet apart, but two of five men were blocked sight of each other in the jungle of growth. Lee's forces were not expected that night, nor the following day. By evening the sounds of chopping and felling stopped and the troops settled. The light was dim, and the calm had a strange doomful weight.

· · ·

Daybreak, he moved forward with the pickets to sight any Rebels scouting Union forces. They passed small canvas tents and the Union hospital, half erected near the Orange Plank Road, and soundlessly penetrated more dense woods. Owls called out a series of warnings. They saw no enemy but the sharpshooter felt a gravity pulsing under him, live as a deep river whose might, curtailed by obstruction, built to implacable force. The others seemed not to feel the low charge of the ground but he trusted his sense and sight, the hallucinatory glow of the skinny trees, and slipped through the pines to sight a small dogwood in abundant blossom. The pink-tipped branches held themselves in conical symmetry, unscarred, untouched. The turn of the open petals brought to mind the smooth inner palm of a woman's hand and he suddenly imagined that Eliza was very near him. He stepped closer. The petals trembled almost imperceptibly, and then again, as though pulsed by distant footfall. He returned to the Union encampment and urgently reported a considerable force marching toward them, but no one had seen sign of a single Confederate in the nearly three mile they'd scouted. His report was dismissed. The pickets were called in and told to rest. Last night's dark had seemed too perilous to admit sleep; the May morning was mellow and men fell to dozing against each other's shoulders. The sharpshooter cleaned his Enfield, disassembling and assembling the works. He'd stopped carrying his sharpshooter's saber. Sabers were heavy and cumbersome, but he felt a keen disadvantage in this place that would likely force one man against another. He thought ruefully that he would need to be at arm's length to triumph in close combat and must take a saber from the first fallen man who no longer needed one. A whippoorwill shrieked its vibrato in the trees, and shrieked again, mocking him. He left off thinking and tried to locate the bird, listening. He knew the look of them, their mottled brown markings and small white spots, with the white necklace on the throat like a preacher's collar. But the whippoorwill fell silent.

.   .   .

Just after noon they commenced a march. Command was muddled not to have sent pickets scouting forward hours earlier. Now their ranks filed in straggled form at a distinct right angle through the trees. They came to the edge of a fallow cornfield. The earth was studded with bleached short stalks, dusty and dry as the brush concealed in the stands of woods. The open ground before them was no more than seven or eight hundred feet, and half as wide across, but they must move down a slope and then up a small hill. Scant movement was seen at the crest, some Union advance group or remnant, for Lee was expected tomorrow. Just as they stepped out, a heightened line of smoke puffed all along the edge of the rise. To a man, their hearts stilled. They fixed bayonets. *Forward. Double time. Charge!* The line yelled together, plunging down the slope in a bombardment of shell and bullets so heavy and deafening it was as though they'd entered a field on fire. The sharpshooter threw himself forward in a realm punctuated by explosion. Men fell to the right and left of him; others leapt over bodies or ran across them. This enraged the sharpshooter, who advanced to the front of the line in search of solid ground. Relief from continuous volley lay only in advancing; he would bayonet every one of the murderers on the hill, for the blood on his face and mouth that was not his own, for the men trampled by their comrades as they died, for a silence beyond any grief and his own death sure to come. He ran to embrace it but made the rise as his battalion streamed behind him, one survivor for every three fallen Federals who'd attacked across the crucible henceforth known as Saunders Field. Reinforcements stormed the hill and the Rebs fell back, melting into underbrush, leaving billowy smoke and the track of the cannon they'd pulled after them. The dense woods hid them as though they were twenty and not a hundred or hundreds of soldiers. The Federals pursued them into the trees and formed haphazard lines as fire rang back at them, staggering pops and cracks that were only camouflage. The massive Confederate force before them was realigning in a dense surround the killing field had only interrupted.

That torturous field! The sharpshooter moved on too quickly to see it covered with bodies, though an unrecognized image of smoke as fine as mist, rising over knee-high grass like so many souls ascending, would stun and confuse him for many years. He found himself without thought or plan in a stalemate of withering fire. Armies a quarter mile apart exchanged a savage fusillade in thick brush, invisible to each other. The sharpshooter stood to the side behind a tree too small to protect his limbs, loading and firing in quick repetition. A soldier to his immediate right took a shell to the gut and rose whirling into the air, flung star-splayed as though before a revelation. The explosion rained down bits of flesh and bowel and bloody entrails on those below; the body dropped to the ground like a bag of wet sand. The sharpshooter, on his knees, cut about the face with gravel or shards of bone, would hear that sound in fractured visions, just behind and to his left, somehow explicit in a roaring instant of pause, and not remember what or when it was, only that the horror and dread still swallowed him when so much else was vanished. The earth reverberated. He spat out a mouthful of dirt and got to his feet, reloading. His hearing was stopped as though cotton stuffed his ears but he could feel the report of his Enfield against his chest like the repeated blow of an insistent fist.

Now their line rallied and moved deeper into the trees; they gained forcefully for a beat of time, driving the unseen enemy before them until a volley seemed to roll round as though unevenly righted. The mix of shell and musket fire came at them like propulsion and concussed them to the ground. The sharpshooter pulled rapidly forward in a fast crawl, calling to the men near him; they were below the fire and could cut the Reb advance at the ankles, shooting quickly all along the line. They sent across a volley and a row of Rebels seemed to fall in a thick smoke of gunpowder, slowing those who must jump and dodge the bodies. The pulsing undergrowth and straggly pines wavered as answering fire forced the Federals to take cover. And so they moved, to and fro over the same hundred yards, the enemy falling back until another brigade relieved them and charged forward, repulsed by Union fire as the Federals came forward in turn, only to be driven back. The angular breastworks here were dry logs and fence posts salvaged from the forest floor; the decimated brigade who'd piled them to shoulder height had retreated. Their dead lay askew across briars and broken branches. Reinforcements filtered forward through the fallen, and the strengthened line held their ground, arrayed in three rows that rapidly knelt to load as the standing line fired over their heads. They were gauging a forward charge when black pine smoke, acrid, redolent with burning sap, rolled up on them in clouds. Gunpowder had so thickened the air that brush and trees ignited. The sharpshooter found a regimental scarf on a bush, tied it across his nose and mouth, and continued firing. He could not see, but the smoke was so dark that he glimpsed white blazes searing through and aimed just above them. Then the breastworks themselves caught fire. Leaping flame enveloped the dry wood and leaf, forcing the men back even as the enemy, seeing their advantage, fired, cutting men down through the flames as they turned to flee. A bedlam of Federal soldiers poured in from adjacent lines. Fires lit throughout the Wilderness and pinnacles of flame shot skyward.

The sharpshooter, his hair and brows singed, fell back enough to glimpse an isolated enemy swarm flail forward around the flaming breastworks, finishing off the men they'd injured, gaining the ground. Men screamed, cut off from any escape. Blazes leapt tree to tree, crackling, whistling shrill otherworldly sounds. A soldier in Union blue, wounded in both legs, rolled away from the flames even as fire pursued him along the ground. The sharpshooter lay down his weapon and ran forward, pulling the man over his shoulder in one motion; they turned, and he heard the man say, *Brother—* A Rebel, his grimacing face covered in black soot, took hold of them both and plunged a knife so deep into the wounded man's back that the sharpshooter felt the blow. Life went out of his burden in complete cessation of the tension and relief so evident an instant before. The sharpshooter grasped the knife and pulled it out, reversing its trajectory full force and plunging it into the throat of their assailant. The Confederate gurgled blood, grasping desperately and bringing them all down. Brush behind the breastworks now lit in a broad crescent; flames doubled in height as fire raced up the trees in whirling pieces. The sharpshooter pushed his assailant aside and was struggling to his feet, still holding the body of his fellow, when a shell exploded nearby, throwing up earth and rock with tremendous velocity. A stone the size of his head struck his right temple a glancing blow and broke his skull. He fell back unconscious as the spattered stone ricocheted into a gully. Sparks flung themselves eagerly over him, igniting a new existence in which he would not know himself, nor this moment, nor the weeks that followed. Two soldiers in retreat ripped off his burning clothes and rolled him naked onto a tent canvas. They were Union sharpshooters, and strong men, for they pierced the heavy canvas with their bayonets, pressed the stocks of their rifles flat together and carried him slung from the long barrels of their guns. His weight pulled the canvas into a tight U shape and his head wound turned it red with blood that stiffened the fabric still more. Despite the hurried retreat to Union ground, he remained stationary, a man in a slit.

Dearbhla

A SEARCH

SEPTEMBER 27, 1864

The journey to Alexandria would be nigh onto a week. Dearbhla kept the brake pole engaged and leaned against the slant as the buckboard lurched on the narrow trail down the mountain. She pulled hard on the reins in the dawn light, voicing a series of hums and clicks. Hey up, hawss, hey up. Here now, hey up. They gained the valley by full daylight. Tossing a few grains of corn to either side from the bag at her feet, she turned the horse from the town, east and north toward the Potomac. Over three year he'd been gone. The high ridges were refuge, but she must bring him back before the weather turned. Lost to himself, the heart of him in shadow, he could not know them, find them. All summer she'd waited, but storms could be early in the mountains, the trail impassable for wagons, a struggle even on horseback.

Here she was Dearbhla, known to her few. The girl, Eliza, that she'd raised from birth, nursemaid to her and her brothers in the place they'd fled. Eliza's child, ConaLee, born months after her father had gone—lost to the War he claimed was his.

Not his, Dearbhla told him: he owed no debt. Eliza begged him to stay, for the child she was carrying. He must go, he said, that no man would force them nor Dearbhla nor any of their kin from this place. The War would be short, winter to spring—the Federals were so vast a force. Dearbhla would help birth the child and they would send him word. They'd winter provisions to last and he'd return a free man who needn't hide, with the fine rifle allotted sharpshooters and a strong mount the Seventh Cavalry would provide. Eliza said she feared he would not be free of the past under a false name. The name he'd fled was the false one, he told her; it was only another scar, a mark on him. He held out his enlistment papers, with the name he'd chosen. Here was his name—a soldier's name no one would question. Better a Union soldier than hiding here, waiting for a victory that could free them. They were all nameless now, but he would earn his soldier's name and come back to claim this wilderness they worked. Though she called him her son, Dearbhla could not dissuade him. So he'd walked off to the War, leaving them the horse for the buckboard.

No news of him, after the first six month. It was as though the soldier *carte de visite* he'd mailed in late '61 had broken apart, his uniformed fellows scratched out, his direct gaze and proud visage an empty outline. Dearbhla knew every detail: the Yankee military jacket too small to fasten across him, his own breeches, shirt, a broad-brim hat. Shaved but for a razored mustache, hair cut close. Another marksman Federal, he'd checked all caution to stand for the Union. The small tin image, four soldiers posed outdoors with their long guns, was dear to Eliza. Country men, on a slant above the thick trunk of a tree they'd likely felled. Their poses reflected various attitudes—dutiful resignation, alert apprehension, wonderment. Only he stood, shoulders set, drawn up full height as though to meet a foe. He wore a farmer's hat, not the short-billed Union caps the others had tilted casually forward or back. Dearbhla hated the *carte de visite*, though she'd wrapped it in muslin and brought it to show Union commanders, or doctors in Alexandria. A city of hospitals, Eliza had read, evacuees from the Virginia battlefields, ferried by train and boat. There'd been a list in a broadside: dozens of hospitals. The biggest held five hundred wounded—the hamlet at the foot of their mountains was home to fewer souls. He would be changed from the image left them. Likely no one truly saw him, senseless or damaged on a cot among many rooms of such, but the scars on his chest would mark him if she found him. She'd rolled his enlistment papers into a tight scroll, wrapped in rawhide cord against any harm—the name might call him to her if she said it, showed it. Even hurt, wounded, he would surely know her, were she near enough. Sense her, if he were blind or bound with bandages. He was strong; naught turned him aside.

Dearbhla had seen him, months and years after he was gone, in steam risen over her summer cook fires, moving through flames in a cloud riven with splintered trees. She'd sensed his strain and peril across distance, through the long War years, just as she felt winter sunlight, or sudden shade falling across her hands.

But no sign had come to her since early May this year.

She'd been tending a cook fire outside in what Eliza called the summer kitchen, rocks built high enough around a fire pit that they could sit out together for warm-weather meals. It was just dusk. Dearbhla kept old customs—throwing a few grains of rice to either side before cooking at an open fire, entering a graveyard, or summoning those who'd passed. Rice was scarce here so she threw a few grains of ground corn as the fire blazed. Chickens uncooped to forage rushed after, never mind that she grabbed one to ream with the spit. She sat to pluck the limp hen, then set it over the fire pit and fed the smoldering embers into a low blaze with twigs and stripes of dried, pungent bark. Then, almost by habit, she closed her eyes, opened her hands to call him, wherever he was. She told herself he shared their daylight, their moonlight, no matter uniforms and distance. Such a spring eve had marked their first vision of this open clearing behind the empty cabin he'd shored up for Eliza. As if in answer to the girl's name, the fire suddenly cracked in a great sear of explosion, throwing blazing pieces into the tangled vines hanging from a balsam. The vines flared in a quick circle of flame and dropped, burning.

Eliza ran out with her rifle as though to meet an attack. She looked at the fiery vines on the ground. Is he dead, then? she asked. Say, Dearbhla.

No, Dearbhla told her. He is not dead. He tells me so.

Tells you and not me, then?

You are here. You see.

Before them, the tangled vines guttered like a candle and went out. A circle of spark lay glittering.

Dearbhla passed her hand near. Look how the glow stays. He calls me.

You can't go, Dearbhla—there will be more summer battles, terrible ones—

You cannot go, My One. And he won't be fighting more battles—he gave all but his death. He is hurt bad, Eliza, but we must wait. See if he come back to us.

They'll let him come back? she asked.

If he heal enough. This wound . . . needs time. It's like fire sunk in, burned deep. He's no more use to them.

The girl uncocked her rifle and leaned it against her. She covered her eyes with her hands as though struck while ConaLee, frightened, cried out from the cabin.

Go to her, My One. She's feared. She knows, like I know.

Dearbhla, she's not three years old! Don't speak of what she knows! Better we don't know, that he suffers, alone, so far from us . . . Tearful, the girl turned and took up the rifle.

Dearbhla waited until Eliza was inside, then stood over the ashes of the vine. She felt of the heat that rose to meet her palms, unsourced heat, for the sparks had finished. It was a grievous wound, then, a heat she could feel from so far. Rebels would not take a gravely wounded captive. They would have killed him, but this message held a bare glow, a senselessness. The circle of ash lay still, as though silenced and alive. He would come to them if he could move, but he could not. She went to the shed for a flat of greased paper and knelt to slip it between the ground and the oval of burned green. The warmth rose hotter, though the ashes were cool. She breathed upon them, pressed them to a mounded line with her fingertips. Rolled the paper tight and poured the ash into a small drawstring pouch she'd fashioned of deer hide. She put it next to her skin and pulled the strings tight around the sash she wore under her clothes.

She turned the chicken roasting on the spit, a cast iron pot beneath to catch the drippings. They must put by extra stores for the winter. He would come back much weakened, or she would go for him. In the buckboard, made up for his bed. She would wait as long as she could, late September, assure him time to heal for such a journey, and warm weather enough to make the trip. The buckboard needed clear passage.

Eliza came out with the vegetables and flatbread, ConaLee trailing after. She sat the child down and tied a rag around her neck. ConaLee must eat with a babbie's sterling spoon from her own wooden bowl. The girl clung to mannerly customs, to her books that she read aloud at night. She'd made the child an alphabet from sticks and resin and played at spelling out words. Dearbhla saw them near every day, in the endless work of putting up provisions, seeing to the animals and gardens. Eliza had learned hunting, dressing, and butchering, but Dearbhla did that work after the birth. Eliza sewed buntings lined with rabbit fur, planted and tended her gardens, cooked, preserved vegetables and wild berries. Game was plenty in their mountains—rabbit, squirrel, turkey, deer. Dearbhla trapped bear near a vast oak full of honeyed hives; she fleshed and tanned and smoked the hides on tree frames. Some female black bear were no bigger than small cows, and

her dogs could bring them down. She stewed the salted meat
with spring onion and their own potatoes and carrots. Venison
made better jerky, and Eliza wore the lighter, smoother deerskin sewn in her winter cloak. The one who'd left had taught
them woodcraft, home craft, trapping, hunting. Together
they used woods medicine, cooked, grew vegetables in sunny
patches of ground. Dearbhla was prideful of him. She'd taught
him much, but his understanding knit one thing with another.
She was not one for Bible phrases but found him in the words,
My strength is made perfect; he turned weakness from him and did
not have nor want what folk called *magic eye*, did not believe in
it. Nor did she, to cast spells, influence others. But they were so
close at heart that Dearbhla could feel his quiet or the mayhem
he moved through, until that day when all fell silent.

· · ·

The son she raised was an orphan child, her dead brother's
child, or so she told in their low country South. She cared
for him first in her one-room cabin in sight of the plantation
slave quarters. Her people were Protestant Irish, poor laborers from starving Ulster two generations past. Indentured
servants bonded to immigration debt, then tenant farmers,
they died off or gave up, drifted off, until it was only her
daddy, a drunken sometime ditchdigger for landowners from
the great houses, her mama, a midwife and woods doctor for
other poor whites who traded what they could for her help.
Dearbhla knew she'd siblings once, boys they were, long gone,
gone young to dodge their father's fists, eat better than they
ate at home. Soon enough her daddy was gone too, gone West
or somewhere, so long ago that Dearbhla scant remembered
him. They were the least, these illiterate Irish, poor by their
own fault and habit it was said, looked down on by whites and
Blacks, but the Black women knew her mother for the dozens
of bunched herbs hung from her roofed outdoor kitchen, for

the woods healing they too practiced. They did not mix then except in passing. Rarely now, Dearbhla might be asked to help birth a baby in the quarters. The Black women, many of them healers, thought her East Ulster Gaelic phrases the lost scraps of a hidden tongue, secret, powerful, like the words of their own languages. Talismans of generations long ago scattered, hurled, chained.

Dearbhla knew only the songs, or the Irish Gaelic phrases seemed songs, and she sang them to the youngest slave children, her only playmates when they were all too small to work. Older, she helped her mother, raising what crops they could, trapping rabbits and foxes, tramping fields and copses of woods for herbs and plants. She helped her mother repair the small cabin, helped her keep them fed and clothed. Every spring the big houses nearabouts received them in the kitchens: delivering a physic for women's troubles, an ointment for gout, whatever was needed, quick, secret. Her mother talked of Dearbhla's gift, and Dearbhla, shown upstairs at fourteen, fifteen, lay hands on women nearing their time, to wash and massage and poultice a dome of child-swole belly. She laid a warmed muslin cloth across and gently pressed the spread of the curled knot inside, sensing the long or short labor to come. So Dearbhla went on as time lapsed, she was twenty, she was thirty, till her mama was near give out, moving chair to bed, the five years she took to fail. Dearbhla did the work, grew vegetables, hunted, traded tonics for food, and dug her mother's grave just beyond the outdoor kitchen, marked only by the largest, flattest rock she could pull with rope and borrowed mule. Was Leena found her the mule, and stood beside her at the grave. Leena, her mother's only friend.

So much put away, kept distant, but Dearbhla still hears, in moments least expected, Leena's soft knock at the slant-hung door of that one-room house. Leena, nearest them in the slave quarters across a mile of field. Small flickers, the outdoor cook fires at night, and they could see Dearbhla's. Leena's was closest. Dearbhla, grown, took some comfort in the glows of light, glad for her own four walls—a stone hearth and fireplace, a wide pallet bed that slept the family when she was small, now hers alone. She thought she remembered those siblings, older boys, fighting their Da for crusts or green potatoes. Leena's soft knock came even then, when Dearbhla was a child, and after her daddy took himself off, and later, in her mother's last days.

. . .

The door swings open, nudged. Leena, a bundle in her arms. Dearbhla makes to rise but Leena puts the swaddled form in her lap. Moving, warm, small as a puppy or runt lamb in the dark Lowell cloth.

Leena pulls back the rough fabric, touches the babe's face. He look white, Leena says. You got to take him.

How, Leena? You know I nursemaid Mistress at the house. The boy she got, after she lost two, he peevish, sickly. She still on bed rest. Wants me there all day but Sunday.

An I helped nursemaid your mama. An taught you some of what you know. You got the healer hand but I filled it, long with her. That why you nursemaid that big house. Let you in, even if you Irish, you an yer mam.

Leena, whose is he?

Who you think? Ole Marse dead these eight months and his babes still getting born. But this one white.

His mother?

No one. The poor yellow gal that birthed him died of it. She gone, her name gone. You take him—he grow up poor, but he free.

He need fed.

You got a goat tied up back yonder at yer summer kitchen.

Now I stole a goat?

No, Ole Marse give her the goat those weeks he pleasure

himself, and I give it to you. No matter the Young Marse hate the Old, Young Marse' wife favor you for nursing her. You know she give you plenty leavings from the big house, clothes, blankets, food—

Not to feed a nursling—

Mistress' wet nurse—she my grandniece's girl. I took her the babe to feed before I come here. You bring him with you and she nurse him, long with the Mistress' babe. Young Marse' son sickly. You tell Mistress, this one good luck. He strong. He bring Mistress more sons, stronger ones. You tell her. You got the goat to milk, an mealy water, to feed him when you here.

Leena, too old for the fields, older than Dearbhla's mother. They'd planted by the signs near the cabin and in woodland swaths. Shared what grew, traded seeds, poultice, tonic. Leena's rheumy eyes and bent frame. Her sidelong gaze the only curb on Dearbhla's father, his blows and shoves. Afraid of Leena. Wisp of an iron-spined slave woman.

Leena, if they turn me out, I got nowhere to go. No way to go there.

She won't turn you out. Thinks you saved her spindly babe, when she lost so many. Could be you did. But this one strong, too strong for that chile that carried him.

But Dearbhla, what's his mama's name?

She got no name, anymore. She under the earth an best if they no mention of her. We got names, any of us? What he know? What you know? You tall as you are from yer runt Irish pappy, an your momma no bigger than me?

Just gossip, Dearbhla said.

I know you come from her, Leena said, I helped birth you. But your daddy? She shrugged. My people sold off when I was three. Raised up in the quarters, just like this babe's mama. But look at him. Why tell him? What he do with that? Say he yer brother's son, brought to you when yer brother an his wife died. Brought to you like I brought him. Or say nothing.

Dearbhla held him out from her. The babe gazed at them

and sighed. Dark roses in his cheeks, wide, light-colored hazel eyes, tight-curled black hair, and lustrous lashes. His palm was open. Dearbhla laid a finger there and he clutched her tight.

See there? Leena said. He know enough. I couldn't save his mama but you give him time. He save you, or someone.

So Dearbhla took him with her in a shawl, back and forth across the field and up the allée to the big house. He stayed quiet there, like he knew, nursed after the babe a few weeks older than he. Dearbhla fed him mealy and rice water at home, talking, singing. He thrived. Mistress lost another babe the next year and called Dearbhla to bring "yer babbie son" to a childbed still twisted and rank, held him, prayed over him. The next child lived, another boy, but the Mistress died in childbirth two years later. Some blamed "the Irish," yet Dearbhla was moved into the house to care for the infant girl, named Eliza for her mother, and the brothers ages two and four.

Dearbhla brought her son and a wet nurse to share a closet room next to the nursery. Those years her boy was like an older sibling to the others, a head taller than the boy his age, herding them along after Dearbhla to the stream to fish, to help collect herbs, roots, berries in fields and forest, learning what she called "woods sense." Later he slept on a cot in the boys' room, seeing to their clothes and slops, helping their tutor keep track of books and slates, absorbing lessons well enough to guide the younger boy while the tutor sat with the older one. When the brothers were sent off to board at a military school, he was indentured, age twelve, to the stable master. A governess took the closet room. Dearbhla moved back to her cabin across the field but became maid and companion to the girl so attached to her. She near raised Eliza, whose father was often away, who said his daughter must always be accompanied.

Eliza missed her "oldest brother" most. Dearbhla had begged he be indentured as her barter, for she was never paid but in goods—he'd a quick mind, a gift with animals, and the stable master, a former schoolteacher, lent him books. He lived at the stables those years, separate from Eliza. Home was Dearbhla's cabin, better furnished by then with castoffs from the big house, enlarged with a slant-roofed room they'd built for his bed. He was fifteen, he was twenty. The cabin glowed as he walked there at night, parting tall grass with his fingertips in the dark. At first, she hadn't known about Eliza and him, then warned him off, pleaded. But it was no use.

Now that place they'd come from was enemy ground. And he was gone off, sharpshooter for the Union, lost in its maw, his hold on Dearbhla unbroken.

. . . .

Wending her way on the valley road, she headed northeast toward the lower Seneca Trail. Federals controlled western Virginia, now the free state of West Virginia, and all the Potomac region. Eliza read aloud any newspapers or circulars Dearbhla brought from town. Since he'd gone to the War, Dearbhla went alone, trading, selling. Years past the dictates of the womb, she was lean, strong with the physical work of woodcutting and hunting, dressed as a laborer in loose overalls, jacket, farm gloves, and paid no mind to her lined, weather-darkened face. A broad-brimmed farmer's hat, pulled low, covered her bundled hair. She knew Union wounded went by wagon and boat to hospitals in Alexandria. A newsprint illustration showed the largest—once a fine hotel with columned front entrance and four floors, large windows facing a city street. Dearbhla had seen some tilted version, broken, in dreams, and trusted her vision. Tall enough, she drove and sat and moved on the buckboard like a man, and spoke little on trips to the town, but she would need help and direction in Alexandria. She would find that largest hospital, and know it. But once she spoke they would know she wasn't a man, or want proof she was kin to the injured. She'd no proof they'd recognize but could show his enlistment papers, say she was sent by the boy's father—an old man too sick to make the journey. They'd let her inside, could be. Eliza's brothers, her father, her kind, were false family, enemies swamped by the War. He was Dearbhla's son, truly. *A woman brought you to me. Said you were my brother's orphan.*

The horse surged forward in the traces. Dearbhla clicked and hummed encouragement and had in mind to go straight on through moonlight. The way leveled, the dirt track widened. The pistol on her lap, easily gripped under a length of burlap, was welcome weight. The War was South now, but few had the means or will to traverse the roads. Anyone she came across would see she'd nothing but blankets and bedrolls in the buckboard, though some wayfarers were lost and hungry, thieving or worse. But the road opened out before her, clear and empty.

Late, she would look for a sheltered copse, a woods with some trickle of creek, to rest and feed the horse. No need for a fire. Biscuit, jerky, hard cheese for respite. Sleep on a blanket roll, hidden from view in foliage dense enough to shield horse and buckboard. Saved for him, the rolled mattress stuffed with new straw, the animal furs, the feather tick tightly wound and roped, to pad the buckboard when she laid him in it. She must find him, and said the words in clicks and hums, song for the horse, a marsh tacky come to this place, like her, near seven year ago. The beasts never panicked in marsh or dune or tidal sink, they proved as sure-footed on mountain trails and mud; this one had carried Eliza into these mountains. They'd kept him, a yearling back then, now so versed, Dearbhla wagered, he'd find his way home from anywhere. The son she sought—if not her flesh, he was her soul—had helped birth this horse, had fed and gentled the foal far from here. He'd found their way in urgent flight to the abandoned cabins highest on the sheltered ridges. They'd shorn up hewn log walls, chinked the gapped wood with mud daub and dried hides, built up slanting hearths with flat stones. Dug a root cellar deep into the side of a viney hill, for storage and refuge. Planted winter garden in the sunlit swaths. Dearbhla's cabin just the ridge above, near hidden in blackberry and pine, was a second habitation if anyone approached too near the first.

And Dearbhla declared she would live separate. To boil your herbs, he'd said, and grind your powders in peace. He'd a quick ear, could speak as they did in the mountain town below, and sold the other two horses they'd ridden in flight to purchase tools, nails, rifles and powder, oil lamps, cast iron kettle, pots, seed. Fashioned wooden shutters they could bar with indoor planks against storm and snow. They'd tacked and sheared rolls of greased paper above every casement to admit a pearly light, winter or summer. He traded game for cornmeal and flour, for the chickens they cooped at night. Dearbhla and Eliza stayed to home before the War. Better they weren't known, nor seen in company. Now the War, division, death made them safer, for who would seek them in such confusion, over such distance, yet the War had taken him.

One day, second summer on the ridge, he came back with a buckboard hitched to the marsh tacky. They all stood admiring, feeling of the buckboard's length and depth, its spoked wheels and leather strapping. The trail to Dearbhla's ridge above was a footpath too narrow for wagon track, but she mused aloud on harvesting roots to sell or trade when he bartered in the hamlet below.

The three sat that night on the porch of the lower one-room cabin, looking into the dark beyond lantern glow, singing rounds, querying one another on what range of sight the sliver of new moon allowed. Firefly light, sweep of bat, sough of murmurous breeze. The shadowy porch and four broad steps he'd built to the open ground before them were mere outlines, glimmering up. Dearbhla saw shifting mist, not ghosts but presence. He stood to see deeper. Some forebear's height had bled through in his stature, his broad shoulders and stance, in his feel for animals and plants. His mind worked at locks or journeys or survival in these mountains as though all were puzzles to solve, but even he could not read the towering evergreens and forests that night, or name the flared canopies that formed their realm of sight. All became looming planes of darkness. Miles of vine and creeper, foxes, owls, preying bobcat and painter lion; the sweeps of dense forest beyond what clearing they managed seemed endless. Yet the vast mountains were sustenance and safety.

That was May, '61, as War fever broke, and battles began.

Dearbhla felt him near again in the sound and creak of the buckboard, the balance of the spoked wheels, the rise and curve of the dirt road.

She went on, bright in her mind with sense of him.

.   .   .

An hour more, and the darkened sky boiled up with yellow clouds. The air took on a green scrim and thunder echoed far-off, a storm rolling down from the mountains she'd traversed. Woods to either side of this valley road were too scant for cover. Dearbhla negotiated a rattling low bridge over a brook and urged the horse to speed, licking the animal's haunches lightly with the reins and calling softly, Gee up, hawss. Go now. The smell of the air was tell enough. The horse needed little urging as the late afternoon light ticked down, darkened to a dusk-laden brown. Hurricanes didn't happen in these mountains, though storms might rage near as hard, and cease as sudden as they began. Dearbhla saw the green thrashed limbs of an evergreen grove as lightning cracked over them. She let the horse have his head until they were off the road, into the trees. The needled ground was layered soft and she slowed the horse to a walk, got as far in as she dared in the time allowed. Rain fell strangely here and there, in cupfuls.

The storm broke as she hobbled the horse and tightened the oilcloth cover over the buckboard. Drenched, she crawled beneath the tarpaulin itself, fearful for the horse still in the traces. The rain whirled in sheets. She cast her mind to calm the marsh tacky, eye to eye, felt in thought the horse's dripping lashes, stroked rhythmically with cadenced phrase, and bade the animal sleep. So the horse stood as the storm poured down. Rain rattled atop the oilcloth like pelting gravel. Dearbhla crouched on hands and knees, arched her back against the oilcloth to turn the fill of the wagon. Runoff slapped the ground under the ratchet of rain. The roar of the wind rocked her and rose to a shriek, and she felt herself near those who'd passed—her mother's death, the stillborn babes she'd brought in dim log-hewn dwellings, and the babes she'd birthed alive, that howled their mother's grief and died. Disappeared. Souls called to the womb like voyagers, then suddenly gone, drifting at will. Dearbhla had turned some when poor women begged her—with herbs, teas, ground bark meant to stop a soul from crossing. Her own soul warned them off, to save them a suffering passage. So many cries, robbed, used, searching, turned away, beat against her, howling in this wind and rain, sheets of rain that slashed and rocked her.

Hail pelted marbles of ice that stung like shot pebbles. She spiraled deeper, into smells and scents left behind, palmetto trails and sea breeze. Live oaks born of bird and wind. Flat, sun-dappled ground. Moss, stirring, twisting, lifted. She knew to grind herbs and roots in the wooden mortar her mother gave her, crush seeds and leaves with a pestle rounded by women's hands. One potion stanched diseases of the blood, another blistered the flesh to turn a rash, or healed a wound. She learned the stones her mother secreted in a doeskin pouch, Ulster runes she'd called them, worn under the breast.

. . .

A week ago, she'd stirred the smooth round stones in her mortar and turned them onto living moss. His head, said the stones. She set burdock and snakeroot to boil, midnight, in her own clearing. His eyes, said the root, curling steam about her head. The boil was fragrant, sugary, but Dearbhla's eyes burned like fires. Torn sheets wavered over him. He could not call her. Others called her for him. She took her food stores to Eliza and packed her supplies. Her dogs hunted for themselves and howled at night to warn any from her refuge.

What if you risk all, for nothing? Eliza held ConaLee in her arms as though to weight her words. It's not safe . . .

Dearbhla only shook her head. I'll keep behind Union lines.

There are no lines! Even below here. It could be one, then the other.

Not if I stay to the northern route, and east. The Federals control all. I'll be back before the snows, even if I must help him some weeks, to gain strength for the journey. Eliza, hear me, and take care until—

Eliza put the child down and took Dearbhla's hands. I know he would tell you not to go and risk leaving us alone. But, oh—if you find him, and he dies then, tell him of ConaLee, and me—

Yes, My One, if I find him. But know—death sees him and looks away.

.   .   .

Now Dearbhla drowsed in storm sounds and remembered words. Roaming, she dreamed the turkey vultures of these mountains, gliding in flight over dying prey, and scattered them from her. She called the sea birds from the salt marshes she knew as a girl, the long-legged stork, ibis, egret. Smelled the sea and salt on their wings. Saw the terns, plovers, skimmers sliding along the sand in lines and clusters where the rice fields met sea marsh, while her mother searched the bracken for plants and birds' eggs. The low sway of the marshes cast a shadow odor, like new milk spoiled with spunk and seawater, rotten, fecund as the turned yolk in eggs the gulls had broken. Here in the mountains, cleansing rain curtained the forests and sheer rock knobs. Winter months, the cold and snow froze decay. No swarm of diseased mosquitos, no shaking fevers and ague. Rivers and falls swelled with snowmelt. Rivulets in abundance, so clear and cold the water ached in the mouth. Freshets of icy runs cast their rapids down the ridges, and Dearbhla dreamed of ConaLee. The child, on her knees by the forest creek she'd known from birth, set afloat an endless fleet of curled leaves that dipped and swirled and plunged.

———

LEFT BULLTOWN on the 26th . . . Got possession of Weston about 5 p.m. . . . Exchange Bank was captured, funds amounting to $5,287.85, were turned over for the use of the Confederate government . . . The road traveled was a bridle-path for sixty miles. My men and horses suffered very much on the mountains for rations.

—V. A. WITCHER, CSA LIEUTENANT-COLONEL,
*Commanding, September 26, 1864 (Official Records, West Virginia
Division of Culture and History, Series 1, Volume 43)*

THIS KNOW ALSO, that in the last days perilous times shall come. —2 TIMOTHY 3:1

Eliza

END TIMES

SEPTEMBER 27, 1864

Eliza propped the muzzle of her rifle against the porch rail. An early cold snap had set the trees turning, but Indian summer held, this last week of September. Her porch rocker, spindly, woven seat sagging, smelled of sun. The warm air was still, nearly humid. She looked down the mountains across canopies of foliage. Breaks in the forest cover, descending elevations glimpsed through bowers of trees, were her stations of transit, her watch over what came or went. She knew, from far off, the gaits and movements of neighbors who lived miles to one ridge or the other, the look of their wagons, buckboards, horses, often lent or borrowed between them. Strangers, threats, moved faster, in uniform or not, always men, rushing in flight, usually up from the valleys on horses urged to speed, sometimes on foot. Home guard, stealing and bushwhacking, avoided the hard trek to the top ridges. Those who came this far up into the hills sought refuge and didn't care how they found it. They were looters, roaming scavengers, deserters, especially from Southern units pressed near to starving this late in the War. Eliza tracked any movement that snaked increasingly closer, ready to fire a warning shot. Neighbors, valleys apart, joined in a volley of shot when they heard gunfire echo down the ridges. Continued shots were a call for help, but you had to have your gun, and room to fire skyward into the echo. The steep mountain trails meant help was not immediate.

Late December '61, when ConaLee was born, Dearbhla had lived with them but made a foray through the snow to her cabin on the ridge above. A straggler surprised Eliza, appeared in daylight on her own porch. Barely up from childbed, she'd heard him test the door of the cabin, then move to rattle the wooden shutters, barred indoors with planks across the windows in the cold. The blaze in the hearth flared up like a signal as he wedged a knife through a sliver of gap in the front shutters. Silently, Eliza placed the muzzle of her rifle an inch to the left and fired. She'd heard the intruder reel backward off the porch, and watched him, through the small charred hole in the shutter, struggle onto a mule and ride away. She'd stuffed a woolen scrap in the hole until Dearbhla could return and patch the wood.

Eliza prized her lookout from this porch, now that there were only women on the ridges. Their cabins withstood the snowy winters. Stone chimneys, hand-hewn hearths, endless forest to chop and stack, if sustenance lasted and hunting sufficed. Most families, with no menfolk to help farm and hunt, had moved to the towns. But the towns were raided by North and South. Dearbhla and Eliza had reason to stay where they were and avoid the War altogether, only waiting for word or news of the one they'd lost, who'd refused their pleas to stay, abide here, not join up. Eliza was barely with child and the War would surely end soon. It did not. So, Dearbhla's journey, today at daybreak, more than three years on, with the buckboard. She believed he lay injured since the spring, unable to make his way to them, one soldier among hundreds evacuated to an Alexandria hospital. Eliza reasoned, pleaded with her not to go, but she'd left at dawn, following slim rumor and outsized hope, to bring him home if she could.

ConaLee, Eliza called into the cabin. Bring the shawl tied closed on the bed. The sheaves inside are just moist.

Mama? ConaLee appeared in the open doorway, arms full. Barefoot in her sleep shift, dark lashed, she was hazel eyed like her father, with his tight black curls that straightened as her hair grew longer.

Lay the shawl there. Come look here at the mountains. Eliza pulled the child to her. See, ConaLee? Miles of colors.

Ours, said ConaLee.

Ours because we know them, but mountains belong to no man. They are forever.

The child looked quizzical.

It means . . . always. Like a story that stays the same, each time you read it. And someday you will read for yourself.

Like Alphabet Pie! D danced, F fiddled—I tell my mirror! ConaLee held up a copper-framed circle of mirror that just fit her palm.

Dearbhla gave you that one.

She said I can see her.

In the mirror? And can you?

I only see my eye.

Hold it away from you, like this. Ah, there is ConaLee. You know, you are near three now, ConaLee. Remember Christmas? And New Year Eve, your birthday? December thirty-one, ConaLee. We had a party. Dearbhla made you a crown.

A fur one.

With bits of holly! You remember. And our feast! Venison, corn pudding, fired potatoes—apple pie, with syrup from our maples.

Like Christmas!

But even better. Know what I have in my shawl there? Sheaves soaked and green, dry enough now to fold and tie. How many dolls will we make?

Three. You, me, Dearbhla.

If you like. Now, lay out the sheaves in three piles. Will you make yellow hair from the corn silk?

We don't have yellow hair.

Ah. But the silk dries in time and turns brown. And crinkles.

No hair. And no faces.

Why no faces, ConaLee?

The child was silent.

Maybe it's best, Eliza said, pausing. So that I can be you and you can be me. And Dearbhla can be us. Flying here to there! Or hiding. Like we practice in the root cellar. And why are you hiding, ConaLee?

Strangers. And the War.

And if anyone asks you about a War?

I don't know nothing about a War.

You don't know—anything—about a War. With strangers, we keep what we know to ourselves.

I don't say I can read my name.

No, you don't say.

Do you say, Mama, that you can read?

I might, or I might not. Eliza winked at her, and bent down to pull the sheaves from the shawl. Now, she said, see here—the smaller for the arms. The fullest husks for skirts.

Or trousers, said ConaLee.

Surely, Eliza said.

The child had never asked about a father. She saw no other children, played with Eliza, with Dearbhla, with the cats, the chickens, with Dearbhla's dogs up the ridge, with blackberry bramble, willow sticks, minnows and toads at the stream. Fathers were in storybooks and McGuffey's lessons that Eliza read aloud. Father in a city hat and mustache, Mother and Sister standing near. *Papa, will you let me ride with you on Prince? I will sit still in your arms.* Such pictures were fancies, as surely as water-babies flying about on dragonflies. Words were play, and play was not true or false. The one they'd lost, gone for a soldier, ah, he was a man. And ConaLee had never known him but in the look of her hazel eyes and dark curls. Eliza could not think his name direct, so soft it was, full like his mouth and tongue, sheltering, strong. His absence deepened like a wound.

Dearbhla had raised him, just as she'd raised Eliza, whose mother had died in childbirth. Eliza's brothers were young. Dearbhla, already their nursemaid, was charged with the newborn. She moved into the nursery and taught the boy she called her relation to fan the babbies in their beds, rock the infant's cradle. Creamy skinned, dark haired like the other children, he shared their lessons and games, and shadowed Dearbhla. Tall, broad shouldered, he seemed older than twelve when he moved to the stables to learn blacksmithing. Eliza's brothers boarded at military school; she had a governess at home, but Dearbhla remained her help and companion. Eliza, at thirteen, began visiting the stables and tending horses with the boy she remembered as an older sibling; they played with the cats and their broods of kittens, parried rhymes and limericks. He would lead Eliza about on her father's big stallion and taught the horse to step in time to *four and twenty blackbirds / baked in a pie* as Eliza recited the words. Dearbhla called them "thee and thine," so close they seemed. But she disallowed any contact between them when she spied them nuzzling in the barn, he not touching, only standing, tensed and still, while Eliza felt of him and pressed her face to his throat.

Mama, said ConaLee, the sheaves are ready.

Eliza dropped her gaze over swells and waves of foliage, then showed the child how to tie off the sheaves near the tops and let the rest fall down over. How to slip the rolled arms through and tie off at neck and waist. Crisscross a green sheaf for the shoulders. Add sheaves for the skirt.

But for Dearbhla's trousers? the child asked.

A wide skirt we'll tear in half, then bind thigh, knee, ankle, for Dearbhla.

Eliza sat forward in her chair. The warm air was hazy. She let her vision go flat, shifted her focus to sense movement rather than detail. Dimly, she was aware of ConaLee, holding up the little mirror to her creation, but felt some whispered alarm and gazed, clearing to clearing, rifle poised. She was edgy, she told herself, and short of sleep from the warm night, ConaLee curled close and Dearbhla gone so far, for what. The old woman thought too serious on a blaze of fire or word she gleaned in town of this battle or that to the South. He'd gone off with his made-up name, sharpshooter for the Union, sending word to a post office box in the hamlet down the mountain, not to call attention to any address. But there'd been no word for so long. Dearbhla said she knew the feel and chime of death, the smell and sound that settled nowhere but moved in the air to what it left behind. Conjure was in the minds of others, she said, not her way, but she cast the stones. And took the horse and buckboard.

Mama, what is that sound?

An owl, ConaLee, confused. Calling by day.

The high-pitched, echoing call was mournful, alarming.

Eliza hadn't told the child of the owl come to reside in the tallest pine, the hemlock whose giant boughs marked the edge of the clearing and shaded the nearly hidden trail that cleaved up and down the ridge. The white-faced owl called at night like a hungry ghost, company when the child slept. These days ConaLee notioned to play under that tree, setting out her nut-shells and dominoes atop years of layered needles.

Eliza stood. Yes, there, just the ridge below. A trace of shud-der atop red-tipped chestnuts and yellow oaks, all rife with squirrels moving branches. But she felt a wet dark seep higher, like a stain gaining ground. A flash of bright dazzled across her cheek. She turned to see ConaLee flashing the little mirror at the sun, dappling the trees with a small bright light, searing through, flashing. Eliza heard a skitter of rocks. She grabbed ConaLee so hard and fierce that the child lost breath and dropped the mirror. They were down the steps and halfway to the back when ConaLee twisted out of her grasp and tried to go back for the makings of her doll. Eliza caught her at the knees but dropped the rifle as she ran for the blackberry bower that hid the root cellar. She put the child in, hissed, *Strangers, stay quiet,* and closed up the dark, turning to run back for her rifle.

But they were there before her, standing to the side of the porch, the reins of their horses slung over the rail of the porch steps. The tall one waited, Eliza's rifle tucked under an arm, smirking, taking his ease. The other was a Yankee, bearded, balding, short and scrawny, his hair gathered in a long skinny hank down his back. His tawny deer hide duster hung past his knees, and the fringe on the shoulders and arms flew about as he jumped and lunged, waving his pistol. He slavered at the sight of her, mad in the eyes, and was after her.

She ran for the chicken coop, for the knife she kept there, sharpened to slice plucked fowl like butter. But she would have to draw him close. She dipped her head and was inside before him, the chickens shrieking and flying. She heard him, smelled him in the low warmth, near but standing aside as the squawking hens flew at his face. He cursed as they tumbled out behind him.

The taller one called in from the yard. Bart, he said, I think you emptied the henhouse.

I get her first, Reb, the Yankee said, hearing the other approach the door.

Go on then, the first said. I got the rifle on her.

She turned to face them and dodged wall to wall, drawing the hawk-nosed, scrawny Yankee deeper in.

The other directed him, sounding amused. I'd say you need full use of yer limbs to hold this one down, Bart. Take off that deer hide duster, fore you get it covered in chicken shit.

The one called Bart shed the long jacket but dragged the saddlebag along. A castoff corncob mattress, folded by the rear wall, was covered with flour sacks. Eliza slid down upon one corner to be certain she could reach the knife. He laid his pistol on a roosting box halfway up the coop wall and was on her, grabbing her ankles from under her and jerking her flat onto her back as the lumpy tick half unfolded beneath them. He pinned her with his weight and jammed one knee between her legs, scrabbling her skirts up to her neck, fumbling his trousers down. She reached behind her as though to hold to the ticking and closed her hand on the narrow handle of the knife. The blade, long, slender, must pierce him full on where his bony ribs met. She featured she saw his heart, a rancid fisted muscle, pumping in his chest, and calculated holding the knife at her own sternum. The stitched border of the cob tick burned in her hands like a flame. She felt him pull down her drawers, exposing her crotch and her belly, and heard the other one come up. Then the taller one was standing beside them, looking down at her, a smile playing on his bruisy mouth. His blue eyes were limpid, flat, like nothing moved behind them.

Grab on, Reb, the other said. You like to watch.

The taller one held her rifle to her head. He leaned down to grasp her left foot with one big hand and slide it free of her drawers, then braced her foot on his chest. He pressed her knee full bent to pull her open. I'll just hold her spread, he said. Catch a better view.

There she be, said the other, stroking himself, his muddy trousers fallen to his knees.

The rifle moved away. She had the knife in her hand and moved it quickly under her bunched dress. He closed his eyes and flung himself down, thrusting inside her as he buried the blade in his chest to the hasp. A grunt rattled in his throat and he lifted up, clutching at the knife with both hands, but the taller one had him by the hair and pulled him off. The fabric of her dress, caught between the blade and pierced flesh, ripped in a straight line. The balding beak-nosed one slid back, knees bent, and the tall one shook him, dragging him onto the coop floor by his scraggly bunched hair.

I hate me a rapist, he said. Specially a no-good Yankee rapist.

The other rasped. Blood bubbled from his throat.

She got you, Bart. Let's not make noise. The one called Reb let him go. Pulled the rifle up to aim its butt end with both hands, and brought it down.

Eliza heard the skull crack. The body pitched forward. She got her feet under her and made to stand.

Stay down, he commanded, pulling the rifle smoothly up to sight her. Pull yer clothes on, Mrs. I was careful not to rip them underthings.

She crouched in her skirts and pulled her drawers over her knees, then knelt forward to pull them higher, clutching her skirts to cover herself.

You stay right there, he said, and grab that saddlebag to you. He took up the pistol that lay on the roost, shoved it in the pocket of his cropped jacket, and tossed her the deer hide duster.

Her heart pounded in her ears. I need my knife back, she said.

Do you now. I'm no rapist, Mrs. But I really don't mind if I kill you.

She felt onto the floor of the coop for the stiff leather strap and pulled the heavy saddlebag toward her. The air was fouled and dim. She thought her sight was shaded in some hysteria and tried to slow her breathing. The chickens had flung themselves out, shapes beating their wings in silhouette against the light. Now the day was pewter tinged, like twilight fallen fast, though it was no more than three in the afternoon. She opened the saddlebag. The money was neatly banded: *First Exchange Bank of West Virginia*. They would have ridden hard a day and night from Weston.

Pull out the money, he said, and stuff it in the lining of that deer hide coat, there. Slip it in careful, just where the stitch is loose. I thank you, Mrs. Not the first time you hid money. Stand up now, and bring them both here.

She walked across the uneven cob surface of the tick, holding both toward him.

Hang that saddlebag around Bart's neck.

He kept the length of the rifle between them. They were close enough that she smelled a flowery tincture and realized he was wearing scent, cologne. It frightened her in a new way, like hot ice behind her eyes.

Now fetch me a shovel to dig this bastard a hole, he said, and a rope to bind you while I do it. You fetch anything else, I'll shoot you dead. He touched her rifle to her throat. You hear me?

She nodded.

Way I see it, I done you a good turn. Helped you kill the hog before it rut. Hangin' offense, kill a Federal in commission of his duty. Lessen' my side wins, a' course. Either way, they dig him up with this saddlebag, they'll be asking you about Union money the Rebs stole. Bart's captive, I was. But Lieutenant Witcher won't find me in any Yankee prison camp and Bart won't be needing no cash. Why would the Federals look up here? Cause someone might send 'em a tip. Now go!

She ran before him to the shed for the shovel. The coiled rope hung on a square-head nail above. It was dark as evening. She could feel the coming storm already in the earth she trod, a dark cool in the dirt. She might call out a hawk's high skrill, a signal to Dearbhla's ridge above her, but Dearbhla was gone. Gone to find no one and nothing. Eliza knew it, she knew it and admitted she knew. He was not bound or kept from them, did not yearn towards them. He'd no thought of them anymore. He'd got them here, to western Virginia's mountainous Alleghenies. Deserted homesteads, high on the ridges. Like a brother in her motherless childhood, then rediscovered, a man she knew as she knew herself. She'd made him her lover, now husband. So close they were, so many years: she knew sudden, now, that he was gone, mindless, never to think, return. He was deep in coastal sea or river mud or wooded ground, in leaves and dirt, or in a field among the dead, unmarked, unnamed, closed shut. She sensed her own end like smoke risen from his, and stopped in the shed, dizzy, grasping the shovel, setting it aside to hang her weight on the coiled rope, trying to loosen the nail. It was the only nail big enough. She pulled but the give was slight. Looped the rope over her shoulder, wedged the blade of the shovel tight under the nail. One foot against the wall, she pulled back on the shovel blade, prying the nail to move, move more. Slowly, she worked it until it sprung free, then closed it tight in her fingers. And ran with the shovel, the rope, back to the Reb.

Look at you run, he said. He'd dragged the corpse out of the coop and stood over it, aiming her rifle full on her. Throw the shovel there, he said. Now the rope. And lay down, face to the ground, here at my feet.

She lay down and he knelt, put a knee hard to her back, pulled her arms straight. He roped them to her sides above her elbows, then rolled her over to sit, and bound her hands in front. She watched him tie a slipknot, run more rope to loop her ankles, and leave a long length trailing off.

I could pull you around, he said, bounce you along. But time's so short. Don't you find? He jerked the rope and flung her full out on the dirt. Answer me!

Time, she said. Yes.

My name ain't Reb, he said, and smiled. You can call me Papa. Say it and I'll sit you up. Say it!

Papa, she murmured, and then louder, Papa!

He sat her before him, a foot or two away, and pulled the length of rope straight out. He stood on it, looming over her, and stripped to the waist, folding his jacket and shirt carefully aside atop the deer hide duster. He took up the shovel and dug, dug fast, practiced, a straight even trench no wider than his own hips. You'll see I'm right handy, he said. Killin' varmints, diggin' graves.

Eliza watched him dig. He was fit and well-fed, his thick brown hair sun streaked. His breeches were Confederate issue, with military buttons on the flap front of the trousers. They fit him like a second skin. Likely he'd stolen them from a man his height, a thinner man or a dead one. She willed herself not to look toward the blackberry bramble and the path, not to glance, and looked past him at the sky arched over the peaks. Clouds to the east had bundled up into runneled, roiling slants of gray. A greenish color moved behind them. She prayed he'd dig faster, wondered if she could say the right things. No, let him talk. The more she said, the less chance. But ConaLee should hear her voice.

You there, Mister, she called. These ropes are tight.

Who you talkin' to, Mrs.? Storm settin' to break. I best make haste. He looked over at her, digging, and slid her a grin. You talking to Papa?

I'm talking to you, she called out.

He pursed his pink mouth and looked around them. Knotted the end of the rope in his hand and stepped into the trench. He was in the dirt nearly to his knees. He dug forward, always facing her. I got to get out of here before that storm hits, he said. These trails will run and pour. Oh, you up in here, you are. Might not have found you without that mirror winking. Reckon you thought we was someone else, signaling us that way.

The dirt flew, piling evenly along the grave as he worked his way deeper in the trench.

ConaLee had dropped the mirror on the porch. Eliza featured she'd seen him snatch it up when she ran back for the rifle and the bearded one came after her.

Where's yer man, he said, rueful. Left you here. No bairns, no horse. Left you for the varmints and the weather. Seems . . . mighty sad. But these is end times. He paused and looked up at the layering sky. Storm about to burst, I'll reckon. Got my deer hide coat, keep this money dry. Or should I stay on with you a few days?

You might stay to supper, she said, loud enough. You finish digging.

I cain't, Mrs. But might be we'll play us a tune before I go. He looked across at her. After, I might be on my way. Let you shovel this dirt back in.

A strike of lightning crossed the roiling clouds. Eliza felt dazed, thinking herself dead and ConaLee unable to stand high enough should the storm last, and water flooded the cellar. Only once had a deluge set their provisions afloat and ruined their store. But the hand-dug cellar was no use for hiding the child if she could stand or reach to crawl out when she pleased. Usually the slant kept the water low, safeguarding the stone shelves that held crocks of potatoes, apples, onions, wooden slabs of dried vegetables, salted jerky, the mouths of the crocks firmed with wax. Still, if he didn't kill her, Eliza would build a crouch of rock to one side, unseen to one who peered in. Better the child had some chance, no matter what happened. She'd told ConaLee many a time not to move from the cellar but to her Mama's hands, but suppose those hands could not reach her.

Eliza watched the dirt fly before her. He was in it to his chest now, strong, not a starving straggler such as she'd defended against in the past. He'd made the War his means. Why tie her and make her watch him dig? He'd buried his fellow to take the money they'd stolen and cover his tracks, but the grave could be hers as well. He wanted something first, wanted her alive when he did it. She gripped the nail, thought how she'd need to admire and feint, near impossible now. He'd seen her stab the other one, even if he'd finished the job himself. How might she lure him close enough to plunge the nail straight into his neck. Rip the big vein long ways so nothing could stanch the blood. He'd have to face her, close, her hands free. She thought how he'd urged the other on and played at watching them. Letting them get so far. He'd stole the Yankee money, surely, and bought Bart off when he interfered, planning to kill him all along—she was only a convenient means, an entertainment. Papa. He wanted puppets. A chill opened inside her. He thought her his rabbit, dazed by the fox's breath. She gripped the nail in her curled fingers.

He was up now, out of the grave. He straightened the corpse, pulled her knife from the chest, wiped it on the grass, and rolled the body in sideways. Held her rifle up for show and threw it in the grave. We might just fetch it out later, he said, to her widened eyes. You'll starve this winter, you can't shoot you a deer.

She saw he had the length of rope in his hand. He came toward her, blue shadow of beard on his face like an animal mask, and pulled her toward the trench. He dropped the end of the rope in behind him and stood over her, brushing dirt from his shoulders, his chest. He took up his shirt and coat and put them on, letting lie the deer hide duster with the money in the lining. Her knife lay atop it. His shirt, unbuttoned, hung open over his trousers. Suddenly he crouched down and slipped the knot at her ankles. He rubbed at the red mark the rope had seared, feeling of her, she thought, before he swallowed her.

Wonder why you didn't use that rifle, he said. I'd wager your aim is good. You might have sighted us through the trees once or twice, but you figured we might stop in somewhere else. You stayed real quiet, hoping I'd misjudge those flashes come from way up here. He stood to pull her roughly to her feet and turned her, pulling her backside tight against him and forcing her bare feet onto the tops of his boots. He walked her to the edge of the grave. Working his hands in front of her, he slipped the knot at her wrists but kept her arms bound. I could put you in this hole with him, he said, his mouth at her neck.

She looked down at the sideways corpse in the narrow grave. The broken boots were just below, and his skinny shanks, the discolored trousers still unbuttoned, skivvied down to show a white slant of hipbone. The saddlebag hung from his neck appeared squarely placed, bank insignia in view. His head was turned up as though looking over it, out of the earth. The features were streaked, the mouth open, half full of dirt. Her rifle lay along him lengthwise, the powder still dry. Hands bound before her, fists still clenched, she imagined, as though in a dream, leaping in as the rope fell away, rolling over with the rifle and shooting the Reb between the eyes. She longed for the feel of the trigger and the kick of the blast.

Take your hair down, he said, and pulled her buttocks against him. Arms bound to her sides to the elbows, she had to bend from the waist to reach into her hair, keeping the nail closed tight in her right hand. He pressed a fist along her spine, pushing her full forward. Throw them hairpins over Bart, he said.

She could just reach. Her hair dropped free and the hairpins scattered down. He pulled her upright and she saw, straight across the stretch of ground, the narrow path between pine and bramble. She knew the rise of hill behind the brush, the dipping bower of blackberry, the fresh pine branches flung across the slanted root cellar. The child could not see him. Could not hear, but for shouted words or screams or gunshots. The child would not know, unless Eliza screamed. Any words would be muddled, all the earth between, the pile of pine, the closed plank door.

He felt of her, stroking, holding her at the waist, pinning her tight. Told you I'm no rapist, he said. I'm a thief, more like.

Take it and mark it, circle back maybe, dig up what I bring round. You do just what I say. Bend over and pull your skirts up. You know I could smell you when I seen that mirror glint, that far away. Bend over now! I like that. Pull yer skirt further up and clutch it higher. Hold it against you.

She felt him move, shifting his grip to pull the fabric up in back.

He moved one hand and pressed it to her crotch, folding his fingers against her in front as though to fix her in position. Do what I tell you, he said in her ear, you might can pull that girl of yours up from her hidey-hole. There back of that path.

A sound came out of her, an anguished breath.

Oh yes, I saw you run with her, drop her in. We been rousting folks out of root cellars, North an' South, taking their precious. But I ain't in the market for no kid. You'll do what I say. You'll give it up. Say so.

She could not say.

You feel my arm across you? Like a vise. Try to move, see how tight it gets. Do it! That's right. So you see. I'll ease off now so's you can breathe. He put his teeth to her ear, tonguing the ridged cup of cartilage and the lobe.

She felt him reach in his loose jacket for the gun. He pushed it up slow across her ribs, shifting the arm that held her fast to grip the gun in that hand and ram it under her breast.

Hear this? He cocked the gun. You jerk sudden, try to twist or move on your own, that fire will burst your heart. Standing here, you'll fall right into the grave. You an Bart in the wet, those midnight locks loose around him. But I want you to do right, Mrs. He moved his free hand across her pelvis, tracing the muscles flexed hard against his touch. He reached in, through the loose cloth of her underdrawers, to the backs of her thighs, stroking.

She said, quick, You don't need to hold a gun on me.

I do, Mrs.

We can lie down, she said.

I'm not like other boys, he said, Moving you is my pleasure. Move you here and there. So you be real still, Mrs. I'll do the work. He kneaded her belly, left off to slide his fingertips only just inside the drawers he'd made her pull on. Your man, now, he was saying, fathered you a girl an went off to the mighty War. Gone for good. Left you here for me. Ah, let's think about him now. He stroked the fronts of her naked thighs, rubbing rhythmically, arching against her, only brushing the side of his hand against her pubis. Then he grasped and cupped her through the fabric, traced the line of cleft with a fingertip. Ah, the mound and the fur, he said, and reached inside.

No— Her plea was guttural, squeezed.

He rubbed her, wetting his hand. Yer lips are wet, Mrs.

He slid her drawers down just enough, running his wet fingers between her thighs. Spread your legs, he said, and gripped her sharply tighter, forcing her breath from her. More! That's right. Why, yer crying all over my arm. Someone learned you to cry silent. If you could lick those tears.

She tensed herself, thighs, belly. But his hand was in her.

Give me the nubbin, he said, and found and stroked it.

That drop of flesh, hooded, hidden, a tear with a pulse, pounded like a minnow's heart. Afraid. Racing away, into her. She felt him stroke it, roll it with a fingertip till he grasped it hard and soft, teasing a radiating pain. He trapped and played it. No, no, no, fled through her mind like an eel in a gash but turned and took up the rhythm, throbbing. A hot pebble the size of a bird's gullet slid up into her throat. She wanted to bellow and press it out of her but a surging raked her with its teeth, forced her mouth open, set her face in a hard grimace. She made a sound. He pulled her up tighter, lifting her just off the ground. Her feet dangled.

One moment, Mrs.

She felt him open his trousers, one fast movement, and push her drawers down in back.

Cleaved like a peach, he breathed. He stroked between her

buttocks, running his finger lightly along. You been took from behind? Some like it regular, and not just the gents.

Panicked, hard knob of the gun at her ribs, she struggled as he held her fast. Felt for the ground with the tips of her toes, minced her feet out in small steps, arched her pelvis away to make any small space. He wet her with his hand from front to back and found the front of her again, sliding two fingers deep in to hook her from inside and pull her back to him. Like a nail to a magnet, he said, and pushed his hardness against her. Oh I could, Mrs., but I'm not that gent. Not today. Oh, you safe, but you going to give it up. Just my hand, and we all go away happy. You first.

He circled his fingers inside her, played her as he held her weight, crushing her tighter as she tilted her hips up to ease the urgency of stroke and pressure. But that opened the way. All around her, inside her, against her, his mouth at her ear, he sucked away the last sliver between them. She willed herself blind and deaf and poured her heart along the bramble path to the cellar dug into the little rise of hill, into the pine branches piled across the door, and cursed herself.

Not a sound now, he said.

He drew the wet throb into his paw, covered and pressed it, darted his fingers in, feeling where the pulse was strongest. She went rigid against him, escaped, seized. A remnant coursed in thin runnels down her thighs before he made her stand, hard against the heel of his hand, her feet flat on the dirt. She was aware first in the soles of her feet, hard against the welcome ground that was her ground. He held on to her, as though her stance kept them both upright, and stroked himself. His groans only meant it would be over. She felt him move his free hand to swab her belly and breast and the rope across her with the jellied gob in his palm. His salt smell mixed with the smell of the corpse in the narrow ditch, and the iron smell of the air. She opened her eyes and looked into the darkening sky. A cut of wind rushed along the tops of the trees, turning leaves to their undersides. Thunder rolled far off. She had opened her hands and dropped the nail. It was there by her foot.

My, Mrs., he said. He threw her to the ground behind him, buttoned his trousers and shirt, moved past her to take up the deer hide duster.

My rifle, she said.

You'll have to fetch it, Mrs.

Untie me, then.

He took up her knife that was still dark on the blade and came near to lift her by the rope that bound her. He cut it once. You'll work yourself free, he said. I'm leaving you Bart's mare. I won't be leading her down in this storm. And I believe I need time to get free of you.

Eliza didn't look at him, only past him.

I'm going, Mrs. But I know my way back. And I reckon I ain't the first.

She sat up and heard him walk off, toward the front of the cabin and the horses reined to the porch rail. Low sounds came out of her as she twisted in the rope, loosening the coils until she could reach an end with the fingers of one hand, move her shoulders and arms to shrug it down. She heard the crashing of the horse as he urged it straight down the slant of mountain. He's gone, she thought, and vomited clear strings of fluid. ConaLee! she shouted, Mama will be there directly! She wiped her mouth and stood to step out of the rope.

The path to the root cellar lay across cleared ground. The bramble seemed to shine with a lavender glow in the dim light, but she knelt to crawl along the edge of the grave. The rifle lay along the corpse, too deep in to reach. She'd no one to hold her ankles and couldn't bear to leave ConaLee alone any longer. He was picking his way down the mountain as fast as his horse could move. If she had the rifle now. If she could run to the porch and sight him. She stepped back along the grave and saw the nail and took it. Shame came up in her as she ran for the path and the bramble, for the sweet smell of tunneling foliage. Lightning cracked once, and again. The first drops fell as she crawled under the sweep of vine, pushed the pine branches aside. She gripped the wood handle of the short, broad door and flung it full open. The child's face appeared before her, pale, luminous, between one dark and another. The small hands reached up. Eliza grasped them and pulled ConaLee to her in one motion. ConaLee, my brave girl. Are you all right?

Mama—I fell asleep. I dreamed—

Dreams are just dreams. But my girl, I dropped my rifle in a hole and the rain is coming soon. Can you play a game with me? We'll make a blindfold and you will reach way down and take up the rifle when I say. Then we'll go inside where you'll be dry and warm while I see to the animals. Can you help me, ConaLee? Very fast?

I can help.

She stood the child beside her and let down the heavy cellar door, pulling the branches back into place. Still in the shelter of the bramble, she tore a length from her ripped skirt and folded it. Here is your blindfold, ConaLee. Let's tie it on so it won't slip and ruin our game. There. Now, turn round. Can you see me?

I can't see you, Mama.

Not by looking above, or below? Are you sure, my babe?

Yes, Mama! The child laughed and put her hands on Eliza's face.

Ah, you know your mama, hands or eyes. Feel the raindrops? We must be fast.

Eliza took her up and ran back along the bramble path. There in the clearing lay the ditch. Eliza knelt by the edge and laid the child along the ground. ConaLee, she said, you are going to lie flat to reach in. I'll hold your ankles fast and tell you where to reach.

There's a smell, Mama.

Yes. Slops are in the ditch. *She cannot see, she will not see.* We must get our rifle before the rain or the dirt damps the powder. Feel how tight I have you? Feel your knees on the ground?

It's a deep hole, too deep for Mama to reach in. Hang down straight. The hole is like the deep well where the Frog King lives. I'll move you forward a little more.

The rifle lay lengthwise, the stock across the saddlebag. The child's small hands, hovering lower, looked almost translucent. Eliza saw through them nearly. She rammed her own knees deeper in the dirt for purchase and hung into the gash to her hips, holding ConaLee's ankles tight. She slid the child a little farther. Now, she said, ConaLee, just before you, reach down. Feel the rifle? She watched as the child touched the wooden stock.

I found it, Mama!

Move your hands up along the steel, a little more, away from the trigger. Now grip the barrel good and steady, both hands. Do you have it?

I do, Mama.

Don't try to lift. Just hold on while I move you back. Eliza pulled the child steadily toward her until she could grab the rifle and swing it overhead to the ground. She held her girl then, rocked back on her heels, saying her name only until a gust of storm wind furled the piled dirt by the grave. She reached for the gun to her right. The rifle's heft in her hand steadied her and she took up ConaLee and fled past the horse tied to the porch rail. The mare nickered, wild-eyed as a flash of lightning lit the way up the steps to the house.

Mama, what's that sound? The child was pulling at the blindfold.

A surprise, ConaLee! Don't look! Eliza slammed the door behind them and put down the rifle, moved the child to the bed and pulled up blankets to cover her. She looked at her muddied skirt, felt of the board floor with her dirty feet. Yes she was inside, where the men had not been, with her child they'd not touched and barely seen.

Here now, ConaLee, she said. Are you chilled?

Mama, let me see!

Not yet! And you must stay in bed till I get back. Eliza loos-

ened the blindfold but little and put her face to ConaLee's.
I see you, ConaLee! Now, stay under the covers. That was a
horse you heard! Someone has left us one who had no home.
But the storm is coming fast. I must put her away, into the
barn.

I want to see! What will we feed her?

Just straw for now, until after the rain. You'll feed her then,
an apple from the cellar. Stay here in this bed until I can get
back and build a fire. Promise me. Do you promise?

I promise! ConaLee was fairly bouncing in the blankets. A
horse!

You stay here. Pretend your blindfold is a fairy's mask and
snuggle down.

Eliza turned from her and was out the door. She took the
horse and led her inside the shed, looping the lead through
an iron ring in the wall. The cow, tied in the opposite corner,
raised her shaggy head, silent. Quickly, Eliza slipped the mare's
bit, uncinched the saddle and blanket and dragged them aside.
There was not a proper stall but she heaped up straw and grass
stored for the chickens and cow. The mare lowered her head
and began to nuzzle, moving her velvety nostrils. Eliza took a
wide-mouthed crock and ran to the ditch. It would be a grave,
this ditch, unmarked, forgotten. She set the crock aside to fill
as the rain splatted down in staggered drops that seemed big
as hen's eggs. She took up the shovel as the rain began to pour.
The long pile of dirt was close to the edge. She didn't look in,
only at the pile of dirt, pushing it in, working her way. The
ditch was deep enough, deeper even than need be. And the
storm would weight the dirt. Midway, she looked up to see
a slant of rain break over the hills on the next ridge, a steely
dark curtain that eclipsed sight. Forward, she kept shoveling,
wishing for Dearbhla. The ditch was near filled when the rain
turned to windblown sheets. She took up her knife from the
ground and let the storm pound her, looking into a blinding
maw of wind and water. Beyond the clearing she could make

out the taller trees lashing to one side and another. She knew her way by feel and moved hurriedly back to the shed with the shovel, carrying the crock, near full so fast. The shed door flew open nearly into her face, but she got inside and put the crock of rainwater by the horse. Even in the roar of the storm, the mare buried her muzzle to drink. Eliza leaned the shovel against the wall and pushed the door open against the wind. The storm slammed it back hard to the shed as she pulled the leather notch tight closed. Wind threw the rain in waves. The ground was an inch of mud already. She fought her way to the chicken coop, feeling with extended arms and open palms until the waving half-hinged door banged her wrists. Inside, the door pulled to behind her, she felt the wet board floor, sluiced by the storm like the deck of a ship. Gradually, she could make out the hens along the back wall roost, piled atop one another. The corncob tick lay twisted and bloodstained before her. Eliza pulled it along the wet floor by an edge and backed out, dragging it full length into the pouring rain. She forced the outer shutters closed over the door to save the hinge, for she knew she could not replace it. The roiling clouds pelted down slivers and marbles of ice.

·   ·   ·

That day, Eliza couldn't bring herself to leave the knife in the coop, though hiding it where she mostly used it had saved her. For years, she would keep it near to hand at night and wear it on her hip by day, sheathed, on a leather cross-chest strap, until snows closed the mountains and the ridge. She kept the nail, scoured it of rust, sharpened the point to feel of it, to press it along the skin of her upper thighs and draw raised bloodied lines on her traitorous body. She could not touch or pleasure herself, thinking as before of the one Dearbhla sought, whose name fled Eliza's heart and mind so that only her bones remembered him. He'd deserted them twice, first to join the force against the enslavers, and again when he drew Dearbhla away to find him, who knew how far from them. Every day, the slice of time left for Dearbhla's return, for the buckboard's course up mountain roads that allowed passage, diminished like a waning moon. ConaLee named the horse Dearbhla, because Dearbhla would know and come back to see, because Dearbhla was no one else's name. It could be a name for the topmost ridges of their mountains and the hidden circling trails between them, for the layered cover of forest upon forest.

Dearbhla

ONE OF MANY
SEPTEMBER 28, 1864

She woke at first light, thirsting, to the sound of running water, close and loud, and imagined the buckboard gentled as though riding a flood. Quickly, she pulled loose the rawhide ties that held the oilcloth firm and saw first the marsh tacky, standing near as though to rouse her. A swollen rivulet tumbled down a gully just below them. All around lay evergreen boughs blown from the trees in the storm. She got down from the buckboard, fetched feed for the horse, calculated how to turn him in the traces on this spongy ground, back up to the road. She removed the bit and fastened the feedbag, then collected the larger, flattest boughs while the horse ate. She dragged branches to the far side, turning in their thick swoops of wet needle to make a wide, layered path. The marsh tacky found his footing. Dearbhla led him, coaxing, urging, up the slant of ground, the weight of their passage releasing the scent of fresh, wet pine. The smell clung to the wheels, to the horse's mane and hooves. The moistened dirt of the road unspooled, letting rise a fragrance of bower for some little time. Dearbhla let it draw her forward. The long past full of whispers, souls, cries, and distance traveled with her. The present was hazy with smells and sounds, for the past was present.

A knock on the door. Not Leena's gentle knock, but a larger hand, flat palmed, desperate, pounding. Not Leena, dead years before, but Leena's youngest, a man in his fifties. *She said you'd hide me, just till they off me.* Rarely, Dearbhla had sheltered men, women in the crawl space under her shanty house till they could be on their way, but never since the Marse saw Eliza glance across a courtyard at the stable boy holding her horse. Not a boy, a man taller than his sons, Irish trash relation of the mick nursemaid his dead wife had insisted on, the root woman who'd helped birth his sons and then Eliza. He'd always refused to pay Dearbhla but in goods and houseroom. Dearbhla moved back to her own shanty when Eliza was nine, but the girl's desperate tears meant the Irish tended her still. He watched Eliza cross the courtyard and make no sign as the Irish groomsman lifted her astride, but saw the spread of the boy's big hands at her waist, his broad shoulders, black curls, and made sure he was accosted by men that night, blindfolded, branded on the chest with the same brand the boy himself used on the plantation's horses. And flicks of an overseer's whip across the wound as well. He would know his place, and Eliza hers, till she found herself living with a Charleston aunt come fall.

The raised scar of the burn, treated, bandaged with poultice, was healing, but Dearbhla knew the two only drew closer, planning, telling her she must come with them or be blamed for their flight.

That evening, Leena's son was barely hid before the overseer and two more rode up in the lowering dusk. Eliza and Dearbhla's Own, riding back from the hidden river copse where they met of an evening, saw the men galloping across the field and made their own way to the cabin through the woods. The overseer and the others had dismounted, dragged out Leena's son as he struggled, thrown Dearbhla to the ground. She heard the crack of stone on skull, felt the overseer collapse over her, dead weight. His fellow lay beside him flat out, bludgeoned with the same rock. The third got away on foot. Leena's son made off on the overseer's horse, whip and pistol in the saddlebags, nodding to them all in silent understanding that he'd strike out on his own. They must take a different route, grab what supplies they could, take their attacker's sidearms and a horse for Dearbhla and go. Weeks of hiding and night travel till they were well away. Her son was a murderer, horse thief, accused kidnapper, Dearbhla thought, until Eliza said it wasn't only the men—she'd struck a blow. The stone came to hand and she'd lifted it with both hands to bring it down. The attacker who fled saw her use it.

.   .   .

Dearbhla's journey east was not their journey north of five year ago. The War had cleaved time, helped hide them even as it slaughtered untold numbers. Dearbhla's haste now was for him, to find him, however maimed or changed. She rationed her sleep, stopping only in full dark, just for a few hours. Biscuit and jerky as she went on, water from her own lidded bucket, refilled at streams or rivers. The forests along the road gave way to infrequent farms and habitations. A grove, an orchard, unmarked crossroads, small hamlets. The road ran straight, mostly, and level. Two days, three. Four. Pulling off near midnight, by the moon. Mostly to rest the horse, take him out of the traces, brush and curry him. Twice, she found sheltered, knee-deep streams, walked the marsh tacky in and staked him, put her own garments aside and bathed. Lay her bedroll in the buckboard wagon under splattered stars. But for the storm early on, the weather stayed fair and dry, cooling, crisp. Urgently, she moved on, closer, as though some force might move him, take him before she could find him. She began to see larger towns and settlements, off beyond her way. Carriages, coaches packed on top with roped trunks, passed by. Once, she offered transport to a dark-skinned woman carrying a large basket of provisions. The woman looked at her levelly, motionless until Dearbhla spoke, then climbed onto the buckboard seat. Dearbhla mentioned Alexandria. Two days on? One? The woman made no reply but to nod. One day. They rode silently, ease and loneliness between them, until the woman indicated a lane off the road. Before she climbed down and made her way, she turned to Dearbhla and gave her a small pie from the basket. Thought you was a man, she said, why I didn't get up at first. Safer to be so, Dearbhla told her, I thank you. The pie, flaky crusted, was lukewarm.

Much later, she pulled behind a copse of trees that hid the road, and ate as the horse grazed the field on a long lead. Apple pie, dense with molasses, a hint of mince and maple. She was not used to company now, and no use to company. Too full of her own creatures. Animal familiars, the horses, her dogs, the chickens and cow at the lower cabin. And wild animals known to her by their night sounds, their scat and tracks on shared ground. The high mountain ridge, teeming with plants and roots, hives and nests. Eliza, a familiar, crossed from one life to another. ConaLee seemed a constellation, her eyes so like her father's. More children, they would have had, if not for the War. Sons, more daughters, never to be, like the babe Eliza lost on their flight North. Time held all. The small tin pie pan, washed in a ribbon of stream, reflected a sweep of night sky lighter than the ground. Alexandria, Eliza had said—a city nigh onto twelve thousand, not near as big as Charleston in South Carolina, but given over to Union hospitals: churches, schools, large homes, even hotels, housed casualties. Ambulance wagons rattled through the streets day and night. Dearbhla must reach him by late afternoon, business hours, when hospitals might receive inquiries.

She was one of many in the streets of the town, managing a horse in the traces. The sounds of wagons, horse-drawn carts, buggies and carriages made a bedlam. Some ways were paved with brick, gullied and worn, but most were wide dirt tracks. She asked the way of a Black servant in livery, waiting in a wagon, to the biggest hospital. The brick one? Used to be a hotel? Row of big windows on the street? Straight on, he told her, to North Fairfax. She pressed on slowly, far to one side. Conveyances streamed past her. She knew the place from way down the street and slowed the buckboard as she came on. A fine building, windows framed above and below with stone, a grand stone balustrade on the roof. It looked to have fallen on hard times. The tall stockade fence of rough-hewn logs, thrown up beside it during the War, stood with gate ajar—a courtyard for deliveries, ambulance, wagons of wounded. Men in uniform milled about in front and stood looking down from a balcony over the four-columned entrance. His brother Yankees, she thought, and felt him held in a mighty fortress, cosseted, for they'd kept him alive, but separate, senseless of her.

She drove the buckboard slowly by, abreast of the big windows, windows so large that a man might step through them like a spirit. She felt him within, near to the street, and continued past, pulling the buckboard around at the end of the block. She drove back on the near side, peering at the first-floor windows. They shone, impenetrable, reflecting the angled light of a cloudless late afternoon. Must be it was early October; she reckoned she'd been on the road six days and it was near five month since that May day she'd felt him injured. Why here so long, if not a captive, or senseless? She could not see within, but might be he could see her. Asleep, he might dream her presence. Emptied of himself, could he stand, move, speak? Several times, she slowed before the entrance and came around again.

Mansion House Hospital, Alexandria, Virginia, circa 1864

A soldier on guard noticed her and signaled her to stop. He surveyed the nearly empty buckboard wagon. Seen you go by a few times, he said. You have business here?

She pulled the reins tight and stood to thrust forward the scrolled enlistment papers. Sir, a soldier, she said. Brought here to Alexandria.

The guard took her in. To this hospital? You had word from him?

No, word about him. You see this name here, on this paper. Again, she offered the enlistment paper. His father sent me, she said.

The guard shook his head. There's talk of measles. I can't take no one into the wards, not even family. No one allowed in.

Catarrh. The boy's father. He mighty poorly. None left but him. He cannuh come. So he send me, before he die. To find his son.

The guard took the papers. Sharpshooter, he read aloud, Seventh Cavalry, West Virginia. You came in this buckboard, from there?

Yessir. A far piece.

Wait here. I'll ask about the name.

She sat, shoulders hunched, but pulled her collar down a bit and shifted the big hat to expose the side of her face. If he was looking, would he know her? She pressed tight to her, under her clothes, the deer hide pouch of ashes from last spring's fiery vine, and called him in her own mind, waiting, not for sound or voice but for any sense of presence. She thought on the plaintive tune he'd played of an evening on the mouth organ he'd loved, even as a child. The slow start of the notes, then the cadence and high refrain. She took his soldier's *carte de visite* from her front pocket, unwrapped it, tilted it toward the oversized first-floor windows as though to focus his likeness through the glass.

The guard was back, holding up the enlistment papers. Sorry, ma'am, he said, respectful. No one by that name. They checked twice. Near five hundred names. And no more Seventh West Virginia Cavalry—pulled into other units after 'sixty-one. Hundreds come in and out of here, but your man's not here now. Not in this hospital.

Dearbhla only stared over the guard's head, along the reflective panes of the second- and third-floor windows. She felt him within, miles and months distant behind each shape of opaque, wavy glass.

I done what I could, said the guard, for you and the boy's pa. You hear me?

She made no reply, gave no sign.

See here now! You must take back these papers— He held them to her face, shook them once.

Even as she took hold of the curled papers, she held out the *carte de visite*, the tintype image, close to the guard's face. Sir, may be he here. Under some other name. If he could not say—

Hundreds are inside there, I told you, and no record of him. You heard me.

You see him here, the tall one, just there— She pointed to the likeness.

The tallest soldier stood far left in the tintype image, his three fellows to his right. Each man gazed askance at the same point of focus, as though peering together toward the same end.

The guard shook his head at the image, refused to take it in hand. How long you carried this?

We had it since 'sixty-two. We been waiting, looking—

His father, eh? Who would send an old woman such a way, in these times? A fool's errand, no matter you dress like a man. As though angry on her behalf, the guard turned and shouted at the men limping about behind him, some of them bandaged, leaning or sitting against the walls, legs splayed out. Should I ask here, he called out, among these layabouts? He turned back to her. I don't see him. Do you?

She only peered over his head, to the large, blank windows behind him.

The guard stepped closer, lowered his voice. See here, you don't owe no one, no matter from when. You done what you could.

She seemed not to hear him. Slow, deliberate, she wrapped the tintype in its fabric. Put the rolled papers and small square image in her clothes.

You been ill-used, sent all this way, he told her. He held up a haversack of provisions. Take this and go, before night falls, and the rowdies from the port stagger drunk up the streets. No place to be after dark—

Dearbhla looked him full in the face. The sack was hard-tack and parched corn, most likely, taken from some casualty. Contagion food—disease killed more men than battle. But she touched a hand to the brim of her hat in thanks, and turned the horse into the street.

You don't want it? he shouted after her. Starve then, old woman!

She went on, unaware of him the moment she'd withdrawn her gaze, so pained in her mind that she barely saw the street before her. She drove through to the outskirts of the town on a thoroughfare, sign of Washington Street, and pulled to the side of the road on a wide green sward. The road was emptier here, quieter. Trees stirred their limbs overhead as yellow leaves drifted down. Hand to her right temple, she cushioned an ache grown so sharp that she caught her breath, and saw, through watering eyes, the low stone wall beside her. A green, unmown expanse was there, the scrubby field studded with wooden headstones. Small piled rocks were mounded up at many graves—a contraband and freedmen's cemetery, unmarked but known to those who sought an end here.

Toward the middle of the field, a procession made its way. Several weeping Black women, and an old man pulling a trundling cart, walked slowly across the uneven ground. The group halted, close enough that Dearbhla heard a low keening, and the halting phrases of a hymn. The hole, already dug, lay open. The man turned to the cart and took up a wrapped form so slight that Dearbhla hadn't noticed it. A piece of winding cloth hung down like a train. He gentled the weight in his arms and the small dark head under the sheeting lolled back, the chin lifted, tilting up. A child of eight or ten, must be. The man knelt at the edge of the hole as an old woman rushed forward. Helping to lower the remains, Dearbhla thought, but saw her resisting the man, trying to pull the body to her in a last clasp or embrace. Had Leena's son got free, made his way? He was no boy those years ago, but a man near Dearbhla's age, strong, scarred. The old woman in the cemetery seemed to feel the child's weight in her arms shift, and she let go as the wrapped form slid into the hole. Crying out, she flattened herself on the ground and reached in with both arms. Dearbhla, in a whirling dizziness, felt herself look up out of the grave at the placid blue sky beyond—but the old woman, whose urgent words she could not hear, whose grasping hands she could not reach, was not Leena but Eliza. Feared for the girl, Dearbhla urged the horse on. She knew the one she'd sought was lost, the soul of the man he'd been fired to ashes in a burning vine.

The Sharpshooter

A WILDERNESS

MAY-OCTOBER 1864

The surgeon at the medical tent saw that his patient was a young man of some form and size who appeared uninjured but for the grievous head wound; the eye was surely lost but congealed blood and matted dark hair concealed the depth of the fracture. He wrapped the head tightly and sent the soldier, still in his bloody canvas, forward in the last ambulance, which would miss the hospital train en route to Fredericksburg but rendezvous with a boat of injured sailing direct to Alexandria. The Union held Washington and environs inviolate throughout the War; naval ships defended the coastal waterway and wounded were deposited on docks reserved for the hospitals.

So it was that an Alexandria surgeon too old for the field, awarded the rank of major for his medical service in this, the largest Union medical facility in a city of dozens of warehouses, mercantiles, bank buildings, and fine houses given over to treatment of the injured, first cleaned the head wound of a soldier wrapped in bloody canvas. He remarked to the nurse who held a tray beside him that the head bandage was the best he'd seen, thinking to himself that it held tightly in place the shattered secrets beneath. He cut closely the dark hair that obscured the man's temple and carefully pulled back the flap of skin that concealed the fracture. He did not probe or disturb the wound but simply removed shards of bone and pieces of skull, one a small triangle so perfect he saved it in a specimen jar. Though he wore the Union uniform he preferred address as Dr. O'Shea and spoke in the soft vowels of Piedmont Virginia. He viewed the riven Union as his own child torn to pieces, like this soldier, who was not scrawny and starved, yet had sustained a wound that would alter his brain if it didn't kill him. The right eye was gone, but the orbital bone was nearly intact. He dripped alcohol and warm water along the tissue away from the wound, sponged the sizable flap of skin that was moist with blood, then nudged it gently with the tip of a scissor so that it fell into the depression in the skull. He packed the cavity loosely with gauze from a glass container and wrapped the head. O'Shea had no idea if the brain would swell or compress, as he'd never treated a man whose skull was broken in pieces. He constructed a gauze tent of sorts across a head frame to keep the head stationary. The man was young and his weakened pulse was steady.

You are my best nurse, O'Shea told the matronly woman beside him. Mrs. Gordon, isn't it? I need your assistance.

O'Shea then asked her to fetch good shears. He stood waiting, aware now of the odor of soot. The canvas and the soldier in it smelled of woodsmoke and burnt pine. The nurse returned and he remarked that there must have been a fire or explosion on the battlefield. Together they cut the stiff canvas, slowly, he wielding the shears and she lifting the fabric away as best she could. When they'd cut it straight through, they exchanged a glance.

Go opposite and lift that side gently, O'Shea said. We will do it together and hope his flesh doesn't come away.

She didn't flinch but watched O'Shea to mirror his effort.

It is all right, said O'Shea, I can see beneath the cloth. We must pull it completely away from under him.

As he'd thought, there were no other open wounds. The body seemed not to belong to the mangled head of the man that lay before them. He was tall, well muscled, singed hairless across the chest and the fronts of his thighs.

His clothes were pulled off in time, O'Shea said. There is redness and singe, but the skin is unbroken. Cool water and mild soap for the bathing.

But what is this, said the nurse. She turned the gaslight higher.

O'Shea saw then the marks on the chest and the long welts that ran from chest to abdomen. They were keloid scars, long and narrow, a dark pink nearly blue. He looked to have been branded and whipped. It is old scarring, O'Shea said, but incurred as an adult. Torturers who do not respect Union sympathies captured him earlier in the War, I would say . . .

The nurse compressed her lips in anger or resignation, but met O'Shea's gaze evenly.

Nothing is truly surprising now, said O'Shea. Have we a urine receptacle here? He took the one she handed across from under the bed and fixed the soldier's member within it, placing the narrow tin vessel between his closed thighs. The nest of dark pubic hair showed no singe.

It's nine p.m., he said to the nurse. You've just come on shift, haven't you?

Yes, Doctor O'Shea.

I'm seventy-four years old and I've been here since six this morning. I would watch this one overnight but I must go home or my wife will be here after me.

She nodded. Of course, Doctor, go. Just give me my instructions.

I wish to treat this case myself, Mrs. Gordon, and I rely on your discretion. Wash his front gently, without moving his head. Cover him with a hospital gown. Check his pulse on the half hour. It's warm tonight, but if his temperature appears to drop, cover him with as many blankets as needed.

Yes, Doctor.

And you must talk to the patient, he said. We know so little about the brain, and his twilight state is likely to persist, with such a wound. He must hear your voice, and mine. Don't jostle him or leave the room open. He's not contagious of course, but put a contagion sign on the door, and require masking if you aren't alone with him. Half a glass of water, on the hour, with an eyedropper, gently into the corner of his mouth. Talking with him, communicate calm and safety. Just as if—

—he was my relation, the nurse said.

Have you sons?

I had. Two sons. Here, at least, I'm of use.

Dr. O'Shea would have taken her hand, but he had not yet washed his own. My condolences, he said. Let us try to save this son. I'll restrict your duties to this end of the ward for tonight. We'll hope he's alive twelve hours hence.

There's no name on the admission sheet, she said, but "Union."

We have no name or documents. He came just as he is. He will need to tell us his name.

Dr. O'Shea, I shan't send for you if there's a crisis—

There's no use, Mrs. Gordon. I've done all I can. Report all to me—one such case may help us with another. But for this soldier . . .

I will talk to him.

Tell him of your boys, when they were children. Or of your own youth. Whatever you can say warmly, as though all were peaceful.

.   .   .

He came and went, as though floating blind in buoyant fluid. He heard voices, measured tones, but no words. He could not feel his limbs and so did not know where he was in space. He seemed to roll or slide easily, but within a dreamless balloon. Perhaps he was not yet born. When the pain came he breathed against it, swimming up, and the pain eased. After some time he could feel his arms and the sensation of touch. A hand grasped his, let off, grasped again. A finger tapped his palm, traced across, then up and down, a fingernail drawn lightly along. It didn't occur to him to respond. He slipped away but came to himself more and more. He tried to move his head and could not, as though he was prevented, but his legs jumped with contractions, and he found he could move his feet. He

Battle of the Wilderness, illustration by combat artist Alfred R. Waud

heard a man's voice, an older man it seemed, kindly, inquiring. Soldier, it said. R. U. What was R. U.? He pictured the letters, circling each other. A woman's voice seemed to converse with itself: It is June today. She was the one who sponged and fed him. Warm gruel that tasted of . . . cornmeal. He felt himself propped up, unmoving, in a bed. It was day. The light from the closed window shone warmly on his arm, a sensation of bright yellow. He knew what yellow was and heard her move a spoon against a bowl. He reached out and she took his hand, holding it with some pressure. He felt her lean closer, and pressed her hand in return.

My boy, she said. Do you hear me?

He could not nod his head. Without considering, he said, I hear you.

She put his hand to her face, near her mouth. Of course you do, she said, so that he felt her make the words. She put his hand down and touched his shoulders and throat, and cupped his face at his jawline. Her fingers traced upward, along the edge of the bandage.

An awareness snapped into place: that was the bandage; his head was kept from moving. He brought his palm to his chest and she joined his hands. He knew then that he was alive: his hands were his own. He could not grasp that he knew little else, but he heard what she said differently, in phrases as she spoke.

You are in a hospital, she said. I am your nurse. You are safe now, and recovering. Shall I call the doctor?

No, he said, for he could feel himself completely startled, and dropping away.

Fine, she was saying, you'll let me know . . .

But when he woke next, the doctor was nearest him.

I'm Dr. O'Shea, he said. Are you with us?

R. U. Yes, he said.

Miraculous, said O'Shea. I'm your surgeon. This is Mrs. Gordon, your nurse.

He could not see, but had the sense they'd joined hands for a moment over him, as though in quiet acknowledgment. It was night, he thought. The hospital was quiet. He wondered if he was blind. He'd no sensation under the bandage.

You were brought in from the Wilderness battlefield in Virginia, said O'Shea, and we are in Alexandria. You have a serious head wound, which is why the bandage and frame keep you from moving your head. The wound is healing. If you'll permit me, I'd like to change the bandage now, while you're awake. We shall prop you up with the pillows. The frame will keep your head still as we help you lean forward.

Yes, he said. So they had changed the bandage when he was asleep, or senseless in the balloon that was receding, the space soon to be denied him, in which he floated, and knew nothing.

Nurse, if you'll bring the tray. There, sir, you feel my hands. I am taking away the frame, which rests on your shoulders. I'll place it on the bedside table. You were wounded in the right temple, here— She is placing a tray on your lap, and we are standing either side yes, now, Nurse Gordon—slowly unwrapping the bandage. The weight of it, gone, will be a feeling of coolness, even tingling.

The weight of the bandage lifted, layer by layer, and the woman's hands took away pieces of batting or cotton. Relieved of the weight and constriction, he felt an upward movement, as though he might bob up to the ceiling like a cork, and placed his hands flat on the bed to brace himself.

You feel my hand on your left eye. We've turned down the light.

He didn't want the doctor to move his hand and wished he were alone with the nurse. But the hand moved and he opened his eye. The room came softly into focus. A small room, the door closed, the shade drawn on a window to his left. The doctor was directly before him, an old man with fair hair and mustache. The nurse, full-figured, middle-aged, stood behind, smiling. She'd upswept gray hair, under the nurse's cap, and brown eyes. She had called him "my boy" and the timbre of her even voice was in his mind.

Here, now. Can you follow my finger? The doctor moved his index finger side to side, up and down. Good, he said. Turn your head, slowly? Yes, good. Can you describe your vision? Is it sharp, cloudy? Different than before your injury?

I see fine, he said, and felt the nurse step forward to take his pulse. He met her gaze and saw behind her a nimbus of light: the gaslight sconce.

Can you tell us your name, soldier? Your regiment?

My name, he said. I—don't know it.

That's all right, the doctor said. Don't strain. You'll remember. You're a strong young man, very strong, or you would not have survived. You were wounded some four weeks ago, in a coma for a week, and then sleeping, with the aid of morphine, which we have nearly withdrawn now. You must tell us of any pain, any sensation. Are you dizzy or muddled? Any headache?

No, but I'm . . . tired, he told the doctor. He gazed at the old man's wire-rim glasses, which reflected the gaslight and its glow, and saw a partial outline of one of the small wall fixtures in perfect duplicate. He wanted the doctor to leave him in peace. He must touch his own face, his own head, and find out what had happened to him.

Of course, said O'Shea. We will bandage your right temple, which is healing well but needs protecting. This bandage will allow you to see but you must rest your left eye, sleep as much as you need. Work on simple tasks as you can, with your nurse—feeding yourself, moving your limbs, holding a pencil—none of which are simple for the recovering brain. You need have no anxiety, here with us. Shall we turn up the light a bit?

No, he told the doctor. Unless, you need— But they were already bandaging his head, wrapping the strips around his right temple completely and partially covering his left. The feel of it was lighter and half covered his face across his nose, below his right cheekbone. He felt them put the frame in place, attaching it somehow to the back of the bed. Wait, he said, and raised his hand. Can you leave off . . . with that.

O'Shea paused. I know it's bothersome. But best to wear it a bit longer, when you're alone. If your nurse can stay with you for a time— Nurse? Yes? Then she'll see to it before you sleep and I shall be back in the morning. And young man, I'm very glad of your progress. It's an exciting day.

He made an effort to meet O'Shea's gaze, surprised that the old man's eyes swam with emotion. The nurse had put the frame on the bed, balanced on his knees, as the doctor left the room. He held it to feel its weight—short rungs on three sides, rungs, he knew, like a library table, with a thin, solid wood top that could lift on a hinge. The bottom had a felt covering along the wood, where it rested on his shoulders.

Shall I put that aside? She moved the frame away and held a glass of water out to him. Use both hands, she said.

He took the glass and drank, small sips. Your name is Gordon? he asked.

Agatha Gordon, she said, and took the glass.

My eye—on this side. He reached toward his right temple.

She gently restrained his hand. You must not touch or pull

at the bandage. Your right eye could not be saved. But your vision is good, and that's a blessing, a great advantage—

My eye is blinded, or gone?

She sat and pulled her chair to his bedside. Your eye is gone, part of the injury. I'm sorry, but we are very glad you're alive, and speaking. What is the last thing you remember?

You talked of a—playhouse. One son, John, told the other—I heard only part.

You remember my prattle? She laughed. You are smiling, a little. It's just as well not to remember trauma, especially as you gain your strength. It may be you will never remember . . . certain things. They are gone for a reason, perhaps.

What reason, he wondered. They had said, "soldier," and "regiment." He knew what a soldier was—an image came to mind, a small tin figure, like an illustration from a book. But "regiment" was nothing but the sound itself, a sound in which he had no interest. Nurse, he asked, will you write your name for me, on a paper, and a question, as well?

Any question? she asked. I will make it simple. She pulled open the drawer of the bedside table, which contained loose paper, and a volume. She used the pencil clipped to his chart and handed him a note.

He read aloud: Agatha Gordon. How are you?

I'm very well, sir, she said. How are you?

He could not return her cheerful aspect.

I've assisted in your care these several weeks, she said. You may ask me—whatever is on your mind.

Will I be a monster? he asked. Am I maimed?

She paused. You will certainly not be a monster. Unless you would like to be. But I think not. And so many are maimed in this War. How I wish I had my sons with me, maimed or otherwise. I live with my daughter now. We are two widows. There, lie back. Shall I read to you?

Better I read to you, Agatha.

It is a Bible, she said, taking the volume from the drawer.

They put them in all the tables. The print is very small. I'll turn up the light.

He watched her rise and walk around his bed to turn the gas flame a bit higher. The sight of her walking, the slide of her skirts, the nighttime light, all were familiar, but he did not know how or why. Perhaps she'd walked so, many times as he lay sleeping or unconscious. He took the volume from her and opened it. The thin pages shone at the edges. It is the King James, he said, printed in Boston.

Yes, she said, peering over his shoulder.

In the beginning, he read, *God created the heaven and the earth. And the earth was without form . . .* He paused, reading the words, and found he could simply say them, looking at her over the pages. *Darkness was upon the face of the deep,* he finished. I suppose many know it.

That is surely enough for now, she said, taking the Bible from him. We know that you can read perfectly well, and even remember the verse. The volume will be here in the table, and I can bring you other books as well. For now you must rest, and I must get on about the ward. She walked by the foot of his bed again, and turned down the gas. The sconce dimmed to a bare glimmer. She settled him back onto the pillows, and put the frame in place. Even for me, she said, this day has lasted long. How do you feel?

Almost human, he said, but for this cage on my shoulders.

Not much longer, I think.

After she'd gone, he looked into the room, memorizing every angle. He was so eager to see that he could not rest until he put his palm over his sighted eye. He dreamed that he could not sleep, had never slept, but saw no image of himself, no shape or form. He was the deep itself, moving between one shore and another.

·   ·   ·

He practiced sitting, feeding himself from a tray, holding his shoulders back and his head erect, though he wanted to turn his sighted left eye slightly to the front. An orderly sat by his bed as he slept without the frame. Then it was removed altogether. He stood, with help. For some days, he talked with O'Shea and Agatha Gordon every morning. He supposed they discussed his remarks or answers. They prompted him for any remembered detail that might help discover his name. No, he was not going back to the War, but if they might trace him to his unit, his place of enlistment, his family. The Wilderness. The Union. The Army of the Potomac. Brandy Station was the winter bivouac from which the Union joined the battle. He was rescued from a battlefield fire, his uniform torn away. Arrived at the hospital by ambulance boat on May 7—but there were so many casualties from the Wilderness, thousands from the Union alone, and the armies were moving so rapidly.

Finally he told them, All that is gone.

But your family, Mrs. Gordon said, have had no word. They are looking for news of you, desperately. She waited, then added, Can you imagine this?

If they are my family, I do not know them. And I am no help to them.

Believe me, Mrs. Gordon said, they want to help you, to know you are not lost.

He is not lost, O'Shea said, a bit reprovingly. He is here with us. Young man, you fought for the North. Do you know why?

He pressed his hand to his forehead, over his eye, across the bandage. I do not know why, he said, but it seems the right thing.

Enough, O'Shea said. I hear a bare accent in your speech, not unlike my own. Many in the border states stood for the Union. I don't think you hail from New York or Boston. Now, is there anything I can get for you?

I want a mirror. And I want to walk about, out of this room. And may I have a notebook? To write in.

Of course, said O'Shea, I will bring a hand mirror. Mrs. Gordon, please measure him for an eye patch. And, sir, you may choose a name, until your own comes back to you. We need a name for hospital records, and as you begin to mix with the other patients, they will need a name to call you by.

John, he said. If Mrs. Gordon doesn't mind.

Not at all, she said, pleased.

And for a last name, O'Shea said, I am happy to lend you mine. Unless you prefer to avoid association with an Irish Quaker.

I don't know why I would, he said.

You may learn why, said O'Shea. But it is yours as long as you want it, and won't shame you while you are here at the hospital, where I believe the name is well thought of.

Certainly, said Mrs. Gordon.

. . . .

He said the name to himself as he stood and shuffled repeatedly around the room, supporting himself heavily against the three walls not taken up by bed, table, chair. His balance varied day-to-day, as did the strength of his grip, his coordination, and his sense of the terrible weight of his head. They said this was a form of pain but he refused any medication. He thought well of O'Shea and Mrs. Gordon, and was conscious of her loss, yet could attach no significance to the words "John O'Shea." Mrs. Gordon brought him a notebook and ink nib, and a small dictionary. He read easily but wrote laboriously, copying out words from the Bible, from one dictionary entry and another, in a slanted text that resembled a child's upper case letters. He was sure he had not written so before, though he'd no image of how his writing may have appeared. He found a small wooden ruler in the bedside table and puzzled over the numbers. He copied them in order and at random, but the shapes did not signify. He read from Genesis first each day, only to see familiar words; "the first day," "the second day," "the third day," he understood. "One" was one thing, "two" was two things: it was two days since Dr. O'Shea had said he would bring a mirror. But the shapes of numerals held no meaning. He wrote words that came to him: "the fruit tree yielding fruit after his kind, whose seed is in itself," and realized the next day that he'd read them in Genesis. He kept the blind on his window up, and the window itself open, though it only looked out on a patch of ground and a back wall of the hospital. One night he was awakened by a thunderstorm. He stood and pulled himself to the splattered sill of the open window, reaching out to drench his arms in torrential rain, and knew with certainty: he was weak but had once been strong.

. . .

Dr. O'Shea brought the mirror. It's not easy to find a mirror in wartime Alexandria, he said, that anyone will part with. This one is lent us by Mrs. O'Shea, my good wife, who would like to visit if you permit it. Now, John, Nurse Gordon tells me you want to see your wound— May I call you John?

He nodded, barely able to restrain his nervous impatience.

I want to describe what you will see. The orbital bone, which frames the eye, is mostly intact, except at the upper right edge of your right brow. You were hit with some force, probably due to an explosion, here—O'Shea measured the wound on his own head, from brow to temple and above—where a narrow portion of your skull was broken. I had to remove the fragments, which were held to the wound by tight bandaging. I laid your own skin loosely into the cavity and this has healed well. Any swelling has receded and the wound closed with no stitches. There is scarring, some permanent discoloration, and a depression. Let me remove the bandage. I've brought you an eye patch, which you may wear in place of the bandaging.

Dr. O'Shea, he said, will I have a glass eye?

I don't think so, O'Shea said, removing the bandage. Glass has a weight. The tissue, the bone itself, is still healing, but I'm not sure it will ever support a glass eye. I've fitted the eye patch. And here is the mirror.

He saw first his good eye, the bridge of his nose, his brow, and the eye patch, which was made of soft brown leather. He looked to be himself, wearing an eye patch. His reflection in the glass was not overly familiar, nor wholly strange. Yet as he moved the mirror to see the half bald head, the forehead, the angry scarred depression from brow to temple to scalp, deep as a half-egg oval, he did not know that creature.

Your hair will grow to cover part of the scarring, said the doctor. I know you are walking a bit, here in the room. You must rest after any exertion, but today I'd like you to walk out to the verandah with Mrs. Gordon, managing your balance and gaining strength, using canes. We must avoid a fall.

Doesn't Mrs. Gordon have anything else to do?

She does. We hope to move you to her ward. I've left the bandage intact and you may wear it when you like.

But I must get used to looking as I do. In the ward. Only, what is under the eye patch—do I have an eyelid? I cannot feel one.

I could not reconstruct an eyelid, John—that is beyond my capabilities, or anyone's, as far as I know. Scar tissue has grown over the optic cavity. You have the mirror. Best to look while I am here, should you have any questions.

He'd imagined a hole, black, tunneling deep into his head to all he'd forgotten. But the scarred empty oval, when he turned up the eye patch, was a small horror, a shallow cavity, inward and blank, bluish, intimately pink. He pulled the eye patch back into place. And what of my other scars? On my chest and front? he asked the doctor, and pushed his untied hospital gown off one shoulder, to his waist.

An old injury, the doctor said, pressing his hand lightly along the skin. An attack against a Union soldier, it would seem, some years ago. You remember nothing of it?

No. If the War were not in the way and I was bent on ven-geance, I might draw the brand and search the South for the man or manor house it represents. And ask my tormentors for information. He looked levelly at the doctor, thinking perhaps he'd already acted vengefully, killed those who'd marked him. A number of them, perhaps. The thought was a neutral one. Aloud, he said, I am—a monster. Would you say, Doctor?

Dr. O'Shea shook his head. I'm not sure you have as much claim to that term as do those who scarred your chest. This War is—purely monstrous. From my standpoint, your recov-ery over these weeks is one of few good outcomes. You look—doubtful.

Do I? I'm grateful to you, that I manage an expression at all.

The doctor shrugged. Our lives are small, our victories smaller. That is the sort of thing I say that my good wife can-not abide. But you must wear the eye patch, to keep the cavity clean, until I can have another device fashioned that will offer more protection, above the eye as well. The hospital works with an excellent draftsman. And here is Mrs. Gordon.

She knocked once and came into the room. I've brought your canes, a robe that may fit, and a sack for your possessions—your Bible and dictionaries. We'll walk through to the ward. There's a bed empty and changed, with a view out one of the front windows. I'll show you the verandah. It's a lovely late June day, not too warm.

He dressed in the robe and went with them out into the ward, slowly, using the two canes. The long room would have seemed crowded, with the narrow beds placed not three feet apart along both walls, if not for the high ceiling, and the nearly floor-to-ceiling windows facing the street. The doctor began his rounds, stopping at each bed. Mrs. Gordon contin-ued on. He stayed by her, using the canes, ashamed he'd had the luxury of a private room all these vanished weeks, of being among soldiers when he did not feel himself a soldier. Many men were amputees or double amputees, with hoops under their sheets to allow their stumps to heal. Some moaned and cried out. Mrs. Gordon asked that he take her arm, and told him in a conversational tone that the hospital's front wards had once been a hotel lobby and looked out on North Fairfax Street. She stood before an empty bed whose white sheets were drawn tight, and placed there a haversack of scant supplies they'd collected for him, taking the Bible from it. They continued on, past the small carts of medical supplies that stood at intervals in the center of the room, through a wide hallway lined with supply closets. The screened verandah to the rear ran the entire length of the hospital and looked out onto a neglected garden with a high fence. The building, Mrs. Gordon said, with its double verandahs—there was another just above, on the second floor—had been the finest hotel in Alexandria. The generous porch space was filled with men on benches and chairs; others walked back and forth or stood looking out. She began to introduce him before he could pull away. Gentlemen, this is John O'Shea, she'd repeat, a Union soldier recovering from a head wound, pausing at one group and another until they reached the end of the verandah. Here several wicker chaises, some fitted with small wheels and cushioned with blankets, were pulled into a semicircle. Soldiers, bandaged, silent, lay back on their pillows; they seemed the least mobile patients well enough to be out of the ward. Others, in narrow wheelchairs, sat smoking or writing letters. Mrs. Gordon said his name.

One soldier reached out a hand. O'Shea, he said, welcome.

She held up the Bible. Would you men like him to read to you? It's Sunday, after all.

He heard himself protest that he was not a religious man. What of it, another said. A youngster, bandaged around the chest and stomach, pushed a chair over. Here, indicated the boy.

O'Shea sat. He read Genesis. *In the beginning . . . without form . . . and darkness was upon . . . the deep.* He heard only some words in the cadence and phrase he spoke, but said them all.

. . .

Weeks later, he was not sure how many, he sat in the ward beside a young lieutenant's bed, facing one of the large windows that looked out on the street. The lieutenant had been raving and slept uneasily, his face twitching. O'Shea loosened the man's restraints but knew he bore watching and stayed near. Officially an orderly and paid as such, O'Shea's duties were more akin to those of an aide. He worked long hours. Being of tireless use was a course of further treatment endorsed by his doctor. The elderly surgeon who'd first lent O'Shea a surname had offered lodging in his home some time ago—a basement room. They were an older couple who could use the occasional help of an able-bodied man, he'd explained. They could pay only room and board, but he would have better food, and could come and go as he pleased through the small back garden. More unearned kindness. O'Shea accepted.

He'd found it difficult at first to walk on the street, back and forth from the doctor's home, difficult to converse with the doctor's kindly wife, who asked that he take suppers with them, for he must continue to build up his strength. He was already strong, but the phrase referred to other things—the need to sit at table and converse, to be among people who were not injured, to hear an anecdote and respond, to remark on the weather. He welcomed the modest hospital uniform, medical in nature rather than military, which saved him any need to buy clothing and allowed him to distance himself from the soldier's life he did not remember. The familiarity of the ward and the staff felt essential. He could be effective here, as he was. He knew, from flashes of dreams, that he'd seen and done terrible things, that he was damaged, like the patients he attended, but he hungered to lose himself in a human endeavor that was not war.

A patient in this same ward for many weeks, hesitant on his canes, he knew the fault was in his brain and not his limbs, and pushed himself to take up one task after another. At first, he'd helped in small ways: refreshing water pitchers, reading letters to men too injured to read their own, reading to those immobile soldiers grouped by nurses at the far end of the verandah. It was understood that O'Shea refused to read newspapers or war dispatches, but chapters of donated volumes, *Uncle Tom's Cabin* or *Great Expectations,* were popular. Mrs. Gordon said he had a following. Stronger, he dispensed with the canes and improved his balance, carrying trays of food to the beds. He lifted men from bed to chair, helped orderlies move soldiers' stretchers, stacked firewood behind the hospital. Stronger still, he wore a felt-lined tin eye patch that shielded his healed wound and dented temple. Thin leather straps held it tight to his head, and he split logs with awl and hatchet, two or three hours a day in the summer heat, stacking the evenly cut wood for the outdoor kitchen, piling up stores against the coming winter. He was good with a raving or confused man, and powerful enough to hold even the biggest men firmly while nurses fitted restraints. Nurses kept O'Shea from his chores to calm such patients, or to sit with those who could not stop weeping. He bade them hold tight the palm-sized India rubber ball he'd used to strengthen his own grip, hold and release, counting, and enclosed a man's fist in his own large hand to supply strength if needed. Smoothly, he opened the hand, stroked the palm flat, replaced the ball. It was a calming, rhythmic ruse that often worked, even with those patients O'Shea suspected would never regain their reason. The young lieutenant was one of these, plagued with fits of crazed panic that rose and fell like fever.

O'Shea's own reason seemed trustworthy if severely limited, like the sight of a horse in blinders. He wanted more duties; he could not imagine how else to alter or fill the days. He was physically strong but unable to sequence numbers properly, or count change the few times he'd bought items in a shop, or think beyond one or two days in the future. Excessively aware, he focused intently on individual tasks and found comfort in repetitive physical work that required brute strength. Chopping wood, hauling coal. Yet he could gentle a disturbed soldier. He pondered as he sat in the chair beside the sleeping lieutenant and stared out the large window opposite.

A summer had elapsed in its frame. The small front courtyard of the hospital, adjacent to the street, was pounded dust and paving stone, and periodically filled with wounded, who lay on stretchers until they could be registered and moved inside. It was early October. Two spindly, straggling trees that shaded part of the courtyard had dropped most of their leaves. Always, a few men slept or lay beneath the trees, veterans too confused to leave when discharged, whom the hospital fed for a time. The street was full of ambulance wagons, coaches drawn by nags, towering supply carts; the window was half open to the noise and dust, and North Fairfax was a major thoroughfare.

O'Shea realized that he was watching the same singular empty buckboard pass back and forth on the street, driven by a lone figure. Hunched over the reins, the driver peered toward the front windows with a penetrating sidelong gaze, steering the buckboard slowly by the front of the hospital, which took up nearly a block, then passing by on the other side of the street. The buckboard passed, again, only to turn and pass by on the near side. The driver, whose face was not visible, gazed from under a farmer's brimmed hat and made the circuit many times. O'Shea watched, idly. The wagon drew up, finally, before the hospital entrance. The driver, tall, thin, stood and was immediately challenged by a soldier posted at the walk. There seemed to be an exchange of papers, and the soldier went off. Rarely, family members with means or connections came through the wards looking for kin. The driver, who must be a servant or intermediary, sat forward, holding the reins close to keep the horse from startling. O'Shea sensed, in the inclined head, the gaze from beneath the shadowing brim of the hat, an intense, unsettling need. The noises of the street were loud—the constant groan of wagon wheels and horses' hooves, the lash of a horse beaten forward, the squeaks and groans of weight and passage. The street was busiest in the hour before shops and offices closed.

Now the driver stood, for the soldier was back, returning the document, shaking it for emphasis. O'Shea could not hear what was said. Then the soldier turned and shouted toward the men in the courtyard. O'Shea heard, *Ask . . . among these layabouts?* The tone of the question was bitter. The guard tried to foist a haversack of supplies on the driver, one he'd taken from a casualty, apparently. But the driver was backing away, steering the horse and buckboard into the confusion of the street.

———————

PART III

1874

Weston, West Virginia, circa 1870

Dearbhla

A PRIVATE TRANSACTION

MARCH 1874

Concealed in spring vine and choke weed, Dearbhla stood midway on the footpath from her cabin, peering down. Weeks since she'd glimpsed him. Papa, as he called himself, left early and returned late, so sure of his hold on this ground. He rode his own gelding on his comings and goings, but today he'd hitched Eliza's horse to the buckboard, and had ConaLee up on the seat. He swaggered, loading a brace of squirrel he'd shot, and the eggs ConaLee would have gathered and packed for barter. She'd tied the chap to her in a shawl so that he faced front on her lap, clutching her hair in one fist and reaching out with the other. Seventeen month he would be, while the twin babes in the cabin were but six or seven weeks. Nursed and napping. Papa had jailed them all, surely as any lawman. He was on a supply run to the town and likely wanted ConaLee to think herself favored, double favored in his allowance she bring the chap—she could not have left him alone with a mother who lay abed. The man had made the girl his skivvy. Twelve she was now, pinched in the face, skinny, seeing to three babbies, cooking, doing whatever got done in the house. Eliza stayed inside, sunk into herself to blunt the sound and feel of him. Close beside ConaLee, he called out Gee! to the horse. Cracked his whip in the air to celebrate himself as the buckboard lurched forward.

Dearbhla stepped back, deeper into purplish choke weed. The thick stalks climbed blackberry bush and bramble, looped from tree to tree, arched a bower over her. Septembers, they'd made ink from the bitter chokeberries for ConaLee's school learning, but that time was gone. Dappled sunlight edged the smaller vines—musky snakeroot, woody nightshade dotted with pink buds, dog fennel capped in yellow. The fading sound of the buckboard rattled down the trail. He was to town, ConaLee with him. No matter, Dearbhla stayed away, lest the child betray her presence. Instead she kept watch, not to risk his anger at Eliza and ConaLee. Mrs., he called Eliza, as though to jeer at the man she'd lost to the War. The War, nine years over, still tangled one thing and another.

Dearbhla pulled up an armful of dog fennel. The fresh weed was protection from sting and bite and she drew the long greens over herself, then twisted the plants from their roots. She folded the greens and bound them tight with a stem, rubbed the roots clean on her sleeve. Tubers thick as her thumb, potent, healing. Boiled in barley water, they made a tonic for nursing mothers. She would hide the roots where ConaLee would find them. But had they barley? And would ConaLee remember, from when the chap was born? The man had bade Dearbhla help birth the babe while he drank in the town. Long since, he'd made sure she knew they'd suffer if he found sign of her on the place.

Dearbhla edged farther up the path, took her horse by the bridle, stored the fennel weed, and put the roots in a poke. She walked to Saturday market once or twice a month, leading the horse she'd packed with burlap sacks and bags of roots and medicinals. Papa, so-called, never traded at market, but at the dry goods emporium where he could barter for spirits. He'd possessed all Eliza had, and would have claimed Dearbhla's old horse, except that she'd stabled the animal at her own cabin the week he'd found them. A little over two year ago—she'd notched twenty-eight month on the door of her place, to know the days and weeks he'd taken. Until then, they'd managed. Stayed to the ridges in the War years. Never went hungry, like those in the towns. They traded for more fowl when privation eased and Dearbhla sold eggs at market. Eliza, changed after the War, believed her husband dead and wouldn't speak of him. He'd made her wife to a false name, she said, though he'd told them the license paper the pastor signed was proof the name was theirs. Alone was betrayed. She was quieter, though still senseful with gardens and plants, and taught ConaLee to read near as well as herself. Then the bushwhacker appeared, like he'd some prior claim. Dearbhla was just back from town with market goods in the buckboard. He stood as she pulled up to the cabin, taking hold of the horse they called ConaLee's, pulling the reins to himself.

Why, I know this horse, he'd said, grinning, clapping a hand to his mouth like he'd told a secret. Get down, old woman. I'll see to my buckboard and supplies. You go in and say howdy. Then you git, and take the little girl with you. Mrs. and me got business.

The man spoke with a Georgia lilt, and Dearbhla went inside. Eliza's rifle was gone from the rack above the door, and she sat blank faced in her rocker, holding ConaLee to her. The child was ten but slept on her shoulder like a nursling.

He took your rifle, Eliza?

And the sidearm, she'd said, but would not lift her gaze. We came back from fishing the stream. It's why I didn't hear him come up. He's kept the guns.

Who is he?

He never said. But he was here before ... during the War. He went away and will go away again. But you must wake ConaLee and take her with you.

Dearbhla bent near. My One, she'd said. The bottle of spirits in the supplies. Get him drunk and come to us in the dark. He won't know the path.

But the stranger was back at the door, holding it open, laughing, shaking the bottle of whiskey. She ain't your One, he said. Take the girl. Mrs. there will let you know when we want her back.

Dearbhla had pulled ConaLee to her feet and stood waiting until he cleared the doorway and she could leave with the child. She'd thought him War trash, a con man, a drifter, with his lanky brown hair and cold, flinty eyes. They'd no clan, no lawman to challenge him. Dearbhla suspicioned he was not the only deserter who'd menaced Eliza during the War, but it seemed she'd kept the child from harm, from seeing or knowing. This one had marked Eliza and returned. Dearbhla stepped past him. Strong, wiry, like he grabbled a living by force and cunning, he seemed to swarm within like hornets afire. He slammed the cabin door behind her and the sound pierced her like needles. She pulled ConaLee with her along the steep path until they reached the safety of Dearbhla's cabin on the highest ridge.

She did not conjure, only saw, knew, took the pulse of person or place. He believed he controlled one thing with another. If his will was resisted, or he was drunk, he raged like a madman.

Dearbhla walked down the path now into the clearing of Eliza's cabin, leading the horse. Swaths of unplanted garden, gone to weeds; the dirt before the broad steps, unswept. Dearbhla made her way to the porch and stepped over the rude gate the man had fastened across. The door was padlocked—Papa's business, this—as though someone might steal his jewel, or Eliza might come to her senses and flee if she could but open her cage. He'd taken the key and closed the wooden shutters across the two front windows, latched them from inside. Dearbhla felt the air he'd pushed and gathered come tumbling back down the porch steps to the ground, flinging itself under the cabin to bear them up and hold them from him.

She led her horse around to the back of the cabin, stepped inside a window whose greased paper pane moved unsecured in a stir of breeze. Dim, closed air, a murmur from the bed in a corner of the wide room. She went to Eliza and stood looking at the sleeping creature on the feather tick.

Dearbhla had last seen her in the fall, faded from herself, swole huge with child, walked about by ConaLee on the porch like a sleepwalker. But not since the twins' birth in February.

Now it was only ConaLee, days Dearbhla saw her, rocking one babbie or the other in the worn porch rocker, while the chap played beside her on the wide board floor. He would stand and jabber and thought ConaLee his mother. Company for her, leastways, while the babbies were work. Work Eliza could not do through another winter, or even the nursing much longer, by the look of her. Dearbhla sat close on the bed and pulled the girl gently to her.

Eliza only stiffened, trembling.

Eliza, do you know me? Dearbhla felt, in the girl's back, the strong beat of her heart. Hiding her strength, then, opposing him in the only way she could. Dearbhla lay her back, stroked her forehead.

The girl's eyelids fluttered open.

Eliza, he is not here.

She grasped Dearbhla's hand. ConaLee, she murmured.

She's to town. He took her with him.

He took her?

I keep watch over her, best I can. She cares for the little ones, and stays close—She would come to me, seldom, with the chap. But never since they're born, with you so poorly.

Make him go, Dearbhla.

He's crossed you, My One—but he must decide himself to leave, to see his own advantage. Eliza, I told you to only talk when he's gone, but talk to me now. Tell me—

Help ConaLee, Dearbhla . . .

She won't leave you, Eliza, nor these babbies. Least he'll stay away more, if he thinks you senseless, mute. But talk to me, My One, find your strength. Do you hear me?

But Eliza closed her eyes and turned away.

. . .

Dearbhla feared the man would spill himself into Eliza until he dumped her in a grave. The nursing babbies might stop her getting with child, if only a while longer. He favored ConaLee as a threat, to make Eliza submit, yielding now if not pliant. For he'd played her once, bestirred her those first weeks he was on the place. Eliza seemed shamed and feared but would not defy him. She let on Dearbhla was only a neighbor, fond of ConaLee, who began to stay with her "neighbor granny" days at a time. Eliza was with child almost at once. He bade them all call him Papa as though he intended some dominion, and was away most days. Dearbhla took ConaLee to read to Eliza or brush her hair, while Dearbhla saw to the gardens, the cooking. Soon enough she'd found Eliza alone out back, motionless, by the door of the chicken coop. He'd tacked up snakeskins, the molted forms of copperheads, on the aslant door—farmers did such, to scare snakes from fowl—but the door was nearly covered. The heads of the snakes, still attached, were dark lumps. Dearbhla went inside to look for eggs and Eliza followed. The chickens piled atop one another in a corner as Eliza stumbled forward, pulling at her clothes. Dearbhla felt of her and lifted her skirt. She'd nothing beneath but a thick rope tied tight around her hips, its bulging knot just at the cleft of her.

Dearbhla cut the rope with the blade in the coop as Eliza collapsed against her. Why this binding? Dearbhla asked.

To keep me here, by the coop, till he return.

It's only a bit of rope, Dearbhla said, coiling it in her pocket. It doesn't tie you here. And you afraid to cut it yourself. I'll take it—let him ask me for it. Now come, eat the food I'm making, bathe, rest. He asks, say you woke in your bed and have no thought of how. Or say nothing.

Eliza nodded, stricken. I won't speak . . . before him.

And not before ConaLee, Dearbhla cautioned. She's burdened, and too young to keep your secrets. Could be your silence may protect her.

The man lived to punish and favor, to poison and provoke, but his cruelties could move against him. That very night his horse shied from a snake and threw him. Dearbhla spied him the next day, from above on the path, limping, jagged cuts to his face and head. He believed her a witch who'd cursed him. He raged, lashing the horse. His anger was more danger. In those days, when he was away, Dearbhla brought food and strengthening tonics, helped ConaLee sew flour sacks for diapers and swaddling. He stayed to town more as the birth neared. ConaLee came to fetch her the day the labor began, stayed just beside her as they brought the babe. The child helped Dearbhla cut and tie the cord, and wash the scrawny infant in water they'd boiled and cooled. Eliza would not hold the boy, but suckled him if ConaLee held him to her. Nursing relieved her swollen breasts and Eliza seemed able to care only for her own relief.

Weeks and months after, she rose from bed only if Papa was gone, or walked about if he dressed her, moved her here and there. He seemed roused by her vacancy at first, used her how and when he liked. He'd put himself a chair near the bramble and the root cellar, out of sight of the house, and pull her onto him, play her like a doll, turn her like the hands of a clock. Dearbhla could see them, a blur through the trees, hear him, though Eliza was silent. ConaLee, mother to her mother, Dearbhla seldom near, was never without the boy babbie who walked and jabbered after her. She seemed not to remember a different life and came to Dearbhla with the year-old chap, to say her mother was swole huge with child again. The twins were born three month later. Now, since their birth, Eliza lay abed.

Dearbhla stood. She laid hands on Eliza, a light touch, passed her palms over head, throat, shoulders, then, slowly, just above the shallow-breathing body, warming a form above the form. She heard Eliza's breath deepen, slow to a true sleep, and turned to look at the babbies. They lay side by side in blanket-lined dresser drawers, atop the broad bureau. Nursed and dry, they slept. ConaLee could do some, but not enough. A washboard and washing tub, half full of soapy water and soaking nappies, sat in the center of the room. Flour sacks ConaLee had torn and washed and stitched—once taught, the child remembered. She knew to rinse them in vinegar water, dry them outside on the porch line she'd strung eave to eave. A low stool, likely the child's station, was drawn up to the tub. There she'd sit, Dearbhla visioned, scrubbing, the chap beside her tapping the vinegar water, Papa coming and going. Dearbhla feared he would lay hands on ConaLee if Eliza no longer satisfied.

I must move him from this place, Dearbhla said aloud.

She saw that the girl twin had Eliza's broad forehead, and held a palm above each babe. She did not feel him in them. He'd cut the cords that bound them and taken no notice since. It was ConaLee who tended them, tended the chap, nursed and fed her mother. The man wandered, hunted, moved about, catching eyes on Eliza, on ConaLee, but so many babes were a bother and burden. He would be looking for a way to leave, not be here through the coming winter, rainbound, mudbound, snowbound, unable to travel the mountain trail and towns about, gamble, drink in company. And Eliza, faded from herself, offered little. But he needed a means. One he could see as his own trickery or sly fortune.

· · ·

Dearbhla, in town, went first to the dry goods emporium. A dead-end alley beside the store allowed for private transactions. Years she'd traded her roots and medicinals for goods, the storekeep, careful never to brush her fingers or look her in the eye, was quick, so that no one saw. He kept her herbs and roots on hand but no one knew where he got them; he wrapped them in brown paper and handwrote the labels, according to Dearbhla's instructions: "for gout," he'd mumble as he wrote, "for digestion," "for women's physic." He sold goods for far more than he paid, the better to buy rugs and lamps for his upstairs rooms, and lady's fashions for his young wife. She would stroll the town, leering, free with the easy virtue he'd purchased, until he kept her off the streets. Now Dearbhla leaned close to the alley door and knocked.

The storekeep opened, red-faced, his eyes bloodshot, marking pencil askew behind his ear. Be quick, old woman, he said. I've a pained head.

Dearbhla began reciting her list of barter and saw the storekeep's wide-eyed wife come up behind him, swinging a key on a string over her head as though to lasso her graying husband. The key flicked hard against his ear as she mocked him, chittering like a squirrel.

Wife, give me that key—when I get my hands on you! To the Asylum soon enough! The storekeep turned from the door as his wife dodged, one side to the other, trying to squeeze past him into the alley. Shrieking, still in her night shift, her hair wild, she leapt back into the shadowy store. Wait there, he told Dearbhla, and half shut the door.

Dearbhla stepped back. The wife was young, a child-wife with a girl's slim feet. Hers were bare and dirty. Likely he'd found her in the saloon, used and willing. Now the girl appeared less and less, peering over his shoulder, mouthing words, darting her fingers here and there as though in secret message. Dearbhla watched the storekeep through the open gap of the door. He caught the girl up, strapped her arms to her sides with his belt, knotted the buckle around her flailing. Her noise stopped as he gagged her with a bit of fabric and threw her over his shoulder.

Wait! he shouted at Dearbhla again, and was off with the girl, to the quarters over the shop. The back staircase let out near the exit to the alley—Dearbhla heard his pounding steps, and the girl kicking the wall with her heels, as they made their way up.

Dearbhla kept her back to the street and held her bulging haversack before her. She traded medicinals at Saturday market: ginseng and tea root, dried lavender, tincture of penny-royal, sage bundled with woven grass. Sacks of wood knots soaked in fox urine to save gardens from deer and rabbits. She knew there were stories about the silent old woman who dressed like a man, but stories turned away trouble. These mountain folk did not know her ways or the words of her talk. Except for the herbs they purchased, the milled grains or flour they traded, she turned them from her. The poorer whites, worn down, traded for Dearbhla's bags of roots to save themselves the wearisome trek to dig their own. She bartered with the storekeep in the alley. He traded in secret with those he received here. Moonshiners, from the look of him.

Dearbhla pulled her brimmed farmer's hat low and looked toward the street.

The town was not spires and grilles, balconies or harbor or masts of rocking ships, but dirt road and wooden flats put down for walking, shambled buildings, pigs and stray dogs in the streets. At first, living in the high ridges above the town, fifteen year ago, she'd seldom ventured down the mountain, and Eliza not at all. Her One was a man then, not a boy, at twenty-two, and Eliza was seventeen. He said to stay up the mountain and made few trips down for supplies. Now it was different. War's end had swole the place. In the years since, strangers came and went. Free Blacks, Italians, German-speaking laborers from cities up north. Competing timber operations were cutting forests nearest the town, taking the big trees and floating lumber to cities in the north and east. Timber rights, so-called, cash for strapped farmers.

The storekeep was back and pushed the screen door rudely open. Here's your usual, he said, holding a box of provisions. He motioned Dearbhla closer. Look here, root doctor. I keep her locked up but she's sly, took the key to the room when I was . . . indisposed. She raves all night. Have you some tincture, some root or mixture, to calm her?

Dearbhla shifted her haversack. I have it, but it is dear.

I'll pay your price. Then I must pay theirs—at the Asylum over to Weston. Rich people are there. She can put on airs and rage as she likes.

She needs rest, Dearbhla said. Warm soups.

Warm soups? I would push her through the Asylum gates in her bedclothes, dead of night, a charity case, to keep them from bankrupting me. But I must pay, and calm her to make the trip. What have you?

Dearbhla searched among her stores. She showed him a small pouch, and a vial of ground roots in a whiskey tincture. The pouch is jimson leaves, she told him, ground to a powder—steep a bare teaspoon in a quart of water for a tea. Two drops of tincture in the tea—no more! It is ground nightshade and black cohosh, here they call it snakeroot—

I don't care what it is, woman!

You have a paper, an empty vial?

He fetched them quickly and watched her pour a bit of the powder into the folded paper. But he reached out as she counted the drops of tincture and tipped more into his vial. Give it me, he said, and took it.

That is five days' dosage, Dearbhla said. She will calm, with just two drops in the tea, and sleep the night. Honey to mask the bitter.

What do I care about the bitter? I would buy it all if you'd sell it. He turned as the bell jingled over the double street doors of the shop. A voice called out. It's that damn Rebel swindler, said the shopkeep. Name your price, woman, and be quick.

Dearbhla knew the voice. Papa had come to barter. The supplies, at least, she could give to ConaLee.

Add more to this box, she told the shopkeep. Two pound cornmeal, pound of barley, ream of jerky, one of bacon. Quart bottle of vinegar. Sorghum molasses. And candy sticks, spearmint. She slanted her eyes at him. The storekeep feared her and she used it when she could. Don't cheat me, she told him. You know better.

The storekeep only glowered.

Then give it all to that man, she told him, the swindler.

Give it him?

Like I say. With what he barters for or buys, like as a good price. And say you don't need the eggs.

Why, old woman?

His wife and children, Dearbhla said, starving while he drinks in the saloon. Give it him, all of it.

The shopkeep only shook his head at her as he took the paper and tincture. Then he turned to Papa's roiling summons behind him, Dearbhla's provisions in his arms, and pushed the door shut.

Dearbhla moved near the wall to the streetfront, leading her horse close behind her. She saw the buckboard pulled up in front of the dry goods store, with ConaLee and the chap in the back. Soon enough Papa was loading the provisions, pleased he'd cheated the storekeep out of such bounty for a few dead squirrel. He gave the loaded egg basket back to ConaLee, and the candy, and headed to the saloon. Dearbhla waited, then walked quickly to the buckboard.

The little chap was busy with his candy stick. ConaLee near stood, surprised, but Dearbhla hushed her. Here, child, take this pouch of fennel root and boil it with barley water—you remember. A tonic for your mother.

Oh Dearbhla, she is poorly.

Cook when he's gone, ConaLee. With the tonic, she'll eat. Barley mash, boiled eggs, cornmeal cakes with molasses. Bacon and fried eggs for you and the chap. Feed yourself, you must stay well. And if he's drunk when he's finished in the saloon, tie the chap to you. Say you'll drive the buckboard to let him take his ease.

I know—it's why he brings me. ConaLee clasped Dearbhla to her. I hear your heart, she said.

That is your mama's heart, strong though she seem weak. Dearbhla breathed in the fragrance of the child's dark curls. And you are strong. Remember, I was not here.

ConaLee released her. Come to us? He's gone near every day.

Child, he would know. But I see you, ConaLee. I'm with you.

Dearbhla walked quickly away, the horse pulling back on the lead as though to tug at her every step.

. . .

A week later, her own provisions short, Dearbhla was back in the town. A showy wreath of black crepe hung on the street door of the emporium. It was custom here, as in the South, to mark a death with such. The wreath was done up in black satin bows, curled black ribbon, black silk roses the storekeep would sell as fancies soon enough. Dearbhla went to the back entrance. She did not knock, only put her hand on the alley door. She waited, for she knew he'd seen her pass by in the street.

He opened the door, combed and clean, spectacles in place. What? I've a business to run.

You gave her all, then. You took from me and gave her all.

Shut up, old woman. You stand here if I let you. He fixed her with a furious, baleful gaze and lowered his voice. Take her trunk, her clothes. Combs and geegaws.

That man who came in, called to you, when I gave you the tincture.

Him? Rebel con man. Here more, since you gave him those provisions.

Put the best of her clothes and personals in her trunk. Next you see him, give it him. Say you want to rid yourself of her trifles, no need now for the Asylum. Giving them away. And he happens by.

Eh? Why him? I can sell her pins and brooches, after some time—

Only your dead wife's best clothes in the trunk—a silk jacket, skirts, underclothes, stockings. And slippers. Leather boots. Hairnet and combs.

Or what? he sneered.

Or some may know what we traded.

Witch, he said. No one would believe you.

But they would talk. How sudden she died, and you telling about the Asylum. She told others.

How? She was locked in her room.

She called from her window, at night, when you lay drunk. She called out she was feared of the Asylum, and your fists. Yelling down into the street. Singing and wailing.

He reddened, for it might have happened. Sweat broke out across his broad forehead. Go away, he said.

Your wife, Dearbhla said. She was the witch. You feel the heat of her.

She was a lunatic. She's gone. Buried in the churchyard.

What did you tell the pastor, the town? Crazed, she drank poison?

He looked askance. She fell down the stairs. 'Twas a knot on her head.

You waited till she slept and threw her down. She is angry. Lunatic, you say? The mad have the strength of ten, strength to haunt, confuse—

And he looked over Dearbhla, behind her, as though a fiend faced him.

Rid yourself, but only to him. That loud one you call a Rebel con man. Tell him of the Asylum. How your wife wished for her rest and cure but you waited too late, and now rid yourself of her things. He will take her power from over you, into himself.

A large dragonfly darted between them, buzzing. The storekeep staggered back, afraid.

Pack her trunk, Dearbhla said, and hang the key from the lock on a ribbon. Give him, the con man, the trunk. If he wants to see inside, bid him open it, rifle through her things. Don't touch them. Tell him, silks, a woman of quality. He will take her anger with him. And if you give him her jewelry, he will take it sooner. Far away. You won't see him again.

The storekeep wiped his brow on his sleeve. I will do it, he said.

Then you will save yourself, Dearbhla told him, and pulled the door shut between them.

.   .   .

From her vantage on the ridge, she waited and glimpsed Papa, as he called himself, but he gave no sign she could read. The storm of him buzzed like a whirl in the trees. She kept herself apart. There were comings and goings, then silence. When she could wait no longer she walked down the trail. The cabin door stood open. All were gone—all. And provisions taken from the larder, cook pots, feather tick, blankets—the bed was but its frame. ConaLee's pallet gone, but her clothes left. Dearbhla saw, from the back window, the cow fallen dead on its side, swole as though to burst.

We was afraid to butcher the cow, said a voice behind her, since we didn't know what killed her.

Dearbhla turned round to see the widow woman, from the ridge farm to the east, bobbing on her feet to lull the babe tied to her in a shawl. Might be I'd have saved her, Dearbhla said.

You're that root doctor from up above, the widow said. She came closer, to show the sleeping babe. I took the girl twin. I could never have children, so I'm blessed to receive. And he said to take whatever stores we could use, not to waste. He gave me his own horse, that we rode here.

She was so poorly? Dearbhla asked. No need of her horse?

Oh, she was give out. Mute, she was, near senseless. He took her in the buckboard, three day ago, to the Asylum. He said it's like a hotel. Rest and cure, he said. She was dressed nice, clothes he got in town. I fixed her hair, to suit a magazine picture the daughter fancied. The older widow, over to that side— she took the boys. She lost her sons, you know, in the War.

Where is ConaLee?

The daughter? She went with him, to help with her mama.

He went off with a twelve-year-old child?

Went off? He's her father. She called him Papa. We all did. He helped about my place now and again, being the only man on these high ridges.

Dearbhla met her gaze. The widow, not young, was still of childbearing age. Likely he'd bedded her regular, and she not even his prisoner. You called him Papa? Dearbhla asked. He never said his name? What man, living legal, calls himself Papa?

The woman shrugged. I don't get your meaning.

No matter, Dearbhla told the widow. You've a beautiful babe. Healthy. She'll tell your fortune when she's grown. Her poor mother, to lose all.

He spoke of cures, the widow said. But life here is too hard for such as her. This babe had no clothes but this wrapping— I'll make her some. She moved the shawl from the babe's face, and traced her forehead with a light touch.

Dearbhla turned behind her, to the old blanket trunk. She opened it and searched, moving quilts aside, for ConaLee's things. She held up the knit woolen bunting Eliza had made the winter ConaLee was born. Take this, she told the widow. Lined in deerskin. For the winter—her sister wore it.

The widow took the bunting and held it to the babe. Oh, she breathed, I thank you.

I hope Eliza might come to me, Dearbhla answered, if she is ever well. But I can't care for a young one. You'll keep the babe, then, raise her as yours—

Oh yes. I promised Eliza, though she paid no mind. The widow looked away and seemed to consider. You know, she said, I have two horses, and would just as soon not feed a third. Why not take her horse, to your place? Then, if she might return—

If you like, Dearbhla said.

It's a pleasant walk back for us, on such a day. I'm sorry you didn't know—of Eliza's going. It was very sudden—

Dearbhla nodded. For the best, she said.

They walked out together. Dearbhla stood watching until the widow was out of sight. Then she took hold of the horse, adjusted the saddle and empty saddlebags. The widow would not have cared for ConaLee's books that had been Eliza's, but Dearbhla took most of them, and the small flow blue plate from her One's girlhood room, a room larger than this cabin. Eliza had asked, when she was but three year old, if Dearbhla could be her mother. Told that her mother had passed, the child had lisped, Then, Dearbhla, say I'm your One. Dearbhla had allowed it, though truly her One was the boy who stood near them, brushing Eliza's hair.

Dearbhla went into the cabin and breathed across the small mirror on the wall, only to see the vapor disappear, but she hoped to vision ConaLee wavering there, running in a field, calling for her mother, not feared, only following. If Papa had kept the child, Dearbhla thought she would sense such. The scoundrel, free of them all, had surely left both mother and daughter at the Asylum gates and never shown himself, to go off with the widow's jewelry and the buckboard. Likely he'd sell it, and his mount, and go far—use the funds for trains or coaches. Likely the horse he'd thrashed so viciously would turn toward home, given a chance. Dearbhla pulled the wooden window shutters closed and set the planks in place across them. Took ConaLee's clothes, rolled up in the castoff blanket. The open padlock, thrown down on the front porch, had the key within the lock. She bolted the closed front door and kept the key—to save, at least, what was here. He'd poisoned the cow, Dearbhla knew, to fluster ConaLee, but she would have gone with her mother, no matter. Later, when the cow was naught but weathered skeleton, Dearbhla would rope the bones to the porch rail and stake the skull to the doorstep. Not conjure, but protection. Warning and caution, if others approached.

And so she left the cabin abandoned. Astride the horse, she urged him up the foot path and felt a paper of cracked grain tucked under the saddle horn. Some of the chickens had escaped capture and the widow had intended tempting them. Dearbhla dropped a thin trail behind her, all the way up the path. She looked back to see six or eight pullets, the youngest, agile hens, come from the woods and trailside, hop-flying, stalking along. She would close them into the lean-to that drew heat from her cabin, build them nests along the shelf, set a couple of dogs to guard them. She'd plenty of straw and feed, and the eggs would help her through the colder weather. She saw, in glimpses, Papa's broken grasp. ConaLee and her mother would not starve, would not freeze. Some force beyond conjure had drawn them to a safety Dearbhla could not provide.

Some whose cases are chronic . . . are among the most pleasant and agreeable patients . . . It is somewhat presumptuous for us to say that a recovery is impossible . . . When patients cannot be cured, they should still be considered under treatment, as long as life lasts.
—DR. THOMAS STORY KIRKBRIDE, 1854

ConaLee

MORAL TREATMENT

The key turned in the lock. The young attendant, older than me but younger than Mama, wore no rings or jewelry. Maybe none of them did. Her uniform was plain—the starched bit of white cap sat just at her hairline, the long-sleeved black blouse and skirt, the broad white apron with its wide shoulder straps and high bib front. A set of keys on a chain disappeared into her pocket. I felt ashamed of my own clothes.

Ladies, she said. Good morning. Please follow me to Dr. Story's office. We shall pass along Ward B, down the stairs, to the rotunda room and entry floor of the hospital.

Obliged, I said. I am Miss Eliza Connolly, and my patient is Miss Janet—

She only stepped back and bid us come through.

Mama smiled as though pleased. I crossed the threshold after her. The nurse, if she was called such, locked the door of our room and turned without another glance.

I took Mama's arm and kept pace. There was noise and commotion, all of a piece, like off-pitch music. The hospital was awake and seemed a town of sorts, all the parts moving. A line of patients passed us, going in the opposite direction, following their own attendant. Others sat on the sofas and rockers along the corridor, at needlework or reading. One woman had attached many feathers to her upswept hair and stood watching us through the fronds of a tall palm. I kept my gaze forward. Mama seemed calm enough. Everyone had surely come out of their rooms, into the wide hallway—the doors to the rooms were shut and the wide corridor hummed. Women's voices were all around us, like blind birds wheeling through a tunnel. The corridor was sunlit from the large window at the far end, and we seemed to move through many conversings that rose and fell. Suddenly all was quiet. Our attendant had locked the ward doors behind us and we were on the stairs.

.   .   .

Dr. Story stood before us, having dismissed the attendant. He was not handsome or imposing, not old, but had an older man's calm way about him. His dark hair was combed to the side, longer in back. Thick brows, very black. The eyes, deep set, blue-gray, seemed almost turned down at the corners and gave him an air of patience or sadness. He wore thin mutton-chop whiskers, a starched white collar and navy silk cravat, a plain suit. He smelled of soap. His mouth was relaxed and his voice warm, as though time never marked this place or rushed his words. I knew Quakers were mostly Northerners, and Abolitionists all. That would mark him here. High in the mountains, Mama and me were slaves to the weather and staying fed, to Papa's moods after he found us. Not chased like Eliza in the story, not whipped. Yet Papa had used us as he liked, and sold us, in his way.

Please, Dr. Story said, and showed us to the upholstered chairs that faced his desk. We sat. I imagined a tea set, and china cups, like we were on a visit, until he spoke.

Matron Bowman tells me, Miss Janet—here he looked at Mama—that you were brought to us by a passing stranger, and that Miss Connolly accompanied you on your journey.

Mama looked up, attentive, and never glanced at me.

He moved to sit in the chair just beside her and leaned toward her. He seemed about to take her hand. But I saw that he would not.

Was it a difficult journey? he asked.

She too leaned forward, and nodded slowly, several times. Perhaps she would speak to him. I almost hoped.

Did anyone hurt you on the journey? Dr. Story paused. Or before the journey?

I held my breath, afraid she might reply. It seemed to me Papa hurt her every day, not to strike her or any of us, but in his look and touch, in holding us fast as he chose. She stood or sat or lay senseless under him and he seemed to play at rousing her to noises. How would she answer? She looked away then, into the room. I hoped she would speak to him, and convince him of our story.

Miss Janet, Dr. Story said, I hope you will speak with me in time. We shall meet every other day, here in the office, to help you acclimate. You will be staying with us for some while. Shall we assign an attendant to ease your transition? Or would you prefer that Miss Connolly stay near you, accompany you in your regimen—your activities during the day—

My mother turned to him. Oh, she said. Yes.

It was a soft voice, her new voice, that struck no chord in me. I thought I remembered that we had sung and shouted and laughed. That she would read to me long and long until I fell asleep. Years when we were alone, with only the seasons and the animals and Dearbhla, and other neighbor women—more of them, in that time before—

Very well then, he told Mama. Please bear with us. I must talk with Miss Connolly, but I hope you will let us know your thoughts.

Mama put a hand to her mouth and nodded.

The doctor turned to me like a warmth that searched and found me. Miss Connolly, he asked, how long have you known the patient?

Two year, about, I said, careful. But I seldom heard her speak in that time—like she did just now, to you.

Matron Bowman provided me with the information you gave her.

I could not answer many of Matron Bowman's questions, I said.

Matron Bowman is not involved in medical decisions, he replied, though she offers her observations. Can you tell me the cause of the fire that destroyed Miss Janet's home?

He seemed generous but saw into me, I knew.

Was the cause discovered? he asked.

It was at night, I answered. A lightning strike, some said, or spilled kerosene. No one knew. But the family I worked for . . . moved North the next day, to their kin, because someone . . . killed their stock—their chickens, the cows, the two horses—the night of the fire.

I'd said too much. Now he might ask for names, the home-steads, the family, the town. But he did not.

Many have suffered, he said, and suffer now, especially here, in this border state. The fighting has ceased, but not the grief.

He seemed to read my thoughts better than I could think them. But I pulled close the pounding heart of the rabbit on the lawn, and the sound of the owl beating his great wings, flying to find the rabbit and tear it open.

What can you tell me about Miss Janet? he asked. Her interests, her diversions.

She had lots of books, I said, and would choose one for me to read to her. She liked Wordsworth, Shakespeare's sonnets—sometimes pages from a novel. Or a children's book. *The Water-Babies*, she had, with drawings in it.

You read Shakespeare to her? You are educated?

Only at home. My father was a schoolteacher, strict about lessons, till he went to the War. My brothers went as well. No one came back. My mother . . . passed, when the War was over. I have no family, and I worked, living in, these last years. Miss Janet had a piano, and a garden that looked near tended even after it was wild. Yes, I would say she likes books, and talk . . . about books.

He included Mama in every glance, as though to involve her in the conversation. And Miss Janet has no family? he asked. No children? I notice she wears no wedding ring.

Where was her ring? She'd worn a plain gold band, ever since I remembered. I felt the white owl drop, talons spread above some scuttling creature. Mama's children were my children, yet I was one of them.

Miss Connolly? Whatever you know of the patient is most helpful.

She has no children, I managed to say, far as I know. No one mentioned such. She was always called Miss Janet. It may be she was betrothed, but so many went to the War. Paintings, portraits like, of her parents, grandparents, hung on the walls—it was the family home.

And why did Miss Janet not employ someone to attend her? As you were employed? Perhaps you don't know the answers to these questions.

I don't, sir. She wasn't able, I think. She seldom went out. My mistress told me to take suppers to her from our table, and baskets of food. I went evenings and ate with her—my family that employed me, had known hers, her father was a judge, I think, but that, had been long before—

He interrupted me. Miss Connolly, there is clearly a bond between you. I would like to employ you as Miss Janet's attendant, to share her room and look after her, and accompany her on her assigned regimen. But I can pay you only in room and board—for the present, until we can ascertain your continued positive effect. Perhaps you might learn our approach, and report to Matron Bowman concerning Miss Janet's progress.

Dr. Story, I told him, I want to stay, very much.

On a trial basis, he said. This must be understood. You see, Miss Connolly, books are all very well. Miss Janet and I will certainly discuss books—he nodded at Mama—but a strict regimen, including physical activity—a walk of some three to five miles a day, croquet or hoops on the Lawn, carriage rides in late afternoon, is essential. We encourage meaningful diversion each morning, mental stimulation in company, conversations on topics of interest, useful activity. For women, sewing and embroidery, sketching in pastels, simply for expression, for pleasure. Some evenings, lectures, performances, open to all able to enjoy them.

I nodded, wondering if he would discover who my mother really was. I did not know truth from memory, myself, anymore. She'd shot deer and killed and dressed them, always with Dearbhla. I remembered them working in brimmed hats, leather gloves to their elbows, pulling and cutting, the slide of steaming guts tumbling out on the ground, and the carcasses hung up. I heard the crack of a rifle in the woods, the thud of running and scuffling near my hiding place, smelled the earth of the root cellar. I pushed at the cool stones set in the walls and did not know why. But Dr. Story was speaking. His voice gathered me in.

You will see, Miss Connolly, he said. We provide firm, sympathetic structure, healthy air and food, a refuge from family and strife. We counsel responsibility and participation. Our approach is known as "moral treatment." Many can be cured with humane treatment, and the incurable, treated humanely.

It seemed a riddle but the interview was over. Dr. Story had taken my mother's arm as he showed us to the waiting room. Matron Bowman was there, to discuss us, most likely. She followed him into the office and shut his door behind her.

I felt almost dizzy. My thoughts were jumbled and I could not exactly recall his words or mine. He'd said I could stay. Was that right? Mrs. Bowman would surely say no. The floor seemed to shift underfoot like the icy floes in Eliza's river, whilst her enemies shouted and snapped their whips across the frozen distance. I'd met so few men who truly looked at me. There were the marauders I never saw during the War, and knew only for the terror I felt—small, hunched, hidden. And Papa, the marauder who stayed to abandon all he sired and ruined. The babbies would be weaned now, peevish, pained in their stomachs from cow or goat milk. The boys would at least have each other, and the chap was near enough to home that he could walk to our cabin across the ridge, were he older, and see the ruin of it. I wondered how long he would remember the stories I read him, the games of Fox and Goose, the finger rhymes, his cunning wooden cup, the handle carved like a squirrel's tail, that I kept aside for him. He wouldn't nap or sleep till I read to him from *Water-Babies*. I made a joke of Tom's *What are bees?* and *What is honey?* because our chap knew both and lisped the words. I told him that life he could not see made him grow. So then it might be fairies that made the world go round—the Tom from the book might become a water-baby, minnow small, and long to be a dragonfly. Our own chap's heart was so close to mine, even after he began to walk—I wore him against me in the shawl, clasped to my front, every day of his life as I went to and fro about the place. It was the two of us, until the twins. If he only remembered someone had held him, fed him, talked fond to him, I supposed it was something.

Mama reached to take my hand, as like she felt me falter. Surprised, I clasped her slender fingers. Her wedding ring was gone, for how long I didn't know. *I am not yer Papa, nor have I ever been. I never laid eyes on you or your mama* . . . surely he'd taken it to sell, to help fund his new adventure. Now I shut my eyes to think of my *Poets*. I read to Mama at night, at home, if he was gone and the little ones asleep. It surely did her good and was some comfort to me, afraid Papa would arrive soon, or come back at daylight, sick from drink. I was tired since the twins and read from books of poems that I could open to any page. Words, *life's star, the soul,* came to me now. I could hear voices then, in the office. The transom above the office door was open—an oversight. I could not say so, lest they blame me for listening, or stir, lest they know I was memorizing every line. Matron Bowman curdled hers with disapproval. I heard her pause. She would be pursing her lips.

And you wish to employ this, Miss Connolly, this—Eliza? We know nothing about her.

Only that she's had some education, Dr. Story replied, and seems to have the absolute trust of the patient. And what do we know of the other attendants? They are men and women, young, many of them, from Weston or towns nearby. We could not begin by firing staff, for we are the strangers here, along with Mr. O'Shea, who arrived two years before us. He admitted to assuming the name of the Quaker doctor who saved him during the War, and supplied a medical record and letter from the same. O'Shea is an excellent Night Watch. We can't always predict.

I could hear him pace, unhurried, just in front of the windows. Mrs. Bowman was seated nearest the door, in the chair I'd occupied. Her voice carried clear.

Mr. O'Shea has exceeded his charge, she said. He gave these two coffee and johnnycakes at dawn, as though we are to feed all who appear at the doors, no matter the hour. I spoke to him severely.

Mrs. Bowman, my uncle asked us to make this journey from

Pennsylvania together, more than two years ago. You and I learned firsthand from the man who defined "moral treatment," and I am grateful every day for your presence.

But Dr. Story, O'Shea admitted them on his own authority—

I imagined the doctor holding up one hand, gentle, to silence her.

In rare cases, Matron Bowman, trusted employees must exercise their judgment and inform us immediately. Remember, my predecessor here was a Weston town father who spent time in Union prisons. Weston may seem to us a mere clearing of woods and fields, but it was a Confederate town, occupied by the Union for most of the War. Our own Great Lawn was home to two thousand infantrymen. Their white tents are gone, but we must make friends among the town. O'Shea's kindness, especially to one of Miss Janet's gentility, is to the good. In fact, I shall tell him so.

I see, she said.

I'm sure it's an isolated incident. As to Miss Connolly—Eliza, is it? Miss Janet, not her surname, I think, may never remember who she was, but perhaps she can accept who she is. Clearly, she suffers severe melancholia and trauma, but shows no signs of delusions or mania. She is occupying a double room; there she will stay, with the girl as personal attendant, until she improves—in some weeks, I expect, if she keeps to the assigned regimen. I made no mention and no promises, but if Miss Connolly learns well and adapts, she might work with other female patients who suffer variations of Miss Janet's condition.

I looked out into the waiting room and could not breathe. Would I dress in that uniform, so clean, so—

The woman is a charity patient, said Mrs. Bowman, despite her "sensibilities." And we must take on paying another salary—

I negotiated terms, Mrs. Bowman. The young woman has agreed to room and board only, until her patient improves to our satisfaction. If she then begins to work with other patients, that decision . . . will be yours to make. I rely on your high standards.

There was quiet in the room.

Assign her to shadow one of your best younger nurses, Dr. Story said, minding a talkative patient, someone who will encourage conversation. Miss Connolly can learn our regimens best by taking part. I've told her I will hear your report, and interview her in this office, to consider future progress. Are we decided then, Mrs. Bowman?

The floor creaked as she stood from her chair. I heard Dr. Story hasten to the door and open it, murmuring his thanks, and I made haste to smooth a strand of Miss Janet's hair. Matron Bowman passed into the waiting room like a ship bearing heavy ballast.

Come with me, Eliza, with Miss Janet, of course. We must discuss Dr. Story's recommendations.

. . .

Dr. Story's treatment office, said Mrs. Bowman, is on the third floor. It's like a drawing room, with dark wood desk and file cabinets, many framed maps on the walls, and a globe of the world held fast in a low brass table. She nodded, as though pleased to tell us.

A globe of the world? I wondered if it would turn like a ball. Mrs. Bowman's office was plain. A desk with two straight chairs before it, and closed cabinets behind.

Our relation is now professional, Mrs. Bowman began. You must call me Matron, and you will be Nurse Connolly to staff and patients. We refer to our male and female attendants as nurses, though your duties here are not medical. Any medical concern must be reported to the Matron—myself—and in the men's wards, to the Steward. You will help maintain calm on your assigned wing, observe how to shift the patients according to schedule, communicate with housekeeping and laundry.

It was as though a light turned on. Relief wet my eyes.

She paused to glare at me, then at Mama. For the present, she said, your only charge is Miss Janet, or whatever her name may be—

I nodded, as though I agreed to uncertainties about Miss Janet.

—your permanent hire depends on her progress. You must remain with her at all times, unless she is occupied and otherwise supervised. Accompany her daily on her assigned regimen, including meals. Her room is large enough for a personal attendant. In fact, the gentlelady who has left us was provided her own nurse by her family, well-placed people—

I glanced at Mama, who wore her fine dress so well.

Mrs. Bowman looked away. I'll have a cot and linens moved back to the room, she told me.

Thank you, Matron, I said. Over the desk between us, she'd opened her ledger to a list of employ. I saw columns and figures, but none I could make out.

She closed the ledger and stood, holding out a pile of clothing. Here are two uniforms. You agreed to room and board only until you prove yourself. Your attire is to be clean and pressed and your cap starched. Nearly all women who live in as attendants share rooms on the uppermost floor. Clean uniforms are delivered each Wednesday and Saturday. For now, your uniforms will be delivered to your room.

I will change right away, Matron—

You must observe our work with patients and encourage Miss Janet to interact. You will keep pace with a particular attendant, Nurse Blevins, and her patient, Mrs. Kasinski. Your daily regimen will be identical for a few weeks. Mrs. Kasinski is—expressive, and may incline Miss Janet to communicate. Nurse Blevins will call at your room in one hour. Do you have any talents, Miss Connolly?

I—read well, aloud. I can recite . . . poems, or—

You don't play an instrument. Or sing.

I can play the harmonica—

Harmonica is not an instrument, she said, and looked at me askance.

I could, perhaps sing, with others—

We have an Asylum choir, for religious services on Sundays, and a Singing Group, for staff and patients. They entertain with standards twice a week. Your participation would be noted. We have lectures on topics of interest, theatricals by the town Players, and traveling companies. The debate and glee clubs from the local school perform in our auditorium. Certain patients enjoy carriage rides on the grounds, with staff of course.

How . . . nice for them, I said. I had never ridden in a carriage, though I had seen them in the town, times Papa had taken me along to help collect goods in the buckboard. Mama likely knew of carriages—she had so many books, at least thirty or forty, and she had not always lived in our mountains. Surely she knew of many things, if only she could tell me. But after Papa came, she said less and less until she stopped talking, even if he wasn't there.

Mrs. Bowman addressed Mama. Miss Janet, she said, you too might enjoy the carriage, if you adhere to your regimen. And communicate your interests.

Yes, I said. Miss Janet is pleased to be here at the Hospital. And she has many interests—

Matron Bowman clasped her hands. You may go, she said.

SCHEDULE OF A COMPLETE ORGANIZATION WITH RATE OF COMPENSATION.

—The following list . . . is believed to include only those that are necessary about a State Hospital for the Insane, when containing 250 patients. There is a loss to the afflicted and the whole community, by every such attempt to manage an institution with an inadequate force.

—DR. THOMAS STORY KIRKBRIDE, *1854*

One Physician-in-Chief,	$1,500 per annum,	
with furnished apartments and board of family.		
If living detached and finding his family,	$1,000 additional.	
One First Assistant Physician,	Board and $500 per annum.	
One Second Assistant Physician,	" $300	"
One Steward,	" $500	"
One Matron,	" $300	"
One Male Supervisor,	" $250	"
One Female Supervisor,	" $175	"
One Male Teacher,	" $200	"
One Female Teacher,	" $150	"
Sixteen Male Attendants,	" $168	"
Sixteen Female Attendants,	" $108	"
One Night Watchman,	" $168	"
One Night Watchwoman,	" $108	"
Two Seamstresses,	" $96	"
One Farmer,	" $200	"
Two Farm hands,	" $144	"
One Gardener,	" $200	"
One Assistant Gardener,	" $144	"
One Engineer,	" $240	"
Two Firemen,	" $144	"
One Baker,	" $150	"
One Carpenter,	" $240	"
One Carriage Driver,	" $168	"
One Jobber,	" $144	"
One Cook,	" $150	"
Two Assistant Cooks,	" $100	"
Four Female Domestics,	" $80	"
One Dairy Maid,	" $100	"
Three Washerwomen,	" $100	"
Three Ironers,	" $100	"

ATTENDANTS OF A KIND, CHEERFUL AND AFFECTION-
ATE DISPOSITION . . . may see to patient schedules . . .
joining them in their walks, rides or work . . . Judicious
conversation . . . a brisk walk in the open air, or simply
directing a patient's attention to a new object, may . . . prevent a paroxysm of grief, or an outbreak of violence.
—DR. THOMAS STORY KIRKBRIDE, 1854

ConaLee

A BRISK WALK

We stood at the locked door of our room. I felt in the pile of clothes and found a round key ring in a pocket. It held only one key. *Your only charge is Miss Janet.* One day, I hoped to have many keys, like the other attendants. For now I let us in and locked us in our room. It seemed magical that my key fit the lock from both sides. I turned to Mama but she sat on the bed as though tired out by her few words. Still, she'd spoken. Someone had brought a cot for me, and bedsheets. I helped Mama undress to the waist and used a sheet to press out her milk. The linen towel beside our pitcher and basin made a binding for her breasts.

It won't be long, Mama, I told her, before your milk dries up. Rest now.

She nodded and then lay back on the bed. Dr. Story, she said, as though musing.

He seems patient, Mama. And you must talk to him, but stay to *our* story. Here, sit up, and practice with me. I drew our one chair over beside her and sat near, as she would in his office. Suppose I am him, I told her, and I ask you, Miss Janet, what are your favorite books?

Mr. Dickens . . . , she offered.

Or you could talk about Shakespeare's sonnets.

Shakespeare's sonnets, she said, as though to herself.

Mama, you used to say them to me. You knew some by heart. You taught me—the one about Time's fool and never writ.

116, she said.

Can you remember the lines? I can't, but once you start to recall—you surely will. He would lend you the book. We could read it to each other.

Might you lend me, she began, the sonnets . . .

I heard her talking softly while I changed. I threw off my dirty clothes and stood on them to wash, filling the basin from the pitcher, sponging with cold water and scant lather from a slice of lye soap. I longed to be clean and scrubbed myself, then stepped into the closet and blotted my damp skin on the drying bed sheet.

Mama, I said. They gave me a uniform! Don't look until I tell you—

She nodded as I chattered on, for I must talk to someone, and now she truly listened. A chemise and undergarments were folded inside the pinafore. Mrs. Bowman required a certain attire, even underneath. I pulled the long gray dress over my head, and the starched white pinafore that buttoned tight at the waist. The stiff linen collar was separate. It fastened under a seam, with hooks and eyes. And the organdy hat—how must it attach? I looked in Mama's carpetbag for hairpins and comb. There was a hairbrush, monogrammed with a P, but no pins. I loosened my braid and pulled out the plaits, throwing my hair over my head and brushing hard. The dead woman's hair would be in the brush, silken or wiry as before. I tried not to think on it but sat before the mirror, twisting my hair into a rope I could knot and tuck.

ConaLee, my mother whispered, and reached toward me across the bed.

Oh, Mama, I said, and went to her. You're getting better. Only don't say my name but here. I'm your nurse, like at home, but you must call me Nurse, or Nurse Connolly. You must be Miss Janet . . .

She didn't answer, but held to my wrist. She looked away then, and closed her eyes. What to say and when? If Dr. Story could help her, or this place, did it matter what truth she told? We could leave, if she got well, and find our way to Dearbhla—Papa was gone, surely, far away. What would he want with us now? He'd given away or sold all we had.

I went back to my chair and picked up the organdy cap. Filmy, starched into shape, it weighed nothing. I put it on and picked up the mirror with the plaster roses. My reflection, the cap fastened just at my hairline, struck me silent. The uniform, my hair pulled back severely—it was not ConaLee in the glass. I tried to remember the story I'd told of Nurse Connolly . . . a father and brothers taken by the War, a mother gone. It could be my story, almost, though I'd not seen the War except in what it ruined. The vanished wedding ring, my father gone, whoever he was, the babbies split up, the cabin empty, claimed already or soon enough—so many wandered, still, even as high as our ridge. But the neighbor women would take the chickens, take what they wanted of the tools and goods, leave the sick cow for the coyotes or bobcats. Late in the autumn, I told myself, Dearbhla would fetch the bones. She must know Mama's surname, and mine. I didn't even know Mama's given name. Papa had said he was not my father, and I felt in my heart it was so. He called Mama "Mrs.," or no name at all. Dearbhla called her "My One." How would Dearbhla know what he'd done with us? She stayed out of sight of the neighbor women, and there was no one else to tell her—unless she conjured our path to this place, but she'd bade me never think the word of her. Mama's round mirror fogged then. I had sighed across it.

. . .

Someone knocked, *tick tick tock*. Nurse Blevins was that way, I'd learn, sharp and quick. I stood listening on the other side of the door. A narrow slat snapped open before my face and I saw her eyes as she saw mine.

It's Nurse Blevins and Mrs. Kasinski, she said.

I unlocked the door and they came in. Our transom was open, and one of the windows, but they seemed to fill the room like a wind. Nurse Blevins's patient, a short, round woman, paced, touching the walls here and there, talking under her breath. She smelled of patchouli and wore mourner's black. But it wasn't proper dress. Her bonnet was tied on with a black scarf and she wore many shawls one over another, and bits of crochet tied in her hair. An old commemorative ribbon of some kind was pinned near her collar.

Mama sat up on the bed. I moved to stand near her.

Nurse Blevins came to shake my hand. I'm Eira Blevins, she said. You are Nurse Connolly. Do introduce me.

This is Miss Janet, I said, and felt myself flush. I'd very nearly said, This is my mother.

Eira Blevins curtsied, as though to a lady. She was round faced and bosomy, her sandy curls in ringlets to either side of her cap. And this is Mrs. Kasinski, she said, who likes to hum a tune when she isn't speaking one. Isn't it true, Mrs. Kasinski?

The older woman hummed a dirge and smoothed the faded ribbon she wore like a medal. But she stopped and sat on the bed to stroke my mother's hand. The poor thing, she said. Has she lost her Abraham? Suffered a murder before her eyes?

My mother drew back, alarmed. Had she seen such? She would not have told me, I knew, and I moved close beside her. Miss Janet must not be startled, I said, quick, to move the woman away.

Eira Blevins's blue eyes seemed to dart with lights. Now, then! she told her patient. You are Ruth Kasinski, as I said.

The woman stood and turned away, and broke into a low, chant-like reverie. *They carried him to Petersen House and forced me from the room! Is it a wonder I don't sleep?*

Mrs. Kasinski, said Eira Blevins, and pulled her firmly away.

Come here now, and see this lovely little mirror. See the roses, molded along the frame? You might draw such roses tomorrow, in your lesson with Mrs. Morrison.

The woman moved to smile into the mirror as Eira Blevins held it up. She hummed aloud to her image, louder and then softer, peering closely.

Eira Blevins led her to the window. Just you look there, Mrs. Kasinski. A fine day for a brisk walk, as they say. The trees are bright green on the ridge, just in the top leaves.

I stepped up to look myself, but what she called a ridge was only a rise across a meadow.

Mrs. Kasinski went on, addressing her reflection in the window glass, shouting out a word or two—*Nor RIDE the mourning train to Springfield, FLOWERS THROWN so thick my Robert trod them like a carpet in the rain, all the colors beaten black—*

Oh no, Mrs. Kasinski, said Eira Blevins. You go too far.

Mama caught my eye, and stood to smooth her skirts.

Miss Janet, I said, I must fix your hair, and mine, before we go.

Mrs. Kasinski dropped her voice to a mournful whisper. *Whilst they built the bier, RIFLE SHOTS in every hammer blow—*

Eira Blevins took her arm, held her tightly, and hummed a familiar tune into her ear. Mrs. Kasinski took it up, humming along.

I didn't remember Lincoln myself, only that Papa swore oaths to cheer the murder and kept a newsprint photo of Lincoln laid out in his casket. I feared Papa and so believed Lincoln was good.

How sad for her, I said to Eira Blevins. Has she taken on so these nine years, ever since the President was killed?

Eira Blevins shook her head at me and held a finger to her lips. I would learn never to dignify a patient's ravings, but to distract them and talk of the present.

Mrs. Kasinski has her own good husband waiting for her here in Weston, said Eira Blevins. Don't you, Mrs. Kasinski.

Oh yes, Mrs. Kasinski said. I pretend so for his sake.

But you know the truth of it. He's a postmaster and visits Ruth every Sunday without fail. Doesn't he, Mrs. Kasinski? Eira Blevins held my cap. She twirled it on her finger and winked as Mrs. Kasinski remained silent. We must get on, she said.

I've done up my hair, I told Eira Blevins, but I've no hairpins to pin the cap.

Oh, I've plenty. Sit here before the mirror. She took two from her own bundled hair. Sit. You've lovely hair, isn't it? There. Pins are fine but hatpins work better. I hide mine in my hair. I'll tell you why when we're walking, and bring you one or two—

Do I look all right? I asked, standing and flaring the skirt.

Why, you're a picture! Tall enough you needn't hem the skirt. Come along, then. We'll walk into the meadow and up along the woods, early, while most are at lessons.

Mrs. Kasinski reached to take Mama's arm but I moved between them as Nurse Blevins urged her patient toward the door. She hummed the same racing tune her nurse had suggested. I realized it was "Camptown Races," but quick, as it's meant to be sung.

·   ·   ·

We left by the main entrance door and began on the Great Lawn, as it was called. Eira Blevins meant to show us the grounds.

It's a credit to the town and the state, she said. Nearly ten acres inside, over nine hundred windows, and the wings stretch along a quarter mile.

I remembered to ask about the child who'd seen Mama and me arrive, and the Night Watch, and the dawn hour. The child with the long blond hair, I asked, wearing the woman's duster—the boy that dresses like a girl? What is his name?

Oh, said Nurse Blevins, that is Weed, as Cook calls him.

He's her pet and does as he likes. He's small and quick. Weed goes where he will.

Weed? Are his eyes two colors? Is he the cook's relation?

Mrs. Hexum's relation? Not hardly! Eira Blevins laughed as though at her own joke. We call him "one-eyed Weed" amongst us. He's a great match for Mr. O'Shea, our Night Watch. But O'Shea was injured in the War, and is much respected. Weed is likely a thief.

Who is Weed, then?

Eira Blevins shrugged. Mrs. Hexum lets him sit in the cellar train cars that run under the kitchen between the dining rooms, to help with putting up the food.

A train? In the cellar?

Not a real train. A few small flatcars that go back and forth on a narrow track, for taking hot food to the dining rooms in each wing. They send the trays in open cars and haul up the platters on dumbwaiters!

I didn't know what she meant but kept silent. I'd seen railroad tracks in town, and a train passing. How would such fit in a basement?

Ever so many from around the town work here, Eira Blevins was saying. Dr. Story sets a tone, and has influence, connected as he is to the great man, and the Pennsylvania Hospital.

Who is the great man?

Why, Dr. Thomas Story Kirkbride, she said. This is a Kirkbride building, like many asylums. Dr. Story is Dr. Kirkbride's nephew, you know. We are not as fine as the Pennsylvania Hospital—I hear it has a circular rail track on the front lawn. Train rides to amuse the patients on fine evenings! But Dr. Story arrived in one carriage, and Matron in the other, with the four horses, fine ones, not farm drays. So now we have the carriages. Some who do well, and do not chant when they should talk, take lovely rides. Isn't it so, Mrs. Kasinski?

Mrs. Kasinski, holding to my mother's arm, paid her no mind. We walked past the fountain on the paved walk beside the flower beds. Low boxwood borders, bluebells, azaleas. Spidery yellow witch hazel that I knew from Dearbhla's garden. The Asylum was three long wings to each side, each set back to catch the light. I heard noises, faint wailing, shouting, from rooms at the farthest end of one wing, as we walked around to the back.

Those are the worst off, Eira Blevins said. We've nothing to do with them—they have their own guards.

Mrs. Kasinski and my mother walked a little ahead. Eira Blevins urged me to keep pace. I could hear that Mrs. Kasinski had changed her tune. She was humming "Darling Nelly Gray," as though serenading Mama. We'd come across the side lawn to the marked paths in back of the women's wards. A tall hedge separated them from the men's acreage. One trail, scored with carriage tracks, opened up wide as a road. I walked up even with Mama, to see if Mrs. Kasinski was a bother.

Miss Janet, I said. Are you enjoying the walk?

Eira Blevins came up beside me. Leave them be, she said softly.

I was startled to hear Mama humming along, ever so quiet. Could be Dr. Story knew his business, and this older woman would be a help.

Ladies, called Eira Blevins, this way.

She led us across a clearing where I supposed the carriages turned about, onto a smaller footpath. We were walking uphill amongst so many very large trees that I couldn't see far in any direction, except to glimpse our forested mountains in the distance. Birds were singing and flitting, and the spring air was warm as summer. Weeds, pinks and yellows, flowered in clumps. Here and there we encountered steps of piled stone, with wooden handrails. Mossy boulders to each side marked the trails.

It seems so easy to walk off into these woods, I said to Eira Blevins. Do many patients run away?

Not at all, she said. If they do leave, and they are always men, it is into the town. They come back on their own by suppertime, or a townsman brings them. They're known on sight—all quite harmless. The more disturbed, in the wards in the far wings, are not allowed on the grounds at all. Until they earn the right, as Matron says. Those in the Women's Wards above the medical offices all have privileges. Ladies of good family, especially the younger ones like your Miss Janet, love the carriage rides, afternoons or evenings, with Matron or the doctors.

I wondered to hear my mother included in "the younger ones." They seemed to think her younger than she was.

We have performances some evenings. Staff takes part as well, in the ward sitting rooms. We have a pianoforte. Someday, Miss Janet might sing, or play. You might join her.

Oh, I can't think—I never had lessons, and she—

Yes, I know. She doesn't speak, perhaps by choice, but she is not at all insensible and does well with Ruth, so quickly. Our Mrs. K. needs a reason to control herself. She can, if she tries.

The trees met over us and a few green leaves drifted down. The way widened and we came out to a high meadow. The tall hedge between the men's and women's walking trails was a distance below us, beyond an orchard of fruit trees and a flat field enclosed by a low stone wall. Just there where the grass was scythed short, a man stood near an open wagon, his horse roped to a tree. He was breaking ground with a long shovel and flinging dirt to the side. A mound of earth grew as we watched. Mrs. Kasinski stopped her humming. We stood in silence but for the sound of the breeze in the trees.

Who is that man? I asked.

Oh, he is the gravedigger. And that is the Asylum graveyard.

He's from the town?

No, he was a soldier who lost his mind, sent here during the War, an old soldier, for he's old now. He recovered but didn't want to leave, and began tending the graveyard. Now he digs the graves.

And that grove between us, I asked, is that an apple orchard?

The tops of the crooked trees ruffled in even rows. They would be covered with blossoms later in the spring, if we were here to see them.

Oh yes, said Eira Blevins. We have fresh apple butter year-round, and apple pies aplenty, from the canned apples—oh, Miss Janet, wait—

She was off after my mother, who strode down toward the orchard so rapidly that Eira Blevins lifted her skirts and broke into a run to catch up. Mrs. Kasinski gasped and took off lumpily after them, flapping her arms to keep her balance, her many black layers flying. Nurse Connolly! I heard. Eira Blevins was put out to be chasing my patient. Glad I still wore my own boots, I fisted my skirts in one hand and ran. They all gained the middle of the meadow. Mama seemed to float in pale yellow grass to her hips, her jacket a shade or two brighter. I heard Eira Blevins call, Miss Janet! Stop! But Miss Janet had turned to wait for us.

Eira Blevins was still panting as I reached them. Miss Janet, she was saying, running away sudden is not allowed!

She was not running, I said, breathless. She was only walking quick, so that we would follow.

I'll say who was running! Eira Blevins shot back.

I put my arm about Mama's waist. Miss Janet, I said, you must listen to Nurse Blevins. Tell us if you mean to change the way, and make it a fair race! But look, we're nearly to the orchard. Can we walk among the trees there?

Well, said Eira Blevins, we might have taken the path, and not bolted across the meadow.

Let us go to the orchard! Mrs. Kasinski cried out.

Very well, if I don't hear you sing, Mrs. Kasinski, and we all walk together. Agreed? Miss Janet?

My mother nodded.

What was that, Miss Janet? Are we agreed?

Yes, said my mother.

Nurse Blevins looked at me in bright-eyed triumph. I knew

Mama might have said more, but Mrs. Kasinski stepped forward and gently took my mother's arm in hers. We all turned toward the orchard, moving at a stately pace.

Eira Blevins said to me quietly, Stay right up on them. Your Miss Janet is full of surprises. See you are quick enough.

I'm sorry. But it's a good sign. She speaks more, especially when we're alone, and Mrs. Kasinski is raving less.

We'll see how long Ruth stays calm, said Eira Blevins.

Is she . . . incurable?

Oh yes. She'll go on about "the fiend who came from behind and shot his poor brain from his head." But she's harmless. And she does go home, usually at holidays. Though I'm afraid she prefers to be here with us.

And what is that ribbon she wears?

It's a piece of a train card given out to those who saw Lincoln's funeral train, that she stitched onto a brooch with a mourning ribbon—she raises a ruckus if we don't let her wear it. Her in-laws can't abide her, and she must live with them. It's reasonable they don't get on. She embarrasses them, and likes an audience, and they are no admirers of Lincoln.

They were Secessionists, you mean.

Most were, hereabouts.

Why, do you think?

Not to defend their plantations—they had none! They had to run to Virginia to sign up and fight for the very ones that called them "Westerners" and "frontiersmen." Too ornery to take orders from Federals, who thought them backward, or because their people had come up here from the South. Most counties to the north and east were staunch for the Union, but Weston folk figured Northerners had slighted them most, and they've long memories. I was glad to see a Quaker take charge of the Asylum, and put away the cribs.

Cribs? What could she mean? I meant to ask, but we were in the orchard. All the knobby trees stood in rows. I saw that Mama was headed straight across to the graveyard, but she didn't let on, and walked as though meandering; Mrs. Kasin-ski did the same.

They seem to get on, I said to Eira Blevins.

A bit too well, perhaps. Ladies, she called out, keep to the path. We must be back on time for lunch.

We'd missed breakfast—a gap in the regimen, or perhaps Matron Bowman had intended to starve us. We'd walk double the intended distance by the time we were back in the ward. A great crashing sounded behind us then. Eira Blevins pulled me aside and put her hand to my mouth. We saw, there in the trees, two huge stags, their heads down, tangling their racks of antlers, forcing each other back and forth. Struggling, they cracked thick branches into fragments, white slather dripping from their jaws. One half-tossed the other onto a sharp broken limb. Speared, trapped, it kept its feet, but the other stag drove on, pushing it deeper as the sharp branch pierced it through, held it fast as a red froth bloomed between them. Suddenly a brilliant jet of heart's blood shot up, slashing across their faces as though to blind them.

Eira Blevins was pulling me slowly backward, off the path, straight across the orchard. We turned to sprint some distance and a surge of lit red seemed to rush after us. I thought of my way here, the lurching buckboard stopped beneath the giant beech. Shadows came up around me but I glimpsed my moth-er's jacket, and then Mrs. Kasinski's square black form, in the flat field beyond the low stone wall. We'd run to the graveyard. But I saw no lights, felt no dark sleep coming. I took deep breaths and leaned down to steady myself on the cool rocks of the graveyard wall.

Here now, Eira Blevins said beside me. You've gone pale. Mind, your cap is on the ground.

She gave it me, with the hankie she'd used to blot her face. I pressed the hankie to my eyes, then felt for the pins in my hair and fastened my cap as best I could. That was terrible, I said.

That was venison for dinner, even so—three hundred pound, I'll venture. We must go back quickly and tell Cook. She'll send the farmhands to haul it back and dress it. Step over the wall now, and hurry up about it. See? They're headed for the gravedigger. What a pair!

We were over the wall. Mama and Mrs. Kasinski were strolling slowly across the mowed ground. The man didn't look up, only kept to his task, standing in the grave itself now, digging, digging.

Should we stop them?

Too late. No, we'll follow. Miss Janet is showing an interest, for whatever reason, and Ruth is surely getting her exercise.

But Matron said men and women are strictly—

He's not a man, really. He's the gravedigger, and a good one. Learned in the War, they say. You see that hut in the shade of the poplar? He built it and lives there in good weather. He digs graves for the town as well and makes a wage, but likes to stay near the Asylum and be fed his meals.

There are no headstones here, I said.

They're marked with numbers. To spare the families.

I saw markers then, studding the ground, short iron badges thrust down in perfect rows.

No one wants their family name in an Asylum graveyard. Many are here in secret, even in life, like the fine lady who lived in your room.

Matron Bowman seems to hold her in high esteem.

Of course, because the family paid handsome. For discretion and special favor.

I wondered how long Miss Janet would merit favor, but kept my gaze forward and didn't read the numbers. Rows of them. And room for many more. We passed the gravedigger's wagon, and the ladder leaned against it. A wicker coffin lay on the ground, awaiting burial.

We came to the edge of the grave. The gravedigger was in the hole to his shoulders. He was short and bald, with muscled shoulders and arms, and bushy white brows. A thick mustache covered his lips so that his mouth seemed a bare crack. His old-fashioned bowler hat was on the grass. A stout flat board, muddied with his boot prints, was wedged to an end, and he was digging at the other. Mama stood looking down from one side. Mrs. Kasinski, directly across, peered down from the other. He looked up at them and I saw that he was old, his blue eyes like bright dots.

Good day, I said.

Eira Blevins caught Mrs. Kasinski firmly by the arm. We'll be going, she said.

But Mrs. Kasinski spoke into the grave in march-like cadence. *Seek not your son among the dead he is not there he lives today in Paradise.*

Mrs. Kasinski, Nurse Blevins said. Come away.

We sent Willie's coffin with his dear Father's, she chanted, *guarded every moment train to train–* She pointed down into the muddy grave, filled as it was with an inch or two of water. *There is the stream beside the Oak Ridge vault–*

The gravedigger took no notice and splashed about in the bottom of the pit, firming the sides of the grave with a long flat spade. The willow casket seemed forgotten, he was so taken up with smoothing the form of the hole. Now he propped the long shovel in an angled corner and measured with spread palms, one hand after the other, the depth's exact dimensions. The water was deeper at one end than the other, eddying and puddled, like grief was in the ground itself, sluicing up through meadows and fields, even into our mountains that were so steep, flinging themselves ever higher. *The fighting has ceased, but not the grief.* I could not think where I'd heard the words, then remembered Dr. Story saying them.

Mrs. Kasinski chanted louder in hurried phrases, shouting some words as though lashing them into the grave. *We had taken our seats in the box the play commenced MY DEAR HUSBAND took my hand. I said to him BUT WHAT WILL MISS HARRIS THINK OF MY HOLDING ONTO YOU SO.*

Eira Blevins pulled at her, urging her back. Mrs. Kasinski stood firm, as though pressed by terrible weight, weeping silent, streaming tears.

But Mama reached across the grave to take her hand and asked, What then?

The gravedigger paused in his labors, his feet in the muck, and seemed to await the answer.

Mrs. Kasinski didn't sing the words, but spoke them.

He said she wouldn't think anything about it. And that was the last he ever spoke to me.

Ah, my mother said.

———————

Reasons for Admission
1864 to 1889

Intemperance & Business Trouble
Kicked in the Head by a Horse
Hereditary Predisposition
Ill Treatment by Husband
Imaginary Female Trouble
Hysteria
Immoral Life
Imprisonment
Jealousy and Religion
Laziness
Marriage of Son
Masturbation & Syphilis
Masturbation for 30 Years
Medicine to Prevent Conception
Menstrual Deranged
Mental Excitement
Novel Reading
Nymphomania
Opium Habit
Over Action of the Mind
Over Study of Religion
Over Taxing Mental Powers
Parents Were Cousins
Periodical Fits
Tobacco & Masturbation
Political Excitement
Politics
Religious Enthusiasm
Fever and Loss of Law Suit
Fits and Desertion of Husband
Asthma
Bad Company
Bad Habits & Political Excitement
Bad Whiskey
Bloody Flux
Brain Fever
Business Nerves
Carbonic Acid Gas
Congestion of Brain
Death of Sons in War
Decoyed into the Army
Deranged Masturbation
Desertion by Husband

Dissolute Habits
Domestic Affliction
Domestic Trouble
Dropsy
Egotism
Epileptic Fits
Excessive Sexual Abuse
Excitement as Officer
Exposure and Hereditary
Exposure and Quackery
Exposure in Army
Fever and Jealousy
Fighting Fire
Suppressed Masturbation
Suppression of Menses
The War
Time of Life
Uterine Derangement
Venereal Excesses
Vicious Vices
Women Trouble
Superstition
Shooting of Daughter
Small Pox
Snuff Eating for 2 Years
Spinal Irritation
Gathering in the Head
Greediness
Grief
Gunshot Wound
Hard Study
Rumor of Husband Murder
Salvation Army
Scarlatina
Seduction & Disappointment
Self Abuse
Sexual Abuse & Stimulants
Sexual Derangement
False Confinement
Feebleness of Intellect
Fell from Horse in War
Female Disease
Dissipation of Nerves

MANY OF THE POSITIONS about a Hospital for the Insane require persons of particular qualifications . . . Their example never fails to exercise a favorable influence on others of a less decided character . . . an idle, vicious, or faithless one may be worse than none.

— DR. THOMAS STORY KIRKBRIDE, *1854*

ConaLee

MRS. HEXUM'S BUSINESS

The dining room was set with white cloths, folded napkins tucked into water glasses at every place. Our lines began to move. The tread of our shoes and the brushing of many ladies' dresses along the matching rows of chairs was calming. Out the window, I saw Eira Blevins talking to a heavy, ruddy woman in uniform whose reddish graying hair was piled high on her head like a bulging crown. This must be the head cook who ruled the basement kitchen, and the garden beds of herbs and lavender bordering the walled kitchen yard. Bricked walls with locked gates were back of every wing—patients not allowed to walk the wood or meadow could meander safely enclosed. The kitchen yard though, open to the Asylum grounds and the barns and fields behind, was only for the help. Eira Blevins turned away as Cook hastened down the wide slant of stone paving to the kitchen entrance, moving her hamlike arms in urgent motion. I saw a small boy then, running past her up the same steps, in the direction of one of the barns we'd passed today. Weed, as they called him, in the woman's hooded duster that covered him below his hips—the same boy I'd seen with O'Shea, the Night Watch, when we'd arrived at the Asylum. He ran like a boy, pumping his knees high. News of the stag. The first barn was likely a horse stable, and housed the carriages and wagons. Farmhands would be about.

Eira Blevins had said to be quick on our way back, and told Mrs. Kasinski that she would not be walking out tomorrow, due to too much singing—she would dine in her room, to calm herself after her "upset." She quieted so completely though, holding close to my mother, that I asked if we might reconsider. And so we made our way upstairs to the ward, lay aside our wraps, and joined the women as they lined up for lunch. Now Eira Blevins was back, taking her seat to my right in the dining room.

The Asylum, she reminded me, is a quarter of a mile long. You see the speaking horn in the wall there, at the staff station, near the dumbwaiter? Covered tins of hot food come up. Later, the empty vessels go down. I told you about the basement rail track. Mrs. Hexum's Weed saves some poor kitchen wench from crouching small enough to ride the railway car and put the food in the dumbwaiters, and he likely thinks it's fun. Funny that she calls him Weed—then again, he's not an exotic flower!

I leaned toward her amidst a commotion of shifting chairs. I suppose not, I said. But where does he live?

A few children live in the basement laundry, she said quietly, and the drying rooms that are warm even in the winter, and stay cool in summer, and they play in the walled kitchen yard, out the back. It's not as bad as it sounds. The basement is nearly all aboveground and well lit—only the cellar is underground, for the airshafts and the train cars.

But, whose children?

She shrugged. A patient might arrive already with child, or with an infant the family won't claim. Or perhaps a "gentleman" patient, a guard, a laborer, gets his way. Oh, it happens. Or did, before Dr. Story. Those infants that can't be placed, a very few, are put in Mrs. Hexum's charge.

Her charge? How many?

That is Mrs. Hexum's business, Eira Blevins whispered. We say Mrs. Hexum is the true Superintendent, though she's no Physician. I stay on her good side. Cook can be a powerful champion, all below stairs, and not only at feeding us.

I thought of my chap and the twins, wishing them so near me. And the children who don't stay here, I asked. Are they placed in the town?

No one here or anywhere would adopt a lunatic's child! They're taken far off if they look normal, to Washington or Pittsburgh foundling homes. A pig in a poke, I'll tell you! I won't be raising any babies but mine. And better sooner than later.

I thought of the little boy, no longer in sight, running up the kitchen steps, odd clothes in motion. And Cook, I asked Eira Blevins, that is, Mrs. Hexum—is she good to the ones in her charge?

Seems so. They crowd around her like so many chicks and do her bidding, as you see. She keeps them close but for Weed, who goes where he will.

I saw him running to the barn. Why does he wear a girl's duster?

But Eira Blevins had turned away to address the table, snapping her napkin open with a flourish. Look! Here is the soup! And it's Mrs. Kasinski's favorite. Isn't it so, Ruth?

It is, agreed Mrs. Kasinski. She rubbed again at what might be a spot on the tablecloth.

The ladies arranged their napkins on their laps as kitchen maids carted food to the tables in covered tin bowls or platters. They began serving up and down the rows: sorrel soup thickened with mashed carrot. My mother, to my left, ate her soup as others did, and when the bowls were cleared, carefully took up her fork and knife, cutting small bites of sliced mutton and potato. She didn't talk to anyone, but nodded and smiled and seemed to agree to others' remarks.

I'd never sat at table with so many. One woman across the way waved her arms, and another stood and sat, stood and sat, but most might be dining at an inn. All seemed jolly. At home, it was me and the chap at table, him on my lap as I helped him with his spoon. I couldn't remember meals in company. I knew that most families had given up their farms on the ridges during the War, and moved to the towns. Some, those last years, stayed and hid in the cabins. I came to know we were hiding too, by the way Mama sat on the porch during the days I was four and five, fixed so she could see between green hills, down the winding road to the valley. She kept her rifle near and I remembered, like a long-ago dream, counting beans beside her, or writing letters in chalk on the rough board floor.

The mutton is from local sheep, Eira Blevins was telling me. My in-laws, let us hope they prove so, sell meats and corn to the Asylum. They've shoats and lambs, chickens, acres of corn—

The midday sun just then fell straight across my face and I squinted up at the tall dining room windows. Sheer white curtains hung halfway to the sills, dazzling the eye. In a bright slice of instant, I seemed to hold in my hand the small round mirror that Papa bade me use to neaten up, that first dawn we arrived at the Asylum. I knew suddenly that the mirror was mine, not his, and from so long ago—Mama must have given it me for a toy. What I'd forgot came to me like pictures on a spool, and my palm so small the mirror filled my hand. I'd tease the sun's flare with my plaything, turn the round glass here and there, but my mother was suddenly grabbing me up, running to the back through the yard, squeezing my breath out of me. I heard her feet thud the ground and the swish and rip of pine boughs, fresh ones that still smelled of trees. She flung them to the side to uncover the short plank door of the root cellar, set into its square-framed hole. The cellar, dug into the side of a hill, was a four-foot drop. She lowered me in feet first, holding to my wrists, and let go. The dark slammed shut.

Where are you, Nurse Connolly? asked Eira Blevins. Shall I show you my hatpin?

What? I said. Her words seemed to drift past me, squat and pressed as flattened raindrops. I felt myself fall down and down.

Beside me, Mama grasped my arm. I thought she whispered, You! ConaLee! Chimes sounded around her voice as though she spoke from the world of spirits. But the sound was only the attendants, one at the head of each table, standing to ring small silver bells. Miss Janet withdrew her touch.

Dessert! announced Eira Blevins. A and B Wards only, she said quietly.

It was sponge cake, tinged with preserved strawberries.

———————

Dearbhla

A RETURN

She'd sold her stores of eggs and medicinal roots, packed her sacks and saddlebags with traded goods, and left the market. The road to the mountainous path was soon empty. Sounds from the hamlet left behind, groans of wagon, a dog's bark, faded. Dearbhla reached the path amongst the trees and stood pondering before mounting her horse. She'd much to occupy her thoughts but considered the moment she would pause astride and look at the deserted cabin below her place. How many days now was Eliza gone, and ConaLee with her? Three days, four? The place was shut best as Dearbhla could manage, but sat waiting, deserted. If they could not come home to this place, they could not come home to her. Not for her any town or street among many, any rural hamlet that told and talked. Nearer to Weston, she could not live safe, private, as they'd once lived together here. After War's end nine year ago, discovery surely no longer mattered, but the height of these ridges, the far-flung promontories, were her dominion. Their refuge would last her time, or she would bend her time to suit herself, for she knew how. But she waited for ConaLee, for Eliza, to know them safe if not returned.

She did not hear the faint sounds coming up on her left, where roads crossed and the track to Weston skirted the ascending forest. But a flick of shadow crossed just beyond her vision, like an unseen bird overhead, or a fast blur of insect wing flown close and gone. The horse, when she saw it appear on the hilly road, moved head down, dragging the traces, and the buckboard behind creaked driverless along the rutted dirt. The apparition wavered. Dearbhla tied her mount to an overhanging maple in the cover of the woods and walked toward it. Not till she laid hands on the sweated animal could she believe its strength. Holding to its muzzle, feeling of its neck and ears, she saw long strings of weedy grass coiled in the bit—starvation food the horse could scavenge in the traces. Here now, she murmured, you drank but ate little. Left him in some saloon, did you. Come, walk on.

She led the lathered horse to the shade of the path, far enough into cover to take the bit from its bruised mouth, unhitch the buckboard. Likely the wretch had found himself transport better suited to a man of means. Her own horse would have found its way but this one was Eliza's, scarce a yearling when it appeared on the ridge, saddled and ridden hard, so Eliza said, the rider a casualty or prisoner. Or a thief, Dearbhla thought, finding the horse in the shed on her failed return from Alexandria. Failed, for she'd flung her soul's inquiry through the walls and windows of that hotel turned hospital, and heard no answer. ConaLee had named the horse for Dearbhla as though to bring her back, but Dearbhla didn't hold with naming animals. No military serial number was burned into its hoof, so it stayed to the ridges, partial to ConaLee, who fed and petted it, rode it by the time she was eight or nine, when the three of them foraged or hunted far enough—until that day the con man arrived. *Why I believe I recognize this horse.* ConaLee was ten. Late summer, '72.

Stay now, Dearbhla murmured, stay. She harnessed the older horse to the buckboard, moving holdback, traces, shaft into place, lifting the gelding's livery away but for bridle. The flesh was marked and banded, not broken, but she'd no water to offer. The horse knew her, knew this place. Spared the weight of its burden, pulled up the path behind the buckboard, it followed their slow upward progress. The sound of the creaking wheels, the ghost repeat of hooves in the dusty clearing, seemed even emptier at Eliza's abandoned cabin. Dearbhla pulled round behind the shed that was barely long enough to conceal the buckboard. Left her traded goods and the livery while she unharnessed her horse, then led both animals back of the cabins to the stream. Water cascaded in a spring torrent from behind Dearbhla's top ridge, but back of Eliza's cabin the flow rattled and meandered, calmer, dappled with few leaves in this summery spring. Now Eliza had gone in ruse and story, escaped her prison. Whose place was this anymore? These woods, forest upon mountain forest, mountains beyond mountains. The shuttered cabin that had thrived, the gardens gone to seed, the labor lost, the bounty of soil and stream and hunt, all lost, were his, sacrificed for a Union that held by dint of death. Yet if he'd returned, though food and sustenance remained, the poison of what lay below in the towns gained ground, despite a War won. The truths she'd never told him of his birth deepened inside her and the ache of losing him stayed, a pain naught assuaged. It was what she had of him, strongest in this place. She knelt on the bank to smell the cool of the stream.

The horses found their footing in the water and stood flank to flank, drinking.

ConaLee

A PROTECTOR

I took Mama, next day, to her morning appointment with Dr. Story. The office door transom was closed and I heard nothing but murmurs during their talk, but I saw Dr. Story shake hands with her, saying he enjoyed their conversation. And so she'd—conversed, I thought, as we joined Eira Blevins and Mrs. Kasinski for our shared regimen. First the laundry, where we made teams to fold sheets. Then on to the art lesson, where Mrs. K stood quiet before her canvas but Mama painted a tolerable rose, with many green leaves. The teacher called it "lively" and I heard my mother thank her like a proper lady. After lunch, Mrs. Kasinski kept on with her singing and Eira Blevins said we would meet in an hour for games, that Ruth must calm herself. I asked if Mama and I might walk alone.

Be quiet about it, Eira Blevins said.

We will, I told her.

And so, on a bright, blue afternoon, we found ourselves on the marked path into the woods. She linked arms with me in the way I remembered, and I asked about her talk with Dr. Story.

He did not ask much, she said. But he read . . . to me.

What did he read? Was it Dickens, or—

I asked him to read . . . Sonnet 116. Then, we read it.

Together? I asked.

Yes. He seemed happy that I . . . said it so well—

You remembered it, Mama?

She stopped for us to look down at the meadow from a rise. After a moment, I did. He has . . . a fine mind.

I should hope so, Mama! But is he kind?

Yes, she said, tearing up. It is so . . . surprising.

I put my arm round her. You have a doctor, a protector, I said. But we must go back now, and keep to the regimen. Dr. Story's plan, after all.

. . .

The back lawn, when we arrived, was full of ladies. The women's wards would play at games and roll hoops while the men's wards used the Great Lawn for croquet and foot races, and playing games of checkers, dominos, quoits in the summerhouses. Tomorrow the reverse, Eira Blevins said. Today after games, the ladies would go indoors for sewing and needlework in sit-down company. Now they rolled their dozens of wooden hoops with dowels or wood sticks. Toys that needed a flat of level ground were no use on our ridge back home—I'd no memory of playing at anything but teaching letters to dolls that were husks and twine. Our only leisure was books, and work that Mama made into play. Here all must play and the younger ladies tied knots in their skirts to run along beside their smooth bright hoops. Mrs. Kasinski lay hers aside to explain battledore, thrusting out small rounded paddles stretched with parchment. She used one to bat a feather-edged cork ball that flew at her off Nurse Blevins's paddle, then turned to Miss Janet with excited phrases of "up now up!"

Eira Blevins stepped aside as her charge kept the bit of cork in the air against my mother's paddle. Miss Janet looks surprised, Eira Blevins said. Surely she must have played such games.

Oh yes, I answered.

As though to prove me right, Mama stepped back to increase their distance and managed the turn of wrist Mrs. Kasinski favored. The feathered cork flew and the sewn feathers on one end put me in mind of a captured bird or small battered creature. Mrs. Kasinski began running back and forth to bat the thing, while Miss Janet only angled her arm just so at each effort.

She does volley well, said Eira Blevins. Ruth seldom moves about so much at battledore. We shall make this a regular thing!

Miss Janet was taller and seemed to aim at her companion, but stout Mrs. Kasinski jumped and leaped. That is how she must have fallen, though I didn't see, having turned to watch the wood hoops gleam and roll amongst many pairs of high-buttoned boots.

. . .

Eira Blevins went to fetch Mrs. Hexum. And Mrs. Hexum herself, broad and round and buxom enough to make two of Mrs. Kasinski, three of Nurse Blevins, or four of my slender mother, appeared with a mustard poultice. Her long apron was splattered with flour that brushed off in puffs as she walked side to side, lurching across the grass. I expected a call for a doctor but it seemed that accident rather than illness was blamed on the attendants, and Mrs. Hexum was in charge. She came from the nearby kitchen, and the strange little boy hopped and skipped beside her. He squatted near as she took Mrs. Kasinski's naked foot in her broad hands. *Tisn't sprained nor even bruised!* She drew silence even from Mrs. Kasinski, who looked fearful as Mrs. Hexum wrapped the poultice tightly round the ankle. She bade Ruth s*it still girlie and play some cards,* then looked about to smiles and laughter—cards were strictly forbidden by Quakers like Dr. Story. She raised her big arms and flung her apron out as the boy ducked under, in and out. Her blouse had pulled loose at the neck and her chest heaved with effort as she grabbed the child up, then set him on his feet to run away. Some ladies clapped or cheered as though it was a trick. He was gone in a swirl of long fair hair and pale duster, and she followed, solid as a fattened ox or bull. Her heart surely pumped like a bellows as she made her way. Then she caught sight of Miss Janet and stopped to stare at her. I murmured a "good day" to draw her attention. She slid her gaze over me and winked, slow, one-eyed. *Send them inside,* I heard her tell Eira Blevins. I fancied the ground moved as she passed, careful, stepping slowly. A pungent smell of burnt sugar and sweat trailed after her.

Dearbhla would say that conjure is not real except that it tricks the mind, confuses the eye. Seems to change distance, draw together shades or slides of shadow. Eira Blevins did tell us to go in while the others stayed "to air" and Ruth rested her ankle—but I wasn't sure anyone but me heard Mrs. Hexum's command. Or that anyone saw her one-eyed wink, that slow blink of her left eye, the rest of her broad face completely still. Dearbhla would call it "magic eye," that appeared as it disappeared. Mrs. Hexum had her hand in us, in the food she made or ordered made, in her kitchen that drew unseen lines to garden, dairy, orchard, field, each the spoke of a wheel she turned. Her girth seemed a conjure in itself. All of her was not contained in the bulk she used as her power and her ruse.

We walked away as though headed indoors, up the steps to the narrow back porch of the Asylum, but I pulled Mama aside. I was scared and needed some moments of quiet, to be still, not watched, away. We stood unseen behind an arbor lattice of tuberose and grape leaf, and lifted a cloth of bordered netting to drink from a freshwater cistern used by the workmen and gardeners. We drank again and I pressed the cool of my wet hand to Mama's hair and face, thankful I could talk to her. She was more sensible of my words, in just this day or so of refuge.

Shall we stay here, in this hospital? I asked.

Yes, we must, my mother said.

That woman, Cook—Mrs. Hexum. Mama, don't be near her. She saw me, I said. *I see you, ConaLee,* sounded in my mind.

Mama looked at me with an air of patience and took my hand. Don't fear, ConaLee, she said.

Many will see you, ConaLee. You must learn to turn a gaze. Dearbhla had said that, many a time; I heard Dearbhla in the words as though she was near. I wondered then if I must be careful of Eira Blevins.

Eira Blevins said she would show me her hatpin, I told Mama. I wonder, does she use one—

My mother only arched her brows as though I'd asked a stupid question.

On Mrs. Kasinski? And Mrs. Kasinski told you so? She's not such a lunatic, then.

No, Mama said. Ruth does what she must.

Like you did, Mama? Could you talk, but you didn't, for fear of Papa?

I don't know. I had . . . no other hope, to keep him from me, she said. She took both my hands in hers and pulled me toward her. I'm sorry, ConaLee . . .

Oh, Mama—just get better. You *are* getting better.

She looked across the porch, to where we glimpsed the tops of the tall kitchen windows. The kitchen would be vast—six tall windows, and the double kitchen doors that let into the yard had their own fan-shaped arch of glass above. Doubtless Mrs. Hexum had to do with hatpins, too. Or perhaps she had no need of them.

You cannot, ever, be without me here, I told Mama. You must not be alone.

She fixed her gaze on mine. We are safest here, ConaLee.

Come, l said. Let's go to our room. I want ten minutes of rest.

. . .

We made our way in, and heard sounds of commotion even from the back hall. I tried to slow our progress but Mama would not wait. She seemed drawn to the noise and pulled me with her. We needed to cross through the vast round room to the women's ward stairwell, and came upon a drama in the rotunda. A man in a fine morning coat and Lincoln hat, facing away from us, raged at those gathered about him. Shouting and cursing sounded as we came closer. It was not our fault, I told myself, and no one noticed us. The four or five male attendants were taken up with dodging and cringing. One had collapsed to his knees, calling out what seemed nonsense, trying to grasp the coattails of the well-dressed man who whirled like a dervish, striking anyone that came near. He launched his fine tall hat at another attendant, who fell back as though struck with fists. I heard, *"Cur of hell!" "Satan's demon!" "Yankee whoremonger!"* The maniac seemed to shout a name at each one opposing him. A gentleman, an Assistant Physician surely, approaching from behind, held a file of papers before him as though to ward off blows. The wild man turned full toward us then and I saw that he was Papa, but dressed in fine clothes, his hair and beard trimmed to fashion, raving, his eyes wild. He foamed and slathered from his mouth like a rabid creature and seemed not to know us. I scarce breathed I was so afraid, and shrank back against Mama. He took no notice of me nor anyone but tore the file from the Physician's grasp, launching papers into the air, balling pieces in his mouth, commencing to chew and spit. The Assistant Physician shrank back, shouting,

Oh stay! oh stay! and two other men, more attendants in black trousers and vests, sleeves of their muslin shirts rolled above the elbow, ducked and grabbed. One flung himself at Papa and brought him down, but Papa only twisted in his grasp, squeezing the man's throat with both hands.

The Night Watch emerged from the doors to the men's stairwell. I knew then the nonsense I thought I'd heard was O'Shea's name. They'd all kept shouting for him, though this was not night nor any kind of watch. He moved rapidly, arms at his sides, taller than any of them. Two male attendants behind him carried a narrow bed with a lid and sides made of close-set spools. Then came Mrs. Hexum, as though the bed had to do with her. I thought I saw Weed, the little blond boy, dancing near. But the pale swirl behind her, to one side and another, might have been a turn of her skirts. Perhaps no dominion was beyond her, not even the men's wards. Roused from some privacy, O'Shea was not wearing the dark jacket that came nearly to his knees, nor his cap. He looked fearsome. The leather straps that held the conical eye patch in place were clear to see: a band around his head and a band across the top, like narrow belts with small buckles. The covered cone of the patch stuck out like a strange armor. His wild black curls fell over part of his scar and he stood still in the melee as if drawing the madman to him.

I had hold of my mother but she pulled free of me as Papa whirled round to face O'Shea. *Hound of plague and horn! The very Beast appears!* Snarling about devils, he rushed to fasten one hand in O'Shea's hair and tear at his shirt with the other. The shirt ripped open as O'Shea caught him under the arms and lifted him off his feet, but he bared his teeth and lunged at O'Shea's throat. The attendants had opened the lid of the bed. All made haste, but my mother grabbed at Papa from behind, clasping him around the neck with both arms, throwing him off enough that we could hear his teeth click shut. O'Shea threw him to the floor and clasped my mother to him. Attendants piled atop Papa, binding his hands and feet. O'Shea saw me and covered the distance between us in four strides.

Why have you brought her here? he shouted, handing her off to me, pushing her from him.

I did not bring her! I stammered. We were sent inside—

I left off, silent at the sight of his bare flesh. A slash of scar, a circle of knotted welts, pink, leathery, thick, covered his right breast atop a swell of muscle. My mother lay her palm on his scarred flesh as he tried to cover himself with the ripped fabric of his shirt. He turned away abruptly as Mama fell back against me and the attendants latched Papa into the narrow bed. Its depth barely held him; he could not move but to turn his head side to side and howl. The Assistant Physician shouted *Lock the crib* as they snapped the padlocks shut. They took him up and carried him away. I turned to my mother, to seek comfort or give it, I did not know, but heard myself wailing and covered my mouth with my hands. All the while the attendants walked off, desolate curses and roars rose between them from the closed box. Mrs. Hexum faced us as the Assistant Physician and the Night Watch stepped behind her. I saw the slow wink of her dark eye. She smiled thin lipped and nodded across at us, as though at a job well done.

.   .   .

My mother held me about the waist as we climbed the stairs to our room. Once there, the door locked, I gasped for breath. Mama, he will find us! What will he do to us? Will he try to take us—

My mother embraced me as in days past, when I was her only child. Shhh, shhh, ConaLee. She pulled my hands from my eyes and held my face as she spoke. Child, you saw, she said. They know what he is. He is trapped, and we are not.

I could believe it, nearly. She seemed so certain.

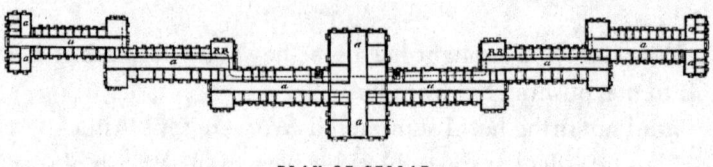

PLAN OF CELLAR.

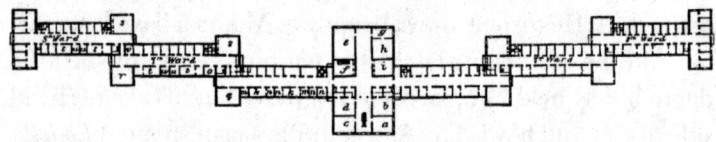

PLAN OF BASEMENT AND FIRST STORY

PLATE NO. I represents the cellar excavated throughout its whole extent
to the depth of seven and a half feet below the floor of the first story.
The centre passage (a) is the hot air chamber, extending though the entire building.
The spaces on both sides of this chamber are for cold air reservoirs . . .
In one of these . . . is a railroad (R. R.) for conveying food from the kitchen
to the different dumbwaiters between it and the extreme wings . . .
Food, prepared in the basement kitchen, and put while hot in tightly closed tin vessels
should be placed . . . so as to pass in its course the bottom
of each of the dumbwaiters. By these means the food is delivered
promptly and hot to every part of the house. Each ward should have
a bell and a speaking tube . . . by means of which whatever articles . . . may be called for
without the attendants having ever to leave the ward or dining room . . .
for any thing from the kitchen, into which they should not be admitted.

—DR. THOMAS STORY KIRKBRIDE, 1854

Weed

A FRACAS

He digs digs digs with his round lead spoon, digging with hands and heels down to where the dirt feels cool, back of the shadowed barn when they're all at chores. Dig every day, the shape scooped out like a slipper his size. The loamy smell and dark grit taste, the dirt sifted, pulled, and grabbed. Cold soft muzzy velvet he can fit himself into. Behind the carriages and the burlap sacks, back of where Zef and Dib curry the horses. The heaped straw shifts. He lies in his dirt nest to listen. One wisp after another settles, whispers. He pulls a burlap bag over himself, breathing through the weave and holes, seeing through crosses and squares. Mouse scuttle, a sound like pattering rice. Rat thump by the knotted corner board. The fat barn cat sits still, swacking her tail, whapping the dusty air. Then it's quiet. A shaft of sun, weightless, warm, a bare tingle, finds him in its wash. He lies quiet and curled, the small dumb arm of something too big to see.

. . .

Hexum's kitchen floats a heat she fills and moves: the long broad room, fan of gleaming window over the double doorway to the yard, the big black stove and its double ovens, the huge scarred table for chopping, beating, folding dough, women hip to hip and the wide flour trough below with its tight closed lid. Windows along one wall rise to the ceiling, taller than the two men who bring cans of milk still warm from the dairy. First light, Zef and Dib trundle the cart from the cow barn. Weed sits among cans tall as himself, banging them with his dull lead spoon. Ole Hexum pound you if you 'sturb those lids chile but he puts his ear to a can to hear the milk slosh. He runs to and fro down the slant to the kitchen while Zef and Dib carry the cans between them, each leaning away like the milk is fierce. Hexum smells and tastes it and fills pewter pitchers for the icebox. The other cooks clutch wide-lipped bowls to their bellies, some already stirring with paddles or whisks. Kitchen mornings ye little uns sit close under the long table while the women work above. Hexum fills their plates: leanest fatback, buckwheat cakes, corn dodgers hot from the oven. There's him and her and him and her and Weed, Hexum's pet, who stays when the others scatter. Fill them baskets wi' blueberries, she tells them, pick what's left of dill and mustard, bring up the pickling jars. Weed stays. His one chore, breakfast, lunch, supper, is only his. What'll I do with ye when yer grown too big? Does any of 'em eat without ye? Not on time, and not hot, sech as the ladies an gents think they deserve!

Weed is smallest, quickest. He rides the dark rumble of narrow cellar railroad because she says he will and she says he can. She gives him the whistle for round his neck and ties on his leather mitts. The covered tin platters never burn him when he shoves them one by one onto open dumbwaiter shelves. He blows his whistle into the speaking tubes beneath each ward dining room. Each tin horn, size of his fist, glints its round ear, shining in the cellar no matter the light. He blows twice to say the boxes are loaded in, then shuttles down the line. Food for the women's wards first, Central Wards A and B, next ward, far ward, farthest ward. Reverse and shuttle back for Hexum to load the men's platters, none but Hexum guarding the food and the platters, none but Weed crouching low on his railroad, moving one car to the other easy as a minnow slips across a rill. The gleam, the roll and clack echoing through the cellar, the narrow track, even the graveled railbed between the ties, are his shades and sounds. The dull thrum and grumbled roar and pitched ringing stay inside him till he rides the sounds again.

Mornings the cellar gets pale light through its small windows. Hexum loads the cars from the double-wide kitchen dumbwaiter. Slatted low wagons on steel carriages, three-inch space between wall and clanking car. Never touch there, my Weed, tha' narrow zipper will take yer fingers off! There now, Pet, ye know yer business.

Twenty-nine minutes start to finish. She times him, waiting while he rides, while the kitchen workers clomp back and forth above, doing her bidding.

But he rides the low cars on the narrow rails. Ladies' wards, gentlemen's wards, farthest wards. He can hear through the dumbwaiter shaft the buzzing noise and slight slipping footfalls of the women, the deeper murmur and scraping boots of the men. Less sound the farther he goes from the central wards, softer noise in the dining rooms or no dining rooms, just the attendants, pulling tins off, clatter of spoons and trays. Now and then a howl like a stabbed wolf has got its head in the shaft, a curdled whoop. Weed trundles back with the empty cars, the ride he likes best, only Weed and his railcars ratcheting through sliding space to Hexum. She grabs him to her, swings him up like a sack of spuds and climbs the stairs to the kitchen. Here now, have yer wire wand my fine Pet, and yer bowl of bubbles. Out wi' ye, into the sunshine!

So he blows bubbles that drift and pop, finds an ant to walk his finger, sets it gently down, blows a bubble round it. She'll call him in to make the trip in reverse, collect tin platters of scraps: sopping breads, gristle and marbled fat, never bones. Bones is sharp as knives, my Pet, if ye splinter em just so. No bones, only flesh picked from bones, an' the garbage a soft mash for the hogs.

Happy for what crazies don't eat, Zef says, happy hogs. Bleating in the pen back of the cow barn, squealing for Zef, blinking their small eyes. Sows drag the shoats along on their teats, each speckled suckling small as a new bald squirrel. Them pigs is smarter than most folks, chile, eat their own in

hard times. Don't be reachin thru that rail fence, now! Weed
aims his spoon from across the pen, breathes *pow, pow, pow.*
The biggest boar, tiny eyed, wet snout quivering, stomps,
leans, charges. Weed steps back, waits for the thud. The boar
lands blind against the rails, snorting, rumbling, stunted tusks
grinding wood. His bristled, dripping snout pokes through,
trembling, quavering. Weed touches his lead spoon to just
above the wet, blowsy holes, rubs gently, up, down, little slide.
The boar snorts. Grunts. Shorter, softer. Boy, you a mesmer-
izer? Step away, leave that boar to himself. You leave off an he
get twice as mad. Go on now. You don't know why them boars
likes you.

· · ·

Weed likes the central ladies' wards, and hiding to watch gentlemen on the lawn. He will be a gentleman, he will sit in the
summerhouse on the Great Lawn on fine autumn days, he
will have shoes with white spats, he will have a monocle and
snap his newspaper that Dib or Zef have brought special from
town. He's not allowed among the gentlemen, only watches
from where they can't see. Hexum says it's what men are,
never be in reach no matter a man's fine coat or collar. Hasn't
she shown him raving men, dressed fine or foul, pressed into
cribs like raging animals? He's to stay near the central ladies'
wards, or be about her quarters, sleep on his sofa or creep
in beside her at night, curled tight as her own pet. Often he
sleeps in the horse barn near Zef and Dib, their rooms behind
the stalls, their rope-hung corncob pallets, their layered rugs
passed on from parlors. They won't hurt ye Pet, they's free men
that earns they wage, no finer help found in town nor field.
They'd tell you same as me, Pet, stay near the gentleladies,
the ones what gives ye sweets an keepsakes. Any trinket that
sparkles ye bring to ole Hexum, eh my Weed? Jewels an treasure. And she opens her locked desk drawer with a key, dumps

out a velvet pouch: earrings that shimmer, brooches and shiny buckles, rings with glinting stones. Lets him hold her round magnifying glass, with the brass handle that snaps into place. He peers at her through it, into her greenish eye and the dot of shine at the center.

Late in the night, he likes trailing O'Shea in the wide, glow-lit hallways. Rounding, O'Shea calls it, walking men's wards A and B, the gentlemen's wards, listening, looking through the narrow oiled slats in the doors with his one eye. O'Shea walks the farther wards alone. Not a boy's business, says O'Shea. Weed goes off to Hexum's room or to the barn to sleep while Night Watch paces the twice-locked wards, up, down, murmurs to night shift attendants. Hexum will say the far wards rouse in phases, waning and waxing, wild as wolves at full moon. Night is day for the Night Watch but Weed naps between chores and wanderings, watchings, curled in cool soil and burlap in the horse barn, swung gentle in Zef's empty pallet, on Dib's soft feather tick, when both men are out work-ing. Empty spaces, absence, waiting. Zef and Dib, Dib and Zef. Evenings, flicker of forbidden candle, kerosene lamps. Sundays, day of rest, but always the dawn milking, the morn-ing milk run. Ain't that right, Dib? Cart us a milk jug or a swaddled babe in the old days. Not you tho, boy, you best off here. Got the run of the place, ain't you? Fetch us water from the barrel an set up the checkerboard. Sit close here, learn you somthin—someday now, you'll best the ole Night Watch, skip-jump 'em and wipe em off the board. You fixin to trail O'Shea tonight? Take them worn-out socks to pull over yer feet.

.   .   .

Hexum likes Weed with her in a fracas. Fracas is what she calls it when she's summoned here or there. She likes Weed run-ning or jumping or hovering to see her do and settle, silence a noise or confusion. She can always find him to trail her across the grass between the girls and women, hoops and sticks and hats and veils. Hexum is her own veil, pulling and spreading, gathering up. Rumpled old Kasinski is on the ground with her battledore paddle, her foot naked as Weed's feet. She looks away, afraid as Hexum cradles her ankle in a big hand, lays on a warm poultice that smells of hot mustard. Hexum gets the women laughing but Weed knows Kasinski's ample shoulders are pricked with Blevins's hatpin when Kasinski will not stop singing. The women shift and circle, closer and farther from Hexum. So quick that no one sees, he grabs up Kasinski's balled silk stocking when they fling it down. Squeezes it soft in his fist as he follows Hexum, darts here and there. She goes back to the kitchen, sends him off.

He flies to the barn to stretch the stocking wide, peers through it at the horses in their stalls, at the barnyard, at the wavering endless walls of the Asylum. The shaped rectangular stones throw rainbows like the ones inside bubbles. He puts one arm and another in the stocking, stretching his fingers wide. Pulls it onto his leg, points his foot in its gloved shine. He wraps the stocking round his eyes and twirls in circles until he's dizzy, tripping in his long duster, lurching between stables and barnyard, past the water trough. He comes to himself in the fenced chicken coop, sawdust layered on his feet, and remembers the new chicks. The hens strut and cluck. He pulls out the crusts he took, crushed soft in his pockets by now, and crumbles them all around. The chicks crowd his toes, climb his ankles, their small spurs prickling like baby fingernails. He hears Hexum ringing her bell and hides the stocking under a nesting broody. The bell is only for Weed. Dinner is not yet but she calls him from the chicken house and tells him they'll visit O'Shea. Eh, Pet? Had our fracas, we did, an yer a far better nurse than any a' these draws a wage.

· · ·

The back hallway to the Steward's rooms, the Assistant Physician's apartment, O'Shea's Night Watch quarters at the end, is so narrow they nearly fill it. Weed treads her skirts. She holds out a plump arm for him to jump astride her haunch of thigh and ride her hip. She stops, back of the hall, Night Watch suite, bedroom and bath, and raps, small raps, on the door. O'Shea, she says. Someone to see you.

Not today, Mrs. Hexum.

I must have a place for 'im just now. Have you another visitor, Night Watch? A laundry wench? A nurse attendant?

I need no visitor, Mrs. Hexum.

Only turn the latch. I'll send im in.

They hear O'Shea rise slowly from his bed and cross the room. Hexum circles a finger at the latch, rolling her eyes at Weed, and finally it turns. The door swings a little open. Weed slides down and darts inside.

See yer not late for the dinner bell, my Pet, she says after. Our Night Watch will want a rest, called so rude from slumber as he was today.

O'Shea shuts the door. They hear the wood floor creak, groaning every step, as Hexum walks away.

The room is dim. Day is night and night is day for the Night Watch.

Excuse my attire, O'Shea says. They pulled me from sleep and a fine maniac ripped my shirt from off me.

He wears a loose muslin shirt over short breeches and turns to kick aside the torn white shirt on the floor. It sails into the air and lands arms asunder as Weed follows him to the fat parlor chair with the rolled arms. Patchy half-worn velvet, deep cushioned, a matching hulk of footrest with sprung buttons and tassel trim. A game board table, a stool for Weed to pull up beside. Iron frame bed behind the curtain, a half-size bureau, no looking glass. A gentleman's valet stand in the closet corner holds his uniform jacket, the folded trousers, the cap. There on the tray like an offering, his eye patch with its leather straps. His short black tie.

O'Shea makes no move to take the checkers from the game table drawer. He regards the boy from his chair. Are you Weed or Pet today?

Weed fixes him with a half smile.

I believe I'll call you James. What about that hair of yours, James? Will Hexum never cut it? Will she have you in hair bows and braids?

Weed shakes his head. Nods his head. Shakes his head. Pulls open the narrow drawer and reaches for the painted checkers. His are black. O'Shea's are red.

All right then. I'll leave you to change your own name. He winces, shifts forward to straighten his back.

I'm the worse for it, boy. O'Shea rolls his neck painfully. The front and open throat of the blousy shirt frames the big head and dark curls, the face and stubble of beard, the one wide hazel eye, its black, flared lashes.

Weed stands looking, frowning.

Talk, Weed, here if nowhere else. Tell me what game is it you want to play.

Checkers, says Weed. He gathers up the wooden pieces in the drawer.

You set up, O'Shea says. I'm not much disposed to checkers today. You'll play for both of us.

O'Shea runs a hand through the shaggy curls that half cover the cratered scar on his right temple. He pulls his shirt off over his head and holds out an eyecup-sized jar of unguent. Here boy, dab this where he raked me.

Weed takes the jar and stands close as O'Shea turns to bare his back. The boy's small fingers trace the cuts, raised now like cat scratches. He takes his time with the greasy ointment, tracing each red swelling beside and between.

O'Shea takes the unguent and caps it, sits forward to let the ointment absorb. Weed looks close at the scar on O'Shea's chest, its raised edges, pinkish welts the width of a thumbprint. Moves his palms to cover the splayed, ragged circle of scar, the purplish flesh beneath.

That's a brand, boy. I'm marked as cattle are marked, or the human slaves of a brute master. I'm a curiosity like you.

Weed opens his mouth to make a word that doesn't sound.

You're Weed, O'Shea says, not James, no more than I'm a whole man. You want to know how they did it, or why, Weed? That's why you need to talk. You need to say words.

How you get that? Weed asks.

The War, O'Shea says, could be. Before they stoved in my skull. Tho my surgeon said not. Scars, not wounds, he said, some past violence best forgot. Old Dr. O'Shea made me his son, near, in offering me his name. Hospital needed a name and I didn't know mine. I was studied because I lived. They saw to my eye patch, gave me a hospital job. Moving patients, wharf to ambulance to hospital, once I was strong. My doctor watched over me near three year. Wrote me a reference when the War was over and I was civilized, back to strength, there to here. A secret for you, Weed.

Weed tilts his head, listening.

You can choose your own name when you want one. Go, set up the board.

Weed likes the round wood pieces that fit one on the other and the painted surface of the tabletop, red and black checks on a black surround. He likes to jump his pieces square to square when they travel fast. He likes the words. Opening. Draw. Capture. The board ready, he seats himself on the stool and looks at O'Shea for the signal to begin.

All right then, says O'Shea. Get my eye patch. I must concentrate to be sure you don't best me.

The wooden valet, Weed's height nearly, brandishes its hanger shape, O'Shea's uniform jacket, and the hinged roller for his uniform trousers. Weed takes the eye patch contraption from the tray. Holds it up, lets the straps fall straight.

Half blinds we are, O'Shea says.

Weed touches his forehead to O'Shea's, his veiled eye opposite O'Shea's good one. He sees with his bright eye's fractured lights into O'Shea's sunken, livid scar, the hole where his eye would be. The skin deep inside, grown fast, is a tender color, mauve as a blush of tongue. O'Shea lowers his head for Weed to fit the straps and holds the felt-lined cone of eyepiece in place. The top strap goes straight back. The second loops the first, back of his head, then skews at an angle in front, across the stoved scar and moon of bald red, into his hair. Weed fastens the small buckles, knowing O'Shea can do it faster.

All right then, says O'Shea. You open. I need my advantage.

It's quiet then but for the tick of the double-belled alarm clock.

O'Shea has taken several of his pieces but finally Weed finds an opening in O'Shea's deepest row and moves, holding his breath.

Well? O'Shea says.

King me, Weed whispers.

. . .

The clang of the staff bell sets him running, long duster floating out behind, feet slapping the hall floor from O'Shea's room, out into the yard, the grass, the dirt round back of the kitchen, the path he pounds back and forth to Hexum, her broad flat face that fills the world. She lifts him to her freckled pillowed front, her throat and cleavage skimmed with talcum powder. Splashes powder under her massive arms and rolls of flesh, the sweet turn of her bitter sweat mixed by dinnertime with tinges of melting butter roasting meat frying pork fat. Between meals the deepest pots and giant cans sit kitchen center, empty, clean, clustered tall as him across a spotless oilcloth on the stone floor. Fry pans and wooden ladles hang on the wooden grid that swings from the ceiling. Always the pounding and making, the women's floor-length skirts turning in their bending moving carrying. Johnnycakes, boiled eggs, oatmeal in the mornings, corn bread, stewed chicken, jelly aspic at lunch, soup, mutton or frizzled beef, corn, squash and pudding suppers. Shouted orders, hot meals three times a day. The women move faster as dinnertime comes on. They take the broom to him if they see him hiding in the cold clean pots, hiding to hear their talk, sliding down to hug his knees. Hexum turns to the workingwomen in their uniforms, their coarse aprons tied at their necks. Now now, she tells them, he's fine as a fiddle, no matter his size or what else. Suppose he grow or don't grow, he's no more blind than any a you. Here, my Weed, wash out that pot, and she gives him a clean wet rag. An the little uns I have workin about here will know their jobs when they're old enough to draw a wage. Why not hire our own? How might they ever get far enough away that anyone would hire em for anything, knowin they come from here? Eh, my ducks? The other small ones cluster round but he's her pet. It's him she picks up and swings.

FOUR-FIFTHS OF PATIENTS . . . should look to walks in the open fields . . . morning and afternoon, at all seasons; and in warm weather, when proper summer houses and seats are provided, they may thus profitably spend one half the entire day in the open air.
— DR. THOMAS STORY KIRKBRIDE, 1854

ConaLee

A CHANCE ENCOUNTER
DECEMBER 1874

It was mid-December, but fine weather still. Everyone said how the warm fall never ended and the seasons were mixed up, bad luck to come, or the Devil's trick. No snow across the hills or highest ridges, animals confused. Churches full on Sundays, revivalists pitching tents in fields. Trees had turned orange, yellow, pale red, but the lawn and meadows were still green. The leather ankle boots in her carpetbag fit Mama well enough. She wore them today on our walk through the grounds, out to the woods and fields. She was better by the summer, talking almost normal, better still these months that should be winter. How scared I was for us both, that day in April so soon after we arrived, to see Papa in the one place that seemed safest from him. Eira Blevins had said he never offered a name or a way to reach his relations, and was locked then to now in the men's farthest ward. It was there or jail, she'd laughed—the "Lincoln maniac," drunk and fancy dressed, raved that a stables in Weston stole his horse and buckboard, and he tried to rob the stableman. A sheriff and five deputies must bind and drag him to the Asylum! I never told her I'd seen him closed in the crib, of Hexum's part, and Mama's. I'd thought him far away, disappeared, but it was like him to see to his comforts: a shave and shine, fine clothes and the Lincoln hat—when he hated Lincoln so—drinks in a saloon on his way to coach or train. No need of horse or buckboard, only vexed he couldn't profit by them. I hoped he'd no "moral treatment" here, to help him connive his way.

Mama seemed not to fear, but I traced a route daily with a stick in the dust or my finger on a page, that the horse and buckboard might take back to Dearbhla. I pretended their trek home was a cord to bind Papa fast—a notion for my comfort. I did not like to upset Mama but I was afraid and thought on it every day. Papa strode into the Women's Ward in my nightmares and flung open Mama's door, or came into my rooms, the ones I shared now with other nurses above the wards, and grabbed me up, confusing me with her, trapping my face and arms in my nightgown. I woke in a wet bed and ran with my sheets to the small lavatory. Soaking the urine smell out in the half tub, washing, wringing, I felt as twisted. I would imagine I saw Papa on the grounds, around the corner of a corridor, looking in through a window, or seated, silent, rageful, with other gentlemen in a summerhouse, Sundays on the Great Lawn.

Mama never mentioned him. Her Miss Janet conversed now, even played the piano for musical afternoons. People thought her "quiet," but she seemed, after near nine month as Miss Janet, so sure a woman of quality that I wondered if I remembered wrong. She had new clothes even, white ones for the endless summer, as it was called, with a gray cape and a white parasol. She'd not worn such clothes in our life on the ridge, for the hard work about the place, and had no piano to play. Between us, she called me ConaLee and heard my mentions of home, but I thought better of asking sharp questions. Little was private at the Asylum now—we were mostly in the company or hearing of others, and she talked with Dr. Story near every day. I would take her to his office but I accompanied other patients during her art lesson, sewing circle, music hour. We still took our afternoon walks, having left off with Mrs. Kasinski, whose walks were confined now to the walled courtyard behind the Women's Ward. She still longed to sit near Mama at meals but was seldom allowed, while Miss Janet dined at "family table" in Dr. Story's own apartments, once or twice a week. These dinners served by staff might include Assistant Physicians and their wives, or town patrons, and always, ladies from the Asylum Auxiliary. Mama didn't mention her new privileges. I did not ask but heard talk amongst the attendants, who said Dr. Story's rooms were plain but grand, with velvet sofas and a harpsichord that Mama played as guests sipped their tea. His balcony overlooked the Asylum entrance grounds, two floors above the vast door I'd knocked upon that dawn morning she fainted across the doorstep, and the Night Watch took her up . . .

You are quiet today, ConaLee, Mama said.

I wanted to ask about the harpsichord but took her arm and kept my gaze on the footpath winding up along the woods. The path was so familiar, for we walked here most days. I felt happiest amongst the meadows and fields and woods, on the paths and trails trod only by women patients granted *liberty of the grounds*. Mama walked with purpose now. We left the Asylum two and three and four miles behind us. The silence around us opened, filled with birdsong and the flit of butterflies, for there were still butterflies, so late. I saw them, as though in a near future, dead all at once, covering the ground like fallen petals. I decided I must know my mother's thoughts and say the words pressing me.

Mama, I asked, why are you not afraid, that he is here, so near us?

She turned, surprised. ConaLee, I don't fear him. I was only shocked . . . to find him here, so changed . . .

But he only pretended not to know us, Mama, and he surely—Papa will find a way— I saw my mother's eyes change expression and covered my own, like a child hiding in plain sight, afraid my words would set him bounding toward us.

She embraced me, speaking low and soothing. ConaLee, *that man* is bound in a cell stronger than any jail. Likely he pretends madness—but if he tells our story, he must tell his own. And he will not.

But I told, when you were not sensible, that he rode us here—he said I would tell the story—

And so you did. But he is a nameless stranger and it was your story, told so well that now it's as true as any other. No one saw him the day we arrived. No one recognized him in his rage and gentleman's clothes but us. She moved my hands away from my welling eyes. Look around you, ConaLee. The meadow below us. The woods and paths we know well. I am Miss Janet and you are Nurse Connolly, with a wage and a skill, and we—

By Dr. Story's graces, Mama. What have you told him?

Very little, ConaLee. Things from long ago, that do not change our story. He has become—a friend. He has told me—he was betrothed, but never married.

And were you betrothed, Mama? You wore a ring, that Papa took. He told me, when he left us here, that he is not my papa. That he only came upon us. Is it true?

She shuddered and turned from me. Her brow shone with moisture.

But you must say, Mama. When did he find us? Why? You must remember, because I don't—

She turned back and grasped my face in her shaking hands, eyes close to mine. He is not your father, ConaLee. He's nothing to you but a torment I could not turn. I am sorry, so sorry—

And the babbies, Mama.

ConaLee, I—do not remember them.

I felt tears track my cheeks. I do, Mama. The neighbor women—one took the boys. The other—

They cannot be ours, ConaLee. She took back her hands, seemed to compose herself, smoothing her skirts as though to take comfort in her fine clothes.

But if they need—

They must make their way. They are not alone.

They are your children.

They were forced upon me. I never saw them, knew them. You know, better than anyone—I was not . . . there. She touched my arm. You feel their loss, but you were a child—

It was not so long ago, I said.

But seems so— Her voice caught.

To you, I heard myself insist, it is very long ago, but for me—

You cared for them and lost them, I know, but we have nothing now in that place. You said, it is all give away. Nothing binds us, and Papa is guarded here, caged as he caged us.

You know how he schemes. Won't he talk his way free?

Suppose he does. The truth will not serve him. We are believed and favored, he is violent, criminal, mad, or acting so.

And we are safe here, provided for. We needn't hunt and trap and cook our food, survive storms and cold, defend against anyone who comes upon us—I could not defend you there.

But, Dearbhla. Why—has she not come for us?

It's not best, that she come. She cannot protect us as this place can—

Who is Dearbhla now, to us? I waited for Mama's answer, but I'd thought on it long. Mama, I said, where is Dearbhla?

Close, Mama said. She touched my hair and lifted a lock in her hand. As close as these strands, ConaLee. She is where she was.

Mama, will we never go home?

ConaLee. Here we are safe.

Dearbhla—

He took nothing of hers.

He took us, I said. And it was all—ours. So much is . . . there still. The cabin, the hearth, the porch, the land. We could look over the mountains, see the wind and storms come up, the stars you taught me—

She shook her head. I cannot go back there, ConaLee. Nor can others.

Mama, what others?

But she only looked away. This is my home now, she said. And your home is with me.

I stepped back. Home? You will stay here forever?

ConaLee, there is no forever. We are on our walk and the day is fine. You must think . . . each day is separate, until a way is clear.

She looked at me so loving, like as her true self. We seemed to stand at a still point in the sloping meadow and ascending woods, the blue sky tilting above, the threads of paths and far-flung trails turning slowly round us. Mama, I asked, who is my father? Where is he?

She looked stricken, and faltered. ConaLee, it is . . . just as in the story you told. He went to the War, from our ridge, months before you were born. He never returned. We never had word. We never knew. His letters . . . stopped.

But—his name? How did you meet? Have you a likeness?

Dearbhla has a *carte de visite*, and his enlistment papers, from early in the War—please, ConaLee, let us walk on— The story, she whispered then, is so painful. Don't make me live in it.

Only tell me, Mama, that one day I will know.

Yes, one day, she said.

She put her arm round me and led me on. We walked slowly, ascending to the highest point above the meadow. We breathed together, her side firm against mine. She was the stronger now. I felt almost weightless to know it, as though I might look down on the yellow grassy fields and drift over them, thinking myself borne up. We stopped, arm in arm, and I felt in my pocket for the palm-sized mirror I carried with me now as a talisman. I took it in hand and caught the glint of the sun, dazzling little knives of light below us, across the meadow, to the edge of the lower woods.

Remember this mirror, Mama?

Dearbhla made a journey, Mama said, when you were two or three. She gave it you. To watch her return, she said.

So the small mirror I'd taken from Papa was not his, but mine. It seemed I might blink my eyes and be back on the porch of our cabin, high on the ridges, before Papa, before the babbies, in the safe time with Dearbhla and Mama. I longed for Dearbhla and imagined she knew of us, saw the bowl of the meadow below us, the swell of trees edging the moving grasses, the forest behind us that climbed higher and higher until it must gain our mountains at last.

This is our view now, Mama said, as though reading the words in my mind.

We'd come out from the trees along the rise. I saw the sloping hillside below us, and halfway across the field, the thick boxwood hedge, taller than a man, that crossed the entire meadow and apple orchard beyond, separating the grounds and walking trails for men and women. Tended and shaped by the gravedigger, the hedge was a thick and gnarly boundary, but from here seemed a graceful line that dipped and swelled.

It seems odd, I said, that a hedge, and not a wall or fence, separates the men's and women's grounds.

If only it were always so, everywhere, my mother said.

Do you wish that, Mama?

I wish some living force had protected all of us. Men hunted, imprisoned us—they enslaved, shackled, burned down the country. And the just men suffered the cruelties of all the others. War scars last. Generations . . .

Do you talk of such things with Dr. Story?

Yes, and I know he agrees. Our refuge is a blessing. Walls to protect, but gardens and hedges, trails to walk, to heal, to please the eye. You know, there's a post and wire fence inside that tall divide, but the hedge has grown over it, so tall and thick, a living wall, if you like. It was on the property, a boundary between farms, long before the War.

Who told you so, Miss Janet? I smiled to tease her with her hospital name.

Why, Dr. Story, she said. He knows the history of the place as though he's always been here.

You ride out with him in the carriage. So say my roommates, the nurse attendants. They say he is courting you.

Perhaps, in his way. He is . . . cordial.

I didn't credit their talk, Mama. Gossip, I told them—

But she turned to me, eyes shining. You must come with us one evening, in the carriage. Why not tonight, after dinner?

That isn't done. I'm only an attendant.

If I ask . . .

Won't he wonder why you ask? It isn't usual—

Because you are my companion, my help, and I want you . . . to enjoy a turn one evening.

Our vantage on all below made me agreeable and I nodded,

wanting to please her. And I longed for a carriage ride. Carriages seemed romantic notions. Standing here, it occurred to me that just the sight of the lower field, across the hedge, satisfied a yearning. I saw something emerge then from a lower dell of woods into the open, a pale dog or fox on all fours, it seemed. Then he straightened and I made out his long pale hair, his form and clothes—it was Weed, Hexum's pet, as they called him. I peered at him, shielding my eyes with my hand. He stopped as well, and seemed to look up at us. Perhaps the rise was just elevated enough that he could see Mama and me. Then he seemed to hurry on, running toward the hedge. I lost sight of him.

Look, Mama, there is that boy they call Weed. He's off toward the hedge, on the men's side. I want a closer look.

At him? Best take it now. He seems a will-o'-the-wisp.

She stayed above, watching me walk down. Closer, I saw an uneven hole in the hedge, a place where the green had withered. It was about waist height, almost a circle, and I leaned down to peer through. The boy looked back at me, as though he'd waited for me to arrive. He was smiling.

Hello, I said. Is that Weed? Are you out walking?

He nodded.

Am I sure you are Weed? I got to my knees to see him face-to-face. Can you say your name?

Weed, he said softly.

If it were darker, I thought, the gloaming hour, he might be taken for a spirit, out here in the field. He had a perfect little face, as though his tawny brows were drawn on, and a pink mouth. I thought of my chap from home, and drew nearer. Close-up, even with the long blond hair, Weed did look like a boy, small, delicate, but not as young as I'd thought. Six or seven, could be. Perhaps he thought the duster more a cloak than a woman's hand-me-down. His one eye was wide and blue. The other was as perfectly formed, but veiled across the iris. The white of it seemed pure, clear. Blind, likely.

You have a milk eye, I said. They say it is second sight. Can you tell the future?

He turned away and put his hand to his mouth, puffed his cheek, and made a sound like a robin's warble.

That's very good, I said. Do you know others?

He only looked at me, pleased it seemed. Small enough, he leaned into the round leafy hole in the hedge to his waist, until he might have touched his face to mine. He laid his hand on the leaves of green between us. The prickly hedge was four feet thick at least, and I reached through to give him my palm. He touched across my wrist to the tips of my fingers, so lightly. I felt the warmth of the meadow, an upward glow of sunlit grass and tangled clover. Deep beneath, a throb of cold held fast, beating like a heart that boomed far off, and shifted.

Do you feel that? I asked. I closed his hand in mine without thinking. He dropped his gaze, a signal it seemed. I let go and opened my palm.

Carefully, he bowed his head and let fall from his mouth a perfect robin's egg, pale blue and moist.

Ah, I said, The nest was empty, then? I cupped my palm to cushion what I could barely feel.

He nodded and clasped my forefinger as a babe might.

Better to save as your own jewel, I told him, than leave for the owl or the raven.

For you, he said. Then he leaned in to whisper, if I heard right, *The bird inside.*

Yes, I said. There is. Or might have been, if the mother had stayed to hatch one.

He seemed not to think on it and only turned a little to make the sound again, a soft warble in his throat that became a low whistle as he ducked down, moving off in the high-grown meadow. I saw him look back at me once, and twice, and then saw only the moving grass, and heard a sound that grew softer as he made his way to the cover of the trees. It was surely a sound I imagined. I could not have heard him across such a distance.

Mama and I returned to find many of the Women's Ward nurse attendants standing out on the grounds, to the broad side of the Asylum. Far off, they seemed white bell shapes, their long white aprons still against the green grass, their hands clasped behind them so that their black sleeves were hidden. They tilted or moved in place, watching some nine or ten gentlemen patients run a footrace across the lowest slope of the Great Lawn.

I hadn't known such was scheduled, but the summery days brought surprises, and the male attendants had moved all the gentlemen outside as spectators. Many were dressed in their best, enjoying iced tea served from trays.

The gentlemen treat their attendants as servants or valets, Mama said, never as nurses.

Until they need strong-armed, I answered.

Ah, yes. That must confuse them. Yet another reason to behave . . . like gentlemen. I hear that many request assistance with more formal dress, their cuff links, shirt collars, spats, while the ladies never do, no matter their past stations.

And who tells you all this, Mama?

She only smiled as we moved along the curved path toward the Asylum, just above the runners' start.

It looked a picture. The sun was low and made a gold sheen on the high stone walls and long, setback wings, bathing the lawns and gardens in yellow glow. The ladies of the Women's

Wards, still at their regimens, locked out of their rooms, could not look down on the race, but the nurse attendants not on duty watched quietly.

The runners are in their knickers, Mama said.

So they were. Large paper numbers were pinned to their undershirts, and most were barefoot. I saw the Steward, the Men's Ward version of Matron Bowman, smoking a cigar at the starting line. Just beside him, head and shoulders taller than the burly Steward, stood our Night Watch. He was in uniform but his cap was in his pocket and he seemed at his ease. A scant breeze ruffled his long black curls as he faced the Steward in left profile, nodding, talking. His eye patch didn't show, and he looked for a moment like any other man.

Walk slowly, ConaLee, Mama said. I shall have to go inside when we arrive.

I slowed my step to hers. A bell clanged and the runners took off in their lanes. They were not running but walking heel to toe, very fast and upright. How funny they look! I told Mama. They are not running at all!

I turned to her, laughing, but she wasn't watching the race. Her gaze was fixed on the starting line. That is speed walking, she said, taking my arm. Very fashionable now, for men. We saw an illustration in *Harper's Weekly*, in my reading circle.

You look at weeklies? I thought you read the better novels.

Oh, most of them prefer lighter fare, though a few of us . . . She paused and turned to face me. Do you know, ConaLee, I'm going to ask that you lead a discussion now and then. Of Dickens, say, any title you like. Copies are loaned by a library in Philadelphia.

Oh, I don't read much, anymore—

But you must read. You were such a reader, when you were young.

I felt a pall, as though the limbs of a giant tree suddenly cast cold shadows over me. She truly did not remember or think of my life during the years she was ill, the work of the place, the chap tied in the shawl to my back or front till he could walk, feeding and petting him, putting the babbies to her breast, cleaning and singing to them all, spoon-feeding and sponge-bathing her, all the while fearing Papa's return. Some days I had time to braid her hair but mostly I only bound it—her masses of dark curls against the pillows might draw his attention, no matter how late, how drunk he might be, how pale or thin she looked.

Mama, I think I will go in as well. My rooms will likely be empty and I . . . will have a bit of quiet.

You must, she said, and rest. Freshen up for dinner, and the carriage ride just after. Oh, I have this for you. She gave me then, from the silk purse clipped to her shirtwaist, a small box. It is rouge, she said, in a light pink. The ladies of the Asylum Auxiliary shop for our sundries—

We had reached the grounds and walked behind the spectator nurse attendants, to a porch entrance. The men's race must have concluded. I heard the attendants clap and murmur before Mama pulled the screen door shut, and half embraced me in farewell.

.   .   .

I had our top-floor rooms to myself, as most didn't return until after dinner. Twelve unmarried nurse attendants, mostly young, stayed here. Narrow beds, with steamer trunks between, took up each wing, six to one, six to the other, with lavatory and sitting room. Many small dormer windows were flung open to the screens, to catch any breeze. The view took in the smaller side gardens and paths, the Great Lawn in front, the long drive from the road. The strip of railroad track was a siding seldom used but for the Asylum, as the main station was in Weston. The narrow river shone, rippling, and the town beyond, and the slope of hills to more mountains. We must turn down the gas wall sconces by nine p.m. and shift beds once a month—to save the mattresses, Matron Bowman said. The corner beds were prized and some girls set up screens at the foot of their beds, or between themselves and a girl to their right or left. The screens were used in the Asylum Infirmary and I'd no idea how some of the attendants had got them, but it felt private to be alone here in the late afternoon. The wings seemed long and empty then. I fancied I heard each tightly made bed whisper one to the other, a sound like curtains rustling, but there were no curtains, only blinds to draw down.

I had the lavatory to myself, to consider my appearance for the carriage ride.

My laundered work clothes from home were hidden in the trunk the Asylum provided. I had nothing to wear but my uniforms, but I put on a fresh apron and cap, and let a few dark ringlets frame my face. Taken from its box, the compact was a thin gold tin, about the size of a pocket watch. The color inside counted its own time, I supposed. The small mirror above the lavatory sink served us all and was not two feet square, but I leaned in close. I was not fair skinned or prone to sunburn but my eyes looked tired. The other girls remarked on my thick dark brows and lashes, but it was as though, these past weeks, Mama grew younger and I grew older, or plainer. I rubbed my cheeks with the pink rouge in circular motion and thought of whirling about behind our cabin with the chap—he loved flying, holding to my hands as I swung him round. I was the world and he followed me about, rubbing with a scrap of rag if I cleaned a pot, stirring the floor with a stick when I cooked, wriggling into my lap or my arms while I held one babbie or another. I was his One. Here, we nurse attendants were no one, all the same, meant not to draw notice. I prized my uniforms, happy to be like the others, but no one loved, or thought of me. Mama talked with me, but was taken up with her new life.

Confusing pains were in my head. I heard Weed—*The bird*

inside—before I remembered him, peering across at me through the hedge. Frightened, I pulled open my deep uniform pocket to glimpse the forgotten blue egg, so small, and lifted it from the dark. It was still perfect. How to keep it whole? I balanced it in the small box that had held the tin of rouge, but a fragile shell must have a nest. I pulled the dark hair from my hairbrush and made a whirl of cushion to line the box. The egg fit just inside, hidden in its lair, and I tied the box with a bit of string.

EVERY THING REPULSIVE AND PRISON-LIKE should be carefully avoided . . . a variety of objects of interest should be collected . . . and trees and shrubs, flowering plants, summer-houses . . . No one can tell how important all these may prove.

—DR. THOMAS STORY KIRKBRIDE, *1854*

Weed

TINY BURST

Weed hides to see and stays hidden to watch.

Hexum's square room on the third floor, once servants' quarters for the Physician Superintendent, is always open. No one but Weed dares enter. She sleeps on two beds pushed together and her tall front window lets out next to the wooden porch rail of Dr. Story's narrow office balcony. Weed slides through her unlatched window, balances a few steps on the porch rail, reaches the tall tree whose largest branches flare high above to the Asylum's fourth floor. Concealed, he climbs along a big branch to the trunk. Sits in a solid crotch of limbs

and leaves. Watches the Asylum driveway below—the circle hedge and flower beds, the fountain in its middle, the Great Lawn beyond, and the latticed wooden summerhouses for taking the air. He sees best because no one sees him, deep in the tree. Climbs down close if he likes. He could hang from a lowest branch, drop down into a cart or wagon, sit atop a carriage pulled close to wait. But he stays still, hears visitors talk, whisper, sob, before the great door. Or watches a covered coach, horse-drawn up the drive, piled high with trunks, pass the circle garden. Rarely the sheriff's black wagon, a closed box with a small round window. But it was noise and clamor the day the raving gentleman came to fracas, men driving in front, standing behind, clinging on, horses urged to speed, snorting, flinging up dust, clots of dirt flying, rattle and clang. The Sheriff's wagon, walls of the box sounding with slams and pounding till the men dragged him out, gagged and bound, twisting, flinging, the Sheriff shouting at Matron Bowman, *Call yer Night Watch an more . . . drunken lunatic . . . robbed a stables and bested four deputies. Step away, woman!* Ah, the great man, Hexum harsh whispered later, off on his calls while fools meddle. Interview a maniac, will they? Ropes gone an gag flung down! Hexum knows where the cribs are stacked, and chains and planks and nets. Cribs gone cause the Quaker says so? Let im take it up wi Hexum. Weed knows to find her and she lets him follow the attendants to her cache of cribs and the men take one up like a plank to batter doors down, through the lower corridors, up the stairs. There in the rotunda, the gentleman maniac, the one, thinks Weed, Hexum's always warned him about, is cursing, raging, tall hat flung aside, coattails flaring. The mad dog leaps atop the Night Watch, slathering his neck, and the lady patient Weed remembers from the alcove, her face wild, clasps arms about the fiend's neck. The men are all on the lunatic when he falls, snapping him shut in the crib, while Night Watch pushes the lady patient away and roars at the girl, the girl who stayed and didn't leave. It's over but for cursing and crying. Hexum turns like a wave pulling an ocean's flow behind her, following the crib.

. . .

Hexum likes Weed about in a fracas but she wants him inside on Sundays when the town visits, pokes about, she says, look-ing and leering, dropping their candy wrappers and greasy papers, guessing who's cracked, looking for tales to tell—as though any but Asylum gentry would be out in that crowd! But the town brings Sunday lunch for all and the great man swag-gers, Hexum says, an her no meal to cook but boiled breakfast eggs, dinner soup, so let them come and promenade. But you stay hid, my Pet, townsmen are some of 'em evry bit the luna-tic, an wiry as any inside these walls.

High up, fine weather Sundays, Weed watches town vis-its from his leafy perch—garden strolls, Great Lawn picnics, spring, summer, long as the weather holds. Town boys play at battledore across a net they pound into the grass, town ladies bring lemonade and sell pies. Someone plays an accordion, a trumpet, even a violin. He's higher, highest in the great tree, never scared. Watches the gentlemen, the gentleladies, loosed from their wards for games and walking about. Sees the long floated bubbles in their minds, the eye in their heads like the eye in his. Different from town folk, different as birds that fly are different from beetles on their backs. Their thoughts wing all around as they walk with their attendants, the gentlemen patients nodding to the lady patients. The gentlemen talk with men from the town and sit about in the summerhouses, where lady patients are not allowed on Sundays lest a man from the town seeks his rest, or a gentleman patient whispers la-de-da. Hexum says la-de-da is the growl men purr before they grab. Lady patients keep moving, only nodding from beneath their parasols. Their attendants say how fine the weather, how lovely the gardens. Dr. Story takes a turn about the paths in his physician's black suit, *hobnobbing,* Hexum scoffs, but Weed's own people are not out. Hexum is in her kitchen, ordering the help, kneading and pounding armfuls of dough wide as her front. In the dairy barn or the stables, Zef is the slide of his rose-blue lips on the mouth organ cushioned in his hands. Later in their dim room, corner of the shadow vaulted barn, Dib is his *uh huhhh* over the checkerboard in the glow of the one oil lamp. O'Shea is a swarm of dark hornets trapped in a mud cell, sleeping in his room before the Night Watch. Hide from Matron Bowman, hide from her knowing heart. Hide from Dr. Story, his glow that sees and slides. Follow the gravedigger, always, a far way behind lawns and fields. The willow caskets are loud with whirling songs and the piled-up dirt is a tumbled country to charge and win. The graveyard is marker badges all in rows and the long hill of field above the orchard is waving grass, the singing blades flitting with hoppers and dragonflies. Evenings, the carriage horses roll their eyes until they're harnessed and blindered, tasting iron bits in their teeth. The cows are a bawled chorus. The kitchen women Hexum orders are only broad arms and heavy feet. They'll wave him out of doors, say he's the devil's bargain with that caul of an eye, that veiled white pupil that doesn't move. Don't you be hexing us, Satan child, nor telling what ye see. Out wi ye! They know he won't tell. They think Hexum doesn't know if Hexum doesn't see.

But Weed sees them all from his tree, even the hidden ones who never come out for town visits. He has his fill of Sunday and eases himself back along a wide limb onto the wooden railing, walking it heel to toe the short distance to Hexum's window, grasping the wide casement, slipping in. She leaves it open a space his size on all but stormy days. Air is a tonic, my Weed, see that ye remember, it's winter air kills disease an calms fever's heat. He runs his fingers along her desk that's high as his chest, feels among bobbins of thread and ribbons and papers and quill pens in stands, account books open in layers. She has a fine candlestick from somewhere and a tall thin candle. Fine as any secret queen might have at her dinner table, eh Pet? Boxes of baubles are in her locked drawer. She shows him on night visits. They light the forbidden candle, play with the rings and earbobs. Her magnifying glass is here on the pages of her accounts, the thick round glass with its handle like the hasp of a knife. She's told him it's glass so fine the sun could burn paper through it, held just so over one of Dr. Story's old dry books. That man, eh, my Weed? Waltzing about with his Quaker this 'n that. Less yeast and bread, is it? More vegetables? My lettuce and parsley and mustard greens not enough? Vine tomatoes now, is it? Waste a water. Zef and Dib planting rows along the walls a the exercise yards, for ladies not allowed on walks to water and harvest, an all must be taught, seldom as they dirty their hands! There must be watering cans, he says, and puts out a call to the town! Him with his old books! She shows off her long brass matchbox full of thin wooden stems. Each one topped wi sulfur, Pet, the devil's fire. Shows off his gaslight to all an sundry but I'll not give up mi kerosene lamp, mi candlestick—let im lollop an wheeze! But it's Hexum who wheezes, pounding about, swinging Weed in their circles. Weed takes up the capped brass tube of matches, shakes the tipped sticks inside, then holds the magnifying glass. Opens and folds it shut, wonders how sun can light a fire. Looks for a book but finds only crumpled paper in a waste can. He lays aside the round glass and puts some paper in his pocket with the bread crusts from this morning, slips out into the hallway, down the back stairs to the kitchen.

He can hear her calling him; Sunday is over. Townspeople must go and the women stirring pots of soup motion him outside. Hexum has a big basin of soapy water, and closed knitting hoops for the children she calls her five ducks. Soon she has them blowing bubbles, big ones that loop and color. The girls chase them all around. The boys jump inside to feel the tiny mist of burst.

―――――――

Thomas Kirkbride Story

DR. STORY'S PATIENT

He saw her nearly every day and wrote his session notes immediately after, as though he's perfected his long-practiced therapeutic method―written recall of phrases exchanged―in preparation for this patient, who appeared so suddenly in this unlikely place. Reading the lines set down in his meticulous hand, he reflected that speech and voice, trust, safety, had begun to free her, allow her an eventual choice of refuge.

What were you called as a child, Miss Janet?
Janet, I'm sure.
Then, Janet is not your surname. You weren't certain.
"Miss" was the polite way, Dr. Story? to address unmarried women . . .

A clue, among many, Miss Janet—to your society, before the War.

But Dr. Story, surely a just society must respect any woman. It is moral treatment, isn't it?

He'd agreed that it was, though they might never see such a world. She encouraged reference to himself in their meetings and questioned him directly. Several times, he'd felt a kind of shift—of space, or light or perception—in her presence. He'd never experienced such and anticipated, or more accurately longed, for her musical performances at Auxiliary or suppers in his rooms. Only then did he have an excuse to gaze at her intensely before others. He told himself all this was preface and saw no harm in sharing certain facts, to which she responded with insight. He'd spoken to her of Thomas Story Kirkbride's introduction of moral treatment at the Pennsylvania Hospital. She asked after his family, his education. Was his mother living? She was not, he answered. His mother, cousin to his mentor, Dr. Kirkbride, had died a decade ago. I'm an only child, and my father remarried soon after her death. Your father made a new life, she observed. I didn't begrudge him, Dr. Story said, but I was away, immersed in my studies, living with the Kirkbrides in Philadelphia. He recalled telling her that he supposed his work was now his immediate family.

Dr. Story, may I ask, what were you called as a child?
I was called Thomas.
Not Tom. No, you are not a Tom.
I was Thomas Kirkbride Story. My mother married
one of the Story cousins and named me the inverse
of my successful uncle's name. That is, she referred
to Dr. Kirkbride as my uncle. We visited often in
Philadelphia. His children were my siblings, in a sense.
A happy home, then, your uncle's home. And the
famous Dr. Kirkbride, a family man.

He'd explained that his uncle was widowed, but after a time married again—a former patient. Restored to herself, she was his unfailing helpmate these many years. He helped her, Miss Janet observed, as you are helping me. When she paused and asked if they had children, he sensed alarm in her question. Several, he replied. His second wife wanted—

That, she said quickly, I could not do. I must never—have children.

He noted her shifted gaze. Then you need not, he said quickly.

He'd moved slightly toward her, and she toward him. Their knees nearly touched. Her recall of childhood, normally a preoccupation of patients, was repressed or cautious, but she was socially conscious and perceptive, observant of others. This in itself had convinced him she was sane even when her speech was halting. Still, he asked direct questions in their sessions. Did she want her memory to return. Did she remember herself as a child. She would only say that she was ... a prisoner, and felt herself a child since arriving here. Each day felt new. And what of the time, he asked, en route to us? The girl, she said, brought her food. Did she mean Nurse Connolly? The girl who accompanied her here? What did you call her, he'd asked quickly, before you came here? Why, nothing, Miss Janet had answered. But here I've come to know her. She is like—a sister, nearly. Then his patient had leaned forward and smiled, her face brightening, and asked if Nurse Connolly might accompany them in the carriage that evening. Of course, he answered, remarking that the weather was fair, that these warm days could not last.

He believed her nurse attendant linked her to past trauma, yet her near-familial ease with a girl so clearly her social inferior spoke well of her ability to form deepening bonds. Her memory loss was self-protective, but she smiled easily now in company. Some, his colleagues and their wives, women from the Ladies' Auxiliary, inquired about her progress, saying she was "a lovely presence" who "so deserves good health."

And happiness, one female benefactress had added, nodding at him in what seemed encouragement. He was careful, very careful, to betray nothing at such gatherings, or before staff. But in their private meetings, he moved their armchairs closer, close enough that he might reach out to touch her hand. But no. Even now, he exercised strict reserve. Her brief mention of childhood moments revealed stability amidst plenty. The guarded looks, the flicking gaze, the startled movements have lessened. She no longer wrung her hands or clasped them tightly. Short responses have given way to dialogue and discussion. She spoke of books they read in common, recalled details of their earlier conversations, narrated accounts of her long walks with Nurse Connolly. He sensed an awakened generosity, a yearning, and could not resist, in privacy, looking into her eyes as one gazes into a fireplace to see the contained flames move and flicker. Today, as their session ended, she had prompted him, drawn him out as deftly as any physician.

It is said, Dr. Story, that you never married.
No. I was betrothed, quite long ago, and—had
attachments, before arriving here these four years past.
But I did not feel then—as I do now.

His words surprised him. Her eyes widened but she gave no sign of receiving a declaration. Shadows dappled the room and sunlight from the bank of windows glanced across her face. Over these past weeks, thoughts of her dawned on him similarly, appearing, quietly insisting, disappearing, leaving a vestige, raising the question of happiness—a question he'd thought himself past confronting. She'd inclined her head toward him, inviting him into a silence. He realized that he was no longer concerned with what she revealed or chose not to reveal.

Dr. Story, perhaps, do you think, when we are alone, we might use our given names? Then I could call you Thomas.

And I will call you—Janet.

Yes. For you, that is who I am.

It seemed so much ground had been gained that he had not interrogated her reply until now. He read the words again. Possibly she only presents an acceptable version of herself. No matter. This evening, the carriage ride, with her attendant. They will talk further, move at her pace. Her attractive qualities, her obviously genteel upbringing, the help she might be in his work . . . he allowed himself to imagine her complete recovery, a new life before her, standing in her white nightgown before his bureau looking glass. Unbidden, he felt the slide of her nakedness in his arms.

He is forty-five. Years ago, a rising Physician at the Pennsylvania Hospital, he'd courted the appropriate Quaker ladies. His intended was considering his proposal when her married sister advised him that their "friend in common" was more interested in another suitor. He composed a note of release and good wishes. Weeks later, the sister made Thomas a carefully worded offer. He was already physician to her household and they met often. Older than he, she'd married a powerful Quaker merchant decades her senior. She wished to remain childless and counseled him pleasurably in all manner of intimacy and precaution, forbidding letters, notes, gifts, sworn oaths or declarations, even as she carefully made herself available monthly to her husband—a responsibility, she called it. His grown children would have considered further offspring an embarrassment and she herself regarded pregnancy as "the Russian roulette women endure." Wealthy, she relied on him only for discretion and fidelity. He fancied himself loved and loving, and they might have gone on indefinitely had not her husband, on reaching his sixty-fifth birthday, insisted on removing his family to the Continent.

Then in his late thirties, he found himself at loose ends and began writing of his mother's death, even as he forced himself to attend dinners, parties, lectures. Extending his responsibilities, he took on a role in his uncle's burgeoning Philadelphia practice and accepted more private patients. An attractive widow confided that her grown son's breakdown was due to his late father's abuse, that her husband had oppressed them both. Though never his patient, she asked counsel while her son regained his reason under treatment. After some time, she'd told him that she'd welcome a continued friendship. They began a pleasant and discreet intimacy. He'd focused on his career while they led separate lives, but left all that behind in coming here. His Physician Superintendent post at the transformed Trans-Allegheny Lunatic Asylum was an ambitious new start. Youngest physician appointed to such a post, he'd dedicated himself to the success of moral treatment in these mountains so far from city streets.

Four years hence, Miss Janet is his patient. Restored under his care, she might be more. His uncle Kirkbride's successful remarriage is lasting evidence that moral treatment, safety, rest, might heal even those whose traumas once rendered them silent. Gratitude for one's survival, Story believes, lasts longer even than love.

USUAL MEANS OF AMUSEMENT ... should not be neglected ... while means of carriage riding seems almost indispensable for many.

—DR. THOMAS STORY KIRKBRIDE, *1854*

ConaLee

A CARRIAGE RIDE

So few were about, this early evening, waiting for the carriages. My apron looked fresh and Mama said she favored my hair and the effect of the rouge, but I half longed to step back inside the Asylum. The air smelled faintly of lilacs though the bulging lacy blooms were long fallen. Then Mama stepped closer, smelling of lilac water and holding a small fringed bag and new silk wrap—all sundries surely gifted her by the Asylum Auxiliary. Those town ladies paid her much attention, while I must not seem too familiar or attached. *You are not her family, but a servant.* Papa had said it in the buckboard that dawn morning we first arrived here. But he was jailed now in the farthest ward and Mama would take me on a carriage ride. She stood a step below me, her hair a sweep of chignon and curls. I wondered how she knew to do up her hair so fancy, or to play a harpsichord and piano. Had she always known such things?

Those waiting for the first promenades stood with us before the broad Asylum steps, while nine or ten well-dressed ladies sat along the garden benches. Two dining room maids served lemonade from trays. These well-behaved ladies had town privileges and took their rides, four to a carriage, up along the wide shady paths to the turn-around higher in the forest. Mama was among them, though she didn't care to leave the grounds and would never walk to town. Ladies like her, different evenings, took carriage rides with Matron Bowman or senior staff.

A clatter sounded. Mama took my arm as the matched teams of horses appeared from behind the Asylum. The drawn carriages sat high up like dark jewels on bright red wheels and set my heart pounding. The horses didn't pause but pulled onto the Asylum's long entrance drive, moving away toward the road and the town. Excitement and muted applause from the ladies, who stood to murmur and admire. The promenade seemed a usual parade of sorts. The drivers turned about on the road, back onto the drive, and the smaller carriage came briskly toward us. There in the high driver's seat, reins in his hands, sat the Night Watch. I felt my own hands tingle—surely he must stay at the Asylum. Late on these unseasonable warm days, the men in the far wings raved and called through the thick bars of their open windows. I always thought I heard Papa.

Mama, does the Night Watch often drive a carriage?

No, never, Mama said.

Bits of green leaf were falling down along the front of my white apron. I looked up to see Weed peering at us from the big tree near the Asylum entrance. He was perched on a lowest branch, throwing down showers of torn leaves. I brushed at my hair and shoulders as the Night Watch pulled the reins tight, tying them to some unseen hook or lever. The horses were nervy and tossed their heads, their combed manes and forelocks shining, and the Night Watch was down now, tending them, calming their nickering. I could see, tilted in the floor of the driver's seat, the stock of a rifle. Another flurry of leaves, whole ones, at my feet. Weed lay along his branch, hanging his arms and legs down like a magic trick. The Night Watch followed my gaze and gave him a glowering look, like a disapproving father. Weed climbed higher, out of sight.

Then Mama pulled me behind her as the Night Watch came

to assist us. He wore a jacket and trousers and a billed watch cap, pulled down to shade his eye patch, but moved as though uniformed, on duty. We three stood suddenly close before the shiny black door of the carriage. Our reflections in the glass of the carriage window seemed a tableau, like an image caught in a bubble that might lift and drift away.

Mr. O'Shea, Mama said, almost under her breath.

The Night Watch only reached to open the carriage door. Mama gathered up her dress and took his hand, stepping onto the metal foot mount. Her skirts trailed inside. The slide of white fabric disappearing into the dark took me so aback that I could not follow. The Night Watch inclined his head at me, and I saw that his one arresting hazel eye was framed with the abundant black curled lashes women envy. I felt his hand at my elbow, my foot on the mount, and was in the carriage, surprised to see Dr. Story sitting opposite. He sat to one far corner and Mama to the other, her dress flared across the seat between them. I took my spot on a sort of shelf seat that Dr. Story pulled down to face them, glad I had no full skirts to manage.

Dr. Story pointed to the leather cords either side of me. Hold just there, Nurse Connolly, he said, should the way get bumpy.

But it is quite smooth, Mama said, after we reach the shade.

The carriage moved off with a start. The windows, hinged shut, took up the top halves of the doors. The glass, aglow with slanted evening light, lit up the inside of the carriage like a little room—the walls, the curved couch of the deep back seat, the bottom half of the doors, even the ceiling, were tufted and upholstered in shiny gray fabric. A pillowed bolster ran along all four walls and I braced myself against it.

See? Mama said. Here are the back gardens.

Dr. Story stood to unhinge the sides of the windows and fasten them inward, attaching their corners to small hooks in the ceiling. The open way on both sides flowed past as though magic, familiar but strange—the laden air and the gardens, the trees and benches, the walking paths trailing across the grass, the greenhouses. Then one barn and another, for we were on the widest path and the way calmed. All seemed to move in reverse. My feet on the floor nearly touched theirs, but it was as though I hurtled backwards, ahead of Mama and Dr. Story. It was so odd to see them enclosed together that I found it easier to look straight across between them, out the narrow back window. Weed's face suddenly appeared there, smiling to know I saw him—he had run behind the carriage and jumped onto the back running board. Appearing, disappearing, he stood up, crouched down, put on a show. I hoped he knew how to jump down when he liked, without getting entangled in the wheels—

Lovely evening, Dr. Story said. He rested his gaze on Miss Janet and seemed to wait for her to speak.

Like . . . May, she answered, tilting her face to her open window.

Exactly so, Miss Janet. Many remark on this autumn that has not happened. But it's very pleasant for us, evenings like this. He was dressed as in his office but seemed different, though still watchful, considering.

Mama had told me, be polite and don't talk overly much. Dr. Story, I said, thank you for inviting me.

Of course. Miss Janet is very fond of you—here he leaned forward—she tells me she views you almost as family.

Oh. Yes, sir. We are grown very . . . accustomed.

Chosen family, he answered, sometimes grow closer in sympathy than any other.

I nodded, not sure what he meant. He put both hands on the rounded silver knob of his walking stick, holding it before him, pleased. In the closeness of the carriage, I saw that his fine, well-made hands were well tended, his frame slim, almost delicate. He would not have made a woodsman or farmer, or built a home from wilderness, but his calm gray eyes drew me in. I wanted to tell him I was afraid of Papa.

The wheels of the carriages are . . . so bright, I said.

Ah, he said, yes, and the festive paint is practical as well. A flash of color to warn off local poachers, who might be about, evenings, after rabbits or pheasant. It's not allowed, of course, but . . . they are hardworking men.

And it's so warm still, with squirrels and birds in the gardens, I said. We'd have snows by now, deep snows— Mama's warning glance stopped my words.

But he agreed. Oh yes, here too, he said, snow most years, mere weeks from Christmas. He inclined his head toward me. Will you be visiting family, Nurse Connolly?

Had he forgotten our interview? Or was he testing me? No, I said, I have no family but . . . here.

The small word hung in the air like a drop too swole to fall. I felt myself trapped inside it and the close padded room of the carriage seemed to glow. The tufted buttons of the dimpled upholstery shone like small lights and sparked a burning heat behind my eyes.

Mama half stood to lean across Dr. Story, her shoulder just touching his vest. Look, Dr. Story, from your window. The meadows are still green, but the orchard's leaves have turned. Like a child's . . . what do we call those stories? The magical ones— She met his eyes. But she'd reached across behind her to grip my wrist and pull me into her seat.

He smiled at her, so near him. Fairy tales? he offered.

Yes, she said, I couldn't find the words. She laughed a tinkling sound that was not hers and sat back, just beside him. Might we shift a bit, Dr. Story? she asked. Nurse Connolly may be one of those who cannot ride backwards, and the air is so pleasant on this side.

I found myself pressed close between Mama and the open window, in the near pillowy corner of the carriage. I closed my eyes to stop the lights and felt her pinch my forearm hard under the fold of her dress. If I slept here, lost time as I did when the lights bade me drift, where would I go? Back to Dearbhla, and time long past—

Nurse Connolly, Mama said, lean far out here and you will see our matched horses in the traces, just as the path opens up.

I leaned out the open window to breathe, her hand pressing me. A fine rain had tamped the dust that morning and the air was sweet and green. I could see the reddish swells of the horses' flanks moving under their harnesses, their black manes flying. We had climbed the incline and were high above the meadow, then curving round to a flat bit of path I knew well. Here we picked up speed. I wished for jingling bells on the harnesses, like the Thanksgiving song about snow and Grandmother's house. *Bell, she said. Or goose.* How different Mama was now, thanks to Dr. Story. The air, the sun-dappled path, the dense trees, even the motion of the carriage seemed his design. I hoped he didn't see through me as clear.

Suddenly the carriage braked so sharp that we skidded along the road like the very sled from the old song, but stopped slung askew toward the woods. The horses were turned half across the path, snorting. I could see them plain from my open window, and a black bear and her three cubs not fifty paces before them. The bear rose up on her hind legs and moved in a careful two-step, pawing the air. She was suddenly taller than the carriage, two splashes of white on her chest, huffing a sound that was not growl nor bark but a pulsing bawl. The blindered horses smelled musk, jostling as the Night Watch tried to rein them in.

Dr. Story banged on the outside of the carriage and called out, O'Shea! Use your rifle—

Quiet! said the Night Watch. No one move.

I looked out the back window, my finger to my lips to signal Weed. He must get into the carriage with us, for the path was too narrow to allow turning about and we could not move backwards in some impossible escape. I felt Dr. Story's light touch on my shoulders as he moved past me and hinged the open window shut. I could see the bear through the glass, stretching full height on her back legs, tilting her big head back, nosing skyward as though to scent the air. When she touched lightly down on her big paws, she seemed swole to frighten us. Sow bears could be fast and vicious, and one of her size— My door was hard into the tall weedy flowers by the side of the path. Mama clutched the back of Dr. Story's coat, as I motioned Weed toward me in frantic silence. They peered from their closed window while I clicked my slanted carriage door open just enough, felt Weed there, and lifted him quickly in. He cowered at my feet as I latched the door shut. If only I could hide us both—

There now, Dr. Story whispered. Wait a moment—they're crossing the road, into the trees.

My mother was in his arms. Why aren't we moving? she asked.

We shall wait upon O'Shea's instincts, he said, touching his hand to the back of her hair. Glancing at me, he stood to latch the other window shut and looked down at Weed, who clutched his own knees on the floor as though to disappear.

I saw him on the path near us and pulled him inside, I said. He must have been wandering the woods. His name is Weed— one of the children in Mrs. Hexum's charge.

I'm aware, said Dr. Story. Child, he told Weed, do not leave the Asylum grounds. It's not safe, these weeks before the weather turns. Do you hear me?

I pulled Weed onto my lap and nudged him to answer. Weed, I said, tell the doctor, *Yes, sir.*

Yes, sir, Weed said.

Dr. Story took his place beside Mama at the window, speaking to her in a low voice. She took his arm as the carriage began to move. The Night Watch was calming the horses, leading them forward himself to pull the carriage back onto the path. He took his coachman's seat then and moved carefully along to the turnabout, and retraced our route at half the pace, as though the Night Watch wanted quieter passage. I clung to Weed in my lap, his limbs heavy against me, his head cushioned on my throat, and envied the bear's fierceness. It seemed to me that I'd already lost my children, young as I was. This stray boy had lost his mother, his name. His story was blank and mine was nearly so. He smelled of dust, and stickiness or sugar, and breathed so quiet I thought he might have dropped into a sleep. But he glanced up at me, the blue of his veiled milk eye pale as pearl. I smoothed his hair to soothe him, soothe myself, but saw our carriage overturned on the path, the glass windows broken out, the horses slaughtered and flayed open, snow falling on their torn flanks. But the Night Watch had saved us, commanding even Dr. Story.

We were descending the path and met the second carriage in the lower woods. Dr. Story opened his window and told the driver to turn about, then looked at us gravely. Ladies, he said, I apologize for our encounter. It seems this strange season has confused nature.

Weed shrank into me. Dr. Story took his place beside Mama and I could hear them murmuring quietly. We began to see the orchard trees, the quiet meadow, the lower gardens, and I breathed easier. Weed, I asked, how old are you? He only pursed his lips. You won't say? I whispered.

Likely he doesn't know, Mama said.

Much was different in the years before I arrived here, Dr. Story said, seeming to address other questions.

I'd thought they weren't listening and wanted to distract them. The Asylum gardens, I said, are so beautiful from the carriage. And it was a most exciting ride—

Overly exciting, Dr. Story agreed. Miss Janet, will you come to my apartments for tea and an aperitif when we return? Purely medicinal. It will help calm you. When Mama only glanced at me, he asked, Nurse Connolly, might you accompany Miss Janet?

Yes, I said, surely.

Good, he said, seeing me as though for the first time. Such closeness, he said then, as between the two of you, carries us beyond the past. The time may come that Miss Janet no longer needs your help, but an experienced, gifted attendant can help many, and receive a higher wage in time. Not all nurses live at the Asylum. Some reside in the town.

I'd no idea where in the town he thought I might live. I—prefer to stay near Miss Janet, I said. I don't mind the nurses' quarters. But thank you, Doctor—

I'm . . . very tired. Mama touched his hand with her gloved one. I must go to my room, but I thank you, dear Dr. Story, for your understanding, every day. We meet tomorrow, yes?

I looked away, for we had stopped before the Asylum. As the Night Watch climbed down to assist, Weed slipped out the carriage door on our side. Mama preceded me from the other and stood a moment, requiring O'Shea's two hands on her waist before stepping down. She said something to him but I didn't catch the words and whispered my own thanks. Behind me, I heard the doctor speak.

We must meet, O'Shea, after you stable the horses. My office.

Mama was so quick to be inside the Asylum that I ran to catch her up and found her standing, watching the two men through one of the narrow windows set to the side of the massive door. She breathed like one who'd run a distance, but stepped back when she saw me.

Miss Janet, I said, I'll see you upstairs.

Yes, do, she answered, but then pulled me closer, holding my hands. ConaLee, she said, take my scarf and reticule to my room. You have a key. I must sit in the garden, there to the side where it's more private.

But you're not allowed in the garden alone—

Leave the room unlocked. And then go to bed. You need rest— I'm sorry to have brought you—forgive me.

Mama, come upstairs with me. The Asylum will be locked.

But she gripped my hand. Do as I tell you. I must have some time.

I turned from her and stood, uncertain, in the alcove under

the stairs to the Women's Wards. My mother had gone but for her small fringed bag and wrap. O'Shea must have driven the carriage to the stables, and Dr. Story entered the Asylum a moment later.

O'Shea

AN ESCAPE

O'Shea did not dislike Dr. Story's third-floor office—his treatment room as the doctor called it. O'Shea thought the room a fantasy he himself might have occupied, in some other sphere, had he lived a different life in a different time. The several oak file cabinets, the typewriter on its separate roll-top desk, the oversized globe in its pedestal table, the framed maps, all spoke of categories and regulated worlds. The Physician Superintendent did not walk the trails and paths of Asylum acreage, seldom traversed the roads and counties of the Alleghenies, rarely took a coach or train to Philadelphia, but his many framed maps pictured pastel regions he might figure at a glance.

Please— Dr. Story indicated a chair and joined O'Shea on the other side of his large desk.

O'Shea wondered with whom else the doctor encouraged this seating arrangement, no doubt meant to ease the barrier of his authority. They met at least monthly, or after an "event of concern." O'Shea always regretted losing the separation of the massive mahogany desk. It seemed to tilt toward them now like a mirrored wall, shining and dark.

Rarely, I have a brandy, said Dr. Story. I hoped you might join me.

O'Shea gave a brief nod, surprised. Neither man used spirits

often, but O'Shea was aware that the Physician Superintendent and the dispensary kept medicinal brandy on hand.

Dr. Story placed two snifters pooled with honey-colored
brandy on the table between them. Each took a glass in hand
but merely breathed the aroma.

O'Shea, seated in the upholstered chair to the right, reflected
that he'd nothing in common with "the nephew of the great
man," as old Dr. O'Shea had first referred to Dr. Story nearly
four years ago. Yet there was familiarity in the smell of the
elixir, the ritual of the snifters. The elderly O'Shea had often
served brandy of a winter's night by the fire, in glasses that
warmed in the palm, like these. It was where they'd discussed
a position open in an Allegheny asylum.

As though reading his thoughts, Dr. Story maintained a
silence.

O'Shea looked straight before him and wondered at old Dr.
O'Shea's absence, a void that translated here into a sense of
presence.

I know we bear no relation, Dr. Story said then, but the fact
that old Mrs. O'Shea was a distant cousin to my uncle—well, I
consider this a connection. And fortunate, as it helped bring
you here, to prepare the way.

Dr. Story was professionally tactful, thought O'Shea. It was
more that the Night Watch had made peace with Mrs. Hexum
by convincing the new Physician Superintendent not to immediately remove the five children she'd collected to an orphan-
age. She petted and cared for them like so many chicks, and
Christian charity demanded they stay (so went O'Shea's argu-
ment) as long as their numbers never increased.

You helped bring the staff along to the changes moral treatment requires, Dr. Story went on. This too is a connection, of
a different kind.

They both knew the changes to which he referred: strict
separation of male and female patients, aggressive if intuitive
vetting of doctors and employees, regimens that included daily

recreation and useful tasks, close supervision of patients by their nurse attendants. Mrs. Bowman saw to that, and still suspected O'Shea because his hire was not her affair.

O'Shea sipped his brandy. All right, he would converse. Only Dr. Story, in this place, knew of O'Shea's Alexandria benefactors. Old Mrs. O'Shea, he asked the doctor, was, what, your father's fourth cousin?

Fourth cousin once removed. Quaker from birth, and converted her Irish suitor during courtship.

Not exactly, O'Shea said. My benefactor admired the faith. And could still serve as a patriot surgeon, saving maimed Union soldiers in his hospital. Though to what end? We did not agree about that.

Yet you are the proof.

Am I? I am the Night Watch.

Yes. And you need only say when you would accept a change of title and more responsibility. As Assistant Steward, you could supervise the regimens assigned the men, with whatever advisory role, attend Physician meetings—

I prefer to work alone, with access to all the men in the wards, and supervision of their attendants. The men see me as their advocate, and the aggressive few remain intimidated enough. As for my Alexandria benefactors, they are gone now, within weeks of each other. Your grant of leave last fall . . . was much appreciated.

It was fortunate that she passed when you were there, O'Shea, helping her settle the old man's estate. I can't help but think of them as your family.

I have no family.

Dr. Story nodded, and drank from his glass. You are not alone in that. It's common in these times. So many of our patients, all classes of society, find themselves sole survivors, nine years on, of our—national catastrophe.

It is still—unspooling, O'Shea said, like malignant thread.

An appropriate phrase, Dr. Story said. His penetrating,

empathic gaze was typical, but in fact he trusted O'Shea. The man was averse to conversation, yet completely discreet. His layman's counsel had proven precise and valuable.

O'Shea didn't respond. His memory of the world before the War remained void. But for vestiges, wisps, he knew only obliteration. It must be worse, he thought, much worse, for those who remembered.

Today is but an example, said Dr. Story. The patient and nurse attendant with me in the carriage—both homeless, seemingly, but for here. Miss Janet does not remember much of her past, no doubt due to trauma. A girl who worked as a servant for family friends sometimes attended her after the War, and accompanied her here.

Then the girl must know her, O'Shea said.

There is a bond. But the girl is nearly a child. The patient was much isolated, alone in the family home, and then burned out, along with the girl's employers. Union sympathizers forced North, most likely. They are still fighting the War in some of these towns, settling scores.

The fire is only banked, O'Shea said.

I'm afraid I agree. Dr. Story met O'Shea's gaze and reflected that he could exchange such words with no one else. Yet he barely knew O'Shea.

O'Shea sat forward. We are here to discuss today, yes? I don't apologize for refusing your order to shoot.

And commanding our silence, said Dr. Story. But I could see your rifle, aimed—

I'm not engaged here as huntsman. The bear was of size, and the cubs—

Not young. Dr. Story allowed himself a rueful smile. The kitchens would say we need the meat.

The cubs were yearlings and might have charged as well, on that narrow road. And there was no escape.

O'Shea, I can hardly complain of your judgment and competence. I thank you, and not for the first time. You know far more of guns and forests than I. This strange season . . . makes the higher paths and trails unsafe.

Agreed. The carriage rides must surely end, until the weather turns.

Not end, Dr. Story said. Patients depend on them. But carriages can stay to the paths near the gardens and barns.

O'Shea nodded. Keep to the routine but alter the route. No more need for armed drivers.

Dr. Story sat forward as well, lessening the distance between them. O'Shea, we depend on you here. I'm sorry to have reminded you of weapons. Of battle, of emergency—

I don't remember, O'Shea said. I remember nothing. But a rifle fits too well in my grip and my aim is keen. I . . . was a violent man.

You were a soldier, O'Shea, who fought evils I was taught to abhor from childhood. I wish I'd not been required to ask your help. But *we* know I was taking precautions against a human interloper, though I think it very unlikely he is anywhere near us.

If his escape had been announced, and a manhunt immediately begun—

It was announced to the police, and the roads are watched, but as we don't have his name or history— The Attendant who assisted him was fired, though maintains he was physically coerced.

Into providing a violent lunatic his gentleman's clothes, and releasing him?

Yes. Seduction is more likely. The patient is a manipulative sociopath. He must have concealed cash or valuables sewn into the clothes locked up since his arrival, and paid his accomplice. I was away when the police delivered him under guard, and he was isolated immediately due to his manic episode. You know too well—I read your report. I met with the man only twice, to consult on our denial of privileges. He's clever, brutal, and has no doubt moved on quickly. We must leave his fate to law enforcement, far from here. His type will come to their attention, and the Asylum would only be harmed by news of his escape.

But if he acts destructively nearby, O'Shea said, and is traced to us, the harm will be greater.

I take your point. But he's intelligent and shrewd, and given that he'd be arrested for assault and attempted robbery immediately outside these walls, his wish would be to get out of the state and region as fast as possible. O'Shea, I depend on your discretion.

O'Shea didn't reply. The large Regulator wall clock ticked behind him, its round brass pendulum moving to and fro, glinting behind glass. O'Shea's thoughts were hard. In this matter, Story was a fraud and a shill, whatever care or safety his "moral treatment" had won for some.

As agreed, Dr. Story said, we must keep all patients close to the grounds now, and concern ourselves with nonhuman animals.

Nonhuman animals. O'Shea felt himself aptly described in the phrase.

· · · · ·

The December evening had grown cooler, like a chill October. A mist rose from the ground like lissome smoke, as though it held the cold to come. He could not fathom spending this last hour before Night Watch in his room after today's events, and so began walking the rectangular circumference of the Asylum. He found himself near the stone walls of the Women's Ward in a nearly hidden side garden, shielded from the ornamental paths and open lawn by tall rhododendron and horse chestnut hedges. The spreading canopy of a large beech tree sheltered rings of shadow on a path below. There, a figure turned toward him as though waiting. A woman, her dark hair unbound. He could not make out eyes or expression. Suddenly, she was closer, though she had not seemed to move, and then just before him, very close, like an apparition.

The figure said, unaccountably, I know you.

Or he might have thought the words himself, never speaking.

She reached for his hand as he pulled away. I was with you today, she said, in the carriage . . . and for many years, when you were lost.

Lost? Her words seemed to him a disembodied echo.

Lost from me, from us. We waited, searched. So many years—

Her tearful voice struck him like a blow. Phantom, he wanted to tell her, go back— Back to the featureless past, he meant, and felt himself in some fluid dimension, as in that time of injured sleep, when he'd floated painlessly, free of memory or future. The very ground, the tree limbs hanging over them, seemed to shift, jolted. Fields, exploding. Knee-high grass, trembling, shaken at the root. The mist was smoke, rising, pale as souls until fire streaked the skies red. The sense that he'd been here and could never leave came upon him like a sudden darkness, blindingly lit. He stepped back but felt her clasp his shoulders with both hands and move with him. She trod upon his feet to reach up, close any distance, press her wet face against his throat. He knew the smell of her. How?

Stop, he said. Leave me.

I won't say more, she sobbed, ever, unless you ask.

Her words whirled past before sound itself roared and paused. Behind him, to his left, some awful piece of clothed remnant, heavy with blood, fell from a height. The smell of bile, putrefaction, was turgid, enveloping. How was she in this place? He felt the ground give and held her against him. Her gasping breath seemed to feed him as she opened her mouth on his and drew him in.

ConaLee

PAGES

The wide hallway of Women's Ward B was empty. All were at dinner in the ladies' dining hall. I turned the key in the door and stepped into Mama's room. The lock snapped closed behind me and I put aside her shawl and beaded bag. To think we had lived here, in this small space, almost as one. We met outdoors for walks now and I'd not been in her room for many weeks. My cot was gone, replaced with a narrow table near the same length and width. A desk it seemed, with one straight chair. The round yellow pillow someone had so prized now padded the seat. What use had she for a desk? I saw a sheaf of papers, a writing nib. I'd no more respect for her privacy and wanted to read whatever words, all the words she wouldn't say to me. I rolled up the loose pages and put them in my apron, a round spear against my chest. Wrong to steal—I knew my Commandments and paused at the window to touch the plaster angel. She was still here on the sill, stuck fast to her square nail, all detail gone from her pitted face. I wanted her, for I prayed to her. My hand hovered near, afraid she might crumble at a touch, and I raised my eyes to look down into the garden. It was nearly dark but the sky was still light, I saw my mother there, her hair damp with mist and fallen around her shoulders. I almost felt her imploring expression as she approached a dark shape before her on the path. Even from behind, I could tell that the tall, broad-backed man was not Dr. Story, but O'Shea, the Night Watch. Surely he'd been sent to fetch her, though he stepped back, raising his arms as like to fend her off. But she pulled him to her, stepped upon his boots to reach him, and put her mouth on his. Was she mad, truly? The two on the path clung tightly and moved as one, deeper into the shade. Their absence seemed to glitter, trailing after them.

I felt my own breath drawn out of me. For the first time in so long, my sight went dark inside bright stabs of light. *Tell them you have fits . . .* I heard Papa say it again, as though he breathed the words into Mama's room: *Yer comin with me. I'll get in this door.* He could not be at my mother's door—surely the words were inside me. It was Papa who sparked the lights in my sight, and the dark after them—I was sure now that I'd had no such affliction before he made us prisoners. He still followed me in nightmares, pursuing me along the hard dirt path to the root cellar. His stride made three of mine until he caught me, threw back the board doors, and took me down, inside, to open a sealed crock and coat the fleshy mound of his thumb with honey—he filled my mouth with sweet in the dream flare and I bit down hard. Lights flashed as he flung me away, slammed me into the dark, stomping the flat wood doors overhead. I felt the blackberry bower shake all round him and fell and fell until Dearbhla came near. She was in the ether that my breath made dense as water. *No matter what that man do, you fly to me in your mind.* I followed her into the roar and saw Mama, running by a dark river that opened deep as a gash. *It's a deep hole, too deep for Mama to reach . . .* I was blind and felt her lay me down, slide me forward, hang me over in the rain and thunder. *Slops are in the ditch.* I reached into the wet but the river stood up and branched off like a tree of burning stars, too big to fall because the Night Watch, O'Shea, held it on his shoulders. Dizzy, I sank in sparks of lights, as though Papa must be near again. Mama's pages were fires that flew up around me.

. . .

I came to myself on the floor beside her bed. *Don't tell them you see lights. Not everyone sees lights.* I felt as though he'd shaken me like a rag, and remembered his grip as though I'd never forgot.

Shivering, I pulled myself up by the bedframe. Mama seemed to gaze back at me from her looking glass as I blotted cold sweat from my face, fixed my fallen cap to my hair. There was silence now and I'd time to leave before the ladies of the ward returned. Dusk was darkness now. I straightened my apron and felt Mama's pages crushed against my chest, not flown, not falling. My mind was blank, empty, like a window closed between one time and another. I unlocked the door, left it ever so slightly ajar for Mama, made my way through the ward doors and up to my narrow bed in our attendants' quarters. I wanted to close my eyes but the pages burned against me.

Weed

HIGHER

Weed sees them below: the Night Watch and the woman. He turns to climb higher, near to the trunk of the tree. This largest beech in the side garden is one of his. Pale lower limbs dip almost to the ground and the highest branches spring with his weight, creak in the air, stretch and rouse. He marks an oval of clear sight through layers of descending leaves. So far above, he watches O'Shea and the woman pressed against him. Set apart from anyone or anywhere, they move deeper under the sheltering branches, to mossy, spongy ground unseen from the Asylum. Colors shift as she lets fall her skirts, pulls off garments, lifts her pale loose chemise and steps into his arms like a child he lifts up to nuzzle. Not the yank pull of calves or goats at the animal barns but a sliding near while she opens his shirt, pulls at his breeches. Not the bull and the cow or dogs in the fields—he holds her front to front. Weed hears him breathe as though stabbed when she moves, shuddering while he stands, holding her until he folds them down, kneels across her and the patch of skirt on the ground.

Weed hears their heaving sounds like he's caught inside, a trick that happens when he hides and looks and sees. They make small noises. Weed sees their slow collapse until they're flat on the ground, like deer he watched one dusk in the orchard. But they are not quiet, settling. Her feet push his breeches down, bare his flanks. Her legs shine, crossed over him, pulling him sharp against her. Weed hears their strangled, urged music and climbs higher, so high he sees but one pale creature below, moving, seeming to fight itself. He tingles, stinging, and sees ants on his hand, ants swarming a broken knot on this high, thick branch. They clasp bits of pale grub and run over one another, piling on top, climbing up, deeper into the tree. Weed shakes them off and sees, far below, the white shape still moving, clasped, swimming. In the instant Weed sucks hard on the stung blush of his palm, the two below pull back to see and breathe. Then the slow swimming begins again, slower, measured, tensed. Weed turns away. A wind is moving him, breathing through the tree, lifting limbs, sighing the leaves. He wants a storm and climbs higher, his bare feet soundless branch to branch.

ConaLee

A RUSE

The writing was spidery, looped all round. Was this a story, a ruse. An entertainment. Or was she a lunatic despite her airs. She'd writ over some words with X's, pressing hard, so I could only read parts, scratchings. *Murderess* was writ here and there. *They were on Dearbhla as We broke through the Trees.* Such had not happened. *Stone in Hand I flung Myself XXXX XThem.* Words were writ across in slides and up and down. Inkblots made of circling stabbing motions. *The Overseer fell.* What was Overseer. I was overseen, Matron Bowman often said. *I Stood to Lift the bootscraperXXXX XXXX.* That was a large stone set to the side of the Asylum steps, with a cast iron edge set in. I seldom used the main entrance and never yet in mud or snow. *His head xxxxxxcrushed in just that Narrow Shape.*

The words made no sense. *One ran away to tell the tale.* A tale she was writing, a story. Dreams, could be. Perhaps she wrote such things for Dr. Story, to assure him she was a lunatic and deserved her careful treatment, her desk, her inks and paper. *Could not feel Reins in my Hands till I Smelled the Creek we Galloped through.* We never galloped through the creek in far past days but walked the horses through ankle deep water to a deer blind that she said my father built. We staked the horses a ways off and waited in the blind. It was dim. The bark and branch walls smelled of damp and we must crouch down to tamp our scent. Strange to remember—no one spoke of my father and the blind was all I knew of him then. I'd forgot I was too small to see through the high chinks. Rifle roar, gunpowder smell. *But Death followed XXXTook our Child.* What child? *Sent Grief to Use and Torture Me.* Papa used her. She'd said as much. One word followed another headlong. I turned the pages this way and that to read the sideways lines, squeezed large and small. *I Fainted to see him so Changed. Woke pressed to his XXXX-Body XXXXXXyet he did not Know me.* I thought of the street I'd dreamed, the grown babbies looking past me. *The child with him, or no child, only a Vapor, the Child XXXXlost on the Journey? XXXXXwhose Spirit found Him and not Me.* Who was lost, who found? Who was changed?

I knew I must leave here, find Dearbhla or call her to me. Distracted so, my gaze swept Mama's lines and snagged on the last phrases. The letters she'd writ were blades she'd aimed to pierce me, sending me to her room, knowing I'd see the pages . . . *had I found him in DeathXXXxx our ConaLee followed Us to Oblivion.* I could not take it in. *The hard Cone XXXxxXEye and Temple seemed Devil's helmet or Angel's armorXXXXXXXe XXXo I could not See but Breathed him bending over Us with the Plate.* She could only be writing of O'Shea, the Night Watch. And Weed a vapor finding him.

Was it true my father could not know us, know me. And she'd known all along, yet never told me, never said! How could he be here? Yet he was. I knew it and ripped the pages to shreds, ripped and ripped till they were snow. I heard the other nurse attendants climbing the stairs. Matron Bowman would reprimand me for not going to dinner. No doubt my mother was in her room, peering from her window onto the path she'd made her secret.

Dearbhla

TURNING

She sits out tonight in the porch hammock, wrapped in furs she keeps here until the snows. Barefoot, she taps her heels to make a motion, as she once swung ConaLee in her lap. The child loved the hammock for a bed, and the black sky splashed with stars. Safe here as nowhere else. Dearbhla told her stories as each constellation turned in its sphere, until ConaLee said the stories and waited for Dearbhla's phrases. How the stories were the same but the stars changed spaces from one season to another. That we are still and stars are turning. Dearbhla feels herself turning though the world is still and clear.

They say in the hamlet below that winter will not come this year. The sun is still warm in December. Too much blood in the ground, coming on ten years after War's end. But the year turns a scant week from now, and the Pleiades, winter stars, make their way as blind Orion surges after them. The seven sisters were ConaLee's, in Dearbhla's stories. The six always visible knew her for the seventh, missing sister, paused in flight. Resting in her journey, Dearbhla said, Orion a beast in the shape of a hunter, with Betelgeuse to one shoulder, his broad belt set with stars. The sisters wept and so brought rain. But why weeping, ConaLee asked, though she knew: their father, borne down with the weight of the world, no longer knew or saw them. Escaped to the sky, they moved forever, the wind of Orion's hunger shredding their garments as they fled. Who knew if the fatherless child thought on the story now. Then, she loved her shining sisters, even when they were gone to the other side of the world and she couldn't see them. The skies marked time's passage in those years.

Dearbhla has worked dawn to dusk through these warm autumn and winter weeks, tracking and hunting, drying jerky and strips of venison, gathering wood with horse and drag, putting up berries, fallen apples, root vegetables grown large in the endless summer, filling and sealing the crocks in Eliza's root cellar. Nights, she remembers the three of them digging out the space, propping the inside walls with stones as ledges and shelves. No ConaLee then. Just themselves, unmolested. A brief time with him that seemed so long and full. She sees, as though from inside, the dark empty space of the root cellar. Her own time is passing. She aches from the work, from the pace she sets, as though her preparations will support those gone from her. She cannot call them back. Her dogs and cats cluster near on the porch, not allowed inside but on the coldest, frozen nights. Weeks ago, a mother cat strayed too far, carried off by coyote or fox, left her mewling, staggering kittens, their eyes still closed. Dearbhla took them in, fed them goat milk she warmed at the fire. Soon enough they ventured out, came back with dragonflies in their mouths. She shut them out to join the others. Now they hunt plentiful mice, rodents, and their absence from bed and hearth sets her thoughts on ConaLee, the child she once held close.

Cold approaches in these cooling nights, as though this warm early winter will cease all at once. She visions the heavy snowfalls of the past, the sounds in the mountains as shelves of drifted snow crack like gunshots and fall, sliding where they will. She feels those snows approach, perhaps in days. True December will surely take hold. She must make the journey to Weston tomorrow, stopping only to feed and water the horse. To see this place, this Asylum for ladies and gentlemen, for those not ladies but treated as such. Eliza, raised a lady, born to it, but what of ConaLee? The Pleiades surge their slow transits away, while ConaLee, Eliza, have come to rest in a place Dearbhla cannot picture. She will journey there, look at the place from the road, for they say a long oval path leads to the entrance. Only to know what it is, know herself near them.

Or she will drive the buckboard to the door of the place, tie the horse where she can, walk inside to ask . . . after a woman and child left off here together months ago. How many came to the place in that way? No telling. She would say she knew of the child, not the woman. Must relay a message to her. Or she could offer the child a home, chores in exchange for board. Such offers were made, she knew, at homes for war orphans. Or if all is well, merely to see ConaLee, to talk in one of the gardens set about. To know ConaLee is well, for no child was more capable, despite all . . . She looks again to the light-splashed skies, rounded beyond vastness, to a moment of flare past Orion's massive belt. A shooting star. Its streak of passage is instant, gone, but Dearbhla sees it. The buckboard is ready, food, water, blankets. She has only to load the revolver she places near her feet, harness the horse. Dawn will do.

The way is brightly moonlit. More than halfway on, she pulls the buckboard under a spreading beech so large the branches might shelter one or two abodes. Or many fairy houses, ConaLee would say. The leaves have darkened, dried, but the branches reach such lengths one over another that she might circle the buckboard and not be seen. Others have stopped here. Piled dirt and leaves, soft shapes for bedrolls or blankets, lie here and there. She must loose the horse from the traces and lead him to drink in a trickling stream just behind. A narrow stone bridge, lapsed into the water at one end, and moss-grown, tumbled rocks. Crouching to drink, Dearbhla remembers a story Eliza told in the War's first winter, shared in lonely talk when she was large with child, sewing diapers, flannel wraps, a bunting. They'd both thought then that he would see the babe in the spring when snows cleared. He would find his way. Hadn't they two letters, care of the general store in the hamlet below? Dearbhla went to the store for mail, and to post Eliza's letters by the dozen.

But there were no trips down the mountain when snows were constant. Shrouded in soughing wind, bright, cold days, nights lit with shining, unbroken drifts, they sat by Eliza's hearth, for she was so close to her time that Dearbhla no longer left her at night. Eliza had no one else to tell, to hear, how in that other place, before flight and War, she'd glimpsed him seldom, those years after Dearbhla forbade them meet. *You saw him, Dearbhla, but I could not.* How she came upon him in a spring meadow when she was sixteen and her horse went lame. Passing near, riding out to check traps for birds and fowl for the kitchen, he took her onto his own horse, leading her injured mare slowly behind. The saddle's movement, the lowering day, their slow progress, bade her close her eyes and press against him, holding him loosely about the waist and closely thigh to thigh. They stopped at the creek and he took her in his arms to swing her down. Shed his boots, waded in to hobble her horse in the cold shallow water. The mare's bruised leg was swollen. He said a few minutes now would make all the difference. She looped the reins of his horse to a live oak dense with hanging moss and ducked under to sit near him on the bank. They were silent. A few minutes, she thought, how many? and turned his face to hers. He was her first, her only love to this day, and she, if not his first, was so deeply beloved that he offered her all he knew, gently, over the next months, until they were lovers, planning escape.

So much for plans, she told Dearbhla.

Back then, fifteen year ago in the place they'd left, Eliza's coming out party was already planned with Charleston relatives. But her father saw her gaze across the courtyard one morning at the Irish stable boy, now a man grown to full height, and observed a strapping dark-haired youth, too secure in special privilege, meet her eyes. Despite his acceptance of Dearbhla, he determined the boy would never climb above his station and had him whipped and branded on the chest, plain to any woman or man should he shed his clothes. Dearbhla bandaged and nursed him. The wound was healing, closed and sore, not a week later, when they left on their sudden flight, taking an attacker's sidearm and horse, and what supplies they could grab from Dearbhla's stores. They'd traveled for weeks, how many they could not tell, by dark at first, dressed as men in rough, nondescript clothes, their faces streaked with dirt.

They'd found refuge. The hard work of it was their sustenance. And so ConaLee was born almost three year later. The child had stopped here, under this beech tree, Dearbhla is sure, on her way to the Asylum with Eliza, eight month ago. They'd passed the night in this very buckboard. But Dearbhla only rests, fills her water bucket, hitches the horse, and goes on.

Weed

LEAVE THE REST

The cooks send Weed to find Hexum as lady patients queue up for breakfast. Often enough she trusts them to preparations but never leaves them to themselves for breakfast or midday meals, afternoon cooking, suppers. Weed climbs the tree beside the Asylum doors high up to her open window and stands close beside her. She's sitting in her chair, her bulk sighed into a fallen weight. Her eyes are open. The treasure drawer is open too, her kerosene lamp lit though it's morning. The knotted cloud of her gray hair is falling out of its pins, too heavy to stay bound. Weed moves around her chair that seems to groan at his careful steps. He waits but she says nothing. He leans near, his eye close to hers, but her shattered green prism stays glassy. He puts his face to her cook's apron, ever so careful, for the scent that tethers him—the milk flour butter smell in her layers of skirts and aprons, the skirts thrown out like foam. Her scattered papers are heaped up in piles and the flame in her lamp burns on, dim in the bright morning. One fleshy unmovable arm wedges itself atop the desk while one pale hand curls in her lap. Oh I were a beauty Pet, ye may not believe it—from my ninth year on evry man I saw came after me, blood relations worse than any. An me too small to stop them flingin me about. Bigger I got the farther away they stayed. Oh I learned to fight Pet, so ye can skate an feather about—none on this place dares backtalk Hexum. My heart pounds fierce when I rush here an there, but they stays out of my way lest I land atop em! Weed knows the words and the pounding of her big heart and wants them again, wants her shout-sing voice. He must wake her, make her talk and be, puts his small hands behind her shoulders. Plants his feet and pushes.

The instant she falls forward onto the desk comes a crack of gunfire, not from here, but somewhere close. Weed knows the sound from trailing the workmen when they shot a horse for its broken leg. The beast dropped down as fast as Hexum, and he thinks he smells the same gunpowder smell. But she is not a broken horse and no shot knocked her down. He throws himself over her broad back, clinging on, clinching his eyes closed in the wet of his tears and the running nose she calls his spigot. Here Pet wipe yer face wi that gentlemen's handkerchief I gave you for yer a gentleman more than any lunatic.

He opens his eyes to see her bulk spread over the desk, her head to the side, her open eyes gazing at a thread of flame running from the fallen lamp she's toppled. The glass globe shatters. Fire widens on the papers, digging a hole in her open account book. That flame stands up first, sparking the flowered paper on the wall. The flowers are alive, opening and crackling. Lamps not allowed Pet nor candles! For Story must have gaslight in his lunatic hotel, but I draw my shades an do as I like. The baubles shine brighter in lamplight, remember it, Pet. See here? All this we save case we light out an leave the rest to this er that! But now her fallen hair is alight, burning a bright nimbus around her as he tries to pull her back, tugging savagely at her chair. Then he runs to the open window he entered to call for help, but the drawn shades have caught on top and fallen to the floor, burning. He leaps over them to the stone window ledge, out onto the tree, into the cool morning. Smoke billows from her window.

Someone has seen. Fire bells are ringing in the yard, ringing and ringing, and the two nurse attendants pulling the ropes are lifted slightly up and down, their hands and black sleeves reaching, reaching for the clanging bells, their aprons so white they might be made of ice.

NO ACCIDENT CAN BE MORE TERRIBLE to contemplate than a fire raging . . . The large iron tanks placed in the attic of the building should always be filled towards night . . . kept full of water at all times; there should be a fire engine and six hundred feet of hose belonging to the institution . . . so distributed that it could be attached to the proper water pipes at the shortest notice.

—DR. THOMAS STORY KIRKBRIDE, 1854

DR. STORY'S WINDOW

She'd sent him a message asking to meet this morning, earlier than their scheduled afternoon appointment. Before breakfast, in fact. Surely she too feels a need to advance matters between them, here in his third-floor office where they've talked long and often. Yesterday on the carriage ride she'd come willingly into his arms, sought his protection so naturally. Perhaps now is the time to state his hopes. He imagines speaking softly, holding her gaze in his. The day is bright, autumnal, cold, as though this aberrant season will right itself and turn to winter. Story steps to the tall oval windows, opens them fully outward to view the Great Lawn, the yellowed road, the narrow river between the Asylum and the town. One might step over the sill, stand on the narrow balcony. Perhaps today, after their talk, he might stand here with her. Story dismisses chance or destiny but believes in the still, small voice that draws one forward incrementally. He will not ask that she convert, only attend occasional Friends Meetings in Philadelphia. She will find Uncle Kirkbride and his wife of some twenty years especially welcoming, and the gracious Friends Meeting House on Arch Street calming, inclusive.

She might be outside his office even now, waiting to see him. He turns, straightens his collar. The women's wards are at breakfast, supervised by Matron Bowman and nurse attendants. He is crossing the room to leave his office door ajar when he hears her quiet knock. A tapping, almost. He opens the door completely.

. . .

O'Shea stands just near her as the door opens, feels the grip of her fingers on his wrist. Story seems surprised, steps back and indicates the chairs before his desk. They've scarcely taken their seats when an apparition appears at the open windows, shouting. His filthy, torn gentlemen's clothes and his raving are instantly recognizable—their escaped lunatic has returned or hidden nearby all along, just as O'Shea warned, climbing the towering tree near Story's office onto the firmly attached drainpipe and balcony foothold. Like a fool, Story has left the windows opened wide as though to assist a violent obsessive in the mission such men live for. O'Shea's dealings with this cunning patient are limited to surveilling him as Night Watch, noting his boastful monologues of robberies, assaults, burning of homesteads, women made to beg, his Southern sympathies a cover for a diseased mind. Now he knows the man for an interloper who called himself Papa, took hostage the cabins, the high ridge O'Shea himself found in the flight Eliza described, for her name is Eliza, and the woman she calls Dearbhla had raised them both in the place they'd fled together. There, she said, the branding of his scarred chest, not the War. Just as the "lunatic gentleman" steps over the sill into the office, waving his gun at Story like a taunt, raving of Quaker devils and Yankee scum, Story stands behind his desk as though to provide an easier target.

Sir, Story shouts, calm yourself! But Story is not in charge. The lunatic cocks the pistol, pupils like pinwheels, the sweat smell of his mania permeating the room like a tinge. Tall Lincoln hat gone or discarded, he shakes his shaggy head as though to clear his vision, opens his mouth wide, lengthens his unshaven face in a series of triumphant yowls and deranged laughter. He has not noticed Eliza though he surely will, for he knows her, has used her, terrorized her, ConaLee his captive, Dearbhla hated, forbidden. Eliza has said all this, weeping, breathing words into O'Shea's neck and mouth through a night more real to O'Shea than this nightmare. She'd removed the hard cone strapped to his head, kissing and touching as though to change what is, for he does not remember, remembers nothing, though felt at last within himself the miracle of a truth known and believed. And now this maniac, birthed in the War and the lost past, is here among them, for the past is the present unrecognized.

Story goes on speaking distinctly, quietly, as though his voice and gaze might affect this avalanche bearing down on them all. O'Shea feels his muscles tense and coil as the lunatic extends the cocked pistol at Story, moving the gun in tight circles as though playing with his target. If he has three bullets, O'Shea thinks, he will shoot them all. As though aware of O'Shea's thoughts, their assailant goes silent and swings his gun arm evenly to sight O'Shea. Eliza sits frozen in her chair, eyes downcast. The gun moves slightly, aims at her head. Story shouts, claps his hands as though to break some spell. Their assailant, long unkempt hair blown about, suit ripped and filthy, turns back toward Story and smiles. Capably, he extends the cocked pistol, using both hands to steady his aim. O'Shea leaps toward him in silence, tackling him from the left, throwing him bodily out the open window as the pistol discharges. Fire exploding in his chest, O'Shea hears someone scream but sees his daughter's face, her panicked hesitation at getting into the carriage with Story and her mother, her eyes and long lashes so . . . familiar. If he had never left her—

Story, standing, speaking, cannot truly believe this flailing threat gone suddenly quiet, extending his pistol's steady aim at Story's head. No more to say, Story thinks, and sees from his desk O'Shea's powerful lunge. An instant, then the maniac's full force catapult into cool, sheer air. There's a thunderous crack, a smell of gunpowder. The shot reverberates, gathering force inside the room as O'Shea falls straight back, the front of his shirt smoking. Miss Janet goes to him, crying out as Story rushes to the window. Mrs. Bowman, suddenly beside Story, sees the escapee below on the drainage stones, flung three stories down, gape-mouthed as though in surprise, long-barreled revolver in his hand. They see a fluid stain blacken under his head, widening as though in haste.

Mrs. Bowman, Story commands her, fetch our surgeon! Send a stretcher here, and attendants.

He is surely not alive, Bowman says.

The surgeon is for O'Shea. Quickly! Now!

She hurries from the room as Story turns to kneel beside Miss Janet, half supporting her. She cradles O'Shea in her arms, holding one palm to his face and the other to his chest as though to stanch the blood instantly reddening his white shirt, pooling in her skirts. Oddly, O'Shea has not worn his uniform to this meeting, but his street clothes. Come away, Story says, thinking only to remove his patient, save her from the discovery of others already rushing toward them, but she looks up to address him.

He is my husband, she says. That is what we came to tell you.

Your husband, Story repeats. He puts his hands protectively on her shoulders.

Fire bells ring in the courtyard. The smell of smoke fills the room as sparking flames and cloudy gray air billow past the window. Some nearby room is ablaze, fired no doubt by the lunatic who reasoned well enough that a distraction would aid his assault. The alarms will bring ambulance wagons, fire carts, townsfolk expecting a blaze, ready with their buckets. *Her husband.* Story feels O'Shea's throat for a pulse—nothing—and rests his hand there, close to hers.

. . .

ConaLee joins her fellows, hurrying the female patients from their breakfast in the ladies' dining room to the kitchen exit back of the Asylum. Hexum's province, a much larger, arching space than she'd supposed, gleams in sun-struck light from many tall windows along one wall. The fan-shaped transom shines above double doors that stand open now, wide as a barn's. The big room is empty of cooks or kitchen help though the broad black ovens continue baking bread as the ladies stream through. The tantalizing smell of browning loaves seems further proof of Hexum's power even as the clanging of the fire bells grows louder, clanging and clanging. ConaLee follows her patients as the women lift their skirts, climbing the wide ascending path that leads past the kitchen gardens.

Across the way she glimpses cooks and kitchen helpers decamped to the barns, where some of their husbands work. Now they stand outside in their long aprons, watching a spectacle of streaming patients as the central wing empties. The wings farther back are in no danger, say the cooks, who watch bare whiffs of smoke rise above the roof and wonder at all the fuss. They must rescue the bread, if only the lunatic ladies would clear the way. Their workmen kin have joined the bucket brigade though some few now drive a low wagon back this way, their only burden a wicker casket. Common enough, this horse-drawn journey beyond the orchard and woods to the meadow and graveyard below, with its low stone wall and staked numbers. The cooks ignore the wagon's passage, remarking on the ladies and their attendants who move like flocks of confused geese toward the front of the Asylum and the Great Lawn. ConaLee can hear the gentlemen's transit beyond the tall brick wall bordering the kitchen garden. She imagines their crowded passage narrowed and lengthened along the garden paths, dividing in flowing channels around ornament and folly. While the women move in a silent cloud of skirts and fashionable boots, the men call out *Huzzah!* and *Bravo!* as though executing a parade march.

Dearbhla

TRANS-ALLEGHENY

She hears the pealing of fire bells before she sees the town. Coming and going from Alexandria during the War, she'd driven through Weston, but the place was bigger now, no doubt freshened by Asylum monies and employ. The wide Main Street was crowded, horses, carts, streaming passersby headed one way, toward the Asylum fire bells, ringing out louder and louder. Suddenly the clanging ceased. Dearbhla followed men and women, children, many carrying blankets and buckets, across a bridge to the smell of smoke and first sight of the Asylum. A wide green lawn, an acre or two it seemed, choked with people, a clock tower and great stone buildings set far back. Tall iron fencing and the gate standing open. Bold brass script on the sign: *Trans-Allegheny Lunatic Asylum.* The narrow river and railroad track to one side. Deep-thronging fire bells silenced but the tinged air ringing with the high-pitched clanging bells of Weston fire wagons. The crowded road opened up once she was inside the grounds, for fire and police wagons had driven over the lawns to crowd against the massive entrance. All was confusion and noise. Dearbhla urged her horse and buckboard faster, toward the smoke furling from two front windows, high up. Slivers of flame, though some in the shifting crowd moved close as though to seek them. She could see men in helmets and great coats throwing objects from the burned-out windows, water pouring out the darkened holes—

———

ConaLee

SPECULATION

The ladies round the side grounds onto the Great Lawn. ConaLee looks for her mother. Mama was not at breakfast and must be here, or safe with Dr. Story, or vanished into her secret life as ConaLee would vanish if only someone knew of her, caught up in this confusing melee, wanting only escape. The ladies prove impossible to manage as they disappear into crowds of townspeople, for the whole town is here, first in alarm and now in curiosity and speculation. The Ladies' Auxiliary has brought blankets no one seems to need—soon a patchwork of wool squares and quilts adorn the ground. Many seat themselves to watch the men—businessmen, shopkeepers, farmers—pass buckets of water to and from the fountain, wetting down the stone of the Asylum walls. The Asylum fire wagon has looped its long hose three floors up onto Dr. Story's narrow office balcony, where two men in helmets stand one behind the other, aiming the hose into adjacent windows that are now charred holes. Flames are no longer visible. Word spreads through the crowd below that the fire is controlled.

The fire bells cease clanging but their sound has carried for miles, as has the smoke of the fire on this clear day. Ambulance wagons continue arriving from surrounding towns and country folk on horseback ride their nags about or loop their bridles on tree branches. A few enterprising town merchants sell meat pies from a cart. Town ladies, the danger passed, raise their parasols and converse. ConaLee sees no flames, only trails of damp voluminous smoke and the passage of many carts and wagons on the road leading from the gate to the columned Asylum entrance. She watches a buckboard negotiate its way, the lone driver . . . standing, sitting, calling to the horse in traces— And ConaLee begins to run, throwing aside her nurse's cap, pulling at her hair to unbind it, not to look like all the others. She raises her arms, shouting, dodging through the crowd, crying out a name she keeps saying even as Dearbhla stops the buckboard and lifts her in.

Child, Dearbhla says, embracing her. Where is your mother?

They look toward the smoke and the charred Asylum walls.

There, ConaLee says. She points to the narrow balcony of Story's office.

The firemen have gone inside. Through a haze of drifting smoke, two figures stand looking down. Though ConaLee cannot see her mother's face, that is her figure that Dr. Story holds about the waist.

We must go now, she tells Dearbhla. Please, now—

Get in the back, ConaLee. I cannot turn in this confusion.

ConaLee moves as the buckboard jerks into motion. She holds to the sides of the lurching wagon with both hands as the conveyance moves forward, Dearbhla negotiating the road that leads past the broad granite steps and Asylum doors. ConaLee looks upward for her mother, breathing in the blistered smell as Dearbhla slows the horse past the fire wagons. Only because she's looking up into the tree beside the Asylum entrance does she see Weed hanging to the lowest branch, swinging his legs toward her. She stands in the slowing wagon, reaching up as he drops into her arms.

Dr. Story

NAMES

In the duration of time, a phrase Story once admired, now abhors, a surgeon, police, fire wagons, arrived. The surgeon to pronounce O'Shea's death "heart shot, instantaneous," as police hear Story's account of the escapee lunatic at the window. Male nurse attendants once supervised by the Night Watch carry O'Shea to the morgue. Casketed by the local mortician, he will be laid out in Story's apartments, but that is hours hence. All is pandemonium now, but the police confiscate the weapon and give Story leave to order the dead assailant on the stones below buried immediately in the Asylum graveyard. The wards evacuated to the Great Lawn, milling about amongst curious townspeople, barely notice a wagon drawn up, concealing their view of a body lifted into a wicker coffin. Dr. Story must lead his patient to his own bedroom to rest while he speaks to the town himself and oversees an orderly resolution. That night, when she explains that Nurse Connolly is her daughter with O'Shea, Story urges her to invite the girl here, to them. She too has had a terrible shock. He calls his patient by her right name, Eliza, and calls her daughter ConaLee, though Eliza says the girl is gone. Back to her home, a day and a half's ride away.

I saw her grandmother come for her, from the balcony, Eliza tells him. ConaLee has a home, though I do not.

This is your home, he says, whatever your name.

PART IV

1864

O'Shea

THE ONLY KEY

O'Shea sits at table each evening with his benefactors, unfolding a cloth napkin on his lap, taking up fork and knife. The elderly surgeon and his wife, he knows, are engaged in civilizing him, offering an experience of home to one who has none, supporting employ that the good doctor has arranged. The hospital is a mere twenty-minute walk. They'd raised an orphaned grandson and lost him at the beginning of the War. The boy had been so young that he hadn't yet left home, except to spend a year at a military boarding school before enlisting. Their son and his wife had died of typhoid when the boy was a baby. O'Shea knows these facts from other suppers, and senses that his presence is a placeholder. Some at the hospital refer to him as "Young" O'Shea to differentiate him from "Old" O'Shea, the much-respected surgeon who's given so freely in befriending his patient. Given too much.

So the recovered patient lives in a generous basement room filled with light from a narrow adjoining greenhouse. He tolerates their talk of the War and spares them every chore he can, splitting wood and stacking it, building the fires, bringing stores from the basement. The Quaker couple, the Irish doctor having converted forty years previous while courting his wife, live simply. They do not employ servants, except to send out the laundry. Turning earth for a garden, O'Shea finds himself hoisting the shovel to his shoulder and aiming it. His hands are sensitive and the sight in his remaining eye is keen. He thinks he knows what and who he was, and resolves never to shoot a gun again. His absence of memory, his maimed head, the slightly conical, shield-like eye patch that draws the gaze of passersby, seems the price he pays for forgetting. He's glad not to know what he's lost and sometimes feels others' overwhelming grief so strongly that he has to turn away, or leave a room suddenly. Shadowy figures envelop him in nightmares, dreams in which he's deafened by concussion and explosion but feels the pounded earth shake, smells the tormented, seared air. After, he sometimes descends, swims a formless dark, falls into a narrow slit of earth. There he struggles, reaching, urged, wanting and wanted as though by death itself. He grasps a woman's hair in his fingers as fragrance and feeling disintegrate.

The elderly doctor and his wife are discussing the Ladies' Aid Committee, and their plans for patients' Christmas meals at the hospital. Should those who are able be invited to various homes, to sit around a table with a family, or should all be fed in the wards, among their fellows?

Dr. O'Shea leaves off speaking to address him. John, what do you think?

I feel that I must not stay here with you much longer, he answers. My debt to you is so great that it weighs on me.

There is surprised silence.

The truth is, O'Shea says softly, I am no one's son, and no one's grandson, much as I might wish it were so.

The doctor's wife seems crestfallen but manages not to speak. She only looks up, inquiring, intent, as though her deep concern might have some effect.

Of course, Dr. O'Shea says quickly. You want to be independent. As does any man. But tell me, John, about this new work of yours at the hospital, calming patients, working with them on hand coordination.

It's a harmless trick, O'Shea answers. But some of them do calm in the moment, and take up the exercise for themselves—squeezing an India rubber ball, such as you instructed me to use in my recovery—when they feel tense or afraid. It's a repetitive motion most of them can manage, in one hand, if they haven't two.

The doctor nods. Nurse Gordon says you're trusted by many in the ward. What would you think of instructing other hospital aides, if the Hospital provided the materials—surely easy to get, and inexpensive. You have a particular way with the men, and that is what you would be teaching.

I have no objection, but—

You would need to be an aide yourself, but you are already doing the work and should have become an aide already. We would ask aides from other wards to observe you with the men. You could then join them in their meetings with medical staff, to discuss other ideas. The War may end in the next months, but there will be no shortage of injured facing long recoveries. The key is this: some therapies might address mental trauma. And soldiers are more trusting of those who understand their experience.

Yes, I think so. They have only to look at me.

Or listen to you, says Mrs. O'Shea.

A good point, my dear, says the doctor. Can one teach an attitude? I think one may try. John, you have an ability that might become a vocation, if it appeals to you. If you gain experience, and find that you can teach others ... to lessen a soldier's anguish, the hospital has even greater need of you. You may continue to live here with us, or not—

Please don't think I'm ungrateful. You've shown great kindness.

Not at all, says Mrs. O'Shea.

We're a well-known hospital, says the doctor. I'm often asked for recommendations on staffing by other institutions. In time, as you continue to gain experience, another opportunity may present itself.

Indeed, agrees his wife.

Up North, perhaps, says the doctor.

O'Shea meets the doctor's gaze and nods. John O'Shea, he says then, fought for the Union.

Oh yes, the doctor says. You fought for the Union, under

whatever name. And institutions will be opening farther South, where need is great also, as the War ends. He pauses, as though considering. More responsibility, he says carefully, may lead to the independence you mention. John, are you willing to take on more duties?

I am, yes.

And you're welcome to stay here with us, says Mrs. O'Shea, until the rest is sorted out. We depend on you, you know.

She looks so pleased that he says nothing more. They continue their meal. He will stay for a time, though he understands that he cannot truly return the familial fondness they offer, or even accept the space in which bonds might grow. He will leave here when time affords and feel no anguish but absence. A blank pulsing thud of heartbeat is the only key he possesses, and it fits no lock. But he's intensely relieved. He thinks of a kite, struggling along the ground, suddenly catching the wind, with the string let out very quickly. He can hear the whistle of air and feel a sensation of buoyancy, as though he gains height over raucous green hills that resound with pleas for mercy.

EPILOGUE

1883

ConaLee

Bundled in their coats, they stood directly across from the First Exchange Bank, one of three in Weston. The cold felt blustery and raw. ConaLee ran a gloved hand along the unpainted picket fence behind them. A *For Sale* sign hung from the sprung gate. Set back from the street, the plain two-story house was spartan but for its faded gingerbread trim and garden lattice. A narrow front porch, near flat to the ground, ran its length. There looked to be an acre or so of land behind, a small barn. Flat for a garden, shade trees to one side. The scrubby, patchy grass allowed a straight dirt path to the house. ConaLee saw, to the side near the trees, what seemed a second-floor sleeping porch. She imagined herself there, summer evenings, watching twilight darken into night.

Weed, you must stand there, in front of the sign on the gate, until I come out.

I'll stand wherever you like, he said.

ConaLee reflected that he was near her height now. She had turned out after all, and he'd turned out too, in his way.

. . .

The bank clerk was a middle-aged woman. ConaLee gave over her father's enlistment papers, with the name he'd chosen, and the account book.

The clerk read the paper, then looked down at the small account book in her hand. You're here about the account of Ephraim Connolly? she asked.

Yes, ma'am. *Ephraim Connolly.* Her mother had named her the name he'd taken—her given name a version of her surname. She was a hint, a riddle, a remembrance.

You are Miss Connolly, then? His family?

I am his daughter, ConaLee Connolly, she said, his only child. I'm unmarried. I'm of age. That's his deposit book, for you to check the dates.

You have his death certificate, or a discharge paper?

We never got such, but it's twenty-two years since he enlisted, June 17, '61, as it says there. She paused and lifted her eyes to the woman's gaze.

A birth certificate then, stating his name?

It burnt. And his unmarked grave . . . is in a wilderness—

It was not a lie, for the Asylum was a wilderness, none knew it better than she, his grave allowed in the narrow, shaded garden her mother had walked that night. Unmarked, according to her mother's wishes, for none of his names saved him. Not a number, not a gravestone, but for the tiny white pebbles heaped under lush grass, leaves, snow, near the large tree where they'd found each other that night. Each spring, her mother circled the tree with handfuls of small stones. The year after he died, Dearbhla and ConaLee made the journey to join her. Weed watched, but took his palmfuls of white pebbles back to the ridges.

The clerk inquired, Have you a date of death?

We know . . . when the deposits stopped. I have this, the *carte de visite* he sent back as a soldier. ConaLee took it from the pocket of her winter coat and laid it gently on the clerk's hand, atop the open account book.

The clerk was silent. The two together barely filled her palm.

Seventh West Virginia Cavalry Volunteers, said ConaLee. That's him on the left, a sharpshooter.

The woman nodded. Not many such, showed a man outdoors, she murmured. She looked up, sympathetic now. Might you have letters from him?

A very few, said ConaLee, to my mother. She showed the yellowed envelopes, addressed to Mrs. Eliza Connolly at a Weston P.O. box.

The clerk glanced over the postmarks. You know, she said, I've been here thirty year. Some of the soldiers wrote on their deposit slips, the date, a place, or a phrase. I kept them in the files. Let me see if I've anything for this name. She left her window and turned to stand before a wooden file of drawers on the back wall opposite.

ConaLee heard the turn of a key and looked away. The winter sky was a clear sharp blue this second day of the New Year, and Main Street of Weston lay dusted with snow. Dearbhla had died a week before Thanksgiving, two year ago, and mere thought, or any look at a bright winter sky these weeks between the winter holidays brought ConaLee the sight of the mounded grave bordered with rocks. That fall, even into November, stayed unseasonable warm, the second such in a generation, it was said, since the winter of '74. They'd dug the grave deep, for the ground had not frozen, and placed Dearbhla in her shroud, with the flat rocks touching edges across the whole of her resting, and then more earth bordered with rounded stones. Dearbhla had asked for many ·stones, and gave ConaLee the name her father had forgot, his bankbook, his enlistment papers. Dearbhla would not travel more, she said, not in flesh or spirit, to any land or ocean, or down from this mountain. She grieved her son, but felt his strength in ConaLee's return to her. They'd lived with Dearbhla near seven year, she and Weed, after the Asylum, ConaLee taking on more of the work, teaching Weed as she went: the trading herbs and tonics at market, hunting, gardening. And Chap was often about the place once he was old enough to ride over from his mother's cabin. The neighbor woman who'd adopted him brought him to see them inside of a few weeks. She was curious, or needing the sound of a woman's voice. The boy twin had died, pneumonia in his third month. And the woman who took the girl twin was long gone from the ridges. Still, ConaLee had missed Chap the most. She knew him at first sight, no matter the time elapsed, and the sight of him as he grew bound her to him. She took care to do favors, invite widow and child to suppers and holidays. Now Chap was twelve, a tall well-made boy who favored their mother. It could be said they looked like siblings, and ConaLee had taught him to read with ease. He should go to school in town. Could be Chap's aging mother might come to help with the cooking and housework, if an invitation was phrased right. They might leave the mountain for the school year, and return to their cabin in the summers.

Weed's light hair had darkened. Slowly, he'd made up some growth. At fifteen, he could read and write but was better at sums than books. Better at hunting and growing things, earning a wage now with the farm crew at the Asylum. They'd come down from the ridges after Dearbhla passed and rented rooms in a Weston boarding house. Hired on at the Asylum, they lived nearby in the town. Occasional visits to the Story apartments at the Asylum became frequent suppers and Sunday dinners. ConaLee found her mother again, distantly at first, then in long talks on the same paths they'd walked what seemed long ago. She knew her mother's stories, and Dearbhla's. Matron Bowman had gone back to Philadelphia and ConaLee worked as assistant to her replacement. Eira Blevins had left after the fire. Mrs. Kasinski, an elderly widow now, lived happily at the Asylum. ConaLee felt nearer to her father in the place where she'd seen him, known of him, and Weed's stories came to seem her own memories. Ephraim Connolly had lost the name he'd taken and never known of his mother, the enslaved girl who'd died so young. *The soft knock at the slant-hung door,* as Dearbhla told it. ConaLee's grandmothers, one the oppressor of the other, had died giving birth. Her mother would have died in a next pregnancy, had Dearbhla not set an imperfect plan in motion. So many died birthing babies, the risk taken willingly or forced upon them. Not ConaLee. She no longer saw lights, or lost pieces of time, but early losses still pained her. She mothered Weed and Chap and was satisfied.

The clerk was back and placed a paper file on the counter. These are his, she said. Deposit slips. He sent near one a month, November '61 to April '64. Most are just his name, always a date and place. But he wrote a line on one or two. Like this one. A quotation or such.

ConaLee touched the slip on top. It was thin as onionskin, folded precisely in half. She opened and smoothed it. His name was on the back in script. And, *Brandy Station, Va.* Below that, *for Eliza and babe–the boat that finds the shore . . .*

The clerk had turned back to her accounts. He has left you a nest egg, she said, the amount, and the interest earned—

What does it come to? ConaLee asked.

Well, some three hundred and forty dollars, and fifty-four cents. To be exact.

I want to ask, ConaLee said, about the frame house across the street. The one with the yard in back. There is a notice of sale.

Just across, you mean? Our bank president owns it—

Is he here? Could I speak with him?

He is not here, but I am his wife, so I can give you the particulars. Our daughter lived there and has moved to a farm outside town. Five children now. We bought them the place. But with so many little ones, they left the house to itself, and the garden is a shambles.

ConaLee nodded. Ma'am, she asked, might you know the price?

We were going to fix the place up a bit. In the spring, we thought . . .

It's fine for me as it is, ConaLee said. My brother is good about fixing things, and I've a talent with gardens. My mother and stepfather will be a help as well.

So you have family nearby?

My stepfather, Dr. Thomas Story, is Physician Superintendent at the Asylum, and my mother, Mrs. Eliza Story, is much involved here in town—

Yes, I know of Dr. Story.

And you are . . . ? ConaLee asked.

I am Mrs. Paine. Pleased to meet you, Miss Connolly. She offered her hand.

Just then, the minute hand of the large wall clock behind her trembled before it moved.

ConaLee removed her glove to take the woman's cool, dry palm. Happy to make your acquaintance, Mrs. Paine. You see, she went on, I'm employed at the Asylum, as a nurse attendant, and my brother is apprenticed to the landscaper and groundsmen there. I have these letters as well, one a letter of reference, and the other, witnessed, from my mother, renouncing any ownership of my father's funds. She's remarried now, as you know. ConaLee reached into her purse for the envelopes. Perhaps you would show these to your husband, on the matter of buying the house.

Mrs. Paine opened the letters and glanced over them. Yes, this, from your mother, is what I need. May I set up an account in your name, Miss Connolly? We can transfer the monies into it.

ConaLee nodded. I've had the account book since my grandmother died near two year ago, but I needed to be of age to claim what he intended for me. Mrs. Paine, I want to offer the full amount—three hundred and forty dollars and fifty-four cents—for the house.

It's not so easy to sell property now, Mrs. Paine allowed. It seems a fair price— And we'll commit, on the bill of sale, to painting the house in the spring, and fixing the fence. All else, as is. Of course I must talk with my husband, but we do want the place to look nice. Well, my son-in-law—he's not one to keep things up, and we couldn't tell him what to do.

No, said ConaLee. She watched the woman mark her ledgers.

There, Mrs. Paine said. I've closed your father's account. I believe . . . it's the last of the War accounts to be settled. And so today is an important day. She looked at ConaLee over her bifocals as her eyes filled. I lost two brothers at Gettysburg. My husband came back, but struggled to be himself.

My father, ConaLee began. For so many years, we didn't know what became of him.

Mrs. Paine nodded. He thought of you, long as he could. And now his account is yours. You must sign this form to establish your own account, and this receipt for the transfer of funds. She watched as ConaLee read through the two pages, and signed her name. And if you think on it, Miss Connolly, and you're still certain, about buying the house . . .

Oh, I'm certain, ConaLee said. It's what my father would have wanted, to provide me a home. Embarrassed, she felt her voice falter. This man, before the War and during, from the day he became someone else and ever after, was her father. She'd found him, despite all odds, come to admire him, even before she learned how he'd died, that day in Dr. Story's office. She would not judge Dearbhla, but mourned that Ephraim Connolly, self-named at last, had never known who he truly was. ConaLee knew him in herself. Mrs. Paine, she asked, shall we meet here tomorrow then, with your husband, and a solicitor?

My husband is a solicitor, and often works with bank clients—

I work with my stepfather's solicitor, a long-standing connection—

Fine, then. Let us meet this time tomorrow.

And might I have his—my father's—deposit slips, when all is done. With his writing on them, as you said.

Surely, Mrs. Paine said. She looked beyond ConaLee, out the large windows of the bank doors. We might have asked your brother in. It's so cold today. And now the snow has started.

Oh, he's strong, ConaLee said. He doesn't mind the cold. Tomorrow, then.

. . .

A mist of powdered snow seemed to lift from behind the house as ConaLee crossed the street, furling her scarf against her face. Weed stood with his back to her but turned as she reached him.

The bank transferred his account to me, she told him.

The Night Watch, Weed said. His account.

He was your father, Weed, as much as mine. You knew him better. And the president of that bank owns this house. I think his wife agreed to a swap. We must go to Mama and bring the lawyer tomorrow. Wait, where has the sign gone?

Weed pulled back his collar to show he'd put it into the front of his coat. You'll want it later, he said.

ConaLee surveyed the house once more. It would be hers. Who lived there, came to stay—would be up to her. *ConaLee, there is no forever. We are on our walk and the day is fine.* Not so many families owned a house. Some owned more, this and that, houses, stores, railroads, vast lands. Others . . . died, or fled, or forgot who they were. Endurance was strength. The courage of the lost swelled and moved, a force separating the days, clearing the way.

Acknowledgments

Thank you to the MacDowell Colony and to Yaddo for residencies that supported me in the writing of this novel, and to the Virginia Center for the Arts, whose residencies sustained my writing and research in Alexandria, Virginia, and at the Battle of the Wilderness site. Thanks to Lemley Mullett of the West Virginia and Regional History Center at West Virginia University Libraries, and to the West Virginia Department of Arts, Culture, and History for help in locating historic images. Thanks to Lynn Nesbit, my miraculous agent; to the entirety of Knopf and especially to Ann Close, my astute and patient longtime editor; to her excellent assistant, Rob Shapiro; to production editor Victoria Pearson; to book designer Maggie Hinders; to jacket designer Kelly Blair; and to Reagan Arthur, whose enthusiasm for this novel was so encouraging. Thanks to reader extraordinaire Pamela Rikkers. Thanks always to my family, who understand, and to my husband, Mark, who helps in every way. Respect and thanks to Quaker physician Thomas Story Kirkbride, whose influential 1854 publication, *On the Construction, Organization, and General Arrangements of Hospitals for the Insane,* influenced the practice of "moral treatment" for the mentally ill for some fifty years, until his humane methods, like all methods, fell out of favor. Among the dozens of books in my *Night Watch* research shelves, I celebrate in particular *The Civil War Told by Those Who Lived It,* four volumes published by

The Library of America, in whose pages hundreds of indelible Civil War–era voices live on. Other helps were *The Art of Asylum-Keeping,* by Nancy Tomes; *The Invisible Irish,* by Rankin Sherling; *Masterless Men: Poor Whites and Slavery in the Antebellum South,* by Keri Leigh Merritt; and *The Lincolns: Portrait of a Marriage,* by Daniel Mark Epstein, which includes oft-quoted lines of Mary Todd Lincoln originally reported in physician Anson Henry's April 19, 1865, letter to his wife. Penned in anguish four days after Lincoln's assassination, the letter is archived at the Illinois State Historical Society. Thanks to Joe Jordan, an asbestos and demolition expert whose interest in the architecture and history of defunct Weston State Hospital (closed since 1994) led him to purchase the buildings from the State of West Virginia for $1.5 million in 2007. Original name restored, the Trans-Allegheny Lunatic Asylum is now a National Historic Landmark open to the public (see TALA .org); three hundred of the original six hundred acres of asylum land are part of the grounds. Thanks to that land and the buildings themselves, the rooms I visited and memorized, the long hallways, the views from the windows, every one of which seemed illumined by the gazes of so many.

Frontispiece: Drawing of Trans-Allegheny Lunatic Asylum, courtesy of West Virginia Archives and History

Page 1: Sketch of Trans-Allegheny Lunatic Asylum, from Thomas Story Kirkbride's book *On the Construction, Organization, and General Arrangements of Hospitals for the Insane*

Page 30: Photograph of Asylum bedroom, courtesy of author

Page 39: Drawing of two women, from *1847 Women's Fashion Books* (PD-150) from Le Bon Ton. From: *Blackwood's Lady's Magazine*, volume 22.

Page 43: Seventh West Virginia Volunteer Cavalry Regiment, courtesy of West Virginia Division of Culture and Historical Records

Page 101: Photo of building used as hospital in the 100 block of North Fairfax Street between King Street and Cameron Street, from Wikimedia Commons

Page 109: Battle of the Wilderness, illustration by Alfred R. Waud, courtesy of Library of Congress Prints and Photographs Division

Page 125: Photograph of Weston, West Virginia, courtesy of West Virginia and Regional History Center, West Virginia University

Page 156: "Schedule of a Complete Organization with Rate of Compensation," from Thomas Story Kirkbride's book *On the Construction, Organization, and General Arrangements of Hospitals for the Insane*

Page 172: "Reasons for Admission," based on Thomas Story Kirkbride's book *On the Construction, Organization, and General Arrangements of Hospitals for the Insane*

Page 174: Photograph of dining room, courtesy of West Virginia and Regional History Center, West Virginia University

Page 188: Floor plan, from Thomas Story Kirkbride's book *On the Construction, Organization, and General Arrangements of Hospitals for the Insane*

Page 209: Photograph of nurses on lawn, from Archives New Zealand

Page 214: Photograph of gazebo, courtesy of West Virginia and Regional History Center, West Virginia University

Page 261: Photograph of key, courtesy of Theo Stockman